# THE
# LAST
# RAVEN

# THE
# LAST
# RAVEN

Riftborn * Book 1

# STEVE McHUGH

**Podium**

*For Vanessa.*
*My love, always.*

Copyright © 2022 by Steve McHugh

Cover design by Podium Publishing

ISBN: 978-1-0394-1501-0

Published in 2022 by Podium Publishing, ULC
www.podiumaudio.com

**Podium**

# THE
# LAST
# RAVEN

# PROLOGUE

### Five Years Ago

"Are you sure you can do this?" Isaac asked me, checking on my well-being for the twentieth time in the last few hours. Isaac had a bald head and was clean-shaven, with dark skin, and eyes that appeared to bore into you. He was over six and a half feet tall and loomed over everything, and everyone, around him. I tried very hard not to sigh. He was only checking up on me. And I appreciated it, but also wished he'd just shut up for a while.

We were stood on the stern of a fifty-foot ship as it bobbed beside the dock of a small island some miles off the coast of Newfoundland. Technically, the island wasn't meant to exist, it wasn't on any maps. Even satellite imagery showed nothing but clear blue ocean.

It didn't even have a name, although after learning about what was happening on it, I'd named it Hell's Mouth.

The captain of the ship, a stout man of about fifty with long grey hair and a beard, left the galley and walked over. His crew, all half dozen of them, were busy unloading the cargo for delivery.

"If you're going, go," he said with slightly more irritation than was deserved, considering how much money he'd been paid to get us there. "Remember, my people know nothing about our deal. As far as anyone is concerned, you're spare crew. We don't want trouble."

"I won't do anything to jeopardise them," I promised.

I checked the earpiece that Isaac had given me, tapping it twice.

"Thanks for that," Isaac said with a slight wince.

We walked down the gangway onto the dock, and jumped up into the rear of the truck where the crates of cargo had been stored. I banged twice on the back of the truck cab, and we set off along the only road on the island.

It was a fifteen-minute drive at a fairly slow pace as the rain lashed against the outside and the wind whistled by the exposed rear of the vehicle.

"Lucas," Isaac said in my ear.

"Yes," I replied, leaning back against the side of the truck and spotting the second, identical truck with the rest of the captain's workers aboard.

"Thank you for doing this," Isaac said.

I let out a slight sigh. "Thank you for asking me."

"I know it hasn't been easy for you," Isaac continued. "I know you're going through some rough times. That you've been going through rough times since . . ."

"My friends were all murdered and I couldn't stop it," I finished for him.

"Yeah," Isaac said softly. "But this could be the start of you finding your feet again."

I nodded, realised Isaac couldn't actually see me, and felt a bit foolish.

The truck started to slow and, a moment later, it stopped altogether. I sat still as the driver spoke to someone outside. The wind made picking up the individual words impossible, but a few moments later, a guard in a midnigh-blue uniform, a black hat, and carrying an AR-15 poked his head around the corner of the truck, looking into the cargo area where I sat.

I waved.

"You comfortable back there?" he asked, chuckling.

"No," I said. "But I drew the short straw, so I get to sit with the boxes. If you like, you can sit back here on the way to the docks."

The guard laughed. "I'm good, thanks." He banged twice on the truck, and after a count of ten, we lurched forward as we were allowed into the compound of the . . . asylum.

The asylum was originally built as a prison in the 1940s when some enterprising monster decided that, as Alcatraz was doing so well, they should build a second one, even further away.

In the 1960s, it changed to Netley Asylum. It was shut down in the 1980s when a reporter exposed the experiments that were being done on the prisoners sent there. Lots of people were quietly paid a lot of money to go away and shut up, but it reopened about five years ago and there were concerning rumours about the place we needed to investigate.

The truck moved through the outer gate of the asylum. The gates were made of iron, painted black, and sat in the middle of a hundred feet of sixty-foot-high chain-link fence. Two guard towers sat at the far end of the front fence. A guard post sat beside the entrance gates, which rumbled closed, all done through a switch inside the hut.

I looked out the back of the truck as it drove through the front court-yard of the asylum grounds. Our info showed the asylum was one main building with an entrance at the front. It had two more at the rear—which wasn't accessible unless I wanted to climb an electrified fence, and more guards patrolling the black tiled roof of the building. There were two loading bays either side and a smattering of other exits, secured by ID cards, which we didn't have.

The front entrance—two large, imposing metal doors painted red—was shut, and the truck continued to the side of the building, reversing into a loading bay where two guards waited.

"You new?" one of the guards, a large man with a military-style haircut and tattoos on the back of his hands, asked me.

I pushed down the ramp at the back of the truck. "Yep," I said, stepping off the platform and making sure it was anchored to the bay.

I turned to find the man stood directly behind me, staring at me. He was a similar height to Isaac, so a good few inches taller than my own five-eleven.

I ignored him, walked back into the truck, and unloaded the first plastic container.

I worked there for a half hour until the second truck came in and the guards got bored watching me.

The truck was nearly empty, with most of the contents on the loading bay as the guards started to check everything.

"You can start moving it into the building," the tall guard told me. "Just keep your nose to yourself."

He actually flicked my nose, and it took me a good few seconds to remember I wasn't meant to leave a body count behind.

Restraining myself, I pushed one of the plastic containers through a set of open double doors and into a large storage area. I'd studied the blue-prints, so I knew that there was a door halfway down the storage room.

The door was hidden behind a tall set of shelves stacked with tins of various foods.

You wouldn't even know it was there unless you went looking for it. The door was painted the same white as the wall. Even the door handle was painted white.

I looked behind me, checking for guards, and opened the door, step-ping through into a stairwell and quietly closing the door behind me.

The stairwell was dingy; it had been a long time since it had been used on a regular basis, but there were strip lights at the top of each set of stairs, so at least I didn't have to make the climb in complete darkness.

Four flights later, I came to the only exit. The second floor. I wished the light above my head was off, but breaking it might set off some kind of alarm somewhere, and I wasn't about to risk it. I pushed open the door and found myself in a small room, with a black-and-white tiled floor. The light was dim and had a black shade, illuminating very little. It was enough to see the door only a few steps in front of me. I pulled the door open and stepped into the brightly lit hallway beyond.

There were windows down one side of the hallway, with six doors opposite—a fact I'd memorised from the blueprints. The last door on the left was my target. I had maybe twenty minutes before I was missed. Before the trucks headed back to the ship. Maybe thirty if I was lucky.

I jogged to the end of the hallway, paused, and peered around the corner, down the hallway that ran perpendicular to the one I was in. No one there. Maybe luck was on my side after all.

The dark wooden door looked like every other door on the second floor of the asylum, except for the metal name plate on it, which read DR CALLIE MITCHELL in black capital letters. I knocked three times. Waited. No answer.

I tried the door handle and found it unlocked. The whistle-blower who'd reported to Isaac said that she never locked her door.

I pushed open the door and darted inside, closing it behind me. I immediately understood why Dr Mitchell didn't lock her door. There was little to worry about being stolen.

There were no cupboards, just a table in the middle of the room, with a chair, a computer, and several coloured plastic envelopes. A sideboard with locked drawers sat under one long window that showed off the doctor's various awards, and the walls were decorated with her qualifications. I wondered if they were real or if she'd fabricated them along with the reason for the island's existence.

"Get in, get out," Isaac said in my ear.

"Seriously?" I whispered.

"I hadn't heard from you in a while," he said as I walked over to the envelopes on her desk and started going through them. Each one had a different name on them.

"You have ten minutes," he said. "My contact says she's in the garden right now; she does it every day. Talks to a different patient out there, shows them the futility of where they are."

"You are not helping," I said through gritted teeth. "The files on the patients aren't all here. These envelopes just have stuff about names and ages but nothing about what she's actually doing here. They're perfectly ordinary files. She's got a locked sideboard; they must be . . ." I stopped.

"Lucas," Isaac said, worry creeping into his voice.

"*Shit*. She has a Raven Guild medallion," I said in horror, staring at the object. It was copper in colour, made from hardened stone, and was in the shape of a buckler shield with a sword and hammer crossing over each other in front. A steel raven sat on top of the shield, as if holding it. The whole thing was about the same size as the palm of my hand. It took a lot of effort not to reach out for it.

There were seven Guilds, each one named after a different bird, but only one Guild had been massacred. My old Guild, the Ravens. I felt my heart race.

"Lucas," Isaac warned.

"Why does Dr Callie Mitchell have the medallion of one of my murdered Guild members?"

"I don't know," Isaac said. "But we don't have time for this now."

"Isaac, I *need* to know," I told him. "They were my family. My friends. My Guild. I was meant to protect them. I was . . ." I stopped, and picked the medallion up, feeling the emotions crash inside of me.

"Lucas," Isaac said, almost a whisper.

"Give me one week," I told him.

"Have you lost your mind?" he hissed.

"There's no intel in here; we're no clearer on what's happening here than before we arrived," I bargained.

"You're only meant to go there to find those files," Isaac said. "My contact assured us they would be there."

"The files are a bust," I said. "They're *not* here."

"So, it's a setup?" Isaac said.

"Looks like it," I said. "Guess I'll just have to find out what's going on. One week."

"Lucas," Isaac started, before sighing. "If they find out who . . . or what you are, you're dead. You know that, right?"

"Yep," I said. "I'm going to have to go dark, Isaac. No comms."

"Damn you, Lucas Rurik," Isaac said. "Not like I have much of a choice, is it?"

"No," I told him, hearing footsteps outside in the hallway, running toward the room. "Guards are on me already. That seems unnaturally fast.

Get Hannah to make me a realistic backstory. Reporter, my normal name. Got it?"

"I'll make sure of it," Isaac said.

"You don't hear from me in one week, come get me," I said, mentally preparing myself for whatever was about to happen.

"If I don't hear from you in one week, I'm tearing this fucking island apart," Isaac assured me.

"Stay safe," I said.

"Stay alive," Isaac said.

I removed the earpiece and smashed it underfoot, picking up the medallion and taking a seat in Dr Callie Mitchell's chair as the door burst open and the tall, sneering guard ran into the room, his sidearm aimed at me. He screamed at me to get on the floor, to lock my fingers behind my head. The usual stuff. I complied and still got a kick to the ribs for my trouble.

I looked up as Dr Mitchell strolled into the room. She was forty-ish, with long dark hair touched lightly with grey, piercing blue eyes, and olive skin. She wore a black-and-white dress that stretched down to her ankles; her arms were bare, revealing a sleeve-effect of mixed tattoos in picture-perfect ink. Each tattoo was a different bird: falcon, owl, eagle, hawk, vulture, kite, and lastly, raven. The latter of the birds sat wrapped around the wrist on her right hand, and the sight of it made the anger inside me surge.

I was dragged to my feet and forced to look at Dr Mitchell as she picked up the medallion and turned it over in her hands. "Who are you?"

"I am the King of Finland," I told her.

The guard punched me in the stomach.

"Who are you?" Dr Mitchell asked again.

"I am the Queen of Finland," I told her.

That one got me a smash in the face with the butt of the AR-15.

My vision went dark as Dr Mitchell leaned over me with a chilling smile. The last thing I heard were her words: "Welcome to the asylum, Your Majesty."

# CHAPTER ONE

*Now*

The Stag and Arrow was pretty unique as far as bars in Brooklyn went. The barman was from Philadelphia, while his husband, George, was from Edinburgh. They'd purchased the bar and transformed it from a trendy wine bar into a full-fledged British pub, about four years previously. It served wonderful food and decent, imported beer, but none of those things were what made the bar special.

The Stag and Arrow was a bar for those people who were born—or re-born, depending on what you were—from the power of the rift. The umbrella term for all the different species—both people and animals—was *rift-fused*.

There were bars like the Stag and Arrow across the globe; the human side of the rift-fused of the world liked to have a drink too, preferably without the staring and prejudice that could occur in human bars. As the only hybrid bar in Brooklyn and, conveniently, within walking distance of my apartment on the opposite side of Prospect Park, it was my preferred watering hole. Finding a great pub that you can walk home from—usually slowly and a bit unsteadily—was, in my view, an important part of life.

"Lucas," Bill Hawkins, barman extraordinaire, shouted.

I looked up as he gestured at a freshly made mug of tea with a querying look. Shaking my head, I got out of my booth, leaving my work where it was, and walked over to collect it.

"I would have brought it over," Bill told me.

"I'm capable of getting it myself," I said. I knew that Bill was referring to my walking cane that leaned up against the booth. The cane was made of blackthorn, with a gnarled shaft and a sandalwood pistol grip. Steel bands sat around the middle and bottom of the stick. It had served me well over the years.

"Yeah, I know," Bill said. "You only use it because you'd prefer to have it with you and not need it than not have it and need it." He'd repeated what I always said about it, practically word for word.

"Thank you," I told him, and he nodded as he went to deal with another customer.

The interior of the bar was divided into three parts. The first was directly upon entering the establishment, where people ordered drinks. The counter was in a horseshoe shape, with dozens of bottles of various spirits hanging in front of gleaming mirrors. Fridges sat below the mirrors, each full, while several craft ales and beers were available from one of the three pumps.

There were several tall tables around the counter, and they usually got full fast when the place became busy, especially at the weekend. The booths directly either side of the doors filled up quickly too, but tonight, only I'd taken up residence in one.

It was a Wednesday, though, and the snowfall had been heavy, so people were staying at home. As it was now ten o'clock, the two dozen people there were probably as busy as it was going to get. There were a group of five people around a table, all in smart business attire—presumably, they'd come straight from work.

The second part of the bar, to the left of the entrance, had tables and booths for people to sit and eat. It doubled as an overflow when it got busy, although today there were three people in one booth and a couple in another. All of them looked to be in their early twenties, and they kept to themselves. The booth with just two appeared to be a date, considering the amount of hand-touching each of them was doing.

The final part of the bar was on the right of the entrance and, mostly, just tables and chairs. There was a step that led up to several arcade machines, two pool tables and two dartboards; they were all occupied by a large group of a dozen or so people, some regulars that I'd seen in there before.

I sat back at the booth I'd been in for three hours. I'd picked one a few back from the bar doors—mostly to stop the draft of wind from flowing over me every time someone came in or out.

"What are you working on?" Bill asked as I looked up from my reading.

Bill was a revenant, as were, I presumed, most people in the bar. It was hard to tell—not something you'd pick up on just by looking at them, as, externally, they still looked human. Revenants were created at the moment of a human's dying; a dimensional tear opened and power from the rift beyond filled their bodies. The energy merged with the human "soul," bringing them back to life and giving them abilities at the same time. All revenants looked human until they shifted, and then each of the revenant species looked very different. I'd never seen Bill's true form—which was what they called it—that was something reserved for either their closest companions and friends, or people they were about to tear in half. The latter of which was not always an exaggeration.

Once someone had been rift-fused, they could no longer have children unless they stepped through a tear into the rift itself. It's why the rift-fused numbered in single-digit millions on earth and aren't the main species on the planet they might have been otherwise.

"Something for a friend of mine. She's a professor of rift science at Columbia University," I said.

"Meredith Pincher?" Bill asked, sitting down opposite me.

I nodded, not surprised he knew her name. Meredith was a bit of a rock star among revenants, seeing that she was one of the few who actively sought out revenant input into her work. "She asked me to look into some of the research she's doing. She's trying to figure out if there's any trend in how the rift gifts individual humans with a specific revenant species. She thought another pair of eyes might catch something new."

"And?" Bill asked, genuinely interested. Even revenants themselves didn't really know how they'd been created, why they'd been chosen, or how tears opened and closed, seemingly at random, all around the world.

The rift was a dimension attached to our own. A place where in the far north sits a giant cloud of power known as the Tempest. Occasionally, that power releases itself like a pressure valve and creates a tear between the rift and earth. And that's when the magic happens.

The power that leaks through the tear can do a lot of things, depending on if it touches a human or animal, and the state of their physical health.

The rift-fused have been around for thousands of years as a species, and while we hadn't been open about our existence until only a few decades ago, no one had taken it upon themselves to do a lot of research into the hows and whys of the revenants' creation.

"And we have no idea," I said. "It's seemingly random."

"What about riftborn and fiends?" Bill asked.

Fiends were animals that were touched by the energy from the rift, and riftborn were those humans who, when almost near death, were actually transported into the rift, healed, and given exceptional powers. Like superheroes but without the matching outfits.

"Pretty much the same," I said. "All rift-fused: fiends, riftborn, practitioners, riftwalkers, hell, even primordials. All born of chaos and randomness. At least that's how it appears."

"Well, three of those we don't see many of," Bill said. "So, I guess that makes it more difficult."

Practitioners are born like humans are—biologically—but only in the rift. Riftwalkers are either a mythological being or so rare they might as well be extinct, depending on who you talk to. And primordials were . . . really bad, but no one has seen one in centuries, so no one wanted to tempt fate by going looking.

"There's even less information on them," I said. "Fiends, being essentially dangerous animals for the most part, aren't exactly the talking type, and riftborn are rare and also aren't the talking type, but for different reasons."

Bill heaved a sigh. "Yeah—there's a lot we don't know about any of it. George was talking to me the other night about a case he's working on."

George was a defence attorney who specialized in crimes involving those raised from the rift. He did a lot of work with the RCU—Rift-Crime Unit— a multi-nation agency who investigate crimes committed by, and against, those touched by the rift. I'd met a few of them over the years, and they'd been good people who were expected to bridge a gap between law enforcement and a world most people didn't even know about until the 1970s, when it was decided to introduce the rift-fused to the world and finally become an open part of society instead of hiding in the shadows.

"Kid died in a car crash and came back to life a revenant while being transported to the morgue," Bill said.

"Not unusual," I said.

"Yeah, well, he freaked out and attacked the morgue attendant, hurt him pretty bad," Bill said sadly. "All he said during the interview was he didn't understand why he'd been brought back. Why him?"

"How's the morgue attendant?" I asked.

"Good now," he said. "Broken arm, few ribs, probably felt better. Doesn't blame the kid, although some would have. Not sure how; he's a kid who woke up after dying and turned into a spined revenant. The attendant is lucky he wasn't turned into a pincushion."

"And the kid?"

"They want to charge the kid with assault, but George thinks no judge in the country would take a nineteen-year-old to court over this," Bill sighed. "Honestly, it's a mess. More people need to do research into us. I don't see another way forward that doesn't include more incidents like this one."

I nodded. "Meredith is doing good work, but she has a team of six, and that's just not enough. So, I try to help where possible."

"You're a doctor, right?" Bill asked. "Not like a proper doctor, but . . ."

I chuckled. "I have a doctorate in rift-science, yes."

"How many revenants have the same doctorate?" Bill asked me.

"There are twenty-two people with a doctorate in rift-science in North America," I said after a few seconds of thinking about it. "It's only existed as a qualification since the early 2000s. And since then, only three people who aren't human have even bothered trying to qualify."

Bill whistled. "And in the world?"

"I have no idea; probably not many more," I told him.

Bill waggled his finger. "That might be the problem, doc."

I agreed with him completely; I just wasn't sure how to change it.

"Meredith meeting you here?" Bill asked.

"Should be, yes."

Bill went back to the counter as six men entered the bar. I paid them little attention and went back to my work, only to find a fresh cup of tea placed in front of me.

I looked up at the waitress who had brought it. She was barely five feet tall with dark skin, and her auburn hair was tied back in a ponytail. Her name was Michelle; she'd only worked at the bar for a few weeks. Like all of the staff, she wore a black T-shirt with the name of the bar written on the back and a name tag on the front.

"Bill says it's on the house," she said with a smile.

"Thanks very much," I said.

Michelle glanced over at the six new men, a shadow of concern in her eyes.

"You know them?" I asked.

Michelle shook her head. "Know their type, though," she said, sadly.

I looked beyond Michelle to the newcomers. All six of them were white, wearing blue jeans in various shades and thick dark jackets, giving the overall impression of an incredibly bad 1990s boy band. Two of them were clearly overweight, their checked shirts almost straining as they moved. They looked to be in their forties and had short hair, almost military-style, although I would have bet that neither had seen a day of military service in their lives.

Of the other four, two were younger, maybe early twenties, both with dark hair, one was almost stubble, and one long, the latter's dropping over his broad shoulders. The one with the long hair was also considerably more muscular.

The last two were the interesting ones. One was clearly in charge: he held himself with an air of authority, and the others moved aside so he could get to the bar and order. He had long, chestnut hair that he'd put into a ponytail, revealing a skull tattoo on the back of his neck, next to the letters *S.H.. Damn.*

The last man's name was Dale Winters, and he was the tallest of the group at a little over six and a half feet. He was broad-shouldered, with dark hair and mean eyes. He was the only one of them who had any kind of facial hair, in his case, a short goatee. Dale was a bully, a thug, and possibly a drunk. He also lived in my apartment building and was generally known as a huge dick by everyone else who had had to endure his presence over the last few months since he'd moved in.

"Sovereign Humanity," Michelle whispered, a little bit of fear creeping into her voice.

I nodded. Sovereign Humanity were a minority group of extremists with backing from elitists who loved to cause upheaval, who blamed the rift-fused for everything from stealing their jobs to climate change. As with most groups like this, they were made up mainly of dissatisfied, privileged people who were fed "facts" from social media groups, false news, and conspiracy theories in a perpetual cycle of self-vindication and ignorance. "They been in here a lot?" I asked.

Michelle shook her head. "Came in the other week, had a few drinks, and left; been back a few times since then."

"They caused any trouble?"

She shook her head. "Not yet, but it's coming. I can feel it."

"Bill won't let them start anything," I said.

"And then it'll be all over the news how a revenant bar refused to serve humans," she said bitterly.

"I know for a fact that a lot of humans drink here," I told her, still watching the six men as Bill brought them their drinks—all beer, from the looks of it— and they walked off toward where the pool tables were.

"You know that some of the media won't care about that," Michelle said. "Sovereign Humanity have their allies in the news, in the police—they're everywhere."

"They're scum," I said.

Michelle walked over to Bill and obviously warned him, as he looked over at the newcomers and nodded once.

Keeping one eye on the newcomers, I started to reorganize my work, putting the loose pieces of paper and notepads back into my brown leather bag before closing it up.

It didn't take long for their presence to have an effect, as several customers gave them cautious glances and then left. The Sovereign Humanity guys were all laughing riotously, as if they'd witnessed the funniest things ever seen, and I noticed that there were still a couple of regulars playing pool. A man and a woman, both early twenties, both had arms covered in tattoos, and both were doing their best to completely ignore the Sovereign Humanity guys.

I drank the rest of my tea and took the cup over to the counter. "Thanks for the drink," I told Bill.

"You're welcome," he said, keeping an eye on the pool tables.

"You want them gone?" I asked.

Bill smiled. "Todd and Mikey are upstairs if we need them," he told me.

Todd and Mikey were two massive security guys who worked for the bar while training to become security detail. They'd rented the upstairs apartment from Bill and George months before, and they'd been incredibly helpful at dealing with the small amounts of trouble that had come the bar's way. Turns out most people don't want to make trouble when the clientele consist of people who can literally rip your arms off.

"I want to tell them to leave," Bill said with a sigh. "But I don't want trouble, either."

I stood chatting with him, and a few minutes later, the Sovereign Humanity group walked over to the exit.

"Fucking disgusting," the one I'd thought in charge shouted. "Beasts and monsters sitting down with hardworking humans."

"Get out; don't come back," Bill told him, his tone leaving no room for argument.

The leader spat on the floor. "You sicken me," he said, with so much anger and hatred. "You'll all get what's coming to you."

"I said leave," Bill told them.

Unfortunately, the man was on a roll. "And you," he said, pointing to the woman who'd been playing pool with the young man. "Humans fornicating with beasts. You're just as bad as these creatures."

I spotted the woman take a furious step forward, about to say something, but that would only escalate everything.

"Hey, Dale," I said casually but loud enough that everyone turned to look at me.

Dale stared at me, and all blood left his face in one of the funniest *oh, shit* moments I'd ever seen.

"Lucas," Dale said softly.

"You know this . . . degenerate?" the leader demanded of Dale.

"Not really," Dale said.

"He one of these abominations?" the man demanded, waving his hands about, as the rest of the group kept their eyes on the rest of the bar's clientele.

"No," Dale said, shaking his head. "He's a doctor or something."

"You should not be in here," the leader said, pointing a finger at me.

"Neither should you," I told him, keeping Dale's eye contact until he looked away first.

The leader pointed at me. "You should watch yourself, boy," he said, in what I assumed was meant to be a menacing voice. "Be sure you know whose side you're on."

"I already know," I told him. "Whatever side stands against you and your kind."

He flushed with anger, but before anyone could say anything else, he motioned for everyone to leave.

I looked over at Bill. "You okay?" I asked him.

Bill nodded.

I looked around at the young man and woman. The man's hands were in fists down by his side, and the woman had her hand on his shoulder as if trying to calm him, although she looked incensed herself. "You both okay?" I asked them.

"That . . . bastard," the woman snapped.

"They won't be back," Bill said.

And at that exact second, a brick was hurled through the glass front door of the bar.

# CHAPTER TWO

The brick had bounced off the front of the bar, leaving a gouge in the wood, but thankfully no one was hurt, either by the projectile or the glass, which was all over the floor.

The employees helped Bill clean it up. Most of the patrons elected to stay and help as well, a nice show of solidarity that I was pretty sure Bill appreciated.

It was just after nine p.m. when Meredith arrived, and immediately set about helping.

By the time it hit one a.m., Bill had sent most people home, and I'd finished nailing a large plank of wood over the empty door frame.

"So, this wasn't how I imagined we'd be spending the evening," Meredith said as she sat opposite me at my booth. Meredith had pale skin and was four or five inches shorter than my own height, even with the heels she wore. Her blond hair was tied back in a ponytail, and she had half a dozen earrings in each ear. She wore a pair of dark blue jeans and a black sweater, the sleeves of which were rolled up, revealing the mass of colourful anime characters tattooed over both her arms.

"Not exactly, no," I said. "On the plus side, it's good to see you again."

"You too," Meredith said. "I guess we'll have to reconvene our conversation about my work."

"We can walk back to my place," I said. "We'll talk about it on the way and you can grab a cab back to yours or crash in my spare room."

"Cab it is," Meredith said with a smile.

There was no room in my life for romantic entanglements, and Meredith was focussed on her work, so we were both happy to be good friends and nothing more.

Bill reported the incident to the police, but as no one was hurt, the perpetrators had run off, and there were no signs of a repeat attack, it wouldn't be high on their list of priorities.

Only the young man and woman who had taken abuse from Dale and his cronies were left in the bar with us. Bill sent the younger pair home, too, once it became apparent that everyone was okay.

We waited around until George arrived, then took off, telling Bill to call me if they needed anything. It had started to snow again, and we stood outside for a moment as I put on my hat and scarf before crossing the road, the sounds of New York's nightlife still evident in the distance. The city that never sleeps . . .

The park entrance was further up the street, and I spotted the young couple who had stayed around to help clean up. They vanished arm-in-arm into the park. A hundred or so feet behind them, two men walked toward the park. They were too far away for me to recognize, but I had a bad feeling nonetheless.

"I've booked a cab from your place to mine," Meredith said as we started to walk around the outside of the park. "It's not a long walk for a chat, but it's all we've got, I'm afraid."

I looked back at the approaching two men, and the bad feeling didn't go away. "Can you get the cab from here?" I asked.

"Sure," Meredith said, although the tone was one of confusion. "There a problem?"

"I hope not, but I just want to be sure," I told her.

Meredith made the call and we walked back to outside the bar to wait for the cab.

"I read through your research," I told her, passing her the notes and file that I'd brought with me. "The idea of being able to use the rift energy to heal humans without the need for them to die first would revolutionize the medical industry."

"If it works," Meredith said.

"If it works," I said, keeping one eye on the approaching men. "You're devising some kind of tracking system."

"Yes, we're using computer simulations to do it, but we can't get it to work. There's no rhyme or reason to how the tears open; we don't even know why some people come back as different revenants. Why is one person an elemental revenant and another a hooded revenant? We know so little, but we do know that when the tears open, they revive the person caught in it, and anyone in the immediate vicinity is healed."

"The young woman shot in the bank robbery," I said. Meredith had written about it in her notes. It had been all over the news a few months before.

"Exactly," Meredith said with considerable enthusiasm. "Her body was almost immediately filled by the energy from the rift, and the lady who had been trying to help her was healed of her arthritis. It was as though she had the joints of a teenager."

"You didn't really need me to go through it all and check it, did you?" I asked.

"No, I just wanted you to read it through before I went to the university for more funding," Meredith said bashfully. "I figured if you liked it, so would they."

"You could have told me," I said with a smile.

"I needed you to go in cold," she told me. "Can you imagine it, Lucas? No cancer, no disease, no premature deaths."

I stared at her. "Meredith, if that's possible, then great, but people have tried to do this before—usually with exceptionally bad results."

Meredith sighed. "I know; I'm getting overexcited and thinking about running a sprint before we're barely crawling. I just . . . Lucas, we don't know *anything* about the energy that comes through from the rift. Not really. We know that there are people living inside the rift; we know that there are cities in there, an entire civilization we can never get to."

"Inaxia," I said, using the name of the capital city inside the rift. Home to several million rift-fused.

Meredith nodded. "Not just Inaxia, though. Lots of cities. Some rift-born talk about them. They're the only ones we know of who can go back and forth to the rift whenever they like. We know that tears appear seemingly at random. That the energy that comes through brings back people or animals who died, and that's it. It imbues great power, and frankly, we have a responsibility to find out how and why."

"Did you just paraphrase Spider-Man?" I asked.

Meredith smiled. "Yes, yes, I did."

I chuckled. "Okay, look, I think your ideas have considerable merit, and they're worth looking into. I also think you need to be careful. If you manage to do this, *if* you discover how the rift selects people . . . you won't be the only one wanting that information."

Meredith's smile faded. "Yeah, I know. I've already had several government agencies asking me to work on their own rift-science projects. One of whom wants to create soldiers that fuse humans and fiends. I want to help people, Lucas. It's all I've ever wanted."

"I can't think of anyone else who's more likely to solve it," I told her as the two men came close enough for the streetlights to illuminate their faces. Two from the bar. They both stared over at where Meredith and I stood, then walked into the park instead. "But please do be careful."

"I will," Meredith promised. "So far, it's just me, you, and my assistants. Oh, and the funding committee."

"Just out of curiosity, who asked you to help fuse humans and fiends?" I asked her.

"Her name was Dr Mitchell," Meredith said. "She works for some security-consultant firm."

A shiver of foreboding hit me. My thoughts flashed back to five years previous, my arrival at the asylum. I'd gone there to help Isaac. There had been stories of people experimenting on revenants, on fiends too. I'd stayed because . . . well, because I was stupid enough to think it was a good idea. It hadn't been, and the brutality and horrors I'd seen there had stayed with me for a long time. I saw firsthand the kinds of methods she'd used to get results. I heard the screams; I smelled the blood. She was little more than a psychopath with a doctorate.

"You recognize the name, don't you?" Meredith said.

I nodded. "She's a monster," I told her. "She experiments on the rift-fused to see how they work. I've seen the aftermath of her *research* firsthand."

"I turned her down," Meredith said. "She was intense and, honestly, a little scary. She wouldn't say who backed her, either, which raised huge alarm bells."

The fact that Dr Mitchell was around and still performing her horror science meant nothing good. I made a mental note to call an old friend and ask him to look into it.

An Uber pulled up alongside us, and Meredith asked the driver to wait a moment as she checked the confirmation of its arrival on her phone. You can never be too careful. Which is sensible but also a damning indictment of the state of the world.

"Sorry about the truncated evening," Meredith said. "Thanks for your input. We'll have to do this properly soon," she said, getting into the car just as it started to snow again.

I looked across the road and into the park, hoping that the two Humanity Sovereign members hadn't caught up to anyone or done anything I needed to deal with. They'd been more than enough of a pain for one day.

Better to be safe, though, so I headed after them.

I'd crossed over a small bridge when I heard the first scream. It came from deeper in the park, and I quickened my pace.

Another scream, and I was flat-out sprinting until I spotted the two rotund men a few hundred feet down the path. One of them held the woman from the bar, while his friend kicked someone—presumably the man she'd left with—on the floor.

"Hey," I shouted. It had the desired effect of stopping the two men as they looked around to see who had seen them. They spotted me as I walked under a streetlamp.

One of the men pointed at me and laughed while the other kicked the prone man in the side again.

"What do you want, old man?" the man who'd laughed said.

"Old man?" I asked. "That's uncalled-for; it's not like either of you are spring chickens."

"Yeah, but we don't need a walking stick," the second man said as the woman helped her friend up and started to move away.

"Get going, you two," I told them. "Get him to a doctor."

She looked at her friend and nodded.

"We didn't say the mutants could go," the kicker said with a sneer.

"You think we won't beat your crippled ass?" the joker said.

"Humans drinking in a revenant bar," the kicker said. "Drinking with the damned soulless. It's disgusting."

"I don't like that word," I said slowly, making sure that there was enough distance between us that both men would have to take a few steps before they could do anything.

"*Cripple* or *soulless*?" the joker asked, laughing like he'd said the funniest thing of all time.

The kicker and joker stood in front of me, the latter removing a brass knuckleduster from his pocket. He put it on in an exaggerated way, making sure I saw it. Both were about my height, but I was pretty sure that neither of them were trained fighters, just thugs who liked to bully and pick on those weaker than them.

"That stick isn't going to help you," the kicker said.

"I don't know about that," I said. "Either of you want to tell me who threw the rock?"

Both of them laughed. "Dirty soulless don't belong in this neighbourhood," the joker said. "They should be in their *own* neighbourhood, with their *own* kind."

I sighed. There were always people like this. People who thought they were better, who needed someone to blame for the state of their own existence.

The kicker threw a punch. It was a right-hand haymaker, the kind that puts you on your ass if it connects. *If.* I stepped around the punch, pushing his arm away with my right hand while sweeping my left hand under and up the outside of his arm. My left hand also held my walking cane, so I let go of it, catching it in my right hand and driving it into my attacker's ribs as I stepped around him.

He was on his knees, coughing up his lungs, as I continued past him. I swung the cane around at the joker, who was surprised at what had happened, leaving him open for the cane to crack around the side of his face. He dropped to the ground and blinked as blood began to pour out of his broken nose.

I stepped toward the joker and smashed the butt of the cane into his face, knocking him out cold, sending him to the snow-covered ground.

The kicker had gotten back to his feet, one hand holding his side, but the other had a switchblade in it. He darted forward and I stepped back and to the side, putting distance between us. The kicker swiped the blade toward me in what I could only assume was him trying to feint, because he quickly shot toward me, lunging the tiny blade like a lance. I stepped to the side and brought down my cane on his wrist, immediately bringing the cane back to my shoulder before bringing it down again, this time on his forearm, following through and ending with a crack on his already-injured ribs.

The kicker screamed, presumably unable to decide which part of him hurt more, and he dropped to a foetal position on the ground.

"Broken wrist, arm, and probably ribs will do that," I said to him as the switchblade hung uselessly between two fingers.

I kicked the switchblade away, which had the not-so-unpleasant consequence of the movement causing him more pain in his hand.

"Who threw the rock?" I asked, placing the butt of the cane an inch above his swelling limb. "Don't make me ask again."

"Brad," he said through gritted teeth. "The one in charge."

"Hair in a ponytail?" I asked. "Had *S.H.* tattooed on his neck?"

The kicker nodded.

I placed the cane against his wrist and pushed as I knelt down beside him. Kicker screamed again.

"I want you to remember that feeling," I told him. "Remember what happens to people who hurt those who are just trying to live their lives.

Don't let me see either of you around here again." I pushed down harder. "Understand?"

The man nodded, gasping for air as I released the pressure on his wrist and took a deep breath. "Phone," I said.

"Front pocket," the kicker said.

I found it where he said it would be; it was some old flip-phone thing that screamed *burner*. I dialled 911, explained the situation, ended the call, and dropped the phone on the ground close to the head of the kicker.

"I was never here," I told him. "I would make sure you remember that." I kicked him in the head, knocking him out.

I continued on through the park without any further trouble. I hoped the kicker would relay my words to his friend when he woke up; I'd hate to think that I'd had to hurt them both for no reason. Well, apart from the fact that they clearly deserved it.

By the time I left the park, any adrenaline that I'd felt from the fight had dissipated, and I felt like just getting home so that I could have a shower and get some sleep. My automatic black Longines Heritage watch told me it was after two a.m. It had been a long day.

I crossed the road and walked over to my apartment building. It was six storeys, and my two-bedroom sixth-floor apartment had wonderful views of the city. Even at night, it was an impressive view. I'd lived there for three years and found it to be a place that I could go to get away from everything.

The foyer to my apartment building was large but fairly unassuming. There was a wall lined with metal post boxes on one side and a large mirror opposite.

I was halfway through the foyer when the door opened and Dale walked in. He looked worse for wear and had the good grace to look embarrassed when he saw me.

"Lucas," he acknowledged softly, his voice barely above a whisper.

I stopped walking. I really didn't have time or energy to deal with him, but the way his friends had behaved still left a bad taste in my mouth. "Your friends are assholes," I told him.

He looked at me. "Now, that's not fair. We're fighting for human rights," he continued without a trace of irony or intelligence in his regurgitated nonsense.

"You're fighting for *nothing*," I said sadly. "You're just trying to find someone to blame because you're pathetic."

Dale's expression darkened and I thought he was going to take a swing at me.

I walked past him and over to the lifts without another word. Dale was not worth my time and effort.

The lift doors opened, I pressed the button for the sixth floor, and the lift started its journey.

The lift doors opened, and I walked down the dark green carpeted hallway to my apartment.

The interior was spacious and light.

I had two dark grey couches, one with two seats and the other with three. The entire place was silent, and I shrugged off my jacket, placing it on the hook next to the door, before walking into the room and pouring myself a large glass of whisky.

I sat on the couch, enjoying the silence as I finished my drink, still feeling on edge about the fight. It had been too easy. Too easy for me to slip into old habits. Four years and no need to hurt someone, to fight. I trained every day, but the second I knew that violence was about to happen, it felt like I'd never stopped.

I looked over at the cane next to the front door. I didn't need the cane, I'd *never* needed the cane, but it was part of the facade that had been created to hide myself. I poured another drink and knocked it back in one, letting the burning fill my throat.

*Enough.* I took the glass through to the kitchen and went for a shower. Keeping the water as hot as possible, I stood there for several minutes, just feeling the heat cascade over my long dark hair and shoulders. I'd half-expected the water to turn pink. It had happened more than once in my life; it was pretty much a certainty that it would happen again at some point.

I opened the shower door and stepped out of the bathroom, drying myself as I walked into the master bedroom.

I pulled the wardrobe doors open, revealing shirts, jeans, and trousers next to two dark grey suits both in dust jackets, neither of which I'd worn in a long time.

Dropping to my knees, I placed my index finger in the hole at the base of the wardrobe and pulled toward me until there was a click. I pulled the base of the wardrobe up, revealing the false bottom beneath it. Inside was a six-feet-square floor safe with a numerical pad beside it. I'd had the safe custom-made the day I'd moved into my apartment. I punched in the numbers 1576, opened it, and revealed the contents inside: a drawstring pouch in black velvet that was large enough to conceal the mask inside, a second identical pouch about the size of my hand, a metal suitcase, and a black duffle bag.

The safe was quite deep, and all the contents fit inside with ease, but I stared at the velvet pouch containing the mask above anything else. I tore my gaze away from it and opened the smaller pouch, removing the Raven Guild medallion from inside. I held it for several seconds before putting it back.

"Not today," I whispered, and closed the safe, putting the false bottom back inside the wardrobe and closing it with another click.

I remained sitting on the edge of the bed for some time, staring at the dark carpet, wondering how long it would be before I had to take the bag and suitcase out of the wardrobe again. I hoped that the fight was a one-off, a momentary return to the world I'd left behind.

My time at the asylum had taught me many things, primarily that I was not in a good place mentally. That I hadn't dealt with the deaths of my friends. That I hadn't dealt with surviving what had killed so many. I walked away from that life and found that the longer I was away, the easier it became to convince myself it was best to keep it that way.

When I finally fell asleep, my dreams were of things I would rather forget.

# CHAPTER THREE

*Five Years Ago*

I'd woken up with a headache and the feeling that I'd like to find the man who had hit me in the face and feed him his own rifle.

I rolled to the side and blinked a few times. My head hurt. A lot. That was a surprise. I'd expected my body to have healed itself, but instead, I was met with pain and the unpleasant sensation that something was very wrong.

Pushing myself upright was a herculean process I'd rather not have to do a second time. My head spun a little, and I had to close my eyes and wait for it to pass. What the hell was wrong with me? Was I drugged?

I swung my legs off the side of the bed and leaned up against the wall, the back of my head feeling the cool touch of stone. Opening my eyes, I realised I was in a cell. The entire front of the cell, door included, was made of bulletproof Plexiglas with several holes drilled into the door and wall. A marked difference from the grey stone that made up the other three walls. A window sat at the top of the cell wall opposite the door.

The cell contained the bed I sat on, a small toilet and shower cubicle with a shower curtain that you pulled around yourself. There was a small table and single wooden chair, and a bookcase that could probably house a dozen books, although it was currently empty.

I ran my hands through my hair and sighed. I'd allowed myself to get captured because I wanted answers about Dr Mitchell's operation. I wanted to know what she was up to, and I also wanted to know why she had a medallion from the Raven Guild.

There was a light tap on the door of my cell.

Dr Mitchell stood in the hallway beyond my cell, with the guard who had hit me in the face. She wore the black-and-white dress she'd been wearing when I'd first seen her.

"You've finally woken up," she said.

"You been out there the whole time?" I asked, looking over at her.

"No," she said with a chuckle. "I have better things to do, Your Majesty."

I vaguely remembered telling her I was the Queen of Finland. "How long was I out?"

"A few hours," she said. "We had to get you dressed."

I looked down and noticed the light blue scrubs. "Brings out my eyes," I told her.

"You're also wearing something quite special," she said. "Under the scrubs."

I unfastened the scrub top, removing it and looking down at the black, skintight top. I pulled the scrub waistband away and discovered it was a bodysuit.

"What is it?" I asked.

"Every guest here wears one," she said. "They stop your ability to tap into the rift. Or, in the case of a riftborn, their embers."

That explained the headache and overall feeling of crappiness. I hadn't healed.

The embers are something all riftborn have. They're a sort of gateway between the rift and earth, but they're like a personal pocket dimension that only riftborn can use. Every riftborn has their own embers, and every ember looks different. To maintain their power, riftborn have to enter the embers every month, and are forced to if seriously injured. Time moves differently in the embers. The more injured a riftborn is, the more time they have to stay in the embers. It'll only feel like a few hours to the riftborn, but it can be days or weeks for time on Earth and the rift.

Wilfully cutting yourself off from your embers means not using your powers for months at a time. It has the benefit of passing rift-fused security precautions by appearing to be human.

"I'm human," I told her. It was a lie, but it was a lie I'd been practising for few months. Isaac had come to me about getting onto the island but needing a human to do it. Three months with no accessing my abilities had left me, for all intents and purposes, utterly human. What they didn't know is that the second I got this damn second skin off, I was going to access my embers. What happened after that wasn't going to be good for them.

"Can't be too careful," she said.

"Why am I here?" I asked.

"Why did you break into my office?" Dr Mitchell countered. "We've spoken to the crew you came with; they're all as mystified as we are. You joined the crew as a new member, you barely socialised with them, and you left the second you could. The captain isn't best pleased at what you've done."

"You didn't hurt them, did you?" I asked.

"No," Dr Mitchell snapped. "I'm not in the habit of hurting people just because a member of their people is stupid. Why are you here?"

"I'm a reporter," I said. "Heard rumours about mistreatment of rift-fused. Of humans. Wanted to find out."

"Did a guard tell you that?" Dr Mitchell asked.

"Don't remember," I told her. "Might have been. Might have been through a Ouija board. One of the spirits of the dead you killed came back to get revenge."

Dr Mitchell's eyes narrowed in irritation. "Ghosts? Really?"

I shrugged.

"Do not feed me bullshit," Dr Mitchell said. "You want to write a story so badly, let me show you the facility. First, you will tell me your name."

"Lucas Rurik," I said, hoping that Isaac had gotten my backstory sorted.

"Rurik," Dr Mitchell said. "There was a king by that name."

"About a thousand years ago," I said. "No relation."

"Against the wall," the guard demanded.

I got up and walked over to the far wall, placing my cheek against the cool stone, as an even cooler breeze wafted in from the window above me.

"Lace your fingers behind your back," the guard snapped. "Any deviation will be met with force."

I did exactly what I was told to do.

There was a hiss of air as my door slid open and I waited patiently while the cuffs were clipped onto my wrists.

"That's a good little boy," the guard said, patting me on the head.

I thrust down the instinct to rip his patronizing tongue from his mouth as he turned me to face him. He smiled and shoved me out into the hallway.

"Follow me," Dr Mitchell said.

The hall had barred windows on one side, overlooking the grounds in front of the prison. The sky was overcast, and there was a smell of impending rain.

The guard shoved me, and I started to walk, occasionally looking outside at the twenty-five-foot chain-link fence that surrounded the entire property.

"You yearning for freedom?" the guard asked with a chuckle.

"Just wondering why the fence is necessary," I said.

"To keep people like you in," he snapped.

"We're five storeys up, there are bars on the windows, dozens of guards, two guard towers with snipers, and, most importantly, we're on an island in the middle of nowhere."

The guard shoved me forward. "Think you're a smart mouth?" He snapped.

"No, he asks a good question," Dr Mitchell said, turning back to me. "We have over a hundred guests here. Some are more dangerous than others. But some of them have dangerous friends. The fencing, the snipers, they're all necessary to ensure that no one tries anything stupid."

We reached the first set of doors, behind which stood two more guards. They let us through without comment, and we continued to the lifts, which we took down to the first floor.

This floor was busier, with several people in lab coats looking over in my direction as we walked along the white-tiled floor to the office at the far end of the floor.

Dr Mitchell stopped to talk to several people, all of whom glanced in my direction, some with disdain, and some with a smile and greed in their eyes. The latter creeped me out a lot more than the former.

We continued on through the floor until we reached a checkpoint with three armed guards. Dr Mitchell spoke to one of the guards, although I didn't hear what she said, and walked to the lift beyond, using a key card to open the doors.

I was bundled into the large lift and Dr Mitchell used her key card again on a small digital panel, which flashed red twice and we set off again.

We were moving down at what felt like a slow pace, although after thirty seconds, I wondered just how far under the island we were.

"I see why you chose the island," I said.

The lift stopped and the doors opened, revealing a corridor with red lights imbedded in the floor, giving it a creepy and unpleasant vibe. Something the whole bloody island had, if I was honest.

There was a large metal door at the end of the hallway, which opened as we drew close, revealing more of the red-tinged hallway as it split off into three. Dr Mitchell took the left turn and we walked past several windows showing one huge laboratory inside.

Dr Mitchell stopped outside of a set of metal double doors. "Do you know what we do down here?" She asked me. "Be honest."

"I was told you're experimenting on humans and rift-fused," I said; there was no point in lying. "I don't know to what end, but I do know you're torturing people. Killing them. That some of the people here are dangerous criminals that you purchased from private prisons on the mainland."

"Which you'll never be able to prove," Dr Mitchell said smugly.

"Well done," I said. "You must be proud."

I got a punch to the kidney for that. I dropped to one knee; the air left my body. I turned back to the guard. "Damn it, I thought we were going to be friends."

He went to hit me again, but Dr Mitchell stopped him. "Lucas Rurik, do you know why you're here right now and not in the ocean being food for the animals?"

"Because you secretly love me?" I asked. "I'm not sure we're meant to be."

Dr Mitchell grabbed my jaw and pushed my head up to meet her gaze. "Because I already checked you out," she said. "You've been out for a few hours. Enough time for me to get your fingerprints checked. Lucas Rurik, reporter for the BBC."

I owed Isaac and Hannah each a beer.

"You're going to write everything you see," Dr Mitchell said. "And once you're done, if I like what I read, you're going to get the scoop on the biggest story you've ever known. Otherwise, we can make you just disappear."

I kept my mouth closed.

Dr Mitchell released her grip from my jaw, and I got to my feet as she used her keycard to open the set of doors, which took us into a large room with freezers along one wall and metal surgical tables in the middle. A morgue. One of the tables was stained red with blood, and there were jars of various parts of anatomy on display on shelves along the far right wall. The opposite end of the room was a metal door, which Dr Mitchell walked over to and pushed open.

"Mr Rurik," she said with a flourish.

I stepped inside, wondering what was going to befall me the second I did, and instead stared in horror at the thing in front of me.

"Guard Tobias Moore," Dr Mitchell said.

I continued to stare at the naked body of the guard. He had been tied to a metal post, in a crucifixion pose, and someone had cut through his chest, opening the cavity to reveal the organs inside—although they were in jars by his feet. The huge flaps of skin had been pinned back, making him look a little like he had wings.

Blood was everywhere.

The smell hit me all at once. The smell of blood and shit.

"Lucas Rurik," Dr Mitchell said. "I believe you know the guard who told you about our operation."

I couldn't speak; I had no idea what to say. What was done to him was nothing more than the work of a psychopathic mind. A monster. I looked over at Dr Mitchell.

"Now you may ask questions," she said with the first genuine smile I'd seen since arriving.

# CHAPTER FOUR

*Now*

A tiny sliver of light broke through the curtains, shining a sunbeam directly onto my face. I tried to swat it away as though it were a fly, and it took me several seconds to realise that it wasn't something that could be removed with an annoyed flail of my arm.

It was after nine a.m., which meant I'd probably slept for five hours in total and wouldn't be going back to sleep any time soon.

After a brief bout of cursing at the curtains' lack of doing their job, I got up and made myself a cup of coffee, using a *Star Wars* mug that Meredith had given me as a birthday gift and was about twice the size of every other mug I owned. Perfect for that first cup of coffee in the morning. I took my first sip just as the phone rang.

I picked the phone up on the second ring. "Hello," I said, hoping it wasn't someone trying to sell something.

"Lucas." Isaac's voice brought back memories of when I'd last spoken to him. He sounded tired, upset. Scared. I'd never heard Isaac sound scared before. It put me on edge.

"Isaac?" I asked.

"I didn't want to do this," he said. "But we need help. *I* need help."

"Help with what?" I asked him, feeling a tightness in my chest. I hadn't spoken to Isaac in nearly four years. "What the hell is going on?"

Isaac took a deep breath. "You know of Gosnell Big Woods Preserve, it's near Rochester?"

"No, should I?" I asked.

"There was a fiend attack there a few hours ago," Isaac told me. "Three days ago, two members of the public were mauled to death. So, the FBI had a team out this morning, with RCU members attached. The team were attacked. Three FBI agents and four of my people were killed. Two more RCU agents are in the ICU. Including Dan."

*Oh, shit.* "Dan is hurt?" I asked. "Sorry, I know you've lost four people, Isaac. I'm sorry about that. Are Dan and the other agent going to be okay? What about Gabriel, Hannah, and Ji-hyun?"

"Gabriel is fine," Isaac said. "He doesn't work for the RCU anymore. Ji-hyun is in Los Angeles. She's working with an RCU team out there. Hannah is at home; she's fine too. Dan and Annie are both in surgery."

The rift-fused are a hardy bunch, and they live long lives, but they can still be hurt. Still be killed. Modern medicine helps heal what the natural body can't, but they're not impervious to pain and damage.

The RCU was a worldwide agency a bit like Interpol but for crimes involving the rift in one way or another. They had several branches just in America, with each branch having up to three teams working for it. To have nearly a whole team wiped out was shocking to say the least. And by fiends was . . . well, it was unheard of.

"What do you need?" I asked Isaac.

"I know you left for time away," Isaac said. "I know you needed that time to sort your head out. But I need your help."

"Whatever you need," I told him immediately.

Isaac said. "The FBI are currently guarding the injured at the hospital. Everyone is worried people higher up are going to start pointing fingers, that there are rumours the RCU fucked up. We didn't fuck up, Lucas. I've stood the rest of Dan's team down until we can find out what the hell is going on. The rest of the branch are still working though, just in case of more attacks."

"Since when did the FBI work on a joint operation with the RCU?" I asked.

"It's a long story," Isaac told me, sounding less than happy about it.

"They're looking to merge you with the FBI, aren't they?" I asked. It had been something that those in positions of power had wanted to do back before I'd walked away. The directors of the FBI had lobbied those in charge of the RCU and had been told to go away and worry about their own organisation. I got the feeling that hadn't changed during my time away.

"I'll tell you all about it when you get here," Isaac said, clearly not wanting to get into it further. "In the meantime, the FBI are investigating, with my cooperation."

"And the fiends that attacked your team?" I asked.

"Dead." Isaac said.

"Good," I told him. "What do you need from me?"

"I've been given dispensation to bring on someone from outside the RCU to help with the investigation," Isaac said. "I want you. This stinks to high heaven. No RCU members are going to get jumped by a couple of greater fiends that they're out hunting. Never going to happen to anyone with even a modicum of experience."

"You want me to look into it?" I said, trying to get my head around the fact that my life had just spun 180 in the last few seconds.

"Please," Isaac said. "I can have the RCU jet meet you and get you to Rochester. I've called in a favour to a friend of mine who lives near you. He's an ex-cop. He's going to pick you up, drive you to the airport. He'll be about fifteen minutes."

"In New York?" I asked, and something dawned on me. "You'd already contacted him. You knew I'd come back."

"You've been out for four years, but I know you, Lucas," Isaac said. "And I doubt very much that you've changed so much in four years that you would say no."

I didn't like that he'd already decided what my answer would be, but he wasn't wrong. I didn't like that much, either.

"Is it going to be on the news?" I asked.

"Six p.m. tonight," Isaac said. "We might have been able to hold it off, but humans got killed. They're being told right now about what happened. Wrong place, wrong time. The FBI are handling it. We managed to get the press to hold off until it was done. It's not like the old days, when people didn't have mobile phones and easy access to share everything they see."

"Is there film of the fiends?" I asked.

"No," Isaac said. "Thankfully. Lots of people on social media talking about having seen fiends in the preserve, though. I'll have someone meet you at the airport in Rochester; they'll drive you to the hospital in Hamble. I'll meet you there."

"See you in a few hours," I told him. "Stay safe."

"Thank you, Lucas." Isaac said. "Your help, it means a lot."

"Anytime, my friend," I said, and disconnected the call as the memories of the dreams I'd had flashed back to the front of my mind. I stood still, frozen in place as the realization of what I'd just done crashed down on me. I hadn't spoken to Isaac in four years. I'd given him my number for an emergency, and he'd never used it in all this time. The RCU had lost people in the most violent way possible, on what sounded like a routine hunt. FBI agents had been killed too. And the human media were about to shine a big spotlight on the rift-fused.

My friend was in the ICU. I hadn't seen Dan in years, but he was a good guy and a good RCU agent. If something had attacked him and his team, it had been something incredibly dangerous. It took me a few minutes to process everything, before I got to my feet and threw some essentials into an overnight bag.

I pushed the thoughts of nerves at returning to my old life, seeing old friends, aside. I did the same to the sadness and anger about what had happened to Dan and his team. Delving into those emotions wouldn't help me right now. I needed to concentrate on what I could actually do. Get a bag ready, get to the airport, get to Rochester. Those were things I had control over.

Getting ready, I realised there was another emotion inside that I'd tried not to think about. I was excited. I was looking forward to getting back to my old life and doing something I was good at.

Within an hour, there was a buzz on the intercom, the video screen showing me a man of about forty with military-styled hair, wearing a black suit that could probably use being let out a bit.

"Lucas Rurik?" the man asked, his accent placing him from somewhere in the South. "Isaac Gordon called in a favour to take you to the airport."

I grabbed my bag, made sure I had a jacket, hat, scarf, and my phone. In my haste, I'd almost forgotten about the cane, and when I picked it up, it felt heavier than usual. Gabriel was the one who had given me the idea of needing a cane, of always having a weapon with me, disguised as an innocuous walking aid. He'd also been the one to suggest keeping my beard and long hair. Isaac and Gabriel had worked with me to remove me from a life that was quickly taking me down a path of darkness. A life I'd managed to stay away from for four years and was about to burst back into. I rested the cane up against the sideboard. I wasn't going to need to pretend to be something I wasn't anymore.

The black BMW SUV was parked on the street in front of my apartment building. The driver's door opened and the large man from the video screen got out, opening the rear passenger door.

"Thanks," I said getting into the SUV and buckling up. "Did Isaac tell you what's going on?"

"Sorry," the man said. "All I know is I'm meant to drive you to the airport."

Upon arriving, I was directed to a Gulfstream G550. The interior of the plane was pretty luxurious. The eight seats were all made of cream-coloured leather, and there were two long couches at the rear of the jet, just in front of where the cabin staff would normally sit, next to a small—even by airplane standards—bathroom.

The flight took about an hour and we landed in Rochester, where a black Chevrolet Suburban was waiting for me. Its driver—a young man who looked like he'd only recently graduated from college—stood outside of the car, waiting for me.

"The Rochester office said you needed to go to Hamble," the driver said to me as I settled into the rear of the SUV.

"That's what I was told," I said. "Any update about what happened?"

"Above my pay grade," the driver said as we set off.

As before, I dozed off to sleep, only waking up when the driver called my name.

"We're at the hospital," he said.

"Thanks," I told him, opening the car door and stepping outside into the hospital drop-off bay.

"Bloody hell," I said, wrapping my coat around me as I fumbled with my leather gloves and tried to remove a wool hat from my pocket at the same time.

I looked up at the ten-storey hospital and felt real fear for the first time in years. Fear for my friends. Fear about how I was going to explain my sudden reappearance.

"Lucas," a familiar voice shouted.

I looked over at the hospital entrance where Gabriel Santiago waved at me. He looked almost identical to how I'd last seen him, except his hair was shorter and he no longer had a beard. He wore a long black coat, and a blue-and-gold clerical band around his bicep. Church of Tempered Souls was the only religion that dealt with the rift-fused. Most of its members were revenants, although there were more and more humans joining as well. Despite having been established centuries before, it had only grown exponentially over the last few decades as the rift-fused had become more and more integrated into society.

The religion didn't worship any particular deity but, instead, dealt with spirituality and generating acceptance for those who became rift-fused, for themselves and those they lived amongst. They discussed the rift itself and the people who lived there, and theorised about what happened after the rift-fused died, too. It was all very supportive and peaceful, a bit like a club for like-minded people who wanted answers and had nowhere else to get them.

"Lucas," Gabriel said, embracing me.

"You're a cleric now?" I asked him.

"A lot has happened in the last few years," Gabriel said.

"How's Dan?" I asked him, picking up my bag and following him into the hospital.

"He's out of surgery," Gabriel said. "They think he'll be okay."

The relief was palpable, and I remained quiet as we walked along the main hallway, past reception where half a dozen people were working, and into the lift taking us to the eighth floor.

"How long have you been a cleric?" I asked.

"Three years," Gabriel said.

"And how is that working out?" I asked him. "You being a cleric, I mean?"

"It has its highs and lows," Gabriel said. "Isaac said you were coming to help out. I'm glad."

"You sound like you believe that this is more than just an unlucky ambush on an RCU team," I said.

"You think Isaac would call you for help for something like that?" Gabriel asked me. "A highly trained RCU unit was all but wiped out by greater fiends. How likely do you think that scenario is?"

"I think that's exceptionally unlikely," I pointed out.

"Something is going on," Gabriel said. "No way Dan's team got ambushed and slaughtered that easily by anything regular."

Gabriel's anger flashed hot and vanished.

"If you'd been there, you might be dead too," I told him.

Gabriel smiled, although it wasn't one of humour. "Four years away and you can still read me that easily."

"I would hope so," I told him. "You always were one to wear your heart on your sleeve."

Gabriel grasped my shoulder. "It's really good to see you again, old friend."

"You too," I told him.

"Let's go see Dan," Gabriel said.

The lift stopped and the metal doors opened, revealing a horseshoe-shaped floor. In the centre of the horseshoe was a large area where doctors, nurses, and the various members of staff were situated. A lot of them were talking to one another or looking at computers. Around the outside of the horseshoe were eight identical doors. There were large windows beside each door, allowing staff to look in at the patients.

Several armed guards stood outside two of the rooms, and as I walked around the outside of the room, close to the doors, I spotted that one of the rooms was a large waiting area with several people wearing FBI jackets.

"That's a lot of feds," I whispered to Gabriel.

"Yes, it is," Gabriel said without further comment.

Gabriel stopped by a door, nodded at the two guards as he opened it and stepped inside, motioning for me to join him.

I paused. The blinds to the window were closed, leaving the room shadowed. Gabriel closed the door behind me as I stared at Dan, who lay unconscious in a hospital bed, hooked up to various machines measuring his vitals.

Dan Parker was a touch over six and a half feet tall, he weighed nearly twenty stone. He was a big man. He was tanned with short dark hair, and was clean-shaven. The memory of him was fixed in my mind. A large imposing presence, a man who talked about honour and doing his duty, about helping people.

He was an arcane revenant. A species of revenant that could open small tears to use the power of the rift to change animals and vegetation around him. He could also cut off the power of another rift-fused within a set distance from him. Only one at a time, but I'd seen him use it to good effect. He was a hell of a warrior.

Despite having never been an agent of the RCU myself, I'd worked with the team on more than one occasion and had grown close to several members. Dan was a good man, a hard worker, and someone who I'd trusted with my life more than once.

"If you get out of bed right now, I'll buy you the best bottle of bourbon you've ever had," I told Dan, to zero movement on his part.

"It's difficult seeing him like this," Gabriel said, taking my thoughts and vocalizing them.

I stood motionless, transfixed on Dan, the beeping of the machines a soundtrack to the bombardment of memories that attacked me. I closed my eyes and took a deep breath, letting it out slowly as I reopened my eyes.

"How did a group of experienced agents get ambushed and slaughtered by two mere fiends?" I asked.

"That's something we'd like to know too," a female voice said from behind me.

I turned to see a young blonde woman in a charcoal suit with a white blouse. She had several piercings in each ear, and her hair was tied back in a ponytail. She offered me her hand, which I shook.

"Special Agent Emily West," she said.

"FBI?" I asked her.

Special Agent West nodded. "Yes." She looked over at Gabriel. "Father, you know you can go home."

"It's Cleric, not Father, but Gabriel is fine," Gabriel said. "Dan's my friend, and I'm still classified as a member of the RCU; I just have other duties."

"And you are?" Emily asked me.

"Lucas," I said.

"Do you have a surname?"

"Rurik," I told her. "I'm just here to see my friend."

"You're not a member of the RCU?" she asked me, removing her phone from her pocket, and tapping on the screen.

"No," I said softly. "I worked with Dan a long time ago. Isaac called me and asked me to come see him."

"Are you a Guild member?" Special Agent West asked.

I shook my head.

"Then you don't have security clearance to be here," Emily said, her tone now hard.

"He's fine," Gabriel said. "I'll vouch for him."

"That's great, Gabriel, but it's not *about* vouching for him," Emily said. "It's about the legalities of the matter. The RCU and FBI were attacked, a whole team nearly decimated. You are not a member of the RCU, you are definitely not FBI, so you have no reason to be here. It's not a visiting hospital, Mr Rurik."

"Emily," Gabriel said, more forcefully.

"It's okay," I told him. "She's right, Gabriel. Can you tell me one thing before I leave?"

Special Agent West considered this for a moment before nodding.

"What actually happened to Dan's team?" I asked. "I don't mean divulging anything that's sensitive, I know that fiends were involved. But what injuries did they sustain?"

"The fiends tore four highly trained revenants to pieces," she told me. "The fifth member, Annie, is currently in surgery having her arm reattached. Dan was the least injured and has three six-inch-long claw marks that raked around his left side, below his ribs, and stopped just above his groin. There was venom in the wound too, although thankfully his body is fighting that. Until he wakes up, we won't know what actually went down."

I looked back at Dan for a second and then turned to Special Agent West. "Thank you," I said. "I need to find Isaac. Any idea where he is?"

Before anyone could say anything, the door behind Special Agent West opened, and Isaac stepped in. He looked almost identical to when I'd last seen him four years before.

"Lucas," Isaac said, engulfing me in a hug. "It's damn good to see you again."

"You too," I told him, feeling a little emotional about the circumstances and seeing old friends after so long.

"Your friend was just going," Special Agent Emily West said to Isaac pointedly.

"That I was," I said.

"I'll walk you out," Isaac told me.

We walked together to the lift, and I felt the eyes of Emily and her team on me. Once we were in the lift, I felt free to talk again. "You want to tell me what the fuck happened?"

"The bodies of two lesser fiends were found close by the attack site," Isaac said. "Both were killed with a rift-tempered blade. General consensus is that maybe Dan or Annie managed to finish them off, but something feels crooked . . . because none of my team were actually armed with a rift-tempered blade."

The best way to kill a rift-fused is with a rift-tempered weapon. It stops revenants from going through to the rift after they die, and it makes sure that anything else killed stays dead. Several revenants have powers that have similar effects—the chains of a chained revenant for one—but rift-tempered weaponry was always the way to go if given the option.

"Exactly why did you ask me to come here to help?" I asked him.

Isaac remained quiet until the lift stopped, and the doors began to open. "I wanted your help because two fiends apparently arranged and executed an ambush on a group of highly trained RCU agents and then were killed by a weapon none of my agents were carrying. Does that sound like a problem to you?"

"Oh, yeah," I said wondering just how awful things were going to get.

# CHAPTER FIVE

Isaac and I didn't speak as we left the hospital and made our way across the car park, stopping beside a red BMW M5.

"Fiends don't work together; they're not pack animals," I said when I was sure that no one was around to hear us. "Even greater fiends are hardwired to hunt solo."

"What if they were elder fiends? They have the intellect and will to work together." Isaac asked.

"There hasn't been an elder fiend in North America in three hundred years," I said. "Two working together . . . that would be bad."

Fiends came in three types: lesser, greater, and elder. The former were both dangerous if you didn't know what you were up against, but it was rare that anyone with the training that the RCU had would come away from a fight against them with anything more than a few cuts and scrapes.

Isaac removed a set of car keys from his pocket and tossed them to me. "I arranged this for you," he said. "I figured you might be around for a few days and would need something to drive."

"So, you're bribing me to stay with a nice car?" I asked with a smirk.

Isaac removed a hotel key card from his pocket and passed it to me. "The Grand in Hamble. Room 718, I had your stuff sent there. Get in; there's something I want to show you."

I took the key card and placed it in my jacket pocket before getting into the car, starting the engine, and syncing my phone with the onboard computer.

"How are the rest of your team?" I asked.

"About as good as you can imagine they'd be," Isaac said. "This was originally the FBI's investigation; we were brought in to provide back-up and support."

"Why was the FBI leading the investigation? Surely, if it was a fiend attack, that's RCU jurisdiction," I asked.

"The two people killed out here the other day were human hikers," Isaac said. "Apparently, they were working with the FBI on something. After the fiend attack, we got involved, but jurisdiction was still FBI, as they had point on the investigation."

"That why you had Dan and company out here?" I asked.

Isaac nodded. "The fiends hadn't been found; people were jumpy. Dan put together a team to help the FBI's investigation. They came out in the morning because they'd had sightings of the fiends. The RCU were running point here; FBI were backup only. They weren't meant to be out here, but higher-ups insisted they take part. Dan was pretty angry he had to babysit humans, but the FBI said they could handle themselves."

"Are the FBI used to killing fiends?" I asked.

"Doubt it," Isaac said. "Something is happening here, something bad. And I'm not entirely sure who I trust. To add to the party, the Ancients got involved."

*Ah, shit.* The Ancients were the oldest, although not necessarily the most powerful, members of the rift-fused. All of them had been Guild members at one time or another, and their job was to ensure that equilibrium among the rift-fused and humans was maintained. They ensured that the Guilds keeping the rift-fused in check were balanced, that the RCU was given time, space, and money to do their job. They had a few other roles, but most importantly, they mediated between humans and rift-fused to ensure a smooth relationship between the two races.

"And exactly what do the Ancients want you to do?" I asked.

"Work with the FBI however we see fit but find out what happened, and find out quickly," Isaac said. "I'm quoting the exact line I was given."

"You think they want it covered up?"

"I think they don't want humans to think we can't stop fiends from hunting them for snacks."

Isaac made a valid point. "I'll be here as long as you need me," I said. "What do you want me to do?"

Isaac removed his phone from his pocket. "These are photos of the two fiends," he told me, clicking a few screens before handing the phone over.

"These were taken in a morgue," I said, noticing the metal table, the sterile-looking environment, and, more important, the fact that I could clearly see the word morgue in the background.

"The fiends were found in a state of decay, but oddly enough, they hadn't dissolved," Isaac said. "They were found under twenty minutes after the attack."

"Who found them?" I asked.

"A man was out walking his dog, found them near a cabin by the lake, about half a klick away from the crime scene," he said.

"How long after they were found were these taken?" I asked.

"About an hour," Isaac said. "The attendants know to get work done quickly when it comes to fiends."

"And there's no decay at all?" I asked. When fiends die, they dissolve to ash. Lesser fiends do it almost instantly all at once, but greater fiends take a while, piece by piece. Elder fiends take hours to fully dissolve, which is why their corpses are sought after by scientists, academics, and trophy hunters. The idea that the two greater fiends hadn't shown any decay at all was not a good one.

"Nope," Isaac said.

I put that thought aside and flicked through the dozen photos. Two greater fiends, both apparently dogs of some kind. They'd been large ones, too, even before the rift had merged with the body and changed them. When part of the rift attaches itself to a dead animal to create a lesser fiend, it makes the animal stronger, faster, and larger, but usually they don't look too different to the animal it was beforehand. Greater fiends are a little different; they're what happens when a tear opens and the rift energy fuses with a living animal. It makes the fiend considerably larger, faster, and usually with a few other unpleasant additions such as armoured skin or the ability to absorb elements.

The two canine fiends were about the size of grizzly bears, with teeth that looked like they belonged to sabre-tooth tigers. Their paws resembled something out of a horror film, with huge, serrated talons coming out of the paw itself. There were multiple lacerations on the bodies, several large holes in the chest, and each one had a cut across their throat. One of the fiends had its chest cracked open, and there were multiple instances of scorch marks around the lungs.

"It absorbed fire?" I asked, without looking up.

"One of Dan's team was an elemental revenant," Isaac said.

Elemental revenants were linked to one element. It let them conjure it, absorb it, even heal from exposure to it. They were powerful beings, but it hadn't been enough to stop two greater fiends. The elemental revenant had poured fire down the throat of the greater fiend, which should have turned its internal organs to barbeque. The scorch marks were superficial; the heat wasn't high. It looked like a half-arsed attempt at hurting the fiend.

"So, no one on the team inflicted any real damage on these fiends. And they died from wounds from a blade no one on the team carried. Where were they found?" I asked, passing the phone back.

"They were found near a lake close to where the attack took place. I've been there; it's a fishing lake, it's relatively small, and rarely used this time of year."

"What's weird about that?"

"According to the FBI, the tracks say that these two killed Dan's team and ended up just over half a kilometre closer to the lake. Without leaving any tracks from the crime scene. How?"

"So, they staged an ambush against highly trained RCU agents," I began. "Then they flew to a different location, and then they died."

Isaac snorted.

I was silent for several seconds. "This is a *fairy* tale," I said angrily. "There's no way two fiends wiped out an entire RCU team, managed to get from the massacre to the lake with no trail, and then, magically, cut their own throats with a weapon no one can find? Obviously, we have someone else out there who killed the fiends. Question is, why?"

"Yes," Isaac said.

"What do the FBI say?" I asked.

"Special Agent West agrees with you," Isaac said. "Officially, Dan's team and the FBI agents heroically died killing two greater fiends. Until we can say otherwise."

"Don't scare the humans," I said. "Special Agent West going to be okay with my involvement?" I asked.

"She doesn't really get a say in it," Isaac told me. "But to keep things on a friendly basis, I'll tell her when she needs to know. As of right now, you're officially deputized as a member of the RCU. You have no rank, no badge, no wage, and don't go around using it to get stuff done."

"Right," I said with a chuckle.

I put the car in gear and drove out of the hospital car park, wondering exactly what was going on in upstate New York.

I wasn't familiar with a lot of the route and hoped the satnav didn't direct me into Lake Ontario or something equally as ridiculous. Thankfully, it behaved itself and I was soon pulling into an empty car park in the middle of a wooded area.

I got out of the car, searching the woodland for any movement. The car park was on an elevated position, which gave me a good vantage point. There was a stream a hundred yards in front of where I stood, and three fallen trees lay along the bank of it. The remains of the trunks jutted out of the ground, wounded and raw.

"It happened over here," Isaac said, and set off down a path at the corner of the car park.

"If those two greater fiends didn't do this," I said, more to myself than anything else.

"Are you thinking it was an elder fiend?" Isaac asked me.

"No," I told him.

"It's something bad," Isaac said, stopping and turning back to me. "And if not an elder fiend, then it's something we haven't seen before. Which one of those two is worse?"

"Let's go find out," I said, motioning for Isaac to continue.

I heard the voices before I reached the site. There were still FBI walking around the scene. I left Isaac to go talk to them, while I followed behind at a slower pace.

I reached the end of the path and the trail below opened out, the snow having covered most of the surrounding area, where law enforcement were camped. I imagined that the whole place looked quite spectacular in the summer months.

The stream wasn't frozen, although touching the icy-cold water made me immediately regret that decision.

"This is where the ambush took place," Isaac said, walking back over to me.

"Agents still here?" I asked, noticing more than a few glances my way, and more than one FBI agent suddenly having to make an important phone call.

"Lots of dotting and crossing," Isaac said with a smile.

"No RCU?" I asked.

"I'm not risking any more of my people until I know what the hell's going on," Isaac said. "The FBI are on cleanup—their case—they get to reassure the locals it's all done with."

I looked around. "How close to a built-up neighbourhood are we?" I asked.

"About ten kilometres," Isaac said.

"Locals are probably safe, then," I told him.

"You know that, and I know that," Isaac said.

Fiends don't like built-up places. They like forests, jungles, and places with caves so they can hide. If a fiend ever went into a residential area, it was either brought there by someone, the animal was already there when it became a fiend, or it ran out of food in its usual hunting ground.

At one point, LA had a big fiend coyote problem. They were fairly harmless until people started hunting them, then you get a super strong and superfast coyote bearing down on you.

I walked around the area of destruction. It hadn't even been a day since the attack took place, and there were still signs that it had been a hell of a fight. There were trees with impact damage and scorch marks. A bloody handprint on one tree trunk, and more drops on the nearby bushes. I imagined the RCU agents fighting for their lives as their own people died.

"Where was Dan found?" I asked.

Isaac pointed off into the distance. "Best we can establish, he was hit and thrown into those bushes. It saved his life."

"And Annie?" I asked.

"Must have thought she was dead," Isaac said, sadly. "She called in a Code Red, and we went from there. By the time we got here, the fiends were gone, and we were left cleaning up. The dog walker called in the fiend's bodies, and things got a lot more complicated."

Code Red: *Agent down, send help.*

I walked off the path, following the mass of human footprints through the snow until I spotted a cabin in the distance. There was a small lake beside it.

"These are fresh," I said, pointing to the prints.

"Lots of law enforcement trudged through here," Isaac said. "But no fiend trails."

I frowned. "The wounds on their bodies, hell, they shouldn't have even been able to walk from the attack site to the lake. And there are no signs at all that they did?"

Isaac shook his head.

I continued on to the bank of the lake and walked along it until I was looking up at the cabin.

I crouched down as the water lapped at the bank a few feet from me.

"Two fiends found here, both dead, both mutilated, neither looking like the kinds of creatures that could take out almost an entire RCU team," I said, running through my thoughts. "They were already dead when they were dumped here, and made to look like they'd died after a great fight."

Isaac gave me a small smile. His own suspicions were obviously confirmed by mine.

I walked over to the dark wooden cabin, which was on stilts keeping it off the lake and wet bank, and tried the door. It was open. I swung the door and tentatively stepped inside. The cabin wasn't very big; a set of bunk beds in the corner, a small stove, a sink, a cupboard, and that was it. I opened the cupboard, which was full of fishing gear and medical equipment.

There was nothing in there of any help. No blood, no evidence that the fiends had ever stepped inside the place.

I left the cabin and looked around. The ground was firm, but there were no tire tracks or drag marks. I walked over to the far side of the cabin and stared over the still lake at the dock on the opposite side. And the two boats moored there.

"You have a theory?" Isaac asked.

"Something killed the RCU and ran," I said. "Not these fiends, something else. The bodies of these fiends were taken by boat from that mooring station and brought here. Might be worth checking if the dog walker was one of the people involved. You know his name? What does he do for a living?"

"I can find out," Isaac said. "The FBI were looking into it."

"Someone was trying to shift the blame of the attack onto these fiends. But that doesn't account for whatever *did* attack Dan and his team." I walked down the steps of the cabin to the ground. "You know I'm . . ." I stopped, unsure I could finish that sentence.

"Yeah, I figured," Isaac said.

"I can't do what I used to do," I told him. "I just can't. I've tried. I've tried to find out how to reverse whatever the hell happened to me. I just want you to know if there's a fight, I will go down swinging, but . . . I'm not the person I was. Not while I'm hobbled like this."

"You've spent four years trying to fix yourself?" Isaac asked. "I thought you just needed time to sort your head out."

"Well, that too," I said. "I'll explain later; I just needed you to know . . . I'm there for you."

"My wife and children would be without me if you hadn't saved my life multiple times over the years," Isaac said. "Whatever you need, I'm there to help."

"Thank you," I said, wanting to move the conversation on. We could talk about everything else once we were done trying to find information about the attackers.

"There was venom inside Dan's wound," Isaac said. "You ever heard of something that can do that? Elder fiend?"

"Deliver venom through its claws?" I asked "Sure. It's not an elder fiend, though."

Elder fiends were created a little differently to lesser or greater. When a tear happened and an animal on earth walked through, just as an animal in the rift walked through, an elder fiend was created. It merged the two creatures and, considering animals in the rift are considerably more dangerous than most of those on Earth, it didn't end well for anyone coming across it. Elder fiends were hyper intelligent and aggressive, but they were rare and they didn't ambush and then wait a bit. They burn out quickly and leave a lot of bodies in their wake before they need to hibernate, to restart the cycle of violence.

"So, if it's an elder fiend," Isaac said tentatively. "And I know, there hasn't been one in centuries, but say that's what this is. Say someone has one that they let loose and it killed people; they covered it up. You ever heard of an elder fiend who willingly works with people?"

I shook my head. "You're thinking it killed everyone, ran off, and people came to cover up the mess?"

Isaac nodded.

I looked around, trying to figure out where an elder fiend would have gone. Isaacs's theory was the best I'd heard, and frankly, when you have nothing to go on, even something you can't usually conceive needs to be considered. "The fiend would have wanted somewhere quiet," I said. "Every other case of elder-fiend attack, there was an outburst of violence, and then it found somewhere safe to hide out."

"There's a lot of places it could go," Isaac said.

"What's up there?" I asked him, pointing to a row of large rocks that jutted out from a slope leading into a denser part of the woodlands.

"No idea," Isaac said as his phone rang. "It's Emily. I need to answer this."

Isaac unbuckled a dagger from his belt and passed it to me. *Just in case*, he mouthed.

Isaac walked away to talk to Emily and I walked over to the rocks. They were much larger than I'd first thought, and there were gaps between some of them that were big enough for someone to walk through, up, and back into the woodland.

I climbed the slope, walking to the side once I'd gotten to the top and looking down into the rocks. The path actually moved sharply to the left, away from the woodland, and down toward a path that led through some overgrown bushes that had been trampled by something big.

"Whatever came through here was in a hurry," I said to myself.

I found a piece of dark brown fur tangled on the remains of the bushes. I picked it up and turned it over. It was matted with blood, and a second piece was almost a metre long by the time I'd untangled it from the thorns it had been caught on. A piece of pink flesh sat at the end of the fur. It would have hurt to have been torn free, but there was no blood trail to follow.

I continued on, finding more clumps of fur, and was halfway through a patch of open land when I heard the sounds of distress. I paused and listened again; it was a long, low howl that was quite unlike any animal. A mixture of wolf, bear, and boar, something cobbled together that shouldn't exist.

The howl sounded again.

*What the hell is that?* I drew the dagger from its sheath and discovered it was rift-tempered. It had a faint purple-and-blue sheen to the metal blade.

Unfortunately, guns didn't always work as well as other rift-tempered weapons. Tempering the gun was fine, but the bullets didn't always absorb the power, and tempering anything with explosives inside tended to blow up, usually when someone was holding it. I wished the knife was a bow; it was the most dependable long-distance weapon that could be rift-tempered. It wouldn't keep me in one piece if it was an elder fiend, but it was better than a solitary dagger.

Even so, I continued on. If there was an elder fiend, it needed to be dealt with before it hurt others. I moved toward the outcrop, keeping low and precise, as another howl sounded. When I was a few feet away, I spotted a cave to the side of the outcrop. It was barely big enough to sit a person, and the fiend was curled up inside of it, watching me with large red eyes. I had no idea *what* it was, but it was not an elder fiend.

Blood had pooled outside of the cave, running in between the cracks of the ground. The creature moved, and I saw that it had the rear of a wolf, the upper torso of a bear, and the head of a boar, but it was all done with humanoid proportions. It had hands and feet instead of paws, and strips of bloody fur fluttered in the breeze, as if the creature were unravelling.

"What the hell are you?" I asked it.

It could only answer with another pained response.

"You killed all those people," I said, taking a step forward.

The creature poked its head out of the shadowy cave and nodded once. Huge tusks jutted out of a chimera face that was halfway between a boar and a human.

"Did someone do this to you?" I asked, my voice full of barely concealed anger.

It nodded.

"Who?" I asked.

The creature screamed, the sound vibrating in my chest.

"This is a rift-tempered dagger," I told it, holding the dagger up for it to see. "I can end your suffering right now. But you killed people. You hurt my friend."

The creature nodded.

"You were controlled?"

A shake of the head.

"Ordered to?"

Another nod.

"Are you alone?" I asked it.

The creature shook its massive head.

"You going to attack me?" I asked it.

A shake of the head. "Can't . . . move."

"I want the people who made you," I told it.

The creature picked up and threw a brown rucksack toward me. It landed near my feet. The creature lifted its head out of the cave, exposing its jugular to me. "Please," it gargled.

I stood before the creature and pressed the tip of the blade against the throat of the creature. "I want you to know," I whispered, "this is better than you deserve."

The creature turned slightly to look at me in the eye, and I jammed the blade up into its throat, tearing open the creature's neck and leaving it to bleed to death on the ground.

I looked back at Isaac as he arrived on the scene, an expression of shock and horror on his face.

"What the fuck is going on?" I asked.

# CHAPTER SIX

A lot of things happened in a short space of time. The first thing Isaac did was call Emily while I went through the backpack of the dead fiend-creature. I really wanted to come up with a new terminology for them, because *fiend-creature* was bad, but my suggestion of calling them "what the fuck was that thing?" was shot down pretty quickly by Isaac.

I had more questions than answers at this point. Who, or what, had created the thing in the cave? How had it been able to kill nine members of an RCU-FBI joint team? Why was it peeling apart? Why had it been left to die? Why go to the trouble of placing dead fiends to take the fall but leave this thing in a cave? The latter question bounced around in my head. Surely, whoever had sent it to kill Dan's team hadn't just wanted to throw away their assassin. If they had, they'd have just killed it. The more information we found, the more questions I had.

Isaac finished talking to Emily and immediately called Hannah, while I started looking through the backpack; so far, I'd found a change of clothes, a wallet with twenty dollars in it and no ID, a piece of paper with several names on it, all of whom belonged to attacked members of the RCU, and a set of car keys to a Toyota somewhere.

"Two fiends," I said to myself. Somewhere out there I'd place good money on a second human-fiend. That idea didn't bring me a lot of good feelings.

"They're on the way," Isaac said, ending the call and sitting beside me, far enough away from the dead thing that we didn't have to smell it any-more. "Any luck?"

"Still looking," I said, poking around in the backpack.

"Remember, you're now officially working for the RCU," Isaac told me. "But not so officially you can tell members of the FBI to fuck off."

"I would never . . ." I said, placing my hand on my heart.

Isaac stared at me.

"Okay, sure, I totally would," I said, picking up the wallet again and turning it over in my hands. It was made of black leather with a red interior. It looked expensive, but there was nothing inside beside the single bill. I turned it over in my hand again.

"He played you," Isaac said. "Got you to kill him, and now we don't have anyone we can ask about what happened."

"He was peeling apart," I said. "He could barely utter a word. I don't know what was done to him, but he looked like he was unravelling. If there were two of those, I imagine there's a second one not too far from here."

"You think there are definitely two of those?" Isaac asked.

I nodded. "Two dead fiends in the cabin. Two of these things. Keys to a car on him. I don't think they were meant to die here. I'm guessing they're meant to be somewhere right now, enjoying the fruits of their job."

"Why not call their employee to let them know something is wrong?" Isaac asked. "I imagine whoever sent them wouldn't want them to be found."

"Can't call anyone without a phone," I said. "And my guess is there's no tracker on it, so whoever sent it expected it to just come home. Didn't work out so well."

"You want to go search for part two?" Isaac asked.

"Not really," I said. "They had a car stashed somewhere. If the FBI are going to be involved in this investigation, they can do the legwork."

"They might strongly suggest that we help," Isaac said.

"Can you strongly suggest that they fuck off?" I asked.

Isaac laughed. "I missed you, Lucas. You were always terrible at the political game. Too honest, wanting to know the truth and not caring about what that uncovered."

"Thank you," I said with a wry smile. I tossed the wallet onto the backpack and carried on sifting through the contents, I noticed an interior pocket I hadn't checked and, opening it, found a business card inside. The card was black with *Sky-High Security* printed in white font. A Rochester address sat on the reverse of the card, but other than that, there was no information on the card.

"What's that?" Isaac asked.

I passed the card to him. "You ever heard of Sky-High Security?"

"I have," he said. "Sky-High Security is a subsidiary of Barnes Pharmaceutical. The former is a private security agency. They've done some work in pretty bad places around the world, and they have some large, and exceptionally classified, government defence contracts. We've had run-ins with Barnes in the past; they're doing research into using the rift for monetary purposes. It's all very classified and probably backed by at least one senator."

"So, it's a no-go area," I said.

"With Sky-High, you're probably okay," Isaac said, passing me the card back. "But Barnes is off-limits. Dan tried to investigate it a few years back and got shut down hard."

"So, what you're saying is that we can't just go accusing them without a lot more evidence than a business card," I said.

"A lot more evidence," Isaac said as voices could be heard coming our way.

"What the bloody hell did you both do?" Hannah shouted as she came into view.

Hannah Jackson was five and a half feet tall, with pale skin, and blue eyes the colour of topaz. Her head was shaved on either side, with the centre being shoulder-length but tied back in a ponytail. The last time I'd seen her, it had been shocking pink, and was now a combination of forest green and silver.

"Nice to see you too, Hannah," I shouted back.

Her stern expression softened somewhat as she got close and wagged a finger in Isaac's direction before hugging me, lifting me off my feet in the process.

Hannah was a horned revenant and strong enough that I'd once seen her tear a car door clean off to beat someone with.

"You haven't answered the question," Hannah said, looking over at Isaac.

"There *are* two of us here," Isaac said, at least attempting to spread the blame.

"I haven't seen Lucas in four years," Hannah said. She was originally from Cork, and despite how long she'd lived in America, the accent had stayed. Something she'd always been happy about.

"It's good to see you, Hannah," I said with a smile.

"Don't you fuckin' dare," Hannah said. "Four years, Lucas. Four. Fuckin'. Years."

"You know why," I said.

Hannah nodded. "I do. I understand, too. I just don't like it. Didn't like it then, don't like it now. You don't sort your head out by fuckin' off to somewhere without occasionally lettin' people know you're okay. And don't start tellin' me about Isaac knowing where you were; Isaac hadn't heard from you in years until today." Hannah's expression softened. "I was worried. I missed you."

Hannah hugged me again, this time putting a little bit of strength into it, so I gasped.

"I missed you too," I whispered as she let me go.

Isaac briefed Hannah about the recent events, while she looked at us as if we were insane. Emily arrived while the explanation was still ongoing, forcing us to start again while dozens of agents scoured the surrounding area, occasionally throwing me expressions of bewilderment or outright irritation.

For my part, I remained quiet. I wasn't even certain that I was "officially" supposed to be there, so thought it best to say nothing until asked.

After an hour of me freezing and a very kind FBI agent bringing me the world's largest cup of coffee—which, I told him, meant that I now owed him my firstborn—Emily West was winding down her interrogation. She'd stopped looking over at me with irritation a while back, especially after she'd seen for herself the unravelling fiend in the cave.

The feds removed the corpse and I looked beyond Emily and Isaac as the fiend's body was moved out of the cave. It was a huge mass of a creature, and its skin had become ribbons, peeling off the body in large strands, leaving large chunks of flesh and blood behind as the specialists tried to get the creature into a body bag. It looked like someone had cooked it for days so that the meat slid off the bone. I wasn't going to be eating ribs again for a long time.

"Lucas," someone called out over the noise of the feds working all around us. I was grateful to tear my eyes away from the horror show and, with surprise, spotted Meredith trudging toward me, in a yellow medical coverall that covered everything up to her neck.

"Hey," I said after walking over to meet her halfway. "Why are you here? How did you get here so quickly?"

"I was going to ask you the same thing," Meredith said. "Got a call at about five in the morning, asking me to come here and help with an investigation. FBI kindly got me here to get involved. You?"

"Similar thing, but the RCU," I told her.

"Dr Pincher is helping us with our investigation," Emily said, appearing behind me like the ghost of federal agents past.

"I didn't know you were working here too," Meredith said.

"Something I'd like to talk to him about," Emily said with a smile that definitely didn't remind me of a predator about to pounce.

I turned to Emily. "Any chance you can give us thirty seconds?"

"We'll see you by the fiend, Dr Pincher," Emily said to Meredith before turning to me. "You've got fifteen. Make 'em count."

I turned back to Meredith. "Okay, I'll explain everything. But I don't have time right now. I'm at the Grand Hotel in Hamble. Room 718. Any chance we can meet up tonight and we can go over some things I need to tell you about?"

Meredith looked a little confused, which I would have certainly been in her shoes. "Sure," she said a second later. "About nine okay with you?"

I nodded. "Let me know when you're there and I'll meet you in the lobby."

"Is everything okay?" Meredith asked as Emily called her over.

"I promise I'll explain everything and answer every single question you have," I told her. "Look, Meredith. I think something bad is happening here, and I don't know what it is, but neither does anyone else. Just stay on your toes."

Meredith smiled. "I'll be fine, Lucas. I'm a big girl." She winked at me and walked off toward Emily.

"Ah, you made a friend," Hannah whispered from beside me.

I turned to Hannah; the huge beaming smile on her face almost made me laugh. "I am capable of it," I said.

"You sure?" Hannah asked. "Your ability to have people try to kill you usually trumped your ability to make friends."

"People can change," I said.

"Yeah, right," Hannah said with a slight chuckle.

I smiled. I couldn't help myself; Hannah always had this slightly mocking edge to her, no matter the importance of the situation.

"We need to talk," Emily West said, once again appearing as from the ether.

Isaac, Hannah, and I followed her to the edge of the clearing, and I wondered if anyone else got the feeling we were about to be told off by teacher.

"Isaac informs me that you're assisting the investigation into what happened here," Emily said. "You do know that the RCU and FBI are joint investigating, yes?"

"Sure," I said.

"That means you don't get to run off and do things on your own," Emily said. "That also means you follow the law. The human law. We need to find out what happened here and, if possible, arrest those responsible."

There were several prisons in the world where rift-fused people were incarcerated. I was happy to try Emily's way. For now.

"Sure," I said.

Emily sighed. "Honestly, you found the Sky-High business card and the dead . . . whatever the fuck that was."

"See," I said to Isaac. "It's catching on."

"And it appears you actually know what you're doing," Emily continued. "Isaac said you worked with him in the past."

"What else did Isaac say?" I asked, wanting to make sure we were all on the same page.

"That you're reliable and trustworthy," Emily said. "Both of which I'll decide on. But I can't stop you being involved, so please just work with me. We all want the same thing here."

"Deal," I said.

"We can't touch Sky-High Security," Emily said. "When I say that, I *mean* it. Barnes Pharmaceutical has more lawyers and money than the United States government. We've tried going after people who work for them before, even had a whistle-blower a few years back."

"What happened?" Hannah asked.

"Whistle-blower developed a case of being blown up," Emily said. "We were moving her to a secure facility, and someone got to her. Killed two US Marshals and an FBI agent in the process. No evidence, no nothing. And we looked, I promise you. If you can help us nail these assholes to a wall, I will take that help. But if you get caught, you're on your own. If you break the law, you better be damn sure you're on your own. There's no cavalry here; there's no backup."

"Thank you," Isaac said.

Emily nodded. "We found a second fiend. By a Toyota on the road. Same state as his friend here. You think they attacked the agents here and just died?"

"I think there's a bit more to it than that," Isaac said.

"Explain," Emily said.

"I think they were sent here to kill the agents here," I said after Isaac elbowed me in the arm, indicating I was up. "They did their job, and someone else planted those two fiends. They were in no state to get from the fight to that cabin, and no one on the team killed them. Money on it the autopsy report shows they were killed a lot earlier, brought here, and dumped. By this point, the two fiend-human things were meant to make their way back to wherever they came from. But unfortunately, their plan fell to pieces and so did they.

"My guess is that one of them started to unravel, climbed into the cave to make sure they stayed out of sight. The second one ran to the car, and the same thing happened there. Also my guess is that they started to unravel when they tried to change from fiend to human. It wasn't meant to happen. Whoever dumped the fiends at the cabin assumed the killers would be long gone, so never went to look for them."

"At some point, they must have known, though," Emily said. "Why not send people to find them?"

"Cops and feds and soon media everywhere," Isaac said. "Can't risk it."

"Find out what you can," Emily said. "If we find something, we'll share it with you, too. Hopefully, we can get this sorted quickly before anyone else dies."

"Whatever we uncover, you'll know," I promised.

"How'd you find the fiend?" Emily asked. "Just curious."

"My father taught me to hunt," I said. "To hunt fiends, too."

"Your father must have been an interesting man," Emily said.

"He was," I agreed.

"Did he teach you how to kill them, too?" Emily asked.

I shook my head.

"What's the plan, then?" she asked. "And please don't tell me if it's going to break all of the laws."

"I have a friend who lives to the west of here," I said. "He knows pretty much anyone in the revenant business. If anyone has intel on Sky-High or Barnes, it'll be him."

"And you think he'll give you this information?" Emily asked me.

"Not for free, he won't," Hannah said with a snort.

"And will it be actionable intel?" Emily asked.

"It'll be intel," I said. "How it was obtained, or whether or not you can do anything with it, isn't up to me. But it might well give us an edge, or at least point us in the right direction."

"For someone who only arrived this morning, you certainly seem to know your way around," Emily said.

"Like I told you earlier," Isaac said, "he's done some consulting for us in the past."

Suddenly, the phones of Isaac and Emily went off, and they walked away to answer them. I watched for a moment with Hannah by my side as the pair of them became more animated.

"When this is over, are you going to vanish again?" Hannah asked. There was no hostility in her tone, but the words stung nonetheless.

"No," I said. "I think I owe you and Gabriel an explanation as to why I left."

"About damn time," Hannah said.

I looked at her and saw the hurt in her eyes. I hadn't meant to hurt people, but I'd also had to do what was best for me. I knew that Hannah, just like the rest of the team, understood my reasoning, but understanding and accepting are two very different things.

"I got married," Hannah said. "His name is Jonas; he's a teacher."

"Congratulations," I said with a smile.

"He's human," Hannah said. "We've been married for two years now."

"I'm happy for you," I said.

"I wanted you to meet him," Hannah continued. "But I wasn't sure whether I was meant to let you know. I'm pretty pissed off at you because of that. And I know that's selfish, but even so, you missed my wedding, Lucas. You missed the happiest day of my life, and I couldn't even contact you to tell you about it. And now you're here because Dan is in hospital and so many of us are dead, and if this is some fleetin' visit bullshit, I'm not sure how to deal with that. You came back because of misery and pain, but you weren't here for the happiness and love."

"I'm sorry I hurt you, Hannah. I really am. I'd really like to meet your husband."

Hannah nodded. "I'd like that too, Lucas," she said softly. "I think Jonas would like to meet you after all these years."

"Let's go see Gabriel and I'll put things right," I said. "Or try to. After that, we'll find Booker and see what truly stupid thing he's going to want to trade for intel on Sky-High, and Barnes," I said.

Isaac walked back over. "Dan's awake," he said.

Emily joined us a second later.

"What has he said?" I asked.

"Nothing," Emily said. "He's barely aware of where he is; it'll be a few hours before he'll be able to talk, and that's if he remembers anything. Trauma does weird things to a person's memory."

"I'm going to go see him," Isaac said.

"Good," Emily said. "If he tells you anything, let me know. I don't want to have to learn information third- or fourth-hand because you decided to deal with a situation yourself."

"What about Annie?" I asked.

"Still unconscious, unfortunately," Isaac said. "They think she'll pull through, but no one can be sure at the moment."

"She's a fighter," Hannah said.

"Yes, she is," Isaac agreed.

"We'll be going too," Hannah said with an exhale. "We'll let you know what we find."

"Thank you," Emily said before looking at me. "I don't know what you are, Mr Rurik, but I assume you know how to take care of yourself."

I smiled. "You remember when I said that my dad taught me how to hunt fiends?"

Emily nodded.

"Well, my dad taught me how to hunt them, but it was my mom who taught me how to kill them."

# CHAPTER SEVEN

While Hannah, Isaac, and I made our way back from the crime scene to our vehicles, Hannah called Gabriel and mouthed *answer phone* to me.

"Must be a church thing," she said. "Only ever goes to voicemail when he's working."

"Okay, how about I go with Isaac to see Dan," I said. "I'll meet you at the church after and I'll explain everything to both of you at the same time."

"You're not runnin' off again, are ya?" Hannah said as she opened the door to her burnt orange coloured Toyota Land Cruiser.

"No," I assured her before noticing the slight smirk on her face.

I climbed into the BMW and started the engine as Isaac got into the passenger seat and strapped himself in.

"You okay?" he asked as I reversed the car before turning it around and driving out of the car park.

"I'm as good as can be, considering what I just saw," I said. "Human-fiend hybrids that peel apart like pulled pork."

"And now I'm never eating pork again," Isaac said with a grimace.

I parked in the hospital car park and followed Isaac inside, letting him talk to any FBI or RCU who happened to be there. It turned out there were none of the latter and quite a few of the former.

There was a light *ping* as we reached the right floor, and the lift doors opened. I continued to follow Isaac around the horseshoe floor to Dan's room. Isaac knocked twice and opened the door before anyone could say anything.

Dan was sat up in bed, drinking water. "Isaac," Dan said, his expression solum. "I'm *so* sorry."

"It's okay," Isaac told him softly. "You're alive; that's something to celebrate at least."

"I don't remember . . ." Dan started, and spotted me. "Lucas?"

"Hey," I said. "Glad to see you're not dead."

"Why are you here?" Dan asked, a slight panic to his voice.

"You got hurt," I said, leaning against the wall and crossing my arms over my chest. "Isaac thought something bad was happening; he asked me to help. I said yes."

Dan drank more water and put the glass on the table beside his bed. "What did you find?"

"We'll talk later," Isaac said. "I'm going to go check on Annie."

"She's alive?" Dan asked with surprise.

"No one told you?" Isaac asked him.

Dan shook his head.

"She lost an arm in the fight; she's been in surgery and is now recovering. It's a good thing revenants heal fast, because she'd be dead otherwise." Isaac gently placed his arm on Dan's shoulder. "I'll be back soon."

I took the chair from by the door and dragged it across the room, putting it by the window so I had a good view of the door. I shut the curtain right behind where I sat. It was force of habit on my part, but that force of habit had kept me alive before.

"Four years out of it and you come back because of me?" Dan asked.

"I saw those claw marks," I told him. "You going to be okay?"

"Docs have said I'll be fine," Dan said. "There was venom in the claws, apparently; it stopped my body from being able to heal. I assume the same is true with Annie. Otherwise, we might not have lost so many."

"What do you remember about it?" I asked him.

"Nothing," Dan said with a frustrated sigh. "The FBI were investigating two hikers who were killed by fiends a few days back. I heard that the hikers were working with the FBI on something. We were meant to supply help to the FBI investigation. The RCU was doing morning patrols of the area every morning since we'd become involved. Some of the agents wanted to go fiend-hunting with us. They figured we might be able to track them closer to dawn as the previous attack had been at first light. The FBI agents wanted to be there early, to get ready. They wanted to look around at night too, see if we could find something. I advised them against it, but one of the agents—I don't remember his name—insisted. We took the FBI to the preserve. I remember getting to the preserve; I remember going down the path, and then I got hit and woke up here."

"Getting hit saved your life," I said. "You got sent flying into some bushes; the fiends couldn't get to you, or forgot about you, I don't know."

"My team . . ." Dan said, shaking his head. "Fuck."

"I'm sorry," I told him.

"Is this how you felt?" Dan asked. "After the Guild were . . . After you . . ."

"After I was the only survivor?" I finished. "Yeah. Survivor's guilt is a hell of a thing. It took me a long time to deal with it. I still get attacks of it even though it happened seven years ago. Isaac will make sure you have people to talk to. People who can help you. It'll be hard at times, but you'll get through it."

"The fiends are dead, yes?" Dan asked. "No one else was hurt?"

"They're dead," I told him. I didn't want to mention the hybrids we'd found; Dan didn't need anything piled on him at this stage.

"Good," Dan said with a large sigh.

"Your team went down fighting," I told him.

"Half of them were fairly new," he said. "A couple of the revenants had only become rift-fused a few decades earlier."

"They knew what they were doing," I said, hoping my words might help but knowing that very little would for a while.

Dan nodded as if he understood and lay back on the bed. "Lots of FBI here."

"They're either helping or leading the investigation; I can't decide which," I said. "Apparently, the higher-ups want to play nice."

"Ancients?" Dan asked.

I shrugged. "They do have an interest in maintaining human and rift-fused relationships. After what happened to you, it was inevitable, I guess."

Dan nodded slowly, closed his eyes, and sighed. "Where have you been all this time?"

"Around," I told him. There'd be time to explain things to him later.

"Wherever you've been, it's good to see you again," Dan said. "Wish it was under more pleasant circumstances."

"Me too," I told him. "You just rest and get better."

"If the fiends are dead," Dan asked after a few seconds of silence, "what are you looking into?"

"Isaac wanted me to run the crime scene," I told him. "There are some things that need to be looked into. The RCU wants to know *how* it happened, obviously. He thought a neutral pair of eyes might go a long way."

"You think it was a setup?" Dan asked me. I knew that he wanted answers, probably more than any of us.

"It's possible," I said. "I think it's suspect, but until I have any information one way or the other, I can't say for sure."

"Your gut?" Dan asked.

"My gut says that all of you were set up," I said. "My guess is the RCU were the target."

Dan sighed again. "Fuck."

"I hasten to say that it's only a theory, and I have no evidence to say who was behind it or why it happened," I told him.

"But you'll find out."

I nodded. "I won't stop until I do."

Dan nodded sadly. "I think I might get some sleep. I'm still feeling pretty wiped out."

"I get that," I said.

I pulled the second curtain shut and left Dan alone in the room. Hopefully, his sleep wouldn't be where his brain decided to decode all of the footage of the attack he couldn't remember.

I found Isaac by the nurses' station in the centre of the horseshoe. "He okay?" Isaac asked me.

"Nope," I said. "He's going to need help. He's going to need people around him who care. And it's going to take time. How's Annie?"

"Unconscious," Isaac said. "The venom in her body is doing a real number on her ability to heal. She'll survive, but they docs are going to keep her in a medical coma until the venom is gone."

I recounted the conversation I had with Dan.

"You think they were set up?" Isaac asked for confirmation when I was done.

"No doubt in my mind," I told him as we walked toward the lift. "Those hybrid things were waiting for Dan and his team. Question is why."

"And who sent them," Isaac said as we stepped into the lift.

"That too," I agreed. "Someone wanted the RCU—you said the FBI weren't meant to be there—team killed off. Someone went to a lot of trouble to set it up, to make it look like fiends did it. Where's the dog walker who found the fiends?"

"You want to go see him?" Isaac asked.

I nodded. "We got a name and address?"

"Sure, Emily told me earlier," Isaac said as we exited the lift.

"Wait," I said when we were outside. I stopped walking and looked at Isaac. "What time did the attack take place?"

"Four fifty-two," Isaac said, removing his phone from his pocket and tapping the screen.

"And you called me at nine," I said. "So, when did the dog walker find the fiends?"

"A little after six," Isaac said, reading from his phone. "Six ten, to be exact."

"The attack took maybe ten minutes," I said. "The fiends would have wanted it done quickly, the ambush taking out as many agents as possible. That's how I'd do it. Eliminate the main problems, deal with everyone else after."

"You have a very scary mind," Isaac said.

"Fair," I agreed. "How long before you and other RCU agents arrived?"

"We arrived at five seventeen," Isaac said. "We were there until the ambulance arrived at five twenty-two. I left with Annie and Dan, and the rest of the RCU agents remained there to do an investigation. That was until the FBI arrived at five thirty-eight. I received a call to tell me that we were to let the FBI into all of our findings."

"Right," I said, my brain spinning with ideas. "Once the attack is done, the cover-up begins. That cabin is a good ten-minute walk from the attack. No one thought to check the cabin for a whole hour after the attack was called in. And thirty minutes after the FBI arrived."

"Why didn't the FBI look into the cabin?" Isaac asked.

"It's a good point," I said. "The lake is far enough away from the attack; there might not be a cordon there. It's certainly possible someone walking their dog there doesn't notice the law enforcement, but I'd have expected the FBI to find the fiends. Way before a dog-walker did."

"You think someone in the FBI is working against us?" Isaac asked. "That they helped set up my team?"

"Not the second bit," I said. "I doubt the FBI set up the RCU and their own people. That doesn't make sense. Emily doesn't strike me as the type to want a bunch of people killed, especially not those she works with. She was as surprised as anyone about the human-fiend hybrids. No, this is about something else. Someone else with power and money set this up."

"Sky-High Security," Isaac said.

I nodded. "My guess is that they sent the hybrids; no idea why, though. The dog walker probably works for them. Had him make the call because it was taking too long to find the fiend bodies and someone needed to push that along. Dog walker calls the FBI. That's the thing. Who, when finding fiends, would call the FBI? If you know what they are, the RCU number is plastered all over the place. And if you don't, you'd just call the cops. Why the FBI? Unless you don't want the RCU to find the fiends because you know they'd spot something wrong immediately, and the local cops would just call the RCU."

Isaac let out a long sigh. "I'll call Emily. Let her know I'm going to put some more RCU people at the hospital. She'll be fine, lets her pull her FBI guys out, and it gives us a chance to ensure we're not about to have something else awful happen."

"Something doesn't feel right," I said. "There's something I'm missing."

"What?" Isaac asked. "About Emily?"

I shook my head. "I don't think so." It was just out of grasp, but my brain couldn't quite get hold of it. "It'll come to me."

"Emily," Isaac said, walking off to talk to her.

"I'll meet you by the car," I called after him. I sat in the front seat of the BMW and tried to get my brain to figure out what I was missing. But every time I was close to getting it, it slipped away. Hopefully, it would come to me.

The passenger door opened and Isaac climbed inside. "She was planning on contacting me about it now that Dan is up and Annie is out of surgery," Isaac said. "She thinks her people are better placed to investigate the original deaths. The two humans. She figures that if those two fiends in the cabin were placed there, who killed the two hikers?"

"You said they were connected to the FBI," I said.

Isaac nodded. "Emily told me. Didn't tell me an awful lot more, though. I got the feeling it wasn't something she was allowed to divulge."

"I think she can divulge now," I said. "Something about this whole thing smells off. It starts with those two deaths, so I think we need to know more about them."

"Well, she's going to look into it," Isaac said. "I'll let you know what Emily says about the hikers. If she says anything. At shift change tonight, the FBI personnel will swap with ours. If there's an FBI involvement in this that's less than stellar, I'd rather they weren't looking after my people."

"Where do you want dropping off?" I asked him.

"Nowhere," Isaac said. "My car is still here. I'm going to take it to RCU headquarters in Rochester. Talk to the Ancient in charge."

"Be careful," I told him. "You know the Ancients have their own motives for getting involved."

"I will be," Isaac assured me. "Take care, Lucas."

I drove to the Church of Tempered Souls and stopped in the car park at the rear of the property.

The church was impressive on the outside. A gothic building, towering over a garden that ran around the outside of it. There was a steeple high above with several ornate gargoyles. I walked through the garden, nodding hello to two elderly women who were sat on a bench, deep in conversation.

Pushing open the heavy door, I stepped inside the church, walking under an archway that led through the pews, above which were several large stained-glass windows. At the far end of the nave were the pulpit and seating area for a choir.

A huge stained-glassed window sat at the far end of the building, depicting rift energies and a glorified image of the transformation of human into rift-fused. It was probably very impressive when there was actual sunshine to come through.

A door behind the pulpit opened and Gabriel walked out. He wore a black suit, which, to be honest, I was a little disappointed about. I figured he'd have been wearing his finest cassock.

"Hannah with you?" I asked him.

Gabriel nodded. "She's making coffee in the cleric house; she told me you had something you needed to talk to us about."

"I do," I admitted.

Gabriel took me through a door at the far end of the church, across a small courtyard with several small trees and bushes. There was a metal table in the middle of the courtyard, with four identical chairs.

The cleric house was a two-storey red-brick building at the far end of the courtyard, with large trees surrounding it. There was maybe a hundred feet between the church and the house, and despite not being far from the road, it was remarkably quiet.

Gabriel opened the midnight-blue painted wooden door and ushered me into the kitchen beyond. "This is the rear of the house?" I asked.

Gabriel nodded. "The front faces the sidewalk on the opposite side of the block."

"You have a lot of land," I said. "A church, a home, a car park. The church takes care of its own, I guess."

"It does," Gabriel told me. "We also pay our taxes."

I chuckled. "I wasn't going to ask."

"Yeah, but you thought it," he said.

"True," I agreed.

The wooden centre counter in the middle of the kitchen had half a dozen stools around it, a metal tray sat on top with a bright yellow tea-pot with sunflowers painted on it, a coffee cafetière, and a small tray of chocolates.

"No sandwiches?" I asked as Hannah entered the room.

"You're more than welcome to make your own," she said. "I'm not your ma."

I sat down as Gabriel poured. When he was done and my cup of coffee was in front of me, I sighed. "So, I guess it's time to tell you what happened."

"You're bloody right it is," Hannah said.

Gabriel said nothing.

I couldn't think of a good way to start, so I just went with the headline first. "I'm human."

# CHAPTER EIGHT

## *Five Years Ago*

I'd been a *guest* of Dr Callie Mitchell's for three days. She had spoken to me, given the tour of the facility several times, but I still didn't understand what she actually wanted me to do.

Dr Mitchell assumed I was a reporter working for the BBC; I got the feeling that if she ever discovered otherwise, I was dead. The second-skin suit she made everyone wear would make sure that the death was permanent for me. Creating a garment that could remove my connection to the rift, to my embers, was something that I didn't think was possible until I'd met her.

Dr Mitchell said she wanted me to document her time there and had given me a notepad, pen, and tape recorder to do just that, but she kept talking about the bigger story. She told me that what I wrote about there was an audition, that no one would ever read the story about her asylum. She liked to mention that if I failed, she would find a new use for me, and I was grateful that I only had a few days left in her company before Isaac came. Before I could be done with this whole charade and Dr Mitchell could be put into a cell in the deepest, darkest prison we could find. She deserved to be forgotten about.

One of the other inmates had told me that the nights were the hardest, but he'd been wrong. I could block out the weeping in the darkness, ignore those who prayed to whatever deity they thought might help, those who shouted abuse at the guards, or begged to be released. Sleep would take me, and I would be free from all of it for a few hours.

The worst part was just after awakening, realising that my dreams weren't reality, that I'd been lied to by my own brain. The crushing awareness that I was not free at all.

I woke up, cursed the world at large, and ran my hand through my long dark hair as I spotted the guard outside of my cell. I didn't know his name, but he was quick to hurt people for supposed infractions. The infraction in question could be anything from someone saying something when he didn't want them to, or looking at him too long.

"Get up," he said. He didn't like me at all.

I took a deep breath but didn't move.

"Doc wants to see you," the guard said.

I swung my legs out of bed. "Can I at least get dressed first?"

"You've got sixty seconds," he said with a huff. "Make sure to bring the tape recorder."

The second skin was on me at all times. I couldn't take it off unless a guard unfastened the small digital lock on the back of my neck. I'd tried to rip it and found it impervious to harm. I had no idea what it was made of, but it was strong stuff.

"Doctor has a special thing for you to see today," the guard told me as the cell door hissed open. He didn't bother with shackles now; I was considered too important to be hurt, although not important enough, should it come to that. The second Dr Mitchell was done with me, I was dead. No two ways about it.

I picked up the tape recorder and made my way to the lift, which we took to the first floor. The guard pushed me along to the right after leaving the lift.

"Can you tell me where we're going?" I asked him after we'd made our way to the far end of the building.

"It's a surprise," he said with a big grin on his face as he unlocked a large metal door, pulling on it, releasing a hiss of air. He motioned for me to go past, which I did without comment. "Wait."

Once again, I obeyed. I was looking forward to a time when I didn't have to obey a damn thing; then we'd see how well he did at hurting people.

The corridor beyond was bathed in blue light and was only a few dozen feet long before a second metal door, identical to the previous one, barred our way.

The guard performed the same routine as before, but as I stepped through the doorway, I got the distinct odour of bleach and the sounds of people talking. I must have waited too long for the guard, because I received a shove in the back for my troubles, and started down a long blue lit metal staircase.

The stairs opened out into a cavernous room, with a metal cage all around a sand-covered arena. There was a staircase to either side of me, and the guard motioned for me to go right, which I did without comment. I climbed the stairs and found Dr Mitchell sat at a desk on top of a metal platform. There was a laptop open in front of her, which she quickly closed before I could get a good look.

"Sleep well?" Dr Mitchell asked.

"As well as I have any night," I told her.

"Today we have a special attraction," Dr Mitchell said, sounding almost giddy about the whole thing. "Are you recording?"

I removed the tape recorder from my pocket and turned it on.

"Come with me," she said, satisfied I was doing my job.

I followed Dr Mitchell off the platform and up another set of stairs to a large metal door. She pushed the door open and motioned me to step into a room with a large window on one side, looking down at the . . . *Arena* really was the only word for it. Opposite it were dozens of computer screens, and at the far end a lift.

"This is the nerve centre of what I'm trying to achieve here," Dr Mitchell said as the lift opened and four people wearing long white surgical overalls and dark blue face masks left, all moving to various stations in the room.

"Do they perform as a techno-pop group on their days off?" I asked.

Dr Mitchell tutted. "I thought you were taking this seriously."

"I am," I told her. "Trust me, I don't have a choice."

"No, that's true," Dr Mitchell said. "Anyway, they're in gowns and masks because they have to go down to the arena floor once the presentation is over. It can be a bit . . . pungent down there."

"Presentation?" I asked her.

"Watch," she said, motioning toward the large window.

Looking down over the arena, I saw that the left-hand side of the entrance I'd walked through led to a platform over two identical metal doors. Each one was ten feet tall and six feet wide, big enough to get a monster through. I knew Dr Mitchell was experimenting on people, but what the hell did she need those doors for?

"Are you ready?" Dr Mitchell asked.

I was about to reply when I realised she wasn't talking to me.

"Yes, Doctor," a female member of the quartet said.

"Proceed, then," Dr Mitchell said, taking a seat on a chair that a guard had brought in for her.

I stood beside the doctor and watched as the two doors in the area were opened with a grating sound that went right through me.

A moose stampeded into the arena and ran around for several seconds. The moose was huge, easily two metres tall and maybe three long. People who have never seen a moose appear to be under the impression that they're not absolutely bloody massive. They're considerably larger than a horse, and if you're a human and you're in their way, your squishy body isn't going to do a damn thing to stop them. They're big and strong, and even a fully grown grizzly bear would think twice before taking one on.

The moose trotted around the perimiter of the arena, its massive antlers occasionally rubbing against the chain-link fence.

"Give it a little jolt," Dr Mitchell said.

The moose almost immediately moved back from the fence.

"Electric fence," I said. "For moose?"

"For whatever we put in there," Dr Mitchell corrected. "Watch."

The second door had been open the whole time, but nothing had come through it.

I thought I saw movement in the darkness beyond the door but said nothing and continued to watch as the staff in the room checked whatever was showing on their instruments.

"Is it shy?" Dr Mitchell asked.

"It's waiting," a male member of the staff said.

"Waiting for what?" I asked.

The wolf that shot out of the darkness was about seven feet tall and looked to be about three times the size of a normal grey wolf. It charged at the moose, which saw it and decided the best defence was a good offence. It ran at the wolf, slamming into it with its antlers and shoving it back.

Blood sprayed over the sand, and the wolf darted to the side, showing the huge cut down its flank. It snarled and charged again, dodging the swipe of the antlers and leaping at the rear leg of the moose, which it clamped down on and just tore free in one motion.

The wolf dropped the leg and walked over to the dying moose, putting its jaws around the massive neck of the animal and clamping down, shaking the moose from side to side as blood sprayed all around.

"What the fucking hell?" I asked. "You have a greater fiend wolf."

Dr Mitchell smiled. "Actually, we *created* a greater fiend wolf. One we control."

"Bullshit," I said to the obvious gasps of the four staff members. "No one controls greater fiends; they're animalistic. They're monsters."

"And now I control the monsters," Dr Mitchell said. "Look down there, Lucas. What do you see?"

"A wolf playing," I said. "Not acting like a wolf. Greater fiends still hunt, still protect their territory, just like they did as normal animals. They still eat. Blood is something they can't pass by; it makes them almost *need* to hunt and feast. Why isn't the wolf eating, why is it just tearing the moose apart?"

"She's not eating the moose," Dr Mitchell said. "Because we haven't given her the order to eat the moose."

"You're creating weapons," I said. "That's all this is about, to create monsters to control."

She grabbed my hand and led me out of the room, releasing my hand as we walked down the stairs and the guard had rejoined us. No point in trying to say I wasn't going to follow her; I'd tried that on day two and almost got a broken rib for my trouble.

We stopped outside of the gates at the far end of the arena, next to where the wolf had entered. The door there was reinforced steel, with similar walls on either side before it turned into electrified fence. Dr Mitchell placed her pass against the card reader and pushed open the door.

"You want me to go in there with a greater fiend?" I asked her.

"You *will*," Dr Mitchell said as I felt pressure on the back of my head. "Or my guard friend here blows your brains out and we feed you to it."

I did as I was instructed. *Two days to go, Lucas,* I said to myself.

The wolf was sat on its hind legs, its entire upper body covered in moose blood, which drenched the sand.

"Come here," Dr Mitchell snapped, and for a second, I thought she was talking to me, but the wolf padded over and sniffed her hand. It could have taken the whole limb off with one bite and used it as a toothpick.

"Go to him," Dr Mitchell commanded, and the wolf walked over to me.

I looked up at it as it stood before me. It was the size of a shire horse and strong enough to tear a moose apart. The wound on its flank was healing. Greater fiends healed fast; it's why once you engaged, you didn't stop until it was dead.

Somewhere in the world, there were three little pigs shitting themselves waiting for this monster to turn up.

The guard grabbed my arm, drawing a blade. I fought back, pushing the guard away, but the wolf growled at me.

"I would allow this to happen," Dr Mitchell said. "You will not die unless I will it."

I let the guard get back to his feet.

"Your arm," Dr Mitchell commanded.

I did as I was told, and the guard drew the blade again. The blue hue of the blade told me it was rift-tempered. He held it against the crook of my elbow and cut down across the forearm. The second-skin slipped away in two, revealing a shallow cut down my arm.

The wolf growled again.

"Your arm," Dr Mitchell snapped. "Raise it."

I did as I was told. The wolf sniffed my arm. The growl that left its maw reverberated in my chest.

"No," Dr Mitchell said. "Back to your pen."

The wolf walked by me as I stood there with my arm in the air, my heart pounding like a drum in my chest.

Dr Mitchell walked up to me, and I lowered my arm. "*I* and *I* alone command that fiend. You've now seen what we do here. We are not just creating weapons; we are going to create the next evolution in human fiend relationships. Wolf 447n will be the first of many. And when I have an army of them, I'll be able . . . Well, that's for another time."

I was speechless.

"Get him a new second skin," Dr Mitchell said. "Get his wound tidied up and let him shower."

"What is the second skin made out of?" I asked as the doctor moved toward leaving the sand.

She turned back to me. "Maybe I'll tell you one day."

The guard took me back up out of the arena and into a shower room on the first floor of the building. He unlocked my second-skin suit and told me to change and shower before he brought me a new one. He left me alone and I almost tore the suit free.

I was done with this. Time to get as far away from these lunatics as possible. I reached out to access my embers and there was nothing. No power, no access, just a void where it had once been. I tried again. And again nothing.

Forcing myself to remain calm as my body started to panic, I turned on the shower and let the hot water run over me. I was stuck there until Isaac came. I had no power and no way to get more.

The panic began to rise in my chest again. What if Isaac couldn't get there; what if Dr Mitchell decided to just feed me to that goddamn thing down there? Well, I wasn't going out without a fight. I couldn't access my embers, I couldn't access my power, but I wasn't helpless.

I breathed in and out slowly as the hot water cascaded over me.

"You done?" the guard snapped.

I switched off the shower, and he threw a black towel at me and placed a second-skin suit over a nearby sink. "Dry, and put some underwear on; the doc wants to check your arm."

I nodded, not willing to say anything as I felt my emotions bubbling up under the surface.

I was human. It had been a long time since I'd been able to say that. All I could do was hope it would end better than the last time I'd been human.

# CHAPTER NINE

*Now*

Are you sure you're human?" Hannah asked.

"Yes," I told her.

"Have you seen a specialist?" Gabriel asked.

"I've spoken to several," I told him. "No one has any idea how to make this better. No one knows if I'll ever access the embers again. No one knows quite why I stopped being able to have access. All anyone knows is that it's really bad. The prevailing idea is that if I get mortally wounded by a non-rift-tempered weapon, I'll bounce straight back to my embers, like I would normally."

"And that's not something you really want to try," Gabriel said.

"For obvious reasons," I said. "Chiefly that if it doesn't work, I'll just die."

"Which would be bad," Hannah said.

"I'd like to think so," I told her.

"So, you stayed away because ya' human?" Hannah asked.

"Partially, yes," I told her. "I kept away because I had pretty terrible survivor's guilt about what happened to my Guild, and I needed time to heal and not delve into a whole new world of trouble. But also because I was . . . am . . . human. I've been riftborn for a long time, and being human again, well, it was difficult to accept at first. I can't do what I used to do. I'm not an asset anymore. I'm a liability."

"Are you bollocks," Hannah snapped. "You're Lucas Rurik. You're never a liability."

"Kind of you to say," I told her. "But I am a hundred percent not the man—or, rather, riftborn—I was."

Gabriel got to his feet, walked over to me, and hugged me. "I am so sorry," he said. "We had no idea."

"It's okay," I told him. "No one had any idea; that was the point. Except for Isaac. I didn't want people to pity me, or for anyone to catch wind of it and think it was open season on me."

"You were worried someone would come after you and finish the job?" Gabriel asked.

I nodded.

"Not gonna let no gobshite come after you," Hannah said.

"Thank you," I said, meaning every word.

"So, we're going to see Booker or what?" Hannah asked.

The three of us left the cleric house and made our way back to where I'd parked the BMW.

"Wait a second; I forgot something," Gabriel said, rushing back off as Hannah and I got into the car.

"Callin' shotgun right now," Hannah said, switching on the heated seats.

"I haven't seen Booker in four years," I said. "I assume you have."

Hannah nodded. "He's a good man who doesn't always do good things. Sounds like someone else I know."

"You have the subtly of a brick," I said.

Hannah laughed. "This fiend you killed. You think Sky-High helped create it? A human-fiend hybrid."

I nodded. "They either did it themselves or they know who did. Too many coincidences otherwise."

Hannah used the car centre console to find a decent radio station, and put on some Disturbed, which wasn't something I was opposed to.

"I'm not sure how happy Booker is going to be to see us all," Hannah said. "He's not exactly someone who enjoys the company of law enforcement."

Gabriel arrived before I could say anything, climbing into the back of the car. He carried a small black briefcase, which he put on the seat beside him.

"What's in the bag?" Hannah asked as the car pulled away and we set off.

"Cash," Gabriel said. "And a sandwich."

"What kind of sandwich?" Hannah asked.

"That's what you're interested in?" I asked her.

"Ham and French mustard," Gabriel said.

"See?" Hannah said, sounding like she'd clearly won an important point.

"Okay, that's a pretty good sandwich," I conceded.

"There's a cook who works at the church," Gabriel said. "She brings in these amazing fresh baguettes. There's no way I'm leaving mine in there to be eaten by someone else."

"Does your church have a big problem with people stealing food?" I asked as we left the town of Hamble, and the roads became clearer of snow. "Because I'm pretty sure stealing is a big no in the Bible, right?"

"I think so," Hannah said. "Something about it being bad. Maybe I read it wrong."

"You're both insanely witty," Gabriel said dryly. "You know full well that we don't follow the Bible. Besides, people are not perfect."

"The sandwich thieves of Hamble," Hannah said. "Maybe when this is over, we can ask Emily to look into it for you, Gabriel?"

"You're both terrible people," Gabriel said.

"I'm pretty sure a man in your position isn't meant to tell us that," I said. "Aren't you meant to be trying to save our immortal souls?"

I caught sight of Gabriel as he narrowed his eyes in the rear-view mirror. "I'm beginning to remember how lovely it's been these last few years," Gabriel said.

"How much money?" Hannah asked.

"What?" Gabriel said, the change of conversation throwing him somewhat.

"The cash, Gabriel," Hannah said. "In the bag. How much?"

"Also, why?" I asked.

"Booker might need to be influenced," Gabriel said. "Do either of you have cash on hand?"

"I've got ten bucks on me," Hannah said.

"You're going to pay him off?" I asked.

"You are, actually," Gabriel said.

"How much is in the bag?" I asked.

"Fifty grand," Gabriel said.

Hannah had been taking a drink of water at the time and almost spat it out over the car's upholstery. "What the hell did you bring that much for?"

"I just took the whole bag," Gabriel said. "It's been sat around for a long time, and I've been trying to figure out what to do with it. This seems like as good an idea as any."

"Why didn't you use it to do church stuff?" I asked.

"It's tainted money, Lucas," Gabriel told me. "After you left, I took it from the RCU for hunting down a revenant who was hiring himself out as an assassin. It was the last job I did. Dan worked with me, told me to keep the money and do something good with it. I know, we can keep proceeds that we find, but it's blood money. Something about using it for the church felt wrong. I used two hundred grand of it to help people in the community, but I knew that I had to keep some back. I just had a feeling I was going to need it."

"You killed an assassin?" I asked.

"Dan did," Gabriel said. "The target was making himself a problem to the Ancients. He took a shot at one. We were asked to track him down and make sure he didn't do it again. He was *not* a good guy."

We talked about old times for the hour or so that the journey lasted, and I was genuinely happy to be in the company of old friends again. I'd felt conflicted about coming back and helping, but seeing Hannah and Gabriel, and spending time with both of them, made me feel like I'd made the right choice. I couldn't run from my past forever; I just needed to learn from it and be better in future.

I stopped the car in a car park behind a long, squat three-storey building that looked like an office block, but I got the impression it was anything but. There were five other cars in the car park, all of which probably cost hundreds of thousands of dollars. The red Ferrari F8 Spider in particular looked like it had cost its owner a small fortune.

"Booker's car," Gabriel said.

I looked behind me at what Gabriel was pointing at and spotted the bright yellow Porsche 911 Carrera 4S.

"What the hell does Booker do for a living?" I asked.

"I don't think fifty grand is going to get us very far," Hannah said.

"He'll be fine," Gabriel said as Hannah got out of the car, pulling her chair forward for Gabriel to exit behind her.

I took a deep breath and left the BMW, locking it behind me as I looked over the roof at Gabriel and Hannah. "How do you want to play this?" I asked.

"Honesty," Gabriel said. "He'll spot anything less and it'll go downhill from there."

We walked together to the nearest door. Gabriel knocked, and the door opened.

"Yes?" a large Hispanic man asked, his huge arms crossed over a barrel-like chest.

"We'd like to see Booker," Gabriel said. "My name is Father Gabriel Santiago."

The large man's eyes widened the second the word *father* was uttered. "He knows you?" the man asked.

"We're old friends," Gabriel said. "You can go tell him I'm here if you like, and he'll decide for himself, or you can let us in out of the cold and we'll wait for you to go check."

The man looked Hannah over before checking me out last. Clearly, he considered us to be no threat to him, because he opened the door and motioned for us to take a seat on a nearby bench. A second man, this one white with tattoos all over his bare arms, sat in a folding chair nearby, a shotgun on a counter beside him.

"Nice ink," Hannah said to the man.

"Thank you," the man replied.

"I like the shark," Hannah continued, while I tried to spot the shark among the mass of colour on his arms.

"Gotta love *Jaws*," he said, twisting his arm as if to look at it for the first time.

"It's a classic," Gabriel said.

"That it is," the man said with a sage nod.

"You worked for Booker long?" I asked.

"A year now," the man said. "José and I started working for him at the same time."

"José, the guy who went to find Booker?" I asked.

"Yeah, we were studying American history at college, and we needed some cash," the man said. "Booker gave us a job, but we had to keep the studying up."

"How's it going?" I asked him.

"Well, thanks," the man said.

"Oli," José said as he returned. "You don't need to tell them our life stories."

"Sorry, man, they don't really seem like a big problem," Oli said sheepishly.

"Apologies for Oli," José said. "He doesn't have much of a filter when it comes to talking to people who don't cower from him."

"It's fine," I said. "Booker always did employ the best."

José and Oli both nodded at that.

"I'll take you to Booker," José said. "He's with Zita."

"Who's Zita?" Hannah whispered to Gabriel as we followed José down a long corridor where I heard snippets of conversation behind several ajar doors. Whatever Booker had going there was a bigger operation than just José and Oli.

We walked up a flight of stairs and down a second, identical corridor, and at the end, José knocked, and pushed open the door for us.

The office inside was large and spacious, with a wooden desk next to a large window that overlooked the car park.

Booker stood behind his desk, his hands behind his back. He wore a tan suit that I was pretty sure cost more than Gabriel had brought in his bag, and had diamond studs in each ear. Booker was six feet tall, thin, with dark skin, and a scar that went from under his left eye, stopping just above his ear. I'd occasionally wondered where he'd gotten it, but I was a hundred percent certain it was none of my business, so I'd never asked.

A comfortable leather couch was under the large window, with a Latina woman sat on it. She wore jeans, a black T-shirt, and high-heels, her brown hair tied back in a high ponytail.

"Booker, Zita," José said. "These are the people who came to see you."

"Thank you, José," Booker said.

We all waited for José to leave.

"Gabriel," Booker said, unfolding his arms from behind him, walking around to the front of the desk and hugging the smaller man.

"Hannah," Booker said, continuing with the hugs.

"It's been too long, Booker," Hannah said.

"Yes, it has," Booker said. "But not as long as when I last saw this guy."

"Booker," I said, looking around the office, taking in the number of paintings on the wall. One of which was of an old plantation-looking house, but it was on fire. "You seem to be doing well for yourself."

"I do okay, thanks," he said before giving me a hug. "Goddamn, it's good to see you."

I smiled as Booker looked over at Gabriel. "Sorry, Father," he said softly.

"We've been teasing him for hours," Hannah said. "I doubt it even bothers him now."

"You all know I *don't* run a Christian church, right?" Gabriel said. "*Goddamn* doesn't mean a thing to me."

Booker smiled, and I caught Hannah looking away to stop from laughing.

"Oh, I'm so sorry," Booker said. "This is Zita."

Zita waved but didn't get up.

"She's not a handshaker or hugger," Booker said.

"She your business partner or girlfriend?" Hannah asked.

"Both," Zita said with a smile.

"She keeps my more . . . outlandish ideas in check," Booker said.

"Like buying Ferraris?" I asked.

"That one is mine," Zita said with a laugh.

"I heard about your team," Booker said to Hannah, suddenly serious. "I'm so sorry."

"Thank you," Hannah said. "That's why we're here."

"You want information?" Zita asked.

"On Sky-High Security," I said.

Booker considered my words for a moment. "Zita, what do you know about Sky-High Security?"

"Run by Mason Barnes," she said almost instantly. "Oldest male child of Barnes Pharmaceutical, thirty-six, rich, asshole. Not necessarily in that order."

"How do you know that?" Gabriel asked.

"I worked for the family," Zita said. "About two years ago, I was doing some accounts work for his father, Dominic, and I had the unfortunate luck to run into Mason fairly regularly. He's one of those handsome-and-knows-it kind of men, the kind who don't really understand the word *no* and think it's a challenge."

"I've met one or two," Hannah said icily.

"Well, Mason is their king," Zita said. "He wants to create the first-ever all-revenant private security team. I know, there are other private security that have revenants, but this is *only* revenants. Ones that are loyal only to Mason and his shareholders. It was something I felt deeply concerned about; I went to Dominic, and soon after, I was fired for gross insubordination. A few days later I start to see goons following me around; I grabbed one and got him to tell me that Mason had hired them to scare me. Obviously, that worked brilliantly. I knew Booker already and came to him for a job, and since then, no creepy stalkers outside my apartment."

"That worked out well that we came to ask for intel on someone and the lady you're dating worked for them," Gabriel said.

"Not a huge shock," Booker said. "I've poached about a third of my staff from that company. Apparently, revenants don't enjoy working for people who look at them like lab rats."

"What is it you do?" I asked.

"That's an excellent question," Booker said, putting his arm around my shoulder. "How about Hannah, Gabriel, and Zita all stay and have a chat about Mason and his machinations for world domination, and I'll show you around."

"Sure thing," I said, letting Booker lead me out of the room.

We tracked back the way we'd come until we were close to the entrance, but instead of making our way toward it, we turned the other way and walked past several doors until we came to an office at the end of the corridor. Booker opened the door, revealing a set of three lifts inside. "There are stairs too, but they're in one of the rooms behind us."

He pressed a button for the lift, which immediately opened, and he motioned for me to go in first. Seeing how my alarm bells weren't sounding, I did as was asked, waiting for Booker to scan an ID card over a numberless box next to the entrance. The doors closed, and we began our descent.

The doors opened, and I wasn't entirely sure I wasn't imagining the scene in front of me.

"Booker, you have a casino," I said, stepping out of the lift into the silence of the cavernous room.

There were a few dozen people cleaning or talking in groups, but other than that, there was no one there.

"We don't open until eight," Booker said.

I followed him down a flight of steps to the casino floor. The mass of machines were switched off, and I was grateful for the lack of sensory overload.

"Why are you showing me this?" I asked Booker after he'd said hello to several members of staff on the floor.

"Revenants like to gamble, but we're barred from most casinos for one reason or another," Booker said, raising his arms in a grand fashion. "We like to compete too, but we're not allowed in officially sanctioned sports. So, I provide what others won't."

"You're a casino owner and sports promoter?" I asked.

"There's another building across town, next to a large field, which I also own. We run physical competitions there. Boxing, UFC, running, basketball, whatever people want to play. We have an actual chess tournament once a month. Last month, eight thousand people turned up to watch."

"To watch chess?" I asked.

"Humans are starting to come too," Booker said with a sage nod. "They want to see what we can do."

"That's brilliant," I said honestly.

"I know," Booker said with a wide smile. "I don't want that bag of money that Gabriel is holding."

"You know about that?"

"Yeah, it's Gabriel. He holds the money like it's about to float away."

I laughed. "Okay, Booker, what do you want?"

"In return for Zita telling you everything she knows about Mason and Sky-High, I want to know what happened to the Ravens, Lucas. I want the *truth*."

I put out my hand. "Deal."

Booker shook my hand. "There's one other thing."

"Don't start adding to the deal," I said with a shake of my head.

"Nothing like that," Booker said with a chuckle. "I think you're going to want to see this."

I followed Booker through a nearby door, with Booker nodding to the large doorman as we went through. He took me down a set of stairs and into the first room we came to on the hallway below.

The room was empty of people and contained just two chairs, a table— all of which were made of metal—and had several Manilla folders in a stack on it. "I had my people set this up," Booker said. "I think you'd like to know away from Gabriel and Hannah."

"Know what?" I asked, taking a seat on one of the chairs as Booker sat on the other and passed me the first folder.

I opened it and took out the picture of the woman inside. She was sat cross-legged and barefoot on a bench, with a drink in one hand and a cigarette in the other. She had short, dark hair and olive skin, and wore a long black dress, but what drew me were the chains that came out of hoods of skin on each wrist.

"A chained revenant," I said.

"Her name is Nadia," Booker said. "We think she's Argentinian. But all we really know is that she's five feet tall and, like you said, a chained revenant. Thus ends the information we have on her. She comes here once a month to fight in one of the tournaments."

"I figured that Mason wouldn't like his people coming here, seeing how you poached them," I said.

"I don't think Nadia is all that close with him," Booker told me. "She's a capable fighter, a scary fighter, too."

I looked back at the picture. Like all chained revenants, Nadia's chains were approximately an inch in diameter and a foot long, although based on previous chained revenants, I imagined she could grow them to be several feet in length and use them like whips, changing the edges to be razor-sharp at the same time.

I'd once seen an X-ray of a chained revenant's arms, and the chains were fused with their radius and ulnar, almost wrapping around them while being a part of them at the same time. Most people who were afraid of revenants were terrified of chained revenants. And for good reason. If there was ever a type of revenant that would kill you for just being there, it was them.

Chained revenants move with a sort of jerky stop-motion movement when they use their powers, which makes them difficult opponents.

"What's she like?" I asked.

"She's scary," Booker said. "Even sat still, she gives off the vibe of being someone you do not want to cross. Her smile is . . . off. As if she's considering how best to end your life. She's quiet but not shy, intelligent, and, more than anything, capable of killing someone without batting her brown eyes. Honestly, Lucas, I like her."

I opened the second file, which had a picture of a large blond man with bushy beard. He wore jeans and a T-shirt, and looked to be standing on a beach somewhere.

"Alexis Capan died in 1889 on the shores of the White Sea on the north-western coast of Russia," Booker said. "He's a bone revenant. Alexis is six foot eight, and weighs nearly three hundred pounds, all of it muscle."

Bone revenants could cover their body in thick bone-like armour and create weapons out of their body. They were strong, dangerous, and not people you want to fight up close and personal if you can get away with it.

"We know that after he was murdered and came back," Booker said, "he hunted down and brutally killed everyone who had taken part in his death. He also killed their friends and family members. And then he left his village, and after several decades, he joined a Guild, but left after less than twenty years. Rules are for other people. So, he became a gun for hire. He's fought here too; he's not the brightest bulb, but he's dangerous."

Before I could open the last file, Booker snatched it away. "Look, the reason I brought you down here was because I need you to see this away from Hannah and Gabriel. I wasn't entirely sure how you would react."

"Is it your mom?" I asked Booker, who smiled, but it only lasted a second.

"I'm serious, Lucas," Booker said. "Don't shoot the messenger."

I took the file as it was slid across the table and opened it. The man in the photo was handsome in a sterile, frat-boy sort of way. He was clean-shaven and had the appearance of someone who would one hundred percent flex in the mirror at every available opportunity.

"This is Mason Barnes," Booker said. "The boss of Sky-High Security, and look what he's wearing."

I didn't answer, I didn't look up. I was focused on why there was a medallion of the Raven Guild hanging around his neck.

# CHAPTER TEN

L ucas," Booker said somewhere in the distance of my hearing.
"Why does he have a Raven's Guild medallion?" I asked without
looking up.

Seven years earlier, my friends . . . my family in the Raven Guild had
been ambushed and slaughtered. I'd spent years searching for who had
done it, almost to the point of exhaustion, both mental and physical. I'd
suffered from survivor's guilt; I'd pushed away anyone who tried to help.
Isaac had been the one who had forced me to accept what had happened,
who had helped me, who had given me a chance at the asylum five years
before to redirect my energies. I thought I'd been ready to jump back in,
and I'd been wrong. Seeing the medallion that had belonged to a murdered member of my Guild, dropped around the neck of someone like
Mason Barnes like it was a piece of gaudy jewellery, brought back a cre-
scendo of emotions.

"He bought it at auction," Booker said. "Paid a lot of money for it. The
photo was taken three years ago, just after he'd claimed his prize."

I sucked down the anger I felt at seeing something with so much
meaning paraded by such a worthless piece of shit. Booker had called it
*his prize*, and the idea of someone thinking of the medallion like that, an
object people had died wearing, made me feel ill.

"How'd you know that we were coming here asking for information on
these people?" I asked, tentatively. "You had this prepared."

"Isaac called and gave me a heads-up," Booker said. "We started looking into it soon after, and I wanted to make sure you weren't in a public
place with anything breakable when you saw this."

"Probably wise," I agreed. "I guess we need to figure out how to get into

Sky-High, and then how to get information on whatever they're doing there. I'm going to have to talk to Mason."

"I don't think I've ever seen you angry," Booker said.

"The medallions mean something," I said. "They're not for rich assholes to buy from other rich assholes."

Booker stared at me for several seconds. "You were there that night, yes?" he asked, his tone tentative, unsure how I was going to react.

I nodded, remembering the cries, the screams, the smell of blood and burning flesh. "I'll tell you everything; that was the deal. But not today."

The pair of us went back up to Booker's office.

"Are you okay?" Hannah asked, seeing my face.

I nodded. "Mason Barnes has a Raven Guild medallion."

"Oh, shit," Gabriel whispered. "You're not going to do anything . . ." He left the last word unsaid.

"Stupid," Booker finished.

"No," I said. "But those medallions don't belong to people like Mason or Callie Mitchell; they belong to the Guild."

"And you're the last member," Booker said.

I nodded. "They belong to me, then."

"Why?" Zita asked.

"If there's a death in the Guild," I said, "the remaining members have to pass the medallions on to new people, to keep the Guild safe and strong. I guess, seeing how I'm the last member, that's up to me. I couldn't do that as all the Raven's medallions were taken the night they were slaughtered. So, I'd *really* like to know how the medallion was found, and I guess Mason is the person to ask that."

"Do not go directly to Mason Barnes," Hannah said.

"I agree with Hannah," Zita said. "It's not clever and he is *not* a man to cross without good reason."

"And right now, he might be the suspect in the murders of several FBI and RCU agents," Gabriel said.

"Yeah, let's not piss on that particular investigation," Hannah agreed.

"There's a better way to get access to Mason and his dealings," Booker said. "Stick to the plan."

"I'm not going to jeopardise anything," I assured them all, although Gabriel still looked dubious. Probably because he knew me best.

"Do you have everything you need?" Zita asked.

I nodded. "We have names of two people who work for Mason; that's a start. We just need a way in."

"Come to the fight night tomorrow," Booker said. "Nadia will be there. She's always there."

"I'll introduce you," Zita said. "I know she works for assholes, but I don't get the feeling she's a bad person herself. She seems to be there because she's waiting for something to happen."

Chained revenants could see their own future or at least one thread of a possible future. Being linked to the rift all the time was not something that was known to be good for your long-term mental health.

We thanked Booker and Zita for their help and went back to the car, where we sat in silence for several minutes.

"You doing okay?" Gabriel asked me, placing a hand on my shoulder.

I patted his hand. "Yeah. There's a lot that doesn't make sense. Why would Mason Barnes risk his company to kill a few FBI and RCU agents? He's rich, powerful, his family have political connections."

"Rich and powerful people are never rich or powerful enough, though," Hannah said.

It was a valid point.

"So," Hannah said after several seconds of everyone remaining silent. "Nadia looks like the best way in to finding out what Mason actually knows."

I started the engine. "Tomorrow night, we come back here and see where we can go from there."

"I'll inform Emily," Gabriel said. "Isaac, too. They'll want to know."

"Can we do this without the FBI?" Hannah asked.

"We can but we shouldn't," Gabriel told her. "Not just because we're trying to work together, or that they've lost people too, but because we're stronger as a unified force."

Hannah let out a snort of derision, and the drive back to Gabriel's church was done with a solemn cloud over the three of us.

I dropped Gabriel off at his church and followed Hannah in her car back to her house. I pulled up and stopped the car outside her three-bedroom detached house outside of the city. A literal white picket fence circled a snow-covered lawn and flower beds.

"It's beautiful in the spring and summer," Hannah said. "You want to come in?"

I nodded. "Sure, do I get to meet the husband?"

"If Jonas is in, yes," Hannah said.

It was only seven p.m., but it was already dark, and while it wasn't snowing again, the cold air bit hard.

The front door opened as we reached it.

"Hannah," a man said, kissing her.

"Jonas, this is Lucas," Hannah said, pointing to me. "We used to work together."

Jonas offered me a fist-bump, which I was happy to reciprocate. "I don't shake hands," he said.

"Probably wise," I told him.

Jonas was taller than me, with a lean build and long, messy hair. He had tattoos all over his arms, a variety of images interspersed with one another, although his right arm looked like the skin was torn, showing the clockwork robot working underneath. It was impressive work.

"Come on in," Jonas said, stepping aside.

"Nice house."

"Thank you," Jonas said, taking my coat. "We got very lucky with the place."

The living room was tastefully decorated, with several paintings on the wall depicting various periods of time in history. "Ji-hyun," I said, pointing to one of Apollo 11's take-off.

"You know her?" Jonas asked.

I nodded. "We've been friends a long time. I have a few in my apartment, too."

"Jonas is a teacher," Hannah said, walking back into the room with three cups and a pot of coffee.

"I teach high-school science," Jonas said, thanking Hannah for the coffee.

I took a seat on one long corner leather sofa, while Hannah placed the drinks on a glass coffee table, and they took their seats on the other end of the sofa.

"You okay?" Jonas asked Hannah.

"It's not been the best day ever," Hannah said. "On the plus side, I got to see Lucas for the first time in years."

I smiled. "Not for the best reason, unfortunately."

"I'm sorry about your friends in hospital," Jonas said before pouring three cups of coffee. "So, what is it you do, Lucas?"

"Not much," I told him. "I live in Brooklyn. I used to work with Hannah."

"You were RCU?" he asked me.

"He only ever worked for us in an advisory capacity," Hannah said for me.

"Sounds exciting," Jonas said.

"He used to help us hunt fiends," Hannah said. "He has a talent for it."

"My parents taught me as a child," I said.

"You a revenant too?" Jonas asked. "That's not rude to ask, right?" Hannah laughed.

"No, it's fine," I said. "No, riftborn, but currently . . . not sure."

"You going to be around long?" Jonas asked, taking a drink of his black coffee, while I added some milk and sugar into mine.

"I hope so," I said. "It's been a long time, and I think I didn't realise just how much I missed everyone and this part of my life. Shame it took something awful for me to realise that."

"Sometimes, you don't know what you had until you take time away from it," Jonas said, and Hannah kissed him on the cheek.

The three of us chatted for a few hours until I made my excuses to meet up with Meredith, who would be waiting at my hotel. I didn't want her to be the last person who knew what I used to be. She'd been a good friend to me over the years, and it felt wrong to let her live in ignorance.

"Good luck with Meredith," Hannah said as she saw me out.

"Pleasure to meet you," Jonas said as I stood on the doorstep. "Don't be a stranger."

"I won't," I said with a smile.

"Thank you for coming," Hannah said. "I've wanted you to meet Jonas for years. I always thought of you as some kind of big brother. And while I am a strong, independent woman and do not need your approval, I still wanted it."

I hugged her goodbye. "I missed you, Hannah. I'm glad you're happy; I'm glad you've found someone nice. The next few days are probably going to be extra special shitty, so go enjoy your moments of calm."

"I know," Hannah said. "Don't do anything stupid."

I made the motion of the cross over my heart and walked back to the car, getting in and starting the engine but taking a moment to decompress from the last few hours' events before I set off.

It wasn't a long drive to the Grand Hotel, but it did leave me with some time to myself to think through the events of the day and call Meredith to let her know I'd meet her in the hotel bar. I wondered just how bad it was going to get before those behind the murders were stopped. It seemed like Sky-High Security was clearly up to its neck in criminal activity; it was now a matter of finding enough evidence that they could be nailed to the wall with.

I stopped the BMW in the hotel car park and got out. It was nearly ten p.m. and the last day had felt like years. I made the short walk to the hotel, nodding to the doorman as I entered the hotel lobby and continuing through to the bar at the far end, which was empty except for a man and woman talking in one of the five booths down one side of the room. I sat in a booth with a good view of the entrance and ordered a glass of ice-cold lemonade. I didn't want to drink alcohol right now, especially with the current mess going on, if I was needed to drive somewhere.

Meredith entered the bar ten minutes later, ordered a glass of wine, and sat opposite me. "How are you?" she asked.

"Tired," I told her. "You?"

"Well, today I saw something that wasn't meant to exist, and I watched it dissolve into a puddle. It was pretty horrible. I've been asked to help out human organisations before with crimes related to the rift-fused, but not usually when the RCU is already involved. Although I guess I'm done now."

"You're done?" I asked, a little surprised.

"Emily didn't know whether to trust the RCU or not," she said. "Didn't know if this was all a big conspiracy, or if they just messed up. Called me in to help check. I did my job. I only know of one person who has shown any interest in a human-fiend hybrid."

"Callie Mitchell," I suggested.

"Exactly her," Meredith said. "You're not human, are you?"

"Technically, I think I am at the moment," I said.

"When we first met, you were asking for help with a problem about a riftborn who couldn't access his embers," Meredith said.

"Yep," I confirmed.

"That you?" she asked, taking a drink of wine.

I nodded.

"I thought you were just another human with an interest in their world," she said.

"Sorry for misleading you," I told her. "Technically, I'm human right now. I needed help, didn't want anyone who might take advantage of that fact coming after me. Or anyone else. We became friends, and I wasn't entirely sure how to tell you everything. I wasn't even sure if there was any point, considering I wasn't the man I was."

"I understand," Meredith said. "You found a safe place and wanted to keep it safe. But now that safe place is gone, and you're back in your old world without your power. How are you dealing with that?"

I shrugged. "I don't know yet. Give me a few days and I'll probably have a different answer."

"Well, you'll have to tell someone else, as I'm going back to Manhattan."

"You're leaving?" I asked, a little surprised.

"Emily feels she can trust the RCU, or Isaac at least. I have work to do, and you guys don't actually need my help. I can study the information about the fiend-hybrids back in my lab. I don't need to be on the ground here."

The TV in the bar lit up with news of the attack and how the FBI members were killed. The bar staff turned it up, and everyone stopped what they were doing and listened in.

"Breaking news," the immaculate-looking male news anchor on the TV said. "And we're going to pass to Mia on scene for an update. Mia."

"Thanks very much, Bryce," a female reporter said. She wore a thick cream-coloured coat and gloves, although her head was uncovered as snow continued to fall. I imagined she would be freezing. She was stood in the parking area where I'd been with Isaac not that long before.

I took a long drink of lemonade and tried to pay attention.

"I'm here in Gosnell Big Woods Preserve near Rochester with an update to the horrific attack that took place in the early hours of this morning," Mia said. "We can now reveal that several members of the FBI and RCU were attacked here by two fiends, resulting in multiple casualties. The families of the attack have been notified, and the investigation as to what happened is ongoing."

"That's horrible, a tragic turn of events, Mia," Bryce said solemnly as they switched back to the studio, with Mia's picture in the corner of the screen. "Can you update on the status of the fiends responsible?"

"The fiends were killed," Mia said. "We've been told that the area is safe for public use, although there will be a heightened law-enforcement presence here while the investigation continues."

I picked up my phone and texted Isaac: *You get the details about the dog walker who found the fiends?*

He texted a few seconds later: *William Stone. 47yr old male. Single.*

A photo accompanied the picture, and I let out a long breath. "Holy shit," I said.

"You okay?" Meredith asked me.

"Meredith, I'm so sorry to do this, but I think I've just figured out how to get at those responsible for this. I need to go see someone. Can I please take a rain cheque on the explanation? The drink and any food is on me;

just add them to my room. Well, technically, it's on the RCU, but we won't quibble about that."

"Sure," Meredith said. "Are you okay?"

I stared down at the face of the man I recognised. "Yeah, when we're done here, we'll get together over pizza and a beer. I'll tell you everything. Promise."

"Take care, Lucas," Meredith said, giving me a hug as I got up.

"You too," I said, and rushed out, got into my car, and sped away as anxiety built up in my chest.

After an hour's drive, I reached a twenty-storey building in the centre of Rochester that sat in a cluster of six much larger buildings all looking down on it. There were no markings outside to say who worked inside or even what they did. I stopped the car in a large car park on the side of the building and got out.

I looked up at the building that housed Sky-High Security and the area around it. There was a large park between the six buildings, and directly opposite where I stood was Barnes Pharmaceutical in a forty-storey monstrosity. After discovering the business card in the backpack of one of the human-fiend hybrids, I'd done a little research, and according to the Sky-High Security website, the building had been unveiled a few years earlier as the largest building in Rochester. Multiple articles suggested that the Barnes family were the darlings of the city. The head of the family, Dominic, was apparently a self-made billionaire—as far as that was actually possible—who had taken over a million-dollar company, and turned it into a multi-trillion-dollar industry that spanned the globe. Of the six skyscrapers, three of them belonged to Barnes Pharmaceutical and one to Sky-High Security, which, according to various websites, was a gift to Mason.

"I wondered how long you'd be," Emily said as she walked over toward me. She wore jeans, boots, and a warm-looking black jacket.

"How'd you know I'd be here?" I asked.

"Hannah called Isaac to say you might do something stupid," Emily said. "Isaac called me and asked if I'd wait here for a few hours. Apparently, you left Meredith with concerns too, because she called me. You *can't* be here."

"I just wanted to ask Mason something," I said.

"And that was?" Emily asked.

I removed my phone from my pocket and showed Emily the photo.

"Yes, he found the bodies," Emily said. "His name is William Stone."

"Four years ago, he worked for Dr Callie Mitchell," I told her. "He was a guard at an asylum for rift-fused who were experimented on, abused, and tortured."

"You sure?" Emily asked.

"He knocked me out with the butt of an AR-15," I told her. "Yes, I'm sure."

# CHAPTER ELEVEN

Okay," Emily said. "So, what does it have to do with Sky-High Security?"

"Meredith told me that Dr Callie Mitchell asked her to help with her work," I said. "She said that Callie was working for a security consultancy firm."

"You sure it's Sky-High?" Emily asked.

"No," I said.

"Well, you can't just walk into Mason Barnes' place of employment and ask questions."

"Why not?" I asked.

"Because his lawyers have lawyers," Emily said.

"You've dealt with him before?" I asked, leaning up against the BMW's door.

Emily nodded. "More than once, unfortunately. You remember the witness who was killed?"

"Yes," I said.

"I was working the case," Emily said. "Witness dies, evidence goes missing, Mason Barnes smells like roses."

"He has friends in high places," I said.

"He has friends in *all of the* high places," Emily told me. "I get that this looks bad for him, but we need *conclusive proof* before we walk through those doors. We can't just go accusing him."

"I wasn't going to accuse him of anything," I said. "I wasn't even going to go inside."

"Why come here, then?" Emily asked.

"I wanted to see the place," I told her.

"You wanted to scout out the area," Emily said with a sigh.

"That too," I admitted.

"You were going to break in?" She asked me.

"Not tonight," I told her. "I was going to just look around, maybe go inside and feign being lost. When I was done, I was going to go see Dan in hospital, see how he was doing. Also see if he recognised this William guy. But while you're here, why were the FBI involved in the first place? Who were the two hikers?"

Emily sighed. "This goes no further," she said.

"Not a peep," I promised.

"Two whistle-blowers," she told me. "They worked for Sky-High. Wanted immunity for intel on the kind of things Mason is doing in there. It's no secret that he wants to create a security service for high-value targets using only rift-fused. Well, apparently, he's preparing the way by having some of his people take part in some shady shit abroad as well as here. They had information regarding the death of the previous witness as well as using rift-fused members of staff to intimidate and, in at least one case, kill people who got too close to him."

"So, Mason had the two killed," I said.

"That's my theory, yes," Emily said. "Although I have no idea why he would then have more FBI agents killed. The victims were headed there to talk to an FBI agent about actionable intel."

"Which agent?" I asked.

"Me," Emily said.

"I think we have company," I said as a large man walked toward us. He wore a dark suit and clearly had a gun under his jacket.

"Mr Barnes would like to speak to you both," the man said.

"Mr Barnes can kiss my ass," I told him.

"Special Agent West," the man said with a slight nod of his head, completely ignoring me, "Mr Barnes has instructed me to tell you that it would only be a few moments of your time so you do not freeze out here. He might be able to answer some of your questions."

"Mason isn't going to answer anything," Emily said.

"You know what," I said, sounding gleeful. "I've changed my mind. Let's go see Mason."

The guard motioned for Emily and me to walk toward the large tower and followed behind us.

"Do not piss him off," Emily said.

"No promises," I replied.

We were led through automatic doors into the huge glass-encapsulated foyer of the Sky-High Security building. The floor was made of grey stone tiles which gleamed. The reception area was a piece of twenty-foot-long granite with a glass top.

We were taken through the foyer to a set of four lifts at the far end of the room. One of the guards swiped a key card over a reader beside them, and the lift doors opened.

The inside of the lift was similar to the foyer: clean, crisp, with dark grey floor and mirrors on the walls. The guard who entered the lift first pressed the button for the top floor, and the lift set off.

The journey wasn't long, and soon the doors opened, revealing another reception area, with a young blonde woman sat behind it. She was talking to a man in a black security uniform.

Something felt wrong. I was playing a game where no one had told me the rules. I put on my best fake smile before we walked through the first set of large double doors into an office that was roughly the same size as my apartment.

There were large windows along one side of the room, and several glass cabinets on the others. Each of the cabinets contained various pieces of armour and weaponry, most of which appeared to be quite old.

As one of the guards closed the door, I noticed the number of rifles that adorned the walls on either side, and the stuffed head of a bear sat above it.

"I killed that myself," Mason said, gaining my attention.

I turned, remembering to smile, and the guards motioned for Emily and me to move. We walked toward Mason, who remained seated behind his desk at the far end of the room. The carpet was red, and the symbolism of it wasn't lost on me. Mr Barnes liked to think of himself as a star.

He stood and walked around his mahogany desk to greet us both. He was a few inches taller than me, with short brown hair. He was clean-shaven like he'd been in the photo I'd seen, with green eyes that held a hint of hostility. He wore a dark blue-and-white checked suit that I was pretty certain cost a fortune. The cufflinks had diamonds in them, and he wore a Rolex Daytona that had a light blue face.

"You like?" he asked, noticing me looking at the watch as we shook hands.

"Rolex Daytona," I said. "Platinum?"

Mason nodded. "Cosmograph Daytona ice-blue. Cost me two hundred grand," he said. "It's a good everyday watch. Nothing too special. I have a few pieces in my collection that put this to shame, but I don't like to be flashy when I have to work."

I caught him looking at my own watch.

"Longines," he said, and I knew he wanted to chuckle. "Maybe one day you'll be able to buy one of these and join the big-boy watch owners." He flashed me his Rolex again and winked.

I wanted to punch him in the mouth.

"You like weaponry and armour, too," I said.

Mason nodded. He clearly liked to be centre of attention and talk about himself. "It's my other passion, apart from watches and cars. What do you drive?"

"BMW M5," I said.

"Nice," Mason said, although he didn't sound like he meant it. "I had one when I was a kid. I have a Bentley Continental GT now. When you own a company that makes as much as this, you're expected own something special."

I bet every time he had sex, he looked at himself in the mirror and winked.

"Special Agent Emily West," Mason said as if greeting an old friend. "When my security told me you were out there, in the cold, I just had to give you the opportunity to come in and say hello. It's been so long. How are you?"

"Why are we here?" she asked.

"I saw on the news about the dreadful loss of life," Mason said. "I know we've had our differences, but I just wanted to tell you that I feel deeply for your loss. If I can help with your investigation in any way, please do ask."

"Can I ask a question?" I said. "Do you know a man by the name of William Stone?"

"Can't say I do," Mason said a little too quickly. "Does he work for the FBI?"

I shook my head. "No idea who he works for. He found the fiends after the attack."

"He's a hero, then," Mason said.

"Sure," I said. "I mean, they were already dead, and were staged to look like they were responsible for the attack, but finding them was hard."

"Staged?" Mason asked, with a truly terrible bit of acting shocked. "You're saying this attack wasn't random?"

"No, Mason, it wasn't," I said.

"Can I ask *you* a question, Mr Rurik?" Mason said, looking a little smug. "Have you ever heard of the Guilds?"

"Sure," I said.

"Six Guilds: Falcon, Owl, Eagle, Hawk, Vulture, and Kite. Each one with between ten to fifteen members, and each of them are created to hunt the most powerful fiends, revenants, and riftborn. To bring to an end the most powerful of their kind. And the only thing keeping them in check is each other."

"Yes, I know," I said, looking over at Emily when Mason turned around and opened a nearby set of doors.

"Come, I want to show you something," he said.

I wondered whether or not it was some kind of elaborate trap, but when he walked through first, flicking on a light switch, I followed suit.

The room was full of antiques and weapons, all of which were kept inside glass cases, and all of which appeared to be rift-touched. The purple glow on the daggers as I walked in made me wary of what was going to happen next.

"All of these are weapons and armour used by the Guilds," Mason said. "Weapons that can kill the rift-fused where simple knives and bullets can't. And Guilds kept them from humans, not allowing us to defend ourselves."

I stopped next to an old Viking helmet that had a faint purple glow around the eye holes. "This is quite spectacular," I said, meaning every word as I continued on past a suit of green-and-red samurai armour that had a similar glow.

"Isn't it just," Mason said, with genuine enthusiasm. "Did you know that a Guild was wiped out seven years ago? Its members killed?"

It took a lot of effort to nod.

"Terrible tragedy," Mason said with no sincerity whatsoever, "but the Guilds report to the Ancients—they're all rift-fused-led. They have no interest in helping in human conflicts, and every day, thousands of us are dying. I want to create Sky-High to be its own Guild," Mason said. "One with loyal soldiers that can be deployed around the world as needed. To help fight human wars. We've only known the rift-fused existed for a few decades, but you could have helped us stop war. You could have helped us stop death."

"The Guilds' job isn't to stop humans from killing each other," I said. "Their job is to make sure that humans and rift-fused live peacefully."

"And how about moving forward?" Mason asked me. "Why shouldn't humans expect their help? The rift-fused want to live on this planet, they want to be a part of this world, they can't then say no when something happens that steps outside of their comfort zone. The rift-fused need to stand beside us, and if they won't do that, we'll create our own rift-fused army who will. It won't be a Guild that sits by and does nothing, that is wiped out because of their own inertia."

Mason stepped out of the way, revealing a glass case. Inside was a medallion: a shield with hammer and sword crossed over the front, and a raven sat atop it. My mouth went dry, my hands started to sweat.

"Where'd you get it?" I asked, not daring to take a step closer.

"Auction," Mason said. "Cost me a million dollars. There were meant to be fourteen of these, but legend has it that there are only four known about. Including this one. Callie was incensed when she'd heard I got it." Mason laughed to himself.

"Dr Callie Mitchell?" Emily asked as I stared at the medallion, knowing I should look away before it appeared suspicious.

"That's right; you know her?" Mason asked.

"By reputation," I told him, finally able to drag my gaze away from the Raven medallion.

Mason's phone chimed, and he removed it from his jacket pocket, reading something before replacing it. "Ah," Mason said, motioning for Emily and me to leave the room. "Work calls."

We did as we were asked, but the second we did and I saw the man and woman seated on the other side of the desk, I knew that things were going to go downhill fast.

"Alexis and Nadia," Mason said as he shut and locked the door.

"A chained revenant," Emily whispered.

"I can hear you," Nadia said with a smile. She got down from sitting cross-legged in a chair that didn't appear to be designed for it, and walked over to us, her movements jerky, her bare feet slapping against the floor. Her long black dress billowed around her, her chains twitching, flicking around her like a snake's tongue.

She stopped in front of Emily and smiled before walking over to me. She looked up at me, and a single tear left her eye, running down her cheek. "Humans," she said softly.

"Excellent," Mason said. "I needed to check, considering how much the RCU has taken you into the investigation, Lucas."

I glanced over at Mason before looking back at Nadia.

"Smoke," Nadia whispered. "The smoke is coming."

I was pretty sure my eyes were wide with shock.

"Not the smoke thing again," Alexis said.

"What smoke?" Emily asked, her voice more than a little concerned.

"She sees the future," Alexis said. "But it's clouded in smoke. She says the smoke is angry. She's been talking about it for years."

"Thank you both," Mason said, with more than a touch of irritation. "You may leave."

No one said anything as Alexis and Nadia left Mason's office, with Nadia occasionally glancing back at me. As she reached the door, I made out one word that she mouthed: *Sorry*.

"Just wanted to check," Mason said when we were alone.

"That we were human?" I asked.

"You can never be too sure," Mason told me. "I believe that your investigation turned up intel about my company. I don't expect you to tell me what it is, but this was the one time you got to see me without you having a warrant."

"So, you're involved, then," I said.

Mason smiled. "I have *no* involvement in the horrific acts that were perpetrated. I hear that two RCU agents survived, both in hospital. I do hope that they pull through and give you all the information you need to put those responsible in jail. It must be awful to lose so many colleagues, Emily."

Emily said nothing.

"And for you to consult on such an awful case," Mason said to me.

"Well, when I find the person who is responsible, the RCU will make sure they're dealt with by the rule of rift-fused law," I said. "The Ancients take a dim view of people murdering their officers. I don't think it would be a pleasant death, but it will be a long one."

Mason smiled. "I'm terribly sorry for cutting our meeting short. I do so wish we could have spoken longer about your investigation, but needs must."

"Does Dr Mitchell work for you?" I asked him as the doors opened.

"I think we're done here for today," Mason said.

"One last thing," I said, to Mason's clear irritation. "I just wanted to give my own condolences."

"For what?" He asked.

"The two members of your staff who were murdered in the same park a few days earlier," I said. "I hear they were hiking. Probably blowing whistles and disturbing the fiends."

"They probably thought they were safe," Mason said, darkly. "It's an easy mistake for the inexperienced to make. Goodbye, Mr Rurik."

Emily and I were marched out by the same guard who had brought us into the building in the first place, and we were left alone once we were back outside in the cold night air.

"That was eye-opening," I said as Emily and I walked back to the car park.

"He threatened us," Emily said. "He knew your name; he knew you were helping."

"I heard," I said, using the key fob to unlock the car. "It was a fishing expedition. He wanted us to be surprised he knew I was working there; he wanted you to know he was keeping tabs on the investigation. I'm heading to the hospital."

"It's a bit late for visiting," Emily said.

"Mason mentioned the hospital; he mentioned hoping that Annie and Dan pull through," I said. "If he really helped send two monsters after the FBI and RCU, he won't think twice about killing a bunch of nurses."

"The order went for the FBI to stand down from protection," Emily said. "They were to wait until released by RCU agents, who, according to my people, arrived about an hour ago. Dan and Annie should be safe, but I get you wanting to check it out yourself. You want me to come with you?"

"That's okay; go home and chill out," I said.

"You're not a consultant, are you?" Emily asked as I opened the car door.

I looked back at her. "I promise you I am," I told her.

"You're a terrible liar, Lucas," Emily said.

I got into the car and set off to the hospital. It was another hour-long drive, and I pulled into the car park and entered the practically deserted hospital, nodding to the RCU agent sat in a chair by the reception area.

I took the lift up but found Dan's room to be empty. There were a dozen RCU agents on the floor, and I asked a nurse on shift where Dan had gone and was told that he'd gone to the roof.

It was only a short few flights of stairs to the roof, and the door was ajar, so I stepped out to find Dan sat on a chair, looking over the town of Hamble. He looked back at me, and his eyes went wide.

"Hey," I said.

"What are you doing here?" he asked me.

"Nice to see you too," I said.

"Sorry, I've just been poked and prodded all day and needed some time off," Dan said. "I only brought one chair."

"I'll stand," I said.

Dan had on a large coat and thick boots, along with a pair of black combat trousers. A thick blue blanket covered him. He looked warm even in the cold night air. "It was meant to snow tonight," he said. "Snow at night is always pretty."

I nodded. "I went to see Mason Barnes."

"How'd that go?"

I shrugged. "I didn't kill him, so about as well as could be expected. There's something I want to tell you."

"Sure, what's up?"

"I'm human," I said. "Been human for years. Can't access my embers; can't access my power."

"Oh, damn," Dan said. "That's awful. So, what happens if . . ."

"I can't heal quickly anymore," I said. "And if I get seriously hurt, I can't get into my embers to heal there. Short answer, I have no idea."

"That really sucks," Dan said. "I'm sorry." He paused for a moment. "You know, I still can't remember what happened," Dan said. "Been trying to. It's just out of sight. So, are you here because Mason threatened me?"

"Something like that," I said.

"He won't do anything," Dan said. "I've met his kind before. Money and power but no actual balls."

I laughed. "He could be dangerous."

"His family have connections," Dan said. "They're not people I'd want to cross. You think he's involved in the murders?"

"I think he had two informants killed with a pair of fiends," I said. "The fiends were killed and deposited to make it look like they'd attacked your group and died in the fight. But we found the two responsible. Human-fiend hybrids, one of whom had a card for Sky-High Security. I don't know why Mason had the FBI and RCU killed, but I know he did. Maybe you were too close to the investigation into the dead whistle-blowers."

"The FBI weren't sharing intel about them," Dan said. "That's pretty much all I know about it. It had been an FBI investigation before their deaths, and we were just there to help. You still think it was a setup, and you're still going to keep kicking over rocks until you find something."

"That's about the size of it," I said.

Dan's arm appeared from under the blanket, a phone attached. "You mind if I take this?" He asked. "It's a . . . lady friend of mine."

"A lady friend?" I asked with a chuckle. "I'll see you back at your room."

I left the roof and walked down the stairs to the floor where Dan's room was. I pushed open the doors and stepped into the carnage inside. The three nurses in the station were all dead; two slumped in their chairs and one on the station itself; it looked like she'd tried to get away. All three had been stabbed; the two seated had their throats cut from behind, the third repeatedly stabbed in the back.

I dropped to a crouch and moved around the room, pushing each door open to check for hidden attackers, or survivors. I made it all the way around to Annie's room, opened the door and stepped inside. She was dead. Shot twice in the head, once in the heart.

I left the room as Dan walked through the door.

"Dan," I whispered, waving him over.

"What the hell happened here?" He asked.

"No idea," I said. "No guards, and Annie is dead." I turned back to the room as pain laced my back.

"I got them to let you live," Dan whispered in my ear as he stabbed me again and pushed me down to the floor.

Two men and a woman walked into the room, all of whom I'd thought were RCU agents.

"What?" I asked.

"When the Ravens died," Dan said pleadingly, "I asked them to keep you alive. And you wasted it by coming here and involving yourself in something that you had no business in. Four years, Lucas; four years you were away, and you could have just stayed away."

"You got them to let me live?" I asked, the pain in my body almost unbearable, my words barely above a whisper.

"You should have *stayed* away," Dan said, this time a little sadder. "You always wanted to be the hero, Lucas. Well, heroes die and are forgotten. Just ask the Ravens."

One of the guards gave Dan a gun. "Unfortunately, the gun lost its rift-tempered charge after it shot Annie," he said. "But seeing how you're human, I guess it doesn't really matter."

Dan shot me twice in the chest, and the world around me went dark.

# CHAPTER TWELVE

## *Five Years Ago*

Day seven in the stay at Netley Asylum had started the same as every other day. A guard had arrived at my cell. He'd woken me, told me to get ready to see Dr Mitchell. I'd done as I'd been told. But today was different. Today was meant to be the day I got out of this piece-of-crap prison where torturing and experimentation on innocent people appeared to be all they did.

The guard had informed me that Dr Mitchell was waiting in the garden to see me. That was new.

He shoved me into the hallway and marched me down it, continuing on to a set of double doors beneath flickering lights.

He unlocked the door with a swipe of his ID against the black card reader, and pushed one of them open, motioning for me to go through.

We walked down the stone staircase to the gravel path below. The rear of the building was divided into two, with one half being for patients and the other for staff. A fifty-foot fence separated them both, a thick line of fir trees on either side, presumably to hide the fence. I once wondered if anyone had ever climbed the trees to try and get over, but the barbed wire top of the fence made a successful climb all but impossible.

A gazebo sat at the far end of the path, beside several flower patches, the colourful petals standing out against the gravel and vast amount of green grass.

"You will behave yourself," the guard whispered into my ear, although the wind that whipped across the island made him only just audible.

When I reached the edge of the gazebo, the guard grabbed my shoulder, digging his fingers into the flesh, making me wince as he held me in place.

When my task was complete, I was going to burn this place to the god-damned ground.

"Mr Rurik," Dr Mitchell said casually, looking up from her cushion-strewn seat inside the gazebo. She placed the book she'd been reading on the seat beside her.

"Doctor," I said as respectfully as the bile in my body would allow. I'd spent seven days in her company and knew she honestly believed that she was going to usher in a new age of mankind, but in reality, she was just a psychopath with a fancy degree.

"You can leave us," Dr Mitchell said to the guard dismissively.

I leaned up against the gazebo entrance and crossed my arms over my chest.

Dr Mitchell smiled at me, although it wasn't one of humour. She turned around and reached under the seat, retrieving the Raven Guild medallion that I'd seen when I'd first arrived.

"Do you know what this is?" She asked me.

"It belonged to a Guild of murdered men and women," I said.

Dr Mitchell turned the medallion around in her hands and stared at it. "Is it yours?"

"No," I said.

"You are not *just* a reporter," Dr Mitchell said. "I've read the online accounts of your work but, Mr Rurik, there's something else you're hiding. You're human, we have chained revenants who work for us so would have known if you were anything else, but there's something about you . . ."

When faced with no good options to say, I remained silent.

"Do you find that odd?" She asked.

"That there's 'something about me'?" I asked. "No, I get that a lot."

Dr Mitchell chuckled with genuine humour for the first time. "I'm so pleased you get to document how we're going to change the world with my control over these creatures."

"They're not creatures. You torture and murder *people*," I said. "You turn animals into fiends to do your bidding. You are, and I can't stress the use of this word enough, nuts."

Before she could answer, there was a crash from behind me. I turned as pieces of brick, plaster, and concrete rained down over the lawn. A horned revenant burst out of the wall of the asylum, its dark grey skin cracked with red like the power inside was trying to escape. Each of the revenant's hands were the size of my head, and it tore into the soft earth where it landed. A horn jutted out of each temple; I knew from previous experience that they were razor sharp and would make short work of anything they hit. The revenant stared at us for several seconds before it screamed in incandescent rage.

"Looks like you don't have as much control as you think you do," I said.

Dr Mitchell didn't even move. She showed no sign of being concerned that the creature had escaped. The horned revenant charged toward us, with hoof-like feet ripping apart the earth as it built up speed. It didn't get halfway before a bullet slammed into the back of its head, removing a portion of the revenant's skull and depositing it, along with part of its brain, on the lawn.

One of the guards on the ramparts above lowered their rifle as the revenant crashed to the ground.

"What a waste," Callie said with a sharp tut. "Now we have to get a new rift-tempered gun. Can't risk it failing."

I didn't trust myself to say anything, so looked away, noticing a dot in the far distance of my vision. A tiny blip in an otherwise-spotless horizon. Good.

Dr Mitchell turned the medallion over. "They're not inscribed with a name," she said, as if we hadn't just witnessed the murder of one of her patients. "Is that unusual?"

"That revenant wanted to kill you," I said. "Doesn't that bother you?"

"Bother me?" Dr Mitchell asked. "It happens. Rift-fused need control. And I aim to give them the control they need."

"Or give it to someone else to control them," I said.

"Or both," Dr Mitchell countered. "If we can harness their power, the power of the rift, we could stop sickness, could heal. It could stop death." There was definite zealotry in her voice.

"And all it takes is a little torture and murder," I snapped. "You're just like every other Frankenstein with a God complex."

"God? God is nothing. His vision was flawed," she hissed. "It was broken from the start. I aim to do better than God."

The dot on the horizon was now visibly a helicopter, and it was coming in fast. I wondered if the guards on the island had seen it.

I looked over to the side of the land where the gazebo sat, to a set of steps that led down to the dock I'd initially arrived at. I contemplated snatching the medallion and whether I'd make it there before the sniper on the roof saw me. Turning my head, I looked over at the closest guard tower. It seemed empty.

"Are you thinking about escaping?" Dr Mitchell asked with an amused smirk.

I looked back at her. "My options are to write this ridiculous piece you want from me to tell you how amazing you are and prove how good I am, so I can be forced to stay by your side and essentially write the biography of a psychopath. Or die."

Dr Mitchell laughed again. "I have enjoyed our little chats, but it's nice to see that after seven days of being here, you have finally decided to show your true character. You're feistier than I expected."

"Happy to exceed expectations," I said with a sigh.

"You could jump off the back of this compound if you really wanted to run," she told me casually. "There are jagged rocks, and near-freezing water, so you might live a few moments before dying there. Have you written the piece I asked?"

"Not yet," I told her. I'd been given an old typewriter to do the work on, but even though Dr Mitchell wanted me to write the facts as I saw them, I wasn't sure she'd have been thrilled about the fact that I'd seen nothing but horror since the moment I'd arrived.

"I'll give you a few more days," Dr Mitchell said. "Then I will judge your work."

"I'll try not to disappoint," I told her.

"You haven't yet," Dr Mitchell said. "I will figure out exactly what you are, Lucas. You can't hide it forever. Take some time out here; maybe you'll get some *inspiration*."

I watched her walk down the gravel path, the door to the building opening when she was nearly there, and the guard exited. They had a brief chat and she disappeared inside the building, while the guard continued on toward me.

There was a slight muffled sound somewhere in the distance, and the guard's face exploded as he fell to the ground before he was halfway to me.

Half a dozen soldiers in black ran up the stairs, five of them heading toward the main building as the helicopter hovered directly above me.

It flew over the building and vanished from view. Chinook HC6.

One of the soldiers came over to me, his suppressed MP5 moving from side to side, tracking for anyone who might be a threat.

"Took your time," I told Isaac.

"Hey, you said seven days," he said with a grin. "You okay?"

I nodded. "Thanks for coming, Isaac. I need to get the hell out of here. Gonna go to the doctor's office first; I want her in restraints."

Isaac stared at me, his expression hidden by his mask. He just nodded once in reply as gunfire erupted across the compound.

I ran toward the hospital, the sounds of gunfire ricocheting all around the hallway as I sprinted through the set of doors leading inside. The noise of the fighting only increased as I barged into Dr Mitchell's office and found it to be empty. One of the windows was open, but no Dr Mitchell.

I screamed in frustration and threw the computer monitor through one of the closed windows, shattering it, before tipping over the desk a moment later.

I'd lied to Isaac. I was not okay.

# CHAPTER THIRTEEN

*Now*

I sat up in a longhouse with a mist-covered floor. The large wooden tables were laden with food, although there was no one around eating it. No animals, either. It was sometimes like this, and sometimes there were people there, laughing and joking about dying and all the horrific things they'd done when they were alive.

This wasn't Heaven—or Hell. I was in my embers. So, thankfully, I wasn't dead.

The embers took pieces of your memories and jumbled them all up before twisting them into some kind of abomination of your memory. The village I found myself in was a combination of places I'd grown up in, a mismatch of architectural styles throughout the years before I'd become riftborn.

Anything that had been alive when the memory was made were now shadows, going about their lives as if nothing was wrong but basically ignoring me unless I interacted with them. Until night, anyway. Night was when everything changed, and you had a whole lot to worry about.

A stag walked into the longhouse, its impressive antlers matching those of several animals whose heads hung on the walls of the building.

I sighed. "You know it would be much quicker if the exit was right here."

"Tough shit," the deer said, its small fluffy tail flicking from side to side.

"Maria?" I asked.

The stag nodded.

Despite there being flowers, fruit, food, and a host of other things that you'd smell during a normal day, there were no smells in the embers. It often surprised me how strange that was. You don't realise just how many background scents there are in your life until there's nothing at all.

"It has been a long time," Maria said.

Maria was an eidolon. Every embers had two—mine were Casimir and Maria. Both were separate—but they shared memories and knowledge. They were, in reality, neither male nor female, despite the names given to them. Essentially, I'd had to name them when I'd first arrived over two thousand years ago, and the names were permanent, but beyond that I had no control over them. Eidolons were, for want of a better term, the groundskeepers of the embers. They made sure that nothing harmful arrived—nothing that wasn't already there, anyway—and when something occasionally did arrive, they either dealt with it or notified me of the problem. Apart from that, eidolons generally lived their existence in whatever way eidolons did. It had been five years since I'd last come back to the embers, of my own free will, and nearly twenty since I'd been forced to return due to serious injury. I tried not to make a habit of the latter.

Time moved differently in the embers. The more injured I was when entering, the more time passed on Earth and the rift before I could leave healed. It didn't feel like much time at all, but it meant staying the night, which was dangerous. It also meant I had no way of knowing just how much time would have gone by when I returned; could be a few days, or a few months, or in one particular unpleasant episode where almost my entire body was broken, and I'd lost so much blood I wasn't sure I'd had any left, a whole year. Getting shot and stabbed was probably not going to be a quick visit.

"It's good to see you," I told Maria, who transformed into an eagle and flew onto the head of a nearby chair, stretching out their massive wingspan.

"You were missed," Maria told me.

"Thank you," I said. "How are you and Casimir doing?"

"We have tended to your embers," Maria said, turning into a huge black wolf and following me out of the longhouse.

The sky above was a mass of swirling colour as dark grey mixed with streaks of brilliant blue and yellow. It reminded me of Van Gogh's *The Starry Night*. It was simultaneously beautiful and foreboding, as if the tempest from the rift was trying to break though.

The street beyond the longhouse had the same swirling mist over the ground, and the houses that I'd once seen stand proud and colourful were now falling apart, their roofs collapsed, their walls in disarray.

"You cut yourself off," Maria said.

"It wasn't deliberate." I said. "This happened because I didn't come here?"

"The power that flowed from here into you had nowhere to go," Maria explained. "So, it started to feed on itself."

Maria and I walked through the village. The only way out of the embers was to either breach the perimeter of it or to find the door that would let you either into the rift or back into normality.

"Why would you hobble yourself in such a manner?" Maria asked eventually.

I looked over at where a blacksmith had once lived, the inferno of the furnace something I'd remembered long after the village had gone. Now the furnace pumped out more mist, and the blacksmith's shadow worked methodically on a sword that would never be finished.

"I didn't mean to make it permanent," I told Maria, turning away. "Something went wrong. I think having to wear that damn second-skin suit short-circuited my ability to access the embers."

"And now you need your power back," Maria said.

I nodded. "I need to get out of here, into the rift. I need to figure out how to restart my power."

"And you know someone who can help you do that, I assume?"

I nodded.

"Fucking hell, Lucas," Maria said after a moment's silence between us. "If you're thinking what I think you're thinking. She's . . . not exactly what you might call . . ."

"Neb is not insane," I said. "Neb is . . . unique."

"That depends on what day of the week it is. Neb spent too long in her own embers," Maria said. "Her mind is fractured because of it."

"And she's still the smartest person I know," I said.

"Might need to change first, then," Maria said, nudging me in the side with their nose.

I looked down at the ruined T-shirt and removed it, showing the two bullet holes in my chest. The bullets would have been pushed out of me while I arrived there, leaving both entrance and exit wounds that would close over time. I couldn't die there, but I could be forced to stay longer because I was too weak to leave.

"I need clothes," I said. "I need to heal. I need food. I need weapons. Not necessarily in that order."

"You don't need half of those in the embers, but you *want* vengeance," Maria said, with a gleeful shiver to their tone. "I can feel it."

"Vengeance can wait until I have answers," I said.

"We won't make the exit by nightfall," Maria said. "You are too injured. Your body needs to heal."

You don't get exhausted in the embers, but being out at night is a bad idea. Especially as I didn't have access to my power. The shadowy people that walked the embers during the day became feral and dangerous at night. They couldn't enter secured buildings after dark, but find yourself too far away from a safe haven, and there's no guarantee you'll live to see the morning.

"How close can we get before we need to find somewhere to hole up?" I asked Maria after several minutes of silence.

"There's a house near the stream," they said.

I smiled at the memory of me as a child playing with the daughter and son of the house's owner. I'd remembered the house smelling of flowers.

I don't know how long we walked, the conversation was sparse, but it felt like no time at all. The closer we got to the house, the greater the sense of dread built inside of me, and I wondered just how dilapidated it would look.

As it turned out, the house was still intact, the flowers still littering the garden in front of it, a mass of stunning colours that appeared to bleed into one another, creating a sort of smudged rainbow effect. The streaks of blue and yellow had left the sky, replaced with a deep red, to make it look like lava about to break through a volcanic crust. It signified that darkness was about to descend upon the village.

I pushed open the door, revealing a large open room with stairs along one side leading to a landing above. Beds would be up there, I knew that much, although the house itself was both familiar and alien to me, the embers not quite getting the details right.

I closed the door and walked up the stairs, Maria behind me. There were openings in the thatched roof up there, letting us watch over the village as it became darker and darker, until I couldn't see anything more than ten feet away. The howls started soon after.

"The shadows hunt," Maria said. "They know you're here. They want your power for themselves."

"Not much good to them when I can't access it," I said, sounding more than a little fed up. I wasn't entirely sure what happened to a riftborn who had been caught and consumed by their own shadows in the embers, but I didn't want to find out first-hand, either. There are some things best left to the imagination.

"The last time you were forced here was when your Guild were murdered," Maria said, settling beside me as I lay down on a comfortable straw mattress.

"Dan betrayed me," I said. "I think he was involved in what happened to the Guild. He tried to kill me, thought that as I was human, he'd be able to remove me as an issue. Turns out he was wrong."

"You didn't expect to not be able to switch your power back on when you needed it," Maria said. "That about sum it up?"

I nodded. "And now I'm here, after my friend betrayed and tried to kill me, and I don't have my power. And I can't do anything to figure out what's going on and protect the people I care about without that same power."

"You fucked up," an owl said from the window.

"Casimir," I said. "It's good to see you, too."

"Lots of shadows around," Casimir said, hopping into the house. "Some of them have become larger than normal. The fact that the power flowing into this place had nowhere to go meant it just hung around, the shadows fed. Some got big."

"Great," I said with a sigh. "And how do we resolve that problem?"

The embers are always linked to earth and the rift; they're like a tunnel connecting the two sides, but one only I can unlock. Unfortunately, as the power flows through the embers to me, it can create build-ups of energy inside the embers itself. Energy the shadows can feed on. Take enough energy and a shadow becomes larger, more dangerous, but sometimes enough power flows into the embers that it turns a shadow into something else. Something monstrous. When that happens, the eidolons will do their best to keep it busy while I'm contacted and expected to come deal with it. They're called the shadow-cursed.

A shadow-cursed left unattended can disrupt the feed of power to me; it can cause, and has caused with other riftborn, untold long-term damage to their bodies and minds. In some cases, it can come through a tear and be set free into the rift or Earth. That would be considered bad on an unprecedented scale.

Casimir shrugged. "Thought you might know, considering you're two thousand years old. Maybe you should have spoken to us before shutting yourself off from your embers."

"Casimir," Maria snapped.

"No," Casimir snapped back. "You feel the same way."

I looked between the wolf and owl. "I'm sorry." What I'd done had felt like the right thing at the time, but maybe I hadn't thought it through as much as I should have done.

"Good," Maria said. "Don't do it again."

I smiled. "Not planning on it."

There were more howls outside the building. Despite the name, you can't start fires in the embers, and at night the cold mists that cover the ground turn cold enough to burn if you're in them for more than a few minutes. Another reason why finding a secure place to stay is necessary.

I finally drifted off to sleep, safe in the knowledge that Casimir and Maria would keep watch over me.

I woke after being nudged in the arm by Maria's nose. She was still a black wolf, but Casimir was now a small sparrow, perched on the top of a nearby set of antlers.

"The shadows have gone back to their dwellings," Casimir said.

"It was quite the evening festivities," Maria said with a sigh. "The power you stopped using has been leaking into the embers; it's meant that places like the hut next to where you woke were saturated with it."

"They destroyed the hut," I said, getting to my feet and stretching.

"One of many," Casimir told me. "Your lack of using your power has disrupted your embers. I believe once you have access to them once again, the shadows should settle down. Until you arrive again, at least."

"How far to the exit?" I asked.

"An hour away at most," Maria said.

It was frustrating that we were so close to the exit but had been forced to camp the night. An hour in the darkness with shadows running after me was an hour I would rather not suffer through. I'd fought shadows before; I'd almost been killed by a group of them a few hundred years earlier. I wasn't entirely sure *what* shadows were; no one was. I'd once heard them described as a magical white blood cell, which I always liked, although that meant I was a foreign contaminant to the body of the embers, which I wasn't particularly keen on.

I left the large hut and saw several shadows walking past, as if deep in conversation between themselves. Behind that were three more shadows. It was much busier early in the morning as shadows went about what would have been their normal lives.

Most ignored the eidolons and me, with only one or two stopping for a moment to watch us walk by. It was a strange sensation, and I was never sure if there was still a little of the hunt left in them from the night before. In the scheme of things, it was a mild threat, but it was one that always sat with me.

There was no way of telling just how long it took to walk, as my watch hadn't worked from the moment I'd entered the embers. It would, bizarrely, show the correct time and date when I left the rift, as if it were moving normally outside of where I was. I'd tried to think about it in deep terms a few times and usually ended up with a headache and a desperate need for alcohol.

The three of us reached a large lake that I'd once swam in as a child. There had been fish the size of my ten-year-old self in there, although I couldn't remember the types for the life of me. I stopped at the water's edge, the mist swirling around my feet, and looked out over the dark lake.

"Something wrong?" Casimir asked as he landed on my shoulder.

I shook my head. "Whenever I see this place, it just brings back memories. My father fishing, my mother trying to teach me how to swim. I didn't realise how content life was as a ten-year-old." I turned away and caught up with Maria, who stood outside of the mouth of a large cave.

"In there?" I asked.

Maria nodded. "I'm coming with you."

Eidolons could traverse between the embers and the rift, so long as the riftborn was with them; unfortunately, they couldn't change shape inside the rift, so whatever Maria chose to become, she was stuck with.

"I'll keep watch here," Casimir said. "I've never liked the rift." He flew off into a nearby gnarled tree, and Maria and I stepped into the cave.

Purple-and-blue power crackled across the tear to the rift, lighting the otherwise-dark cave in brilliant colour.

I placed a hand against the tear, and it drastically increased in size, filling the entire wall of the cave.

"Are you ready?" I asked, turning back to Maria, who had turned back into their large stag form.

Maria nodded. "Let's hope that Neb will be able to help."

I had to believe that she would, because if Neb couldn't help and I was no longer able to access my power, I wasn't sure how I was going to help my friends caught up in Dan's treachery.

# CHAPTER FOURTEEN

From stepping into the tear in the cave to stepping out of the tear in the rift was instantaneous. Maria and I found ourselves in a cave that looked pretty much identical to the one we'd just left, although in the rift, looks could be deceiving.

It didn't take us long to leave the cave, and we found ourselves atop a large hill; the view of the rift stretched out before us. It took my breath away.

Parts of the rift were twisted with power, full of monstrous creatures and danger around every corner, but that was far from Neb's settlement. Far from the vistas we found before us. The plains stretched for tens of miles, with huge mountains looming up in the distance. The grass on the plains was a mixture of green and orange, and spread out as far as I could see. Inaxia, the rift capital city, was far from there; Neb and the council didn't exactly get on.

While there are plenty of animals in the rift that are native to the place, the people living in the rift had all once lived on Earth. Some still moved between the two freely, but a lot of people had settled on living in the rift, even with the dangers. They found a peace or place to call home that they couldn't find elsewhere.

Neb's settlement was called Nightvale, mostly due to the fact that for one week every year, the entire area was bathed in twilight. It was roughly halfway between where Maria and I stood and the mountains. The huge central black stone tower of her settlement loomed among the colour of the plains. I looked up at the sky and found nothing but bright blue and purple clearness above.

"Weather looks good," Maria said, as if considering my own thoughts.

Bad weather in the rift was . . . well, it was bad. Really bad. The kind of awful weather that TV news shows like to put their weather presenters out in to prove to their viewers just how dangerously bad it was. Except, if they'd done that in the rift, they'd lose weather presenters at a huge rate.

The sounds of various animals in the distance were a welcome change from the embers. Just the noise the wind made as it brushed over the grass was something I hadn't realised I could miss. The first time I'd traversed the embers and arrived in the rift, it was closer to a city, and the sounds and smells of everything from normal everyday life had caused me a sensory overload. It was still a lot to take in even after all this time.

"You can ride on my back," Maria said. "It'll be quicker."

I swung up onto Maria's back and they started at a trot, the small animals that had been hiding inside the footlong grass scarpering for cover, but as we reached the bottom of the large hill, Maria began to build up speed until I was holding on to their neck for dear life.

The closer we got to Neb's settlement, the more I realized that it had grown by a considerable amount since I'd last stood before it. A thousand people had lived there twenty years before, when I'd last visited. Judging from the size, I'd guess ten times that amount lived there now, maybe more.

Despite the rift being home to millions of people all from different countries throughout history, I wasn't concerned about not being able to understand anyone. One of the stranger parts of the rift was how everyone was able to understand everyone else. After only a few minutes of speaking to someone in a language you didn't know, you were fluent. Reading and writing took a little more effort, but it too was made easier to understand. No one knew why or how it happened. There were theories it had to do with people who had died in the rift and their essence becoming absorbed by the tempest, their knowledge flowing out of the tempest back into the world, but no one to my knowledge ever got close enough to the tempest to find out without being turned to ash.

"You think she'll be happy to see you?" Maria asked after she'd slowed down enough that it didn't look like we were about to attack the settlement.

I looked up at the ramparts, where there were dozens of guards, all in black and green armour, all probably watching our approach. "I really hope so," I said eventually.

Maria stopped a few hundred metres from the settlement entrance, and I swung myself off, landing on the ground, and walked toward the main gate, where four guards were stood outside, all carrying long spears, all with the same black-and-green armour of those I'd seen on the ramparts.

The armour was a mixture of steel and leather, with steel helmets that had green feathers in them. I had no idea what creature they'd used to get those feathers, but if it had been from something in the rift, it probably hadn't been easy.

"Halt," one of the guards shouted. They walked over to me as I did, with Maria hanging back a few feet.

"Name?" the guard demanded, her voice loud enough even from several feet away.

"Lucas Rurik," I told them.

She stared at me for several seconds. "And the purpose of your visit?"

"I need to see Neb," I said.

"Is she expecting you?" The guard asked.

I shook my head. "I doubt it, but it's imperative that I speak to her. Please."

The guard looked beyond me at Maria, who raised a hoof in a sort of waving gesture.

"Eidolon?" she asked, more inquisitive than demanding.

"Yes, I'm riftborn," I said. "Their name is Maria."

"Wait here," the guard told me, and walked back, their armour the only sound before she reached her comrades and began a conversation.

"You think something bad has happened here?" I asked.

"I haven't heard of anything," Maria said. "I haven't been in the rift for a long time, but we eidolons do stay in contact."

The guard made her way back over to me. "You are allowed entry," she said, and removed her helmet, revealing long blond hair, a stark contrast to the dark armour. "I'm to inform you that you are considered a friend here."

"Hence you removing your helmet?" I asked. There were a lot of customs in the rift about people not wearing anything on their head when greeting a friendly visitor.

She nodded. "If you fail to comply with anything you are asked to do, you will be dealt with accordingly. Do you understand?"

I nodded.

"Please follow me."

I followed the guard to the front entrance, where I was searched. Once allowed through, we continued into the settlement and past two large guard posts, where another dozen guards stood, all watching Maria and me with a mixture of interest and outright hostility. Newcomers aren't welcomed warmly in a lot of rift settlements.

The settlement was, like many rift settlements, built in five rings. The outer ring was the guards and military, the next one merchants of one form or another; after that were living accommodations, and the fourth ring was full of schools, libraries, and places of learning, including military academies. The final ring was the power structure of the whole settlement. Five streets stretched from the inner to outer rings, making navigation easier.

For Neb to have made her settlement so much larger, she would have had to build it from scratch while demolishing the old one. A big undertaking, and I wondered what had happened to create such an influx of new people.

"Have you been here before?" the guard asked as the smells of the merchant area threatened to overwhelm me.

"Not for many years," I said. "When I was last here, Neb's settlement had a thousand people."

The guard looked back at me and chuckled. "At least twenty years, then."

"What happened?" I asked, trying to ignore the mass of delicious food we were walking by.

"It's not for me to say," the guard told me. "Neb saved us all, and we owe her much. That's all you need to know. Everyone here is loyal to Neb."

The threat was implied; *Screw around, and you'll regret it.*

We reached a guard post that stopped people from entering the central ring and, by extension, the tower, and there were several guards training on either side of the tower. "I thought that happened in the military ring or in the schools," I said to the guard.

"Those here wish to advance," she said. "They have to fight in the shadow of the tower and win to be given the chance to advance in rank."

"That's new," I said.

"A lot has changed," the guard said, before turning and saluting to another guard, although this one had silver on their armour along with the black and green.

The soldier also removed their helmet. "You're here to see Neb?" he asked, his voice low. He had dark skin, a bald head, and long black beard that was braided with colourful beads. He looked like someone who knew his way around a battle. He was missing part of an ear, and a wide, ragged scar went from his left cheek across his nose and stopped by his right ear. His face looked as though it had been carved out of granite, and his piercing gaze was hawk-like in intensity. If he ever stepped foot in Hollywood, he would be cast as the villain in every single action film ever made. He stepped toward me and offered me his forearm, which I knocked my own forearm against. You didn't shake hands in the rift, not unless you were damn sure whose hand you were shaking.

"I'll take you to Neb," he said, motioning for me to follow him. I noticed the longsword at his hip, the ornate steel pommel in the shape of a dragon's head.

"Thanks for your help," I said to the guard, who smiled, nodded, replaced her helmet, and walked back to her post.

"I'll wait here," Maria said. "I do not think I would enjoy being in that building in this shape."

"Your deer will be given food and water," the soldier told me.

"Thank you," Maria said, following the guard who had been ordered to take care of them.

I followed the soldier as we entered through the twelve-foot-high dark wooden door and into a huge room with people walking around the hallway in front of us.

"This castle matches the city," the soldier explained. "Five floors, each with five rings. This one is administrative. The higher we go, the more important the jobs."

"Do you have a name?" I asked him, looking around as we walked along the corridor past dozens of people who were going in and out of the multitude of what looked like open-plan offices.

"Kuri," the soldier said.

"Have you been here long?" I asked as we reached a lift. They were powered by rift energy, as were the lights, the doors, and everything else inside the rift, including occasionally the weaponry. It was difficult to use and even more difficult to keep stable enough not to explode and create a tear, so it tended to be used for smaller jobs. Even so, once you'd seen one of the large weapons use the rift to tear apart their user's enemies, it tended to stay with you forever.

"Twenty years," the soldier said as the doors opened, and we stepped inside.

"With Neb?" I asked as we began our slow ascent.

"Yes," he said. "What century is it on Earth?"

"Twenty-first," I said.

Kuri turned to me and nodded. "I've known Neb a long time but never felt the need to leave my home to come to her settlement."

"What changed?" I asked as the lift stopped.

"Many things," Kuri said in a tone that suggested he had no intention of discussing it further.

The doors to the wooden lift opened, a slight blue-and-purple glow around the edges that I noticed for the first time. The smaller uses of rift-powered things were perfectly safe, but they always made me slightly wary anyway.

The top floor of the citadel was considerably quieter than the first one had been, and Kuri escorted me down the corridor where a number of soldiers lined either side, saluting to Kuri as we passed. At the end of the corridor, Kuri knocked twice on the twenty-foot-tall double doors that had ornate carvings in the almost black wood.

The door opened, revealing two guards, both in red-and-black armour, both carrying long spears.

"Lucas Rurik to see Neb," Kuri said.

The guards looked beyond Kuri to me and nodded once. "Any weapons?" one of them asked me.

I shook my head, but the other guard patted me down anyway. Kuri showed no irritation that they were doing something that his people had already done. I doubted very much that anyone would be allowed this close to Neb unless they weren't considered a threat and had been searched.

"You're clean," the guard said. "But if you step out of line . . ."

"Neb will kill me before any of you get a chance," I finished for him.

He looked slightly taken aback but nodded curtly and motioned for me to continue through the large room with its paintings on the walls, and dark-grey stone floor. I glanced out of a stained-glass window at the far end of the room. From the height we were at, I could see across the plains to the River of Ghosts in the distance, one of the largest rivers in the rift that ran from the mountains all across the plains to the far north, where few dared go.

Some people think that the rift is some kind of heaven, hell, or purgatory, depending on what they believe, but it isn't. It's just another place, attached to Earth but separate. The people who come to the rift and die there don't go to another rift somewhere else—not that I'm aware of. Many people still practise their religions that they were part of on Earth and just believe that the rift is another stop on their way to the afterlife.

The guard opened one of the white wooden doors and motioned for me to step through into a large room with tall ceilings and columns that gave the whole place an ancient Greek vibe. There were three large glass doors on either side of the room that led out to a balcony on either side. Colourful drapes adorned either side of the room, cascading onto the polished light-wood floor. At the far end of the room were two sets of double doors, both the same wood as the floor. One of the doors opened and Neb stepped out.

She wore a forest-green tunic that stretched to her sandal-clad feet. Each of her bare, muscular arms had half a dozen gold and silver bracelets, and she wore several earrings in each ear. She was nearly six feet tall, with brown skin, almost-black hair, and slate-grey eyes. She moved with purpose, aware of her position within the rift and the respect that she commanded just by the mention of her name. She looked every inch the leader I knew her to be.

Two guards had entered the room behind her, but both hung back by the door; neither would be needed if there was to be trouble. I'd seen Neb fight; I'd seen Neb kill. She was probably more dangerous than most of the guards at her disposal.

Neb stood before me, looking down at me as I bowed my head slightly.

"It's been twenty years," she said.

"A lot has happened," I told her, looking up.

"The rift changes for us all," she said, still holding herself rigid, still trying to decide if I'd returned an ally or an enemy. "Why have you chosen to return now?"

"I need your help," I said.

"You did not come to see me after the Ravens were murdered," Neb said, and there was an accusatory tone to her voice. It had hurt her.

"I know," I said. "I was . . . I couldn't face telling you. I felt like a failure. I couldn't protect them."

Neb drew a dagger from the sheath on her back that I hadn't been able to see but had known would be there. She held the dagger between us, making sure I got a good look at the rift-tempered blade. "I do not need this," she said, although I wasn't sure if it was a statement or a question.

I shrugged.

Neb smiled, sheathed the dagger, and passed it to a guard, who hurried over to collect it. "Let's go outside and discuss matters," she said to me, her face still poised and regal.

I nodded, and followed her out of the nearby door to the balcony overlooking her settlement. It was windy; the scent of the flowers in bloom closer to the mountain reminded me of my times training in the realm.

When the door to the balcony was closed, Neb turned toward me, enveloping me in her arms. "It is good to see you, Rurik," she whispered in my ear. "It is good to see one of my students again."

I nodded sadly. "I'm so sorry for not coming here before now." I'd sent word to Neb about what had happened, but I couldn't face telling her, and then over time it became more difficult to take that step. It was a failure on my part and the one thing I'd been concerned about coming back there.

Neb nodded. "I understand. But do not think that you failed them; you did all you could, I am sure. You survived, Rurik."

I remained silent.

"The last Raven," she said, looking out over the plains and letting out a sigh. "Tell me what happened, Rurik. In your words. Tell me why the Ravens are dead."

# CHAPTER FIFTEEN

W e were ambushed," I told her. "We were driving along the road when the convoy was attacked. They wore masks, used automatic weapons, explosives, and finished us off with blades. We had just left Russia; there had been a multi-Guild hunt. A suspected elder fiend. It had turned out to be several revenants killing for fun."

"Do you know who carried out such an attack?" Neb asked me.

I shook my head and told her everything that had happened since the attack. After returning from my embers, I'd investigated who might have carried out the attack, had Isaac's help to do it, but we'd found nothing. Dead end after dead end. I ended by telling her about Dan and his betrayal, about my being unable to access my power.

When I was done, Neb stared at me for several seconds. "I understand your predicament," she said slowly. "You need your power back. You need to leave the rift and help your friends."

"Can you help me?" I asked.

"Rurik, do you know that over the centuries, I have been a queen, a king, a general, a wife, a soldier, an assassin, a god, a scholar, a farmer, and probably many other things? But I do not give up the secrets of the rift lightly. You were an exceptional student, possibly one of the greatest I ever taught, but do you know your one huge failing?"

I shrugged; I was pretty sure she was about to tell me no matter what I said.

"You have no *patience*," she said. "You never did. If you didn't need to know something right there and then, you didn't bother to seek out more knowledge about it. The embers, for example. You know what they are; you know how to use them. You knew that if you stopped using your powers, essentially cutting yourself off from the rift, your power would cease. Even chained revenants would believe you to be human. You did this to aid your friend in his quest to stop this Dr Mitchell from experimenting on the rift-fused. The outfit she made you wear appears to have caused this cutting-off to become permanent.

"But you didn't do your research," Neb continued. "You assumed too much. You assumed you could just reactivate your power. You are not a stupid man, Rurik, but you are an impatient one. You should have spent time devising how you were going to leave such a predicament as you have placed yourself in. You did not. That was rash and ill advised."

It wasn't like I could disagree with her.

"I will tell you what you want to know, on one condition," Neb continued, looking back across the settlement.

"Anything," I said.

"Come with me," Neb said.

I sucked down the frustration. If I tried to hurry Neb along, she would take even longer. She was not a woman to be rushed, and she was not a woman you wanted to anger. She had been my teacher for the centuries that I'd been inside the rift. Training to become a Raven. She taught me how to fight, how to become a weapon, an assassin who should be feared. She was a hard but fair teacher, but she was not someone who suffered anyone thinking they knew better. She had something she needed to impart, and we would not be done until she had finished.

I followed Neb across the large room and through the opposite door to the one she'd emerged from earlier.

There was a long corridor beyond, decorated in the same way as the large hall, and she stopped in front of the second of five doors, opening it and waving me inside.

I did and took a seat at the circular table next to a large window. Apart from the four chairs and table, there was a small dressing table sat against the far wall.

"This is my war room," Neb said, closing the door behind her and taking a seat opposite me.

"You at war?" I asked her.

"Yes," she said. "Twenty years ago, a settlement to the north of here was attacked. Destroyed completely. Three more met the same fate. Approximately ten thousand people died. Ten thousand revenants. Ten thousand survived and we took them in here. Took in more since then, too, so we now have a little under forty thousand people. Most live closer to the mountains, tending farms and the like."

"That's a big increase," I said.

"I never wanted to become a leader again," Neb said. "Not of this magnitude. I left Inaxia for that exact reason. But sometimes we must do things we do not want to."

"Why didn't Inaxia step in and help these people?" I asked. "I know those in charge of Inaxia don't have influence this far north, but surely they could have helped."

"They did in their own way," Neb said. "They sent food, supplies, soldiers, but the people who live here live in villages have seceded from Inaxia's influence. People are stubborn, and even aid is often refused if they think it comes with unnecessary rules attached."

"They were scared that it would be a foothold for Inaxia in the north?" I asked.

Neb nodded.

"People came to me for help because I was separate from Inaxia," Neb said. "And now I have thousands of people under my care once again."

"What was destroying the settlements?" I asked her.

"An elder fiend, two of them, to be exact," Neb said.

"That's not good at all," I said.

"The tempest had a surge," Neb said. "Power flowed out, creating multiple tears, and with it came the problems it creates. First surge of that magnitude in centuries."

"Are they dead?" I asked.

"Yes," Neb said. "But what happens here affects Earth. Those elder fiends could have easily made their way through a tear. The result would have been disastrous."

She removed a small wooden box from one of the dresser's drawers and passed it to me.

"I don't think marriage is the answer," I said before I could stop myself.

Neb didn't smile. "You always did have a smart mouth. It must have been hell for you to keep it to yourself earlier."

"It's been hell to keep it to myself for seven years," I said.

"When you have your power back, when you are whole once again, what's going to stop you from falling into the same problems as before?" Neb asked, placing her hand on the box so I couldn't open it. "What's going to stop you from hunting and hunting, and forgoing everything else in your desire for vengeance? I taught you better than that. I taught you how to be a Raven. Your *unkindness* were murdered, I get that, but it is not on you to feel bad about surviving. Would you rather have been with your people? Would you rather have been worm food?"

"No," I admitted. "But the guilt I felt at surviving was my sole driving force in everything I did. I felt like if I could just find those responsible, it would release some of the burden I felt."

"The burden of life?" Neb asked.

I nodded.

"Do you know why you excelled as a student?"

I shook my head. "I knew where to put the sharp end of a dagger?" I asked.

Neb laughed at that. "No, you idiot," she said, although there was no unpleasantness in her voice. "You care about your friends. You care about your loved ones. Contrary to popular belief, caring about people makes you a better killer than living a solitary life with no one. It reminds you that you need to be careful, because if you fuck up, your friends might die. Being a loner eventually means you forget your humanity, you think only of the hunt, the kill. No one can live like that. You were exceptional because people like you, and you don't have to pretend to be someone you're not. People feared you because of that. Because of your ability to switch between friendly and assassin. I'd seen it happen. I saw a switch flick inside of you more than once, and it made people afraid. Rightly so. Do you still have that ability? Because you will need to protect your friends by eliminating the threat toward them, and honestly, Rurik, some of them might not understand."

I stared at Neb for several seconds. "Whatever it takes," I said eventually.

"Good," Neb said, clapping her hands together. "Open the box."

Inside was a forest-green crystal. It glowed faintly until I plucked it from the box, when it lit up like a firework. I held it in the palm of my hand as the crystal, no larger than the nail on my thumb, pulsated like a heartbeat.

"Do you know what that is?" Neb asked me.

"A heart crystal," I said. "Otherwise known as a promise crystal."

Without warning, Neb practically dove over the table, clasped her hand over mine, and held on tightly as the crystal cut into the flesh of my palm.

"Damn it," I shouted.

With her free hand, she grabbed the back of my neck, forcing me to lock eyes with her. "When I need you, you will come? Do you agree?"

Neb's voice was raw, and I knew that saying no would result in something bad happening. Probably to me. Maybe to her. She was afraid of something, I could feel it, but I didn't know exactly what it was.

"Yes," I said as she increased the pressure on my hand before releasing.

I looked down at the crystal in my hand, which I was pretty sure was now beating in time to Neb's heartbeat. The blood on my palm was being sucked up into the crystal itself as it changed, becoming smoother, more oval in shape. I knew where it was meant to go, where I was meant to wear it. The medallion in my home. Looked like the days of my hiding from my past were well and truly gone.

"Warning would have been nice," I said, breathlessly.

"Warning wouldn't have worked," Neb said. "You might have said no."

Anger flashed through me. "And that would have been my damn right, Neb."

Neb's eyes narrowed for a moment before she sighed. "Yes, but you needed help, and this is my payment for said help. You will come when I need you."

"For what?"

"Doesn't matter," Neb said, with a dismissive wave. "You will come."

Heart crystals functioned outside of the rift. No matter where I was, it was linked to Neb. It also meant that she could communicate with me while I dreamt. That wasn't something I was looking forward to.

"You break the crystal and you're brought right to me," Neb said.

I'd used one once before. The forceful movement of being taken from Earth to the rift, bypassing the embers, was about as fun as being repeatedly kicked in the testicles. I put the memory of it aside.

"You want to know how to regain your power, yes?" Neb asked.

I nodded.

"When you stopped using your power, it had to go somewhere," Neb said. "It normally flows from the rift to the embers and into you. But if you cut yourself off, it stays in the embers. It feeds it."

I thought back to my journey through the embers. "The decaying buildings," I said. "The power is stored in them."

"Correct. It becomes a part of the very building itself. The shadows destroy them, releasing the power, which goes to another building and hides again. You break the building, it will flow into the one thing it can flow into. You."

"I need to destroy a building that has the power inside of it," I said, more to myself than to Neb. "How?"

"It's your memories," Neb said. "Seriously, you are two thousand years old, and you never bothered to figure out how your embers worked?"

"Does anyone?" I countered.

"No," Neb said with a smile. "I was probably your age by the time I started to look into it."

"You didn't answer the question," I said.

"Fine, you can fix and break the embers as you wish. You can't rearrange them too much, but destroying a building will be as easy as knowing where to hit or push or pull. Everything has a weak spot, Rurik."

"Thank you," I said, getting to my feet.

"You say that now," Neb said. "Look, whatever you do in your embers, be sure to run. The second you start screwing around with it all is the second the shadows turn nasty. And there are worse things than shadows in there."

"Yeah, I know," I said.

"Oh, that you know," Neb said with a chuckle. "Just be careful, Rurik. You were mortally wounded when you entered the embers, so it might have only felt like you were there for one night, but on Earth and here, it would have been days, maybe weeks."

A lot can happen in two weeks. She was silent for a moment, but I could tell that there was something on her mind.

"What is it?" I asked eventually.

"What are you going to do with the medallions?" She asked. "The Ravens' medallions, I mean."

"I don't know," I admitted. "I have five of them, not including my own, but I couldn't find the rest."

"Less than half," Neb said sadly.

I nodded. I wasn't really sure what to say.

"They are your duty to use to re-establish the Guild," Neb said. "You know that."

I did; I couldn't lie. When a Guild lost members, it was up to the survivors to ensure that the Guild was kept up to strength. "I can't re-establish the Ravens when I only have half of the medallions."

"You could get more carved," Neb said.

"I know, but . . ."

"But those that belonged to your friends are still lost and that feels wrong?" Neb suggested.

I nodded. "Whoever killed my people scattered the medallions; it looks like some were sold off to whoever could afford them. Also, I need to make sure that the people who killed my friends don't just do the same to a new group. It's not as easy as just giving the medallions away and saying job done."

Ned stood and embraced me. "I wish you luck, Rurik. When you are ready to start the Ravens up again, come see me. I'll help however I can. They were my Guild to begin with; I'd like to make sure they stay in safe hands."

"I will," I promised. "Thank you for your help."

"I'll see you one day soon enough," Neb said. "Save your friends, be the man you were trained to be, but stay safe. I'm going to need your help one day, and I don't want to find out you died and can't keep up your end of the bargain."

"I don't plan on dying," I told her. While my embers would take me in should I be close to death, whether I wanted them to or not, a sudden death—decapitation, bullet to the head, et cetera—would kill me too quickly for the embers to do anything. On top of that, being seriously hurt with a rift-tempered weapon would mean it would be much harder for me to head into the embers. Either way ends with me being dead. For good. Riftborn were hard to kill, but it was perfectly possible.

"No one plans on dying, my dear," Neb said. "That's what's so goddamned frustrating about it."

Neb escorted me back through the top level of the tower, standing beside me as the lift was called. There were no guards to go with me this time, I assumed because I'd come out alive from talking to Neb and was therefore deemed no longer a threat.

"Rurik," Neb said as the lift doors opened.

I turned back to her.

"I trained you to do what you needed to do," she said. "The Ravens thought you were a normal member of the Guild; was that always the case?"

I nodded. "Two people know what I was trained to do," I said. "Ji-hyun and Isaac."

"I have not met the latter," Neb said.

"He's a good man," I told her. "I trust him, and he deserved to know. He understood why it had to remain a secret, and he didn't judge me. Two things that I needed in a friend."

Neb sighed and remained quiet for several moments. "When you go back, you won't be able to hunt these adversaries and have your friends remain in the dark about what you were. Not everyone will understand."

"I know," I said, and stepped into the lift. "But it'll be nice to have the burden of the secret removed. I think when the Ravens were killed and I survived, part of my problem was maintaining what I was while trying to find those responsible. The rules state that I was to never reveal what I was trained to do, even if my Guild was gone. The rules suck and aren't fit for purpose. I need to do this my way."

"You will be revealing a large secret about the Guilds," Neb said without any hint of unhappiness at what that might mean.

"Good," I said as the doors began to close. "Keep safe, Neb. I'll see you soon."

"When you get your power back, it might take some time before you're back to full strength," Neb told me. "Try not to do anything stupid in the meantime."

"No promises," I told her with a smile.

"Make them pay, Rurik," Neb said before the doors closed altogether.

The short lift ride felt much longer as I considered Neb's words. She was someone whose opinion mattered to me a great deal. She'd also trained Ji-hyun. We'd bonded early in the training, and even now, centuries later, that bond was unbreakable, even if we hadn't seen each other in many years. Riftborn were rare, and Guild members even rarer than that, but what we'd gone through together, only a tiny fraction of a percentage of riftborn would even know about.

The lift doors opened, and I stepped out, finding Kuri waiting for me.

"I wondered where you'd gone," I said with a smile.

"You seem happier," he said. "I assume it went well."

"It went about as well as it always goes when you want answers from Neb," I told him.

"I hope they help," he said, taking me to Maria, who was hungrily eating a bushel of bright blue apples.

"These are delicious," she said, looking up at me, half an apple the size of my fist falling out of her mouth.

I picked up a nearby sack and filled it with a few dozen apples, using rope to tie it around Maria's neck. "For when we return to the embers," I said.

"Thank you," Maria told me.

She followed me out of the pens, as we nodded a thank-you to the beast master who had taken care of her.

The ride back across the plains was done with a renewed vigour, and we reached the cave with what felt like a good time.

The sky was beginning to darken when we stepped back into my embers.

A large barn owl landed on a boulder beside us. "Hope you had fun," Casimir said.

"I need to find a building that is bubbling over with power," I told him. "A building that's being torn apart with it. I need to destroy it."

Casimir thought for a moment. "We can find something like that. But we're going to have to wait until nightfall."

# CHAPTER SIXTEEN

I didn't want to wait until nightfall. There was a voice in the back of my head that screamed how bad of an idea that would be. But we needed to find the building with the most power leaked into it, and that was easier to do at night.

We waited inside a building that I had vague recollections of belonging to some kind of holy man in the city, although it looked more like a large hut than what someone would have considered to be a church. There was no seating inside the hall, although the interior was lit up by the dozens of torches burning on the walls.

There were several windows, all covered in wooden planks, reminding me of something out of a zombie movie. Not an ideal thought, considering the shadows outside were about to start their night-time activities.

"We'll double-check where the building we need is," Casimir said. "Stay here."

They both set off, leaving me alone in a miserable-looking building as darkness began to descend over my embers.

It wasn't long before Casimir returned, flying through an opening in the roof of the hut and landing beside me. "Got it," they said. "You ready to go?"

I nodded and let out a long breath. "How far?"

"We're going to be running," Casimir said. "A few minutes away. You can't help but see the building; it's humming with power."

I opened the door of the hut and stepped out into the darkness. I locked eyes with Casimir, who beat their wings with panic. Somewhere in the distance, there was a howl.

I sprinted through the almost-total darkness after Casimir, who flew ahead, moving toward the torches that burned in the distance. I wasn't sure who had put them there, or whether or not it was safe, but I trusted Casimir, and besides, I figured being able to see anything about to attack would be a lot better than standing around in the darkness, wondering what was going to kill me first.

I was about halfway to the light—maybe two hundred feet— when a shadow stepped into it. It had been absorbing power from the embers. The power had twisted it, turning it from something resembling a human, into . . . a horror. A shadow-cursed.

I stopped running and stood still for a moment. It was the size of a black bear but looked more canine, its long, gangly limbs were almost bone-thin, and its ribs were pronounced under its dark fur. The skin around its mouth was missing, revealing only a skeletal maw, its teeth reminding me of a crocodile. If the shadow-cursed ever got through the embers to Earth, people would die.

Ordinarily, a shadow-cursed in the embers was a danger but nothing I couldn't have dealt with. However, I was unarmed and unpowered, neither of which were going to make my life easy.

The creature turned toward the village, and I dropped down behind a nearby boulder. The shadows would be in the village somewhere; presumably, I was too far away from them to be noticed, but I was pretty sure that the shadow-cursed was not going to be met with a joyous reception should the two meet. Shadows considered a shadow-cursed to be just as much of a problem to destroy as I did.

The shadow-cursed howled, a low, bass-filled sound of horror and dread, causing goosebumps all over my arms. I wasn't afraid of the creature, but I was cautious about it, and I didn't want to engage it unprepared.

I moved silently toward the light as the shadow-cursed turned and walked back into the village. The mist beside me began to break, and the head of a snake poked out of it.

"Maria," I said.

"We saw the shadow-cursed," they said. "Casimir has gone to find this place of power."

"The shadows?" I asked.

"I made a big commotion on the other side of the village," Maria whispered. "They're all over there, but the shadow-cursed is walking through the town, looking for you, I assume."

"You're probably right," I admitted. "I'd very much like a weapon right about now."

A small robin landed on my shoulder. "Last hut on the left," Casimir said. "Close to the river. It's humming with power."

"Have you thought how you're going to destroy it?" Maria asked.

In all honesty, I hadn't. I hadn't expected to have to deal with a monster in my own embers, either. It had long since turned into a hard day. "I'll figure it out on the way," I said eventually. "Let's go."

I kept low as I ran past trees until reaching a large hut; I hugged the wall, sliding around it, until I could peer down the street to where the shadow-cursed was patrolling. Shadow-cursed weren't especially smart, but they could see well, even in the embers, so stepping out into the open was a good way to get it to charge me.

"Casimir, I need you to go piss off the shadow-cursed," I said.

"Done," Casimir said without hesitation, and was soon flying toward the fiend, where they started to dive-bomb it.

"They are excellent at irritating people," Maria said just before I darted across the road, practically throwing myself behind a large stone wall, the mist swirling over me as I rolled along the ground and came up beside a hut almost identical to the one I'd just left the cover of.

I let out a long breath as Maria—still in snake form—slithered up beside me. "You think we got away with it?" they asked me.

"Run," Casimir shouted as he bombed past at high speed.

"Nope," I said, following them as the sound of the shadow-cursed running toward us filled the air.

"I thought you were keeping him busy," I shouted at Casimir, who was already some distance in front, leading the way. They turned into a large snowy owl, mid-flight, their bright white plumage visible every time light from the multitude of torches touched it.

We weaved through the village as the sound of the fiend giving chase reverberated around me, the night-time making it harder to pinpoint, as if it was everywhere at once.

"Lucas," Maria shouted, changing into a deer and nudging me aside.

I threw myself to the ground, rolling back to my feet as the shadow-cursed impacted with the wall that I'd been close to. The stone exploded all around, but the shadow-cursed got stuck in the wooden parts of the fence, causing an immense noise in the process, gaining the interest of a multitude of shadows, who could be seen descending on our location.

"Damn it," I snapped, and started running again, following Casimir, who landed atop a large hut close to what had once been a stream but was now even-denser mist. Dozens of shadows converged around the building, several of them turning back to me as I stopped in my tracks.

"Well, shit," Maria said from beside me.

"Can we get them to break the hut?" I asked as some of the shadows broke away from the group and started toward me.

"I have no idea," Maria said.

What in the hell was I meant to do now?

"Try not to get hurt," I said to Maria, and sprinted toward the building next to the hut, spinning out of the way of two shadows who tried to grab me from the darkness, and bursting through the front door like it wasn't even there.

I ran up the stairs to the top floor of the building and looked out of the window to the ledge outside. I didn't remember the building from any part of my childhood, but I sure was glad it was there.

The numbers of shadows were ever increasing, and I spotted the shadow-cursed in the distance, pacing back and forth. It wasn't keen on charging into the throng of shadows, and more than a few of them had turned in its direction, seeking out a new target.

Casimir sat on top of the wooden hut closest to me, with Maria—now an owl themselves—beside them. The feeling of power came off the building in waves, crashing into me over and over again. This was clearly where all of my unused power was going, and somehow I had to break the building and release the power back into me.

"You could wait it out until morning," Casimir shouted.

They were right, I could, but that would mean leaving my friends for even longer to deal with whatever awful shit Dan and his allies had done. I walked to the end of the hut, thankful that there were no real rooms built there.

I walked over to the open window and looked down. The building beside the one I was in had a thatched roof and was only a single storey. At least it was a way out.

There was a loud snort and a scream from outside the building, but I pushed it aside and sprinted across the floor, launching myself out of the window and landing on the thatched roof of the hut. Turns out thatched roofs are not built to withstand a full-grown man impacting it at speed. Who knew?

I crashed through the roof and hit the ground next to what would have been a fire pit. The wind was knocked out of me, and I rolled onto my back and looked up at the hole in the roof.

"I bet that hurt," Casimir said, their owl head poking through the hole.

"Fuck off," I eventually managed. Witty comebacks were for people who could breathe properly.

More howls and screams from outside brought me back to the present a lot quicker than just lying there and waiting for the pain to shift ever would have. I was going to have to deal with the shadow-cursed. I couldn't just leave it to run around unchecked. I just had no idea *how* I was going to deal with it. The last one I'd killed had been with a rift-tempered dagger, something I was unfortunately not able to do at the moment.

There was a pounding on the door and more inhuman screams from outside, as the hut shuddered from the impact.

"The shadow-cursed is trying to break in," Casimir said. "It's being attacked by shadows, but it's holding its own at the moment."

The door buckled, and I managed to roll aside just as part of it shot into the hut, taking out a chunk of the far wall.

A wave of power smashed into me, almost forcing me to my knees as one of the shadow-cursed hooves smashed through the door, accompanied with a scream as it was attacked by more shadows. I ran at the wall as fast as I could, slamming my shoulder into the broken wood and feeling another wave of power as I had to steady myself against the wall.

"Little help," I called to Maria and Casimir.

Maria dropped through the hole, changing into a chestnut Arabian horse mid-leap. She landed, spun, and kicked out at the wall, putting both hooves through it like it was paper.

Another wave of power as the entire roof collapsed, and Casimir, who had turned into a rhino, dropped through it. Eidolons had to use a lot of energy to turn into an animal; it was why they mostly chose light or small animals. A horse was about as big as I'd ever seen either of them become. Turning into a white rhino that weighed well over four times as much as a horse was going to have a serious impact on just how long Casimir could stick around and help.

Casimir walked through the wall. They didn't even bother to build up a head of steam; they just strolled through it like it wasn't there. I spotted Maria turn into a bird and fly out of the now-decimated roof as I scrambled out of the hut, trying to put some distance between me and the demolition zone.

I was about ten feet away when the power slammed into me from all sides, forcing me to my knees, my vision going dark. I opened my mouth to scream in pain, but only smoke came out. Dark grey smoke twirled around me as the sounds of the shadows and shadow-cursed fighting became an accompaniment to my pain.

As the pain subsided, I got to my feet and turned to find the shadows swarming over the fiend, tearing it to pieces. They weren't as strong as the fiend, but what they lacked in strength, they made up for in sheer numbers. Like piranhas attacking larger prey. They tore the shadow-cursed apart, ripping off limbs, drenching the surrounding area in blood and gore. They didn't eat; they just killed, and when they were done, when there wasn't enough left of the shadow-cursed for it to be recognizable as once being anything, the shadows turned to me.

I smiled. "Casimir, Maria, you both okay?"

"Yes, boss," Casimir said, their voice distant. They'd need to recharge.

"Go," Maria said. "Help your friends. Don't take so long to return to us next time."

The shadows closest to me started to move my way. "I won't," I told her, and smoke poured out of my hands, covering me as I vanished from the embers.

# CHAPTER SEVENTEEN

There are two places you can leave the embers from on Earth. One is where you consider your home. The second is where you have something personal that means a lot to you. In my case, both of those options meant there was only one place I could go. My apartment in Brooklyn.

I opened my eyes and found myself sat on the floor of my apartment bedroom. My room was still as I'd left it. No one knew that I lived there; the entire apartment and all of the bills were under the name Matthew Nelson, so I wasn't concerned that I'd arrive to a battalion of Mason Barnes' private army.

I wondered if Dale had told his Sovereign Humanity buddies that we lived in the same building, but there wasn't much I could do about that right now.

I opened my wardrobe and unearthed the safe. I hadn't expected to be opening it again so soon, but if my life had taught me anything, it was to expect the unexpected.

I entered the code on the keypad, opened the safe door, and removed the contents, placing them all on my bed. I opened the black-velvet drawstring bag first, staring at the medallion as it tumbled into my hand. It looked identical to the one in Mason's private room: a shield with a hammer and sword crossed over it, and a Raven perched atop. There was a space between the shield and hammer, where the two crossed, and I removed the green gem from my pocket and placed it inside.

The medallion flashed twice as the crystal fused itself to the metal, and when it was done, it flashed once more. The promise crystal would not be removed until the oath was fulfilled. However long that took.

I slipped the medallion over my head, feeling the cold metal chain against my skin. While I knew there was no going back to my quiet life, placing the medallion against my chest once more made everything feel even more real.

I opened the duffle bag, which contained a half a million dollars in bills and five more velvet pouches, each one containing another Raven medallion. I zipped the bag shut. I didn't need them right now. There was also the larger velvet pouch, which I opened, removing the hooded mask inside. The mask was black with a dark grey hood, and there were dark grey marks around the eyeholes, and identically coloured slashes along either side of the mask. The mask of a Guild Talon.

I stared at the mask for several seconds. Talons are trained to remove threats to the Guild. Both internal and external. They're trained to quietly deal with any problems that arise so that the Guild is kept safe and the members don't need to be concerned with such matters. There are two Talons to every Guild, and they're meant to keep their Guild safe. The second Talon had died defending the Guild. We had failed to keep our Guild safe. It was not a failure I would repeat.

The metal briefcase contained a Heckler & Koch P30L. I'd removed it from its case and kept it clean and in good condition every month since I'd put it there. I checked the gun over, making sure it was all okay, before loading the three magazines with thirteen .40 S&W ammo rounds. I removed the leather holster from the case and put it around my waist, feeling the gun against my right hip and putting the two magazines in the back, before removing two long daggers from the case. Both had a blue-and-purple tinge to the blade, although one was larger, with a wider blade, and only one sharp edge. Both were rift-tempered. I wish I'd had them back in the embers. I put one in the sheath against my back, and the other, larger one in the sheath at my left hip.

The last item in the metal case was a set of rift-tempered knuckledusters. I slipped them into my pocket. They were good in a pinch, and while it was unlikely that I could kill a revenant, fiend, or riftborn with them, I could certainly do some damage, and sometimes that was enough.

I grabbed a black hoodie and changed into a clean dark green T-shirt and pair of jeans.

I left my bedroom with the duffle bag in my hand and walked into my front room, dropping the bag, and drawing my gun at Dale Winters, who sat behind my sofa, fear clear to see on his face. A sandwich had been placed on the sofa. Whatever else Dale was, he was not good at hiding.

"Hey, Dale," I said, keeping the gun on him. "I think you're going to have to explain a lot."

"I'm not who you think I am; please don't shoot," he said in one breath.

"Explain better," I told him.

"My wallet," he said, the contents of his sandwich beginning to spill out.

"Take the food off my sofa before you stain my carpet," I said. "Where's your wallet?"

Dale did as he was asked and put the food back on the plate, before keeping one hand up while he removed the wallet from his jeans pocket and tossing it across the coffee table to me.

I kept one eye on Dale as I picked it up and glanced at the FBI ID inside. "You're a fed?" I asked.

"Undercover," Dale said.

"Keep explaining," I told him, not lowering the gun.

"I was put undercover with Sovereign Humanity because they have ties to Mason Barnes, who we're pretty sure is dealing in stolen revenant DNA. He's trying to make his own revenants, or fiends, or something. There's a lot there. Anyway, my bosses put me inside because Mason's security staff are almost entirely linked to Hamble PD."

"He uses cops as security?" I asked.

"Ex-cops, but the cops on HPD just let everything go," Dale said. "The whole Barnes empire is basically allowed to do what they like in Hamble; the police will back them up. I was to find evidence linking Mason and HPD to illegal activities. And I found a lot. Dangerous experiments, bribery, extortion, murder, people vanishing if they piss him off. I gave all of the evidence to my handler. Emily West."

"Special Agent West was your handler?" I asked.

"Not at first," Dale said. "But two months ago, my handler was murdered. He had his head cut off. His family were executed too. Emily took it on, as she was friends with him. Only people who knew were Emily and a few select people in the FBI. She doesn't know who to trust, so she trusts no one."

"Yeah, I got that impression," I told him. "But that doesn't explain why you're in my apartment, eating my food."

"My food," he said before he could stop himself.

"What?"

"I've been here two weeks," he said. "I had this food ordered in."

"Two weeks?" I said more to myself than to Dale.

Dale nodded. "I knew you lived here, but when you vanished, Dan and the rest of the Mason brigade started to look for you, but no one knew you were here. I didn't tell Brad and his people that you lived in the same building as me. I thought maybe having someone who I knew wasn't involved with them might help."

"How'd you know I wasn't involved?" I asked.

"You were at the bar," he told me. "Friends with the people there; also, you beat the ever-loving shit out of two SH members. Gave me a good clue. Emily found out where you lived and contacted me, asked me to keep an eye out in case you came back."

"Emily happen to say *how* she knew where I lived?" I asked.

Dale nodded. "She said . . ." He paused, trying to remember something. "Gabriel."

I lowered the gun.

"This building isn't under your name, is it? I thought it was safe."

"Safe for what?" I asked.

"Two days after you vanished, they went after your friends," Dale said. "They torched a church, they hurt people, and somehow they found out that I was undercover. A week after you vanished, they came for me one night, and I managed to get away. I got back to my place, but I knew it wasn't safe, didn't know where else to go. I came here."

"Your apartment is inhabited with Mason's goons?"

"Brad," Dale said. "And a few others. They turned up looking for me and, I guess, are waiting to see if I'll come back. They patrol the building sometimes; they have badges, tell anyone who asks that they're cops just keeping an eye on the place because I was a terrorist."

Dale looked genuinely upset at the idea of people thinking he was a terrorist, which I couldn't exactly blame him for.

"Have you heard anything about my friends?" I asked.

Dale shook his head. "Dan woke up; they knew they needed to get him out of the hospital soon. No one else was meant to survive, so I hear. The RCU lady did, and as the FBI and RCU were protecting them, they needed a way to get to her and remove the threat. I think it was Dan's idea to attack everyone all at the same night, to eliminate the threat. I bugged Brad's office, heard all about it. You weren't meant to be there, though, and from what I hear, Dan is pretty livid that you survived."

Good. "But not everyone is dead, right?"

Dale shook his head again. "No. After the attack at the hospital, the FBI were stood down."

"Wait, what?"

"Don't know why," Dale said. "I spoke to Emily a few days ago; she was told it was an RCU matter."

"That's insane," I said.

"I don't know what happened to any of your friends, though, "Dale said. "After they burned the church, they went after me, and I spent a few days getting back to Brooklyn."

"So, how long have I been gone?" I asked him.

"Twenty-three days," he said.

I looked up at the ceiling and let out an irritated breath between clenched teeth. "Damn it," I whispered to myself.

He shook his head. "That medallion, you're a Guild member?"

"A Raven," I told him.

"I heard Dan talk about you," Dale said. "He was ranting at Mason. I think he's scared of you."

"Good," I said. "Have you tried contacting your higher-ups in the FBI?"

Dale nodded. "They told me to wait at home, and then Brad arrived with his goons, so I'm thinking there's a leak somewhere, and honestly, I figured I'd stay here a few weeks and then try to work out what to do next. They know I'm a fed, but they will have no problems with putting a bullet in my head."

"So, Dan is a leak for the RCU, and there's a leak at the FBI?" I asked. "They got the FBI to stand down, so it sounds like Mason has some powerful friends. Half a dozen FBI agents killed, plus two whistle-blowers. For what? And why would the FBI want their own people killed?"

"I don't know," Dale said.

"Why would Dan betray us all?" I asked, more to myself than to get a response from Dale. Not just all of us, but to be a part of the deaths of the Raven Guild. Just how long had all of this been in place?

"Way I hear it, he was made an offer he couldn't refuse," Dale said. "Don't know what it is, but it must have been good."

"Okay, so, you can come with me," I said.

"To where?" Dale asked.

"We're going to go see if we can get transport back to Rochester. My friends are there; we'll find them somehow. Then I plan on hunting down Dan and hanging him by his own spleen."

Dale nodded.

"Stay here," I told him. "Get ready to leave."

"What are you going to do?" he asked me.

"I'm going to go say hi to Brad," I told him, and walked toward the door.

"That medallion will mean that what you do is legal, yes?" Dale called after me.

I turned back to him. "I'm in pursuit of dangerous individuals," I said. "So, yes."

Dale shook his head. "Be careful; they might be cops, but they're bad people."

"I will," I said, placing the Talon's mask next to the door, opening it, and stepping out into the empty hallway. "Be prepared to leave as soon as I return."

I closed the door and set off down the hallway. I didn't want to have to use my gun in this situation; last thing we needed was my neighbours to call the police. If Brad and his friends were already embedded with the HPD, there was no telling if that corruption had spread to other police departments.

I took the stairwell to the floor below and quickly checked the hallway there to ensure it was clear of threats.

There was no one in the stairwell outside of the Dale's floor, so I stopped outside of the fire door and pushed it open ever so slightly, listening for any signs of people close by. When there was nothing, I risked opening the door further and poking my head out to check.

Two men stood outside of Dale's apartment, which was the last one on the floor to the right of the of the stairwell, next to a large window that overlooked the front of the building. We were a few storeys up, so throwing them through the window, while tempting, would be loud and almost certain to end with more trouble than I needed right now.

I pulled my hoodie up over my head, made sure that my knee-length coat was done up so that my gun and knives weren't visible, and stepped out of the stairwell toward the two men. They were both large, with short hair, wearing identical black jackets, jeans, and black boots, and both had an air of menace about them. One looked my way; he had a scar over his top lip that stopped just to the side of his nose. His movement made the second look over to see what was going on. He had a black eye that was just the other side of hideous. It looked like he'd been tenderized. It was possible he had.

"Gentlemen," I said.

"What d'you want?" the scared man asked.

"I just want to see Dale," I said. "I heard he was home. Need his advice."

"You want to see Dale?" the man with the black eye asked, repeating my question but adding contempt.

I nodded. "Yeah, man. I've got some information about a revenant." I whispered the last word as if I said it, someone might appear behind me.

"What about it?" the scared man asked, taking a step toward me, a cruel smile on his face.

"I think one of them is living in the building," I said.

The two men stared at each other. That was a mistake.

I dashed forward, driving my elbow in the temple of the scared man, and moving on to the man with the black eye, jabbing my fingers into his throat before he could call out. His friend was unconscious before he'd hit the hallway carpet, and I dragged the other one away from the door, pushing him to the ground as he made an awful wheezing sound.

I took the guns from both men, emptying them and tossing the ammo in one direction down the hallway, and keeping hold of the guns themselves for now. The still-unconscious scared man also had a Bowie knife that I tossed down the hallway.

The man who was still struggling to breathe began to fish in his pockets, trying to get his phone out. I grabbed his wrist and pulled it away, twisting it enough to cause discomfort.

"How many in the apartment?" I asked.

Defiance radiated from his eyes.

I broke his wrist.

The defiance was replaced with agony as he tried to scream, but it came out as a raw, guttural cry. I kept hold of the broken wrist as the man looked up at me.

"Don't have time to play games," I said. "How many?"

He held up his other hand, fingers spread.

"Five?" I asked.

He nodded.

I let go of his arm and he rolled to his side, cradling the broken wrist against him. I considered removing him as a problem on a more-permanent basis, but I didn't think my neighbours would appreciate a dead body in the hallway outside of their apartments.

I tossed the two Beretta 92s into a ceramic bowl filled with potpourri, making a loud clinking noise as they landed, before removing my coat and dropping it to the floor, and trying the handle on Dale's apartment door, finding it unlocked. I pushed the door open, stepped inside, and closed it behind me with an audible *click*.

With only one bedroom, the apartment was smaller than my own, but the layout was pretty much identical. There were three men, all of whom were sat in the front room. None were Brad, although all three of them turned to look at me. I waved at them, which appeared to confuse them more than anything else.

One of the men, the largest of the three, with a big black bushy beard, got to his feet and rolled his shoulders, cracking his knuckles as he walked toward me while his friends finally found their courage.

"We don't need to fight, do we?" I asked.

The big man, who stank of cigarette smoke, ran toward me, throwing a huge haymaker that I ducked, and I smashed my elbow into his ribs, pushing him back toward his two friends, both of whom had drawn knives, despite them having guns in their holsters. I guessed that they weren't meant to draw attention to themselves while they stayed there. Either that or they considered me no threat.

The commotion brought out thugs number four and five, the latter being Brad, whose eyes widened when he saw me. He went for his gun.

I turned toward him, took one step, and turned into smoke. I can create smoke, manipulate it, make it into weapons, harden it, and a host of other things, but turning into smoke itself and moving around in that form was hard work, especially seeing how I turned whatever I was wearing or holding into smoke, too. Except for living tissue. I done it a few times and . . . well, frankly it's bad.

The smoke swirled around Brad, who tried to bat me away like I was an errant wasp. I re-formed behind him, the larger of my two knives in hand, as I spun away from him and drove the knife into the chest of his companion. I pushed him away, the knife sliding out of him with ease, and spun back toward Brad, who had turned toward me, his gun now out of its holster. I turned partially to smoke and moved faster than he was capable of understanding, punching him in the stomach as I moved past him, breaking his arm, and tossing the gun aside before I let go of him.

Brad fell to his knees, screaming in pain, as his three remaining friends stared at me in open horror. I couldn't keep up the turning to smoke for long, but it was usually enough to do it once and let everyone else piss themselves.

The big man surprised me by barrelling into me, taking me off my feet and trying to smash me, head-first, into the wall. I slammed my elbow into his nose, and he changed his plan, releasing me enough to drop to the ground. I pushed him aside and stabbed him under the armpit, twice in quick succession, one slightly lower than the other. Blood poured out of the wound, and he staggered back as I moved toward his two friends, one who was trying to get the revolver out of its holster and died with a blade to the throat before he was able to.

The last one back-pedaled and fell onto the glass coffee table, utterly destroying it with a deafening crash. Blood began to pool around the back of his head, and it didn't take long to realise there was a large chunk of glass imbedded in his neck. I left him where he was and went back to Brad, who was crawling, one-handed, toward the bedroom.

I grabbed hold of the back of his shirt and practically lifted him off the floor, pushing him back toward the living room. He didn't resist and soon found himself sat down, staring at his friend, who I was pretty sure was going to die.

"Dan said you were riftborn," Brad said.

"Good for Dan," I said.

"He told us you wouldn't be back for a long time," Brad continued as if I hadn't said anything, his voice holding a faraway quality of someone whose entire world view of where he sat in the pecking order had just been shattered.

"He said you were dangerous," Brad continued, looking up at me for the first time. "But . . ."

"Not like that, yes?" I asked.

I sat down on the chair beside me. "Brad, Dan lied to you. Dan lied to a lot of us, and I want to know where he is. I want to know where Mason is. I want to know what you've done to my friends, and if I don't like any of those answers, you're going to see what happens when I turn into smoke while I'm holding on to someone else. Spoiler, it's nasty."

"But you were just quiet in the bar," Brad continued. "You didn't do anything. Dale said you were just a professor."

"Yeah, not so much," I told him. "Look, I don't have all day."

"I don't know where Dan and Mason are," Brad said. "Probably in Mason's office building. We burned down your friend's church."

"By *we*, you mean you?"

Brad nodded. "Some of Mason's Sky-High Security guys helped."

"Why? Why go to all this trouble?" I asked him.

Brad said nothing.

"Look, there are dead FBI agents and dead RCU agents; the latter were definitely betrayed by Dan, and I think probably the former too," I started. "This all goes back to those two whistle-blowers, doesn't it? Mason get a little freaked out? Worried the FBI were going to start getting too close to something he's working on?" It was a guess, but it was as good of a guess as I had.

Brad nodded. "Mason didn't expect the FBI to just keep coming though."

"So, do you know of someone in the FBI working for Mason?" I asked.

Brad shook his head. "Not for Mason, no."

"What does that mean?" I asked.

"There's a whole organisation just beyond Mason, an organisation Mason is working for," Brad said.

"What are they called?" I asked him.

"No clue," Brad said. "All I know is that Mitchell is working on creating more of those hybrid things. Needed a test."

"Was that the attack?" I asked. "A test?"

"I don't know," Brad said.

"Sovereign Humanity?" I asked. "How are they involved?"

"We were going to blame them for the attacks on the RCU," Brad admitted. "Dan said it was a stupid plan because no one would ever believe that a bunch of humans killed highly trained rift-fused."

"Dan had a point," I conceded.

"Yeah, well, we'd already set them up, been using them to spread hate and getting people to distrust rift-fused. Dan said there were big plans for SH, but I don't know what they were." Brad sighed. "We were just to keep doing what we were doing. Utterly pointless, if you ask me."

"No one did, I assume," I said.

Brad visibly bristled. "No, they didn't. I spoke to Dan about it beforehand; he was working with some FBI agents. Dan got them to go with him. It was just meant to be the RCU, but the FBI were poking their noses in things they shouldn't have been with regard to Sky-High, so Dan saw it as a good way to eliminate them as a threat. He led them all into an ambush, but he got hurt, and one of the RCU survived. The whole thing was fucked."

"I don't understand why Dan would put himself in a corner like this," I said. "Why kill the FBI and RCU? What does he hope to gain from it?"

"Ask Dan," Brad said.

"Someone is trying to create a war?" I asked.

"I don't know," Brad admitted. "You're going to kill me, aren't you?"

I nodded. "If it helps, I'm going to kill Dan, Mason, and everyone else who was involved in this."

"Dan said you used to be in a Guild," Brad told me. "Said you'd want vengeance."

"Partly because of that," I said, feeling anger bubbling up at the thought of my Guild's assassination. "Partly because you deserve it." I moved quickly and slammed the dagger up under Brad's chin, into his brain, killing him instantly.

I removed the dagger and cleaned it. Rift-tempered weaponry killed humans just as well as revenants, fiends, and riftborn. The biggest difference between the two groups was that killing a human with it ensured they'd never come back as one of the latter.

I made sure that all five were dead before leaving the apartment and finding that the man I'd hit in the temple was also dead. The other man, with the broken wrist, was sat up against the wall, cradling his arm against his chest. I dragged the dead one into the apartment and then motioned for the other to come to me.

"I'm not going to kill you," I said when he shook his head.

He stood up, although it looked like it hurt. I showed him the blood-bath inside Dale's apartment. "There's a rumour that when Genghis Kahn destroyed his enemies, he used to leave one person alive to tell the others what happens to those to cross him. Congratulations."

The man stared at the bodies inside the apartment and slowly looked up at me, terror etched on his face.

"Tell them I'm coming," I said. "And then run. If I see you again, you're going to be alongside them."

I left him in the room with his dead friends and went to find Dale. I got the feeling that by the time I was done, there would be a lot more death in my wake.

# CHAPTER EIGHTEEN

As much as Dale wanted to go to his apartment and pick up a few things, I convinced him that it would be better not to go back in there.

I'd left my blood-splattered hoodie in my apartment and put on a clean pair of jeans and T-shirt. There had been too much blood for me to get away with it. I'd washed my face, too; I didn't want to go to the Stag and Arrow covered in the blood of several thugs.

"How many of them were cops?" I asked Dale.

"Ex-cops," Dale corrected. "A few. Most are ex-military."

We reached the bar, and I opened the door, the din of the full bar crashing into me and making me pause. I let Dale in first. I wasn't really someone who enjoyed lots of people in one place, or loud noises. It's far too easy for someone to get the jump on you when your senses are in overdrive.

"Bill," I shouted over the noise, gaining his attention when I started waving in his direction.

He came over and leaned over the bar. "What's up?" he shouted in my ear, and I only just heard him.

I pointed to Dale, and Bill's expression darkened. "We need to talk," I shouted back. "Now."

Bill looked between Dale and me, and concern spread across his face like oil on water. He nodded and motioned for us to follow him, leading us through the throng of people and into a room at the rear of the bar, next to the stairs that lead up to where he lived with George.

"What the fuck is he here for?" Bill snapped as we entered the room.

"Bill, meet undercover FBI agent Dale Winters," I said.

Dale nodded slightly.

"He's a fed?" Bill asked, sounding more than a little surprised. "And where have you been? What's going on?"

"Short version," I said. "A member of the RCU betrayed his own people; I have no idea why. A man called Mason Barnes seems to have been involved in the deaths of FBI agents, and my friends have been hurt while I've been away. I'm a riftborn. Someone in the FBI has stood down the team who were helping with the investigation. Oh, and a bunch of bigoted idiots were being primed to take the fall for it all."

"That's a lot to take in all at once," Bill said. "Why would anyone want to bring the trouble of the FBI and RCU down on their heads? Especially someone with as much money as Mason? Why would he want to risk losing it all?"

"I don't know why," I said.

"Me neither," Dale said. "I wasn't privy to the finer details."

"I need to get to Gabriel's church," I continued. "I'm pretty sure I can figure out where everyone went from there."

"You want to borrow my car?" Bill asked.

"I was hoping to," I said. "But your car is . . . How can I put this?"

"Slow," Bill said. "You can say it. I have a Chevy Silverado that has a zero-to-sixty time of about two weeks."

"Yeah," I said. "I was hoping that maybe George could lend me his Mercedes."

"I can do you one better," Bill said. "Give me five minutes."

"I have another favour," I said as Bill removed the phone from his pocket and was about to walk off.

"You want the fed to stay here?" Bill asked.

I nodded.

"Do I get a say in this?" Dale asked anyone who was listening.

"No," Bill and I said in unison. "You're someone with a brain full of intel and a badge. They find out where you are and you're dead. As is everyone around you. George has access to several safe houses inside the city. You can become a resident of one for a few days, after which we're going to need you to go through everything that happened."

"I'll talk to George," Bill said. "Go see Michelle; she's in the staff room other side of the bar. She lived in Hamble for a while, moved down here a few months back. Gabriel's church is only one of four in New York State, so Michelle goes back there when she can. She might know where Gabriel is. Dale, you can come with me."

Dale looked between Bill and I, a slight panic in his face. "You think you can keep me safe?" he asked.

Bill nodded. "George's firm has been keeping revenants safe for decades. A human Fed should be easy."

"Thank you," Dale said to me, offering me his hand. "I'm sorry for what I said and did while undercover."

I shook his hand, keeping hold of it when he turned to leave. "George and Bill are good people. If I find out that you're involved in this more than just being undercover, I won't hesitate to bury you alongside your friends in your apartment."

"You know you're threatening a federal officer," he said, a little bit more confidence in his voice.

"I know," I said. "Point stands. I'm not playing, Dale. I just wanted you to know."

Dale nodded, having gone a shade paler, and I left him to ascend the stairs with Bill.

After traversing the still-busy bar, I found Michelle exactly where Bill said she'd be. She was watching a show on the large TV that adorned the wall of the staff room and eating a sandwich. She looked up at me and hastily wiped her mouth.

"Hey," she said. "This is staff-only."

"Bill said to come see you," I said. "Something about Gabriel's church. Do you know Gabriel?"

"You mean my cleric?" she asked, slightly unsure of where the conversation was going.

"You're a member of the Church of Tempered Souls?" I asked. "Gabriel's your cleric? The church is in Hamble."

Michelle nodded and put the rest of her sandwich on the table beside her. "Was," she said as I took a seat opposite her. "It was destroyed."

"What happened?" I asked as a mixture of anger and fear bubbled up inside of me. If they'd hurt Gabriel in any way, I was going to rain down fire the likes of which haven't been seen before.

"They torched it," Michelle said. "Gabriel is safe, but no one has seen him for some time. We have an online group to arrange meets, but no one knows where he is."

I pushed my feelings aside for a moment. I couldn't help anyone if I couldn't find out what had happened and where my friends were. "Did Gabriel ever tell you about how to contact him if you needed him?" Every church has a different method to contact its cleric in times of emergency. The only people who knew it would be trusted members of the congregation.

"I can't say," Michelle told me, keeping eye contact.

"I need to get hold of my friends. I know you made an oath to keep this information to yourself," I said, keeping my voice neutral no matter how much I wanted to let emotion in. "But if you can do anything to help, please do."

"We all take the oath," Michelle said. "Gabriel wanted us to know that we could go to him for help, that the church was a place of peace. I do not want to break the oath I gave. I want to help, but the oath was a personal thing. More than just words; it placed us into a family. Do you understand?"

I nodded. It was obvious that Michelle was conflicted between telling me to help Gabriel and keeping the secrets that she swore she'd keep. I didn't want to add to the burden, but I also needed information. Sometimes, the best way to get what you want is to keep your mouth closed.

"He has camera feeds in the church and surrounding area," Michelle said. "If he wants to see you, he will find you. I hope he's safe."

I thanked Michelle and returned to where I'd last seen Bill, waiting around impatiently for a few minutes until he appeared with George.

"Lucas," George said, shaking my hand. "Thanks for delivering such a steaming pile of shit onto my lap."

"He's joking," Bill said quickly.

"I am," George told me. George was several inches taller than me, Black, with a bald head and dark moustache. He wore an expensive dark blue suit with a white shirt and red tie, with a grey-and-red pocket chief. On his wrist was a black Rolex Submariner. He looked like the word *suave* was invented just for him.

"I don't know what's happening in Hamble and Rochester," I said. "Either of you heard anything?"

"No," George said. "Nothing specific, anyway. Rumour has it the FBI have shut up shop, so to speak, and that the RCU are in charge of everything now. But then, there are rumours that the RCU were all killed, so I don't know how they can both be true. What do you know?"

"Mason is not working alone," I said. "There's more going on here than first thought. Brad said that Dan was going to lead the FBI into the attack, but the RCU members decided to join. He got hurt, and Annie survived, so they couldn't spin it as an RCU attack on FBI. Once she woke, she'd know exactly what happened, so they had to eliminate her and any guards at the hospital."

"No guards were killed at the hospital," George said.

"Wait, what?" I asked. "It was just the nurses and Annie?"

George nodded.

"I saw RCU agents in the building," I said. Why kill the nurses but not the guards? Something wasn't adding up.

"Let me show you something," Bill said.

I followed George and Bill out of the rear exit of the bar into an alleyway behind it. It was dark now, and the cold had firmly set in; somewhere in the distance was a rumble of thunder, and I wondered if we were in for a storm.

There were two large garages at the end, and Bill used a remote to deactivate an alarm system before removing a set of keys from his pocket but didn't open it, instead turning back to me.

"Be careful," I said.

"Thank you, Lucas," George said with a smile. "But I've been working with these people for twenty years; I'll be fine. So will Dale; they won't find him, and we'll make sure that your apartment, and his, are cleaned. I know a few revenants who specialize in removals."

I did not want to know.

"In the meantime, my husband wishes to gift you something very important to him," George continued. "He won't tell you it's important to him, because he doesn't want to make a big deal out of it, but it is."

"George," Bill said in a tone that suggested his husband could shut up anytime he wanted to.

"What's going on?" I asked as George placed an affectionate hand on his husband's shoulder.

Bill opened the garage door, revealing a dark green Audi R8.

"Wow," I said as Bill tossed me a set of keys, which I thankfully caught. Judging from the expression on Bill's face, I was pretty sure that catching them was some kind of test.

"My Audi R8 V10 Spyder Performance Carbon Black," Bill said. "To give it the full name."

"I assume you shorten it," I said.

"You'd think so, wouldn't you?" George said with an almost audible roll of his eyes.

"I did not expect that," I told him.

"He also has an old Shelby GT Mustang in the other one," George said. "I don't remember the year."

"Yes, you do," Bill said.

"Yes, I do," George replied with a large smile. "But I do so love to hear about it when I pretend I don't."

"Thank you both for this," I said. "I don't know how I can repay you."

"Do not break my car," Bill said. "That's a good repayment."

"I promise I'll have it all washed and waxed before returning it," I told him.

George offered me another handshake, which I accepted. "Godspeed, Lucas," he said, serious for the first time since we'd left the bar.

Bill walked over and hugged me, patting me on the shoulder. "Come back in one piece," he said. "I got to know the human Lucas pretty well, and I think I'd like to get to know the real you, too."

"I'll be back for a drink," I promised. "And to return your car."

"More the car," George called out, and was playfully struck on the arm by his husband.

I unlocked the car and got inside, positioning the seats and windows before I drove out into the alley wondering if, despite all of the horrors that I'd seen, and despite me needing to find my friends, it was okay that I was going to enjoy the drive. Take the little bits of happiness where you can get them.

I spotted Bill watching me all the way down the alley, presumably regretting ever passing his Audi to another soul. I drove out of view, and it took me a while to get through New York, which was, as always, busy no matter the weather. But once outside of the city, heading north, I opened the Audi up and smiled. I would take the happiness now, thanks.

Dawn had just lit up the sky in a sea of brilliant reds and oranges as I reached Hamble. I didn't go in for superstitions much, but "red sky in the morning, shepherds warning" was one that always stuck with me.

I stopped the car in a car park close to the church and walked the rest of the way, the rain making me glad that along with the duffle bag—which I'd left in the car—I'd brought a thick raincoat.

The church was a shell. The roof was gone, the glass destroyed. Scorch marks adorned every inch of the exterior walls, and the small garden in front of it was ash.

"Goddamn it," I said, remembering that Gabriel didn't much care about blasphemy.

I walked to the front doors, which were now charred and partially collapsed. Snow had collected just inside the main steps, and I paused to take a breath, preparing myself for whatever I was about to find inside.

"It wasn't me," a voice said from behind.

I turned to find Nadia stood at the bottom of the steps, about ten feet away. Rage filled me.

"It wasn't me," she said, louder as I leapt down the steps and started to walk toward her, smoke billowing all around me.

"Explain," I said through gritted teeth.

"I didn't do this," Nadia said quickly. "The day I saw you and Emily in Mason's office, I left the organisation. It was time to go."

The smoke vanished. "Why?"

"Two reasons," Nadia said. She wore jeans and a black T-shirt under her thick black jacket, which wasn't zipped up. She had no shoes on her feet. I wondered if there was any point to the jacket.

"I don't feel the cold," she said. "The jacket is for appearances."

"You knew what I was thinking?" I asked her.

"I knew what you would ask," she said. "I will explain all, I swear."

"Now," I told her. "The two reasons, you'll tell me now."

"They asked me to kill Gabriel," she said. "I don't kill priests of any religion."

"And two?"

"I met you," she said softly.

"Angry smoke," I said.

Nadia nodded. "My life is intertwined with yours."

"You don't know that for sure," I told her.

"That is true," Nadia said. "I can only see one possible thread of where my life goes, but that thread has smoke swirling around it. I have seen that smoke since the day I woke up a revenant. Sixty-three years I have been searching for the smoke, moving myself to what feels right until it comes into my life. That smoke is you. Or at the very least, it's what you represent."

"And what is that?"

"Vengeance," Nadia said. "That's what you want."

"I want to know where my friends are," I said.

"But you still want vengeance, yes?"

I stared at Nadia, her cloudy eyes almost mimicking my smoke. There were no emotions in them, but no lies either. Chained revenants didn't like to lie, it caused them pain, it altered paths of their thread in ways they couldn't foresee. "Yes," I said softly.

"I shall help you," Nadia said. "I need to be where I need to be."

I stared at her for a moment. She was deadly, probably an assassin, and almost certainly capable of killing me should she be given the chance. There was always a possibility that her thread would reveal that she needed to kill me, and if that was the case, she'd inform me before it happened. Chained revenants had a sense of honour about such things. Some people would find it weird, but it was who they were.

"I need to go inside the church," I told her. "I need to find my friends."

"Mason sent a death squad after me," Nadia said cheerfully as she ran past me up the stairs.

"I assume that ended badly for them," I said, following her.

"I tore one of their heads off and beat another man in the face with it," Nadia said before smiling. "It was eventful."

I shook my head and followed after her, ducking under beams and stepping over rubble until we were in the seating area of the church. I looked up at the lack of roof, which had crushed all of the wooden pews around me. The sky was clear, and it looked almost peaceful.

Nadia sat on the dais at the far end of the room and watched me. "Did your friend die here?" she asked.

"I doubt it," I said. "Hey, Gabriel, you watching me right now?"

The dais began to move. It was slow at first, and Nadia practically leapt off as it sped up, as though it were being unscrewed from beneath. I stepped off the dais and watched it continue to move up, revealing a set of stairs beneath.

"Your friends are down there?" Nadia asked.

I nodded. "I hope so."

"Let's go, then," she said and practically jumped into the stairwell, vanishing from view into the darkness before the lights adorning the walls of the circular staircase ignited themselves, revealing the stairwell to be dozens of feet deep at least.

I followed Nadia down under the church, wondering how there didn't appear to be any damage to the walls of the stairwell. I reached the bottom, where Nadia waited for me, and pulled a lever on the wall that opened a nearby door at the same time as repositioning the dais above.

Nadia darted back behind me, raising her hands. "It wasn't me," she shouted as Gabriel appeared in the doorway, a shotgun in his hands. He took one look at me and lowered the weapon, practically enveloping me in the hug a second later.

"We thought you would be gone for weeks or months," Gabriel said.

"Your church appears to have fallen down a bit," I said.

Gabriel smiled. "It's been a long few weeks, my friend; I honestly hadn't noticed."

I returned his smile. "She's with me," I said, pointing to Nadia. "She's . . . I'll explain in a minute."

"I know Isaac," Nadia blurted out.

I turned to look at Nadia. "You didn't mention that."

"Sorry," Nadia said. "I was feeding information about Mason to Isaac. He was concerned about some horror stories that he'd heard about him. I've known Isaac for twenty years, and he contacted me a year ago, asked me how happy I was working for Mason. I wasn't. I saw my chains continued with Isaacs's involvement somehow, so I fed what I could. Had to keep up the appearance of loyalty to Mason, but when Lucas arrived, I knew where my future lay. I knew I had to leave. Ask Isaac; he'll tell you."

"We need to talk to Isaac," I said.

"Come see the others," Gabriel said sadly. "I think there's a lot you need to find out about."

"Hannah, Meredith, Isaac?" I asked. "What happened?"

Gabriel looked sad. "Hannah is okay, mostly. They went for her at home with her husband. Hannah fought them off, but Jonas got hurt. Not badly, but Hannah sent him to his folks' home in Toronto. Meredith is unhurt; she was already back in New York City when all of this went down. She's flown back home to be with family; it's safer that way. Obviously, everyone is going through some stuff. I've called in some favours to get the families of everyone involved watched."

"And Isaac?" I asked.

"He was in the hospital about two minutes after Annie was murdered," Gabriel said. "He got jumped by Dan, hurt badly. Managed to radio Hannah, but by the time we got there, he was in a bad way. After what happened with Hannah's family, we got Isaac's out of harm's way. Kids sent away, but his wife, Ruby, is here. It's really bad, Lucas. We can't get him to a hospital because we don't know who we can and can't trust. Everyone here is someone we know for sure isn't working with Mason. They've taken some RCU agents. We don't know where they are."

There was a pit of fear that practically filled my entire body in an instant. "Is Isaac . . ." I couldn't finish that sentence.

"He's in a coma," Gabriel said. "I don't think he's going to make it."

# CHAPTER NINETEEN

No one said anything for the five-minute walk through the tunnels under the church. I wasn't sure which direction we were going but was pretty sure we were going deeper underground.

Eventually, we came to a large metal door that wouldn't have looked out of place on a submarine, complete with large locking wheel. Gabriel knocked rhythmically on the metal, creating an echo around us as the large wheel slowly turned.

The door opened and a tired-looking Hannah stood in the doorway. She hugged Gabriel, saw me and smiled, and looked over at Nadia. An expression of hatred swept over her face and she dove at the chained revenant, who didn't move an inch as I intercepted Hannah's path.

"Get out of the fucking way," Hannah snapped at me, trying to shove me aside.

I stood my ground. "She's on our side."

"She's working for them," Hannah almost snarled.

"I work for no one," Nadia said calmly.

"She left the day I went back to the embers," I said. "She had nothing to do with whatever happened after that."

"I did not know that they were going to burn down the church or go after your families," Nadia said. "I was working with Isaac. If I'd known what was about to happen, I'd have told him."

"They went after Hannah's family," I said, "after Gabriel's church, and I assume they would have gone after Isaac's family if you hadn't gotten them out. This was personal. There's nothing to gain by it other than causing pain."

"Mason didn't do it," Nadia said. "Not to say he wouldn't, but he would only do it if there was a long-term benefit to him personally. Burning down a church is effort and time better spent doing something else."

"Dan did this," I said. "I don't know why, but I'd bet money he was the one who decided to go after the church and families."

"What makes him hate his own team like that?" Gabriel asked.

No one had a good answer for it.

"I'm sorry about your husband," Nadia said to Hannah.

"Fuck you," Hannah snapped, pointing at Nadia.

"Hannah, we need help," I said keeping my voice level. "Chained don't lie; chained don't care about the machinations of people like Mason. They arrive where they're needed to get them where they need to go. We're going to find Mason, Dan, and anyone else helping them, and we're going to kill them all. But right now, Nadia wants to help."

"I *need* to help," Nadia said, walking past Hannah and me, through the open door.

"She puts one toe out of line," Hannah said watching Nadia leave. "One goddamned toe."

"I get it," I said. "I'm sorry about Jonas. Is he okay?"

Hannah nodded once and walked back through the hatch.

I followed a moment later, hoping that Hannah wasn't going to do anything to Nadia. While Nadia had been working for the enemy, even though she'd also been working with Isaac, it's hard to keep a grudge against chained revenants. Some people have theorized that they create a bubble of influence around them that lets them join those whose lives they need to be a part of. Whatever the reason, I wasn't about to throw away help.

I stepped through the hatch, Gabriel closing it and locking it shut behind me. "Welcome to the hideout," Gabriel said as I looked around the spacious room.

"We have this room," Gabriel said, gesturing around him to the size-able table and chairs, but other than that, and despite the size, it was empty. "Each of those seven covers leads to a chamber. This whole place is like a large wheel. Down each chamber is a similar-sized room to this one. Each room is connected to the one either side of it."

"What are in the rooms?" I asked. The ceiling was a mural of Inaxia, done in vibrant colours, making it look like something out of a fairy-tale.

"One is a medical bay, kitchen, bathroom, three bedrooms, and the last is where we store, keep, et cetera anything we might need. It's basically an armoury but without large amounts of armour."

I dropped the duffle bag. "Lots of cash, a few other bits," I said.

"I'll take it to the armoury," Gabriel said, unzipping it and removing a medallion. He looked up at me. "Lucas."

I fished my medallion out from beneath my T-shirt. "I'm back in every way that counts," I said.

Gabriel got to his feet and hugged me. He'd always been a hugger.

He went back to the bag and found the Talon mask. He looked up at me and I expected him to ask questions, but he just put the mask back and zipped the bag up.

"That's why you took it so personally," he said. "Your failure to protect the Guild, I mean."

"It was quite literally my job," I said.

"I'm sorry," he whispered. "You should have told me."

"No one is meant to know who the Talons are," I said. "That's sort of the point."

"You have no Guild left to be a Talon of," Gabriel said. "Whatever secrets you were duty-bound to keep shouldn't be kept at the expense of your own mental health."

Gabriel had a good point. "Well, I'm back now, so hopefully I'll make a better go of it this time."

"I know that must have been a difficult decision," Gabriel said. "To put the medallion back on after all this time."

"People are trying to kill me and my friends," I said. "Same people betrayed us. Same people killed my Guild. It might have been the easiest decision I ever made. How many people are down here?"

Gabriel re-zipped the bag before answering. "Hannah, me, Isaac, and his wife, Ruby. I'll take you to see him if you like."

"Please," I said. A lot of churches belonging to the Tempered Souls had excellent medical facilities on site to deal with those who were newly rift-fused or otherwise required care not provided by human-run hospitals. Apparently, that meant they were able to administer to coma patients as well, although I doubted that was something they dealt with all that often.

"Let's go deposit this," Gabriel said, lifting the bag and walking through the first chamber on the right, next to the door.

I followed Gabriel down the lamp-lit corridor. "When was this constructed?" I asked.

"Early 1900s," Gabriel said. "I had it renovated about five years ago. That's why there's electricity, internet, fresh water, et cetera. It cost a small fortune, but I figured it might come in handy. We were lucky about the firebombing. No one was here when it happened; we were trying to make sure Isaac's family was safe. Booker and Zita were instrumental in helping. We owe them our lives."

"I'm sorry," I said. "About the church."

"Places can be rebuilt," Gabriel said, pushing open a metal door. "People can't."

The armoury had two more doors inside and looked pretty much identical in size to the main room. There were over a dozen tables, each one covered in weapons, ammo, various pieces of armour, and, on one table, several large briefcases.

"You're doing okay, then," I said.

"Money and weapons aren't an issue," Gabriel said. "People are."

"What about the rest of the RCU? You mentioned that some of them were taken."

"The rest of the New York branch were attacked the same night as you were hurt," Gabriel said. "Two dead, ten missing. The LA team was also attacked by, apparently, fiends. Several dead or missing there, too. We suspect they were taken hostage as some sort of insurance, but no one can confirm that. We don't know where any of them are."

"Ji-hyun?" I asked.

"Ji-hyun hasn't contacted us," Gabriel said. "No one has heard from her in several weeks."

Ji-hyun was probably one of the toughest people I'd ever met. If anyone was going to survive whatever Mason had concocted for the RCU in LA, it would be her. "Once we're done here, I'll find out what happened," I said. "Any other teams attacked?"

"Not that I'd heard of," Gabriel said. "But if Dan was involved in the attack on the New York branch, he was definitely involved with the LA attack, too. He'd done work for both of them. And it gets worse. Dan is now officially in charge of the RCU New York office. Rumour has it his agents are made up of Sky-High Security rift-fused personnel."

"He did all of this just to get the boss's job?" I asked. "One of his allies said that Dan was meant to lead the RCU into the ambush and make out that Sovereign Humanity had done it, which in and of itself is stupid, but Dan stepped in and said as much. He took the FBI agents with him, set them and his own team up."

"Anything else?" Gabriel asked.

"Brad said that Mason was working for an organisation," I said. "No idea who they are or what they're called, just that they're higher up the pecking order. Sounds like Mason is just one of the cogs in the machine. I think Dan is working for them rather than Mason himself. He told me he was involved in the murder of the Ravens. Said he'd made sure to keep me alive."

"Seriously?" Gabriel asked. "So, he's been working for these people for at least a decade."

I nodded. "Long time to move pieces to the right places, to make sure things are going the way you want them to. The question is, how did Dan coordinate everything? Did he have a secret phone? Did he do it over email? How does someone spend years setting up the RCU, and what did he hope to gain from it? He included the FBI agents because they were investigating Sky-High. They had whistle-blowers who were murdered."

"Hannah has been looking into the computer stuff," Gabriel said. "Dan has a town house in Rochester. Might be worth a look. Hannah's been trying to find anything that might give us a clue as to what Dan's plan is. Apart from trying to kill us all. He's been put in charge of the New York RCU branch, but that can't be his plan. To kill everyone just to take Isaac's place."

"Why attack the LA branch, too?" I asked. "Why not kill all the RCU agents in every branch?

"He worked for the LA and New York branches," Hannah said.

"You think it was just petty grudges?" I asked. "That feels like a leap. Whatever the reason he did this, he must have known that someone would have his back. Otherwise, he's just waiting for the Ancients to send a Guild after him."

"An Ancient working with them?" Gabriel asked.

I shrugged. "No idea. But Mason wants money and power, not a fight with Ancients and Guilds."

"What about Booker and Zita?" I asked. "They okay?"

"They've been left alone," Gabriel said. "I think whatever links they have with us aren't enough to get them put in the crosshairs. Thankfully."

"I might need to pay them a visit," I said. "Maybe they can find out something the rest of us can't. Maybe one of their customers knows him, or works for Mason, or something. Anything we can actually grab hold of and work with."

"Literally?" Gabriel asked.

"If I get to punch someone in the face, I'm not going to complain," I told him.

"Mason never mentioned Dan," Nadia said from the doorway as she stepped into view. "But Mason did take phone calls from someone. Wouldn't say who. Alexis and I were just there to keep him safe, and to liaise with Dr Mitchell."

"What was Dr Mitchell doing?" I asked.

"We didn't know about the hybrids until after the attack on the RCU and FBI," Nadia said. "Dr Mitchell keeps her research very quiet. We just provided protection, although there were several rumours about her. About her using prisoners for experiments, about her taking homeless people for the same reason. I tried to find out what she was doing for Isaac but couldn't. Nothing concrete. Mason and Dr Mitchell are very good at keeping their . . . proclivities to themselves."

"You had no interactions with Dan?" I asked.

Nadia shook her head. "Never even heard of him until a few weeks ago. Sorry, I can't help."

A woman's head poked out of the curtain before it was pushed aside, and she stepped into view. She was Black, with long dark hair, and she wore jeans and a T-shirt. She was just over five and a half feet tall, and looked like she hadn't slept in some time. Ruby kept rubbing her thumb over her wedding ring. She glanced down at the watch on her wrist, which sat next to a bracelet that appeared to be made of some kind of cord.

"You must be Lucas," she asked, in a Southern drawl.

I offered her my hand, which she shook. "I am," I said.

"I'm Ruby," she told me, looking back at Isaac, who was lying in bed, hooked up to several machines, although none that I saw were to help him breathe.

"I'm sorry about Isaac," I said. "And your family."

"Thank you," Ruby said. "I miss my children."

"I'm sure they'll be fine," I said. "Gabriel knows good people."

"Isaac told me about you," Ruby said. "Told me that you were a Raven, that your Guild was destroyed, and that you had issues dealing with it. Told me you went to a dark place, did dark things. He loved you. Sorry, he loves you. You know that, right?"

I nodded. "I love him too. He's like a brother to me. He's a man who just helps people. No complaining. I think he enjoys it."

"He does," Ruby said. "He missed you, I know that. He would often talk about you to our kids and to me. He would tell them stories about the things you did as a Raven. Cleaned-up stories." Ruby chuckled.

"Yeah, I didn't always do nice things," I said.

"But you tried to," Ruby said. "I think that was what Isaac likes about you the most. You try to do the right thing. He told me that some people don't even bother doing that. The easy thing is just too damn tempting."

I smiled; it sounded like something Isaac would say.

"What happens to Isaac when he dies?" Ruby asked. "I mean, I know what happens to revenants when they die; they get taken to the rift to live out the rest of their days there."

"They're essentially ageless in the rift," I said. "They can live there a long time. Eventually, revenants will die in the rift, but it takes a long time. Maybe a thousand years, maybe more. Depends on the person."

"But he was cut with a tempered blade," Ruby said. "Gabriel won't say, beyond the normal church spiel about how his light will transcend us all. Hannah is too angry all the damn time. What happens now?"

"I don't know," I said. "Riftborn, revenants, fiends, anyone who dies at the hands of a tempered weapon doesn't go into the rift. They just . . . go."

"What do you think?" Ruby pressed.

"I think those who don't go to the rift just go to nothing," I said. "I think their energies are sent out across the world to inhabit someone else, maybe several others. I think that once Isaac goes, someone else will be born a revenant in his place. Maybe two or three more; Isaac had a lot of power."

"He had a lot of years left," Ruby said, staring at her husband. "He raised our kids like he was their biological father. I know that rift-fused can't have kids on Earth, but he was never concerned about that. He had a family and he loved us. Are you going to find the man who did this?"

"Yes," I told her. "And I'm going to kill him for it."

Ruby stared at me for several seconds. "Just like that?" she asked.

I looked from Isaac to Ruby and back again. "Easily," I said. "I've been killing since I was fourteen years old. And that was over two thousand years ago. Killing people was never the problem. Losing myself in the need for vengeance, in the need to validate why I got to live while my friends didn't, that was the issue. It helps when you have something to fight for. Killing for the sake of it isn't something I want to do. When you reach that point, you're just a murderer, a monster, or usually a combination of the two."

"I don't think it would be very nice of me to wish pain on those who did this," Ruby said. "I was brought up to turn the other cheek, to live and let live."

I remained silent.

"But fuck 'em all," Ruby snapped. "Burn them to the fucking ground. For Isaac. For all of us."

I didn't bother replying; there was nothing more that needed to be said.

"I have a favour," Ruby said as I turned to walk away.

I stopped and looked back at her. "Of course," I said softly.

"Is there anything you can do to help him?" She asked. "You're a rift-born. Can't they do amazing things?"

I walked back over to Ruby and stood at the foot of the bed, looking at Isaac. "There is something that can be done," I admitted. "I can take him into my embers."

"That will heal him?" Ruby asked. The hope in her voice made me wish I wasn't about to shatter it.

"No," I said, barely a whisper. "Nothing can do that."

The deflation of barely concealed hope on her face broke my heart. I would have given anything to be able to make Isaac better, to give him back to his wife and children.

"I can take him into my embers," I said. "I'd be able to talk to him, heal him to a degree. He might be able to come back, to give you a few days, maybe a week."

"Or?" She asked.

"Or it will flay his mind like peeling an orange, and his screams of agony will be all you remember until he dies a short while later." There was no nice way of putting it. This was an all-or-nothing situation, and the *nothing* part was not something you soon forgot.

"Have you done it before?" Ruby asked.

I nodded. "Three times in my entire life. Twice it worked. Once it didn't. The once is the one time I remember the most. I'll do this; I don't want to, but I will. But only if you agree to it. If it works, then you get a few days with him. He can see your kids, he can die peacefully, and just maybe he'll return to the rift. If it doesn't work, he won't go to the rift. That much is a guarantee."

"You can remove the taint of poison from the blade?" Ruby asked, the hope back once again.

"Sort of," I said. "I'd take the poison on myself, into my embers. I would need to heal while there." I didn't tell her how horrific it was to do, or just what we'd both have to go through for it to be completed, but some hope was better than none.

"I'll consider it," she said. "How long do I have to agree?"

"Twenty-four hours," I said. "After that, I'm not sure whatever I did would make much difference."

Ruby hugged me. I hadn't expected it, but I found myself hugging her back. "Thank you," she whispered.

I nodded and left Ruby to make her decision, while I went back to find Gabriel, who sat with Hannah and Nadia, the latter of whom appeared to be trying not to get close to Hannah.

"I called Booker," Gabriel said. "He wants to meet. But we also need to get hold of Emily and find the missing RCU agents."

"Is she okay?" I asked.

Gabriel nodded. "Think so. Her team was stood down, no explanation. Just someone high above her boss decided enough was enough."

"Despite the dead FBI agents?" I asked.

Gabriel nodded again.

"Okay, arrange the meeting with Booker," I said.

"We might be able to kill two birds with one stone," Gabriel said.

"Do we know *where* Emily is?" I asked.

"No," Hannah said. "Like I said, her team was stood down, but no one has heard from her or anyone else in her team. Sounds like they've been told to keep quiet. I spoke to a few friends in the feds, and either no one wants to get involved, or no one knows more than that. But I'm thinking that this guy does."

Hannah turned the laptop around and showed me a photo of William Stone, the guard in Dr Mitchell's employ back at the asylum. He was stood outside of Sky-High Security, talking to a Mason Barnes.

"How'd you get that?" I asked.

"Took it myself," Hannah said. "It's not like we've been doing nothing since you vanished. We started watching."

"I know," I said.

"I tagged his truck," Hannah said, showing me a map with coloured dots to show where his truck stopped for longer than an hour.

"They're all over the place," I said. "He runs errands."

"Yep," Gabriel said. "There are six places he runs to a lot."

Hannah hit a key and only four dots remained. "That's Booker and Zita's," I said.

"Yes, it is," Hannah said. "The others are a bank, his home, a grocery store, a warehouse complex with maybe a dozen large warehouses, and two other houses. We think one is his . . . lover."

"So, the warehouse, then," I said.

"Yeah, but it's huge," Gabriel said. "Too large to search every part of every building before we get spotted. We need it narrowed down."

"And we need him to talk to us so we can do it," Hannah said.

"I've seen him around," Nadia said. "He's . . . creepy. I saw him at Booker's; he likes the fights. Never takes part, only watches. Watches the women maybe a little too closely. He's there every night. Or every night I was, which was most nights."

"We might be barking up the wrong tree here," I said. "Hannah, can you take me through each of these places?"

"I can," Hannah said.

"Arrange a chat with Booker," I said to Gabriel. "One way or another, our friend William here is going to help us out."

# CHAPTER TWENTY

We drove George's car across the city of Hamble, stopping at each of the destinations in turn, parking far enough away that it didn't arouse suspicion. I wasn't sure if Hannah or my IDs would be out in the world to spot, but we already knew that Hamble PD were on Mason's books, so it was better to not take any chances.

The RCU had tagged William's car with a tracking system that gave us a little blue dot to follow around until he stopped his car outside of his lover's house.

We waited outside, parked up, as his BMW SUV arrived and stopped outside of the two-storey town house.

William Stone, looking much like he had at the asylum, bounded out of the car like he was taking part in a hurdles race and took the steps two at a time to the front door. He stood there, bottle of wine in hand, and knocked.

"Smooth," Hannah said.

"If you're working for a big shot like Mason, he's not going to want you to keep all of your exceptionally criminal enterprises on your phone for anyone to see," I said. "Right?"

"You'd assume so," Hannah said. "It would be pretty stupid to openly talk about illegal stuff on your everyday phone. You'd want encryption software at the very least. Probably a burner phone."

"Would you carry your burner phone around with you?" I asked.

"Probably, yes," she said. "Just in case the boss messages you something urgent. I'd make sure of it. If you're thinking of going in there and stealing his phone, don't. I'm pretty sure if we get caught, we get to find a bunch of dead agents."

"Why would you kidnap RCU agents?" I asked. "What's the endgame here?"

Hannah shrugged. "You're kidnapping rift-fused for what end? Highly trained rift-fused, too. I don't see the end goal either. If you're going to kill them, why not kill them all at the same time?"

"There's a lot weird about this whole thing," I said. "You got any idea where Callie Mitchell is?"

Hannah shook her head. "Not a clue. This is why we haven't been able to do anything. We don't know who is alive, or where they are, or who we can trust. We're treading water here. No Ancients are helping, either, in fact; even though we put through a distress call to them, they haven't even contacted us."

I checked my watch; it was 9:22 p.m. "Looks like the warehouse might be our best bet. Let's check that out."

The drive was short and I parked the car in a car park behind some shops across the street from the warehouses. It was one massive plot of land, with four large warehouses on it and a few smaller buildings. There was an office building attached to one of them.

"Who works there?" I asked Hannah as we stood a little back from the fence, letting the shadows of the nearby trees help keep us hidden.

"Officially? A shipping office," Hannah said. "William goes in there sometimes. Occasionally arrives with something, occasionally leaves with something. Haven't been able to get into the buildings, as there are too many guards. I've tried making a lap of the building, but if anyone is being held in there, I have no idea where. Guards are armed, too, and they look professional."

"You think this is a giant waste of time?" I asked. "That they're already dead and this is just a way to drag us out from hiding?"

"I don't know," Hannah said. "I just know I don't want any more people to be killed by these assholes."

"Up to three weeks as their prisoner," I said. "Can't be good."

My phone started to vibrate. "Booker," I said, answering.

"Are you doing something stupid?" Booker asked me.

"Define *stupid*," I said.

"You're outside the warehouse right now, aren't you?" Booker said. "Those hostages are still there."

"And you know this because?" I asked.

"We got a friend in Sky-High," Booker told me.

"You have an informant?" I asked.

"You remember those two hikers killed?" He asked me.

"They were FBI informants," I said.

"Ah, you do know," Booker said, although I could tell he wished I hadn't. "Turns out one of them had a girlfriend who also works for Sky-High, and she is *not* happy about her beau being turned into fiend chow."

"What did she say?" I asked.

"Hostages are split in two groups," Booker said. "Half in the warehouse, half in Sky-High. You go for one, the others get killed. Et cetera, et cetera."

"Shit," I snapped.

"We have a plan," he told me. "We need to hit both places at the same time. We do one before the other, and a whole bunch of people gonna die."

"That needs more information," I said. "We have to do that right first time."

"According to our source, the doctor wants a steady stream of rift-fused for her . . . needs," Booker said, sounding angry for the first time. "They're all alive, all safe. But that won't last forever. She doesn't want to waste them on just any old research; she has others for that. Sounds like Mason has convinced her to keep the humans safe for now, use them as leverage should they be needed. He was pretty angry that it all kicked off without his say-so."

"What does your inside lady do?" I asked him.

"Lab technician," Booker said. "Her hands aren't clean, and when this is all over, she's going to be having a long, hard conversation with the law, but she knows that. I think she was the one who pushed her boyfriend to go to the feds. She's angry, Lucas, and angry people are oh so helpful."

"Can we meet her?" I asked.

"Tomorrow morning," Booker said. "Already spoke to Gabriel; he knows the details."

"What do they want?" I asked. "Does the lab tech know?"

"She knows bits," Booker said. "She managed to download a lot of intel from the company. She's bringing it over tonight, but it sounds bad. Like *if you read it, they're gonna go kill you* bad. Whatever is going on here got a whole bunch of federal and RCU agents killed, and they didn't bat an eyelid for it."

"I'm going to kill Dan," I said.

"Good, he's an asshole," Booker said. "See you tomorrow. Ten a.m. Gabriel will get you there."

I hung up the phone and stared at the warehouse for a moment.

"Booker got an informant," Hannah said.

"Yes, he did," I said. "If Mason hadn't killed those two hikers, none of this would be happening now, and Booker's informant would probably either have run already or would be dead by Mason's hand."

"You think it's legit?" Hannah asked.

"If Booker does, then yes," I said. "He's too smart to be taken in by a fraud. I guess we find out tomorrow." I told her the rest of the conversation before we got back into the car just in time to see William pull up at the main gate to the complex.

The clock said 10:13.

"It's a fifteen-minute drive," Hannah said with a snort. "He's a love 'em and leave 'em type. No cuddle or anything."

I watched William's car roll across the car park and stop, while I quietened the urge to go over and kill him.

William ran up the exterior staircase and entered the office building, vanishing from view.

"They're in there," I said. "Or the access to them starts in there. No point going to that building to see them when they're over the other side of the complex."

"We can't be certain," Hannah said. "Not enough to get them in time."

I nodded. "We will be." I started the engine and pulled away, driving back to Gabriel's church.

"Can I ask you something?" Hannah asked.

"Sure," I said.

"Why didn't you tell us you were a Talon?" There was genuine hurt in her voice.

"Us or you?" I asked.

"Me," Hannah said. "Who knew?"

"Isaac and Ji-hyun," I said. "That's it."

"We were close, Lucas," Hannah said. "I thought we were, anyway. And then you left without a word; you just vanished. You didn't tell us you're a Talon, or that you're human, or where you were going; you didn't even leave a number."

"Talons can't tell people," I said. "Not because we don't want to, but because if someone ever knew that I was a Talon, it could cause harm to the Guild if I'm ever put in a situation where I have to choose between my Guild and my friends. People would use that information against me, against the Guild. It's happened before, and it never ends well. Ji-hyun knew because I've trained with her for centuries, and Isaac because he was the only one to help me hold it together after the destruction of my

Guild. The more people who knew about me, the more dangerous it was for me—and for them."

Hannah nodded. "I don't understand why Dan is doing this," Hannah said as she leaned up against the car. "Why destroy your Guild? Why the RCU? We've worked with him for years. Been friends for even longer than that, and he tries to wipe us out."

"Some people are really good at pretending to be something they're not," I said. "Sometimes, that something is a good person, a friend, an ally. Dan pretended to be all of those for a long time. I don't know why, but we'll find out."

"Booker said he's working for someone else," Hannah said. "This is beginning to sound like there's a bigger plan here. Not just Callie Mitchell wanting to create monsters for weapons."

Hannah and I returned to the bunker beneath the church, where we found Nadia sitting on a small table just inside the entrance. Hannah took a deep breath and walked away without a word.

"Do you want me to talk to her?" Nadia asked.

"I think that might be a terrible idea," I said.

Nadia nodded as she considered this. "Yes, I am not a good person to do this."

"Have you ever been in love, Nadia?" I asked.

Nadia's face crumpled and I regretted saying anything.

"Yes," she said eventually. "Twice. Once before I was this, once after. Neither ended well."

"I'm sorry," I told her.

"I have done terrible things, Lucas," she said softly. "I have travelled the chains as I tried to get to my future, to my destiny, and I have seen and done things that would have made the human me ashamed. The need to be in the right place is great, but this is the first time I feel like I'm in the right place with people who won't use me for my power, who won't ask me to do something I do not wish to do."

I nodded. "I understand."

"I know how my kind are seen," she said. "We're monsters, murderers, psychopaths. There are chained revenants who open themselves up to the rift too much and see all of the chains all at once. They try to figure out which chain is the right one by eliminating anyone on the other chains. It drives them mad. It makes them monsters. I am not a monster. I have done monstrous things, but I am not a monster. I will help you. I will . . . do the right thing."

I believed her. "That's all any of us can try to do, Nadia."

Nadia climbed down from the table. "Not just because it's the right thing," she said, "but because I have seen the angry smoke. I fear it. I fear you."

"You have nothing to fear from me."

Nadia stared at me for a few seconds. "You told your friends that you were the Talon. They have accepted that, but I have been searching for that smoke for a long time. I have seen the aftermath of places you have been. I have seen your work."

It was more than a little disconcerting to think that someone had been looking for me for a long time, going to places I'd been, seen the things I'd done.

"Not even Dan really knows what you've done," Nadia said. "He thought you were just a Guild member, a rank-and-file. Powerful and dangerous but no more so than any other Guild member. But Talons are . . . not rank-and-file. Things are going to get bad, Lucas. Worse than they are now, and you know this."

"Are you asking me if I'm willing to do what's necessary to get people back?" I asked. "Because you have to know I am."

"I do," Nadia said. "You've been away from all this for some time. I needed to check. Needed to know that you're ready."

"You can't tell the future, right?" I asked.

"No," Nadia said. "Not *the future*. I can see multiple possible timelines and events that happen in them, but I can't see individual people too well. I couldn't tell you that Dan was going to attack, because I wasn't part of it. I couldn't tell you what Mason is doing right now, because there's no timeline where I'm involved. I see what affects me, and I see smoke in my future. That's you. I can see timelines where I am killed before I get here. By Alexis, by Dan, by nameless, faceless thugs. But when it comes to an overall picture, it's not as simple as just seeing a person; it's something about that person. It makes the whole thing infuriating."

"It sounds . . . exhausting," I said.

"It is," Nadia told me. "I'm . . . grateful for you letting me help."

Nadia walked off, leaving me alone in the room. *Help.* We were going to need help to pull this off. I walked back outside of the bunker and called Bill. He answered on the first ring.

"You need something?" he asked.

"We've got a problem," I said. "How quickly can you guys get up here? Bring anyone who can help."

"How much trouble are you about to cause?" Bill asked.

"As much as I can," I told him.

"Give me a day," Bill said. "You okay?"

"I will be," I told him.

I sat there outside for a while, just taking some fresh air and feeling the cold.

I heard the footsteps approaching well before I saw who they belonged to.

"Special Agent Emily West," I said.

"Just *Emily* will do," she told me. "I think we're beyond formalities now, don't you? Gabriel told me about Isaac; I came to see him—I'm sorry. I know you and he have history."

I gave her a grim smile. "I have a *lot* of history. I probably owe you some kind of explanation as to who I am."

"I think," Emily said as she leaned up against the dilapidated wall beside me, "that you're right."

"So, where do you want me to start?" I asked.

"At the beginning," Emily said.

"I was born in 235 BC," I began.

# CHAPTER TWENTY-ONE

S o, the phrase 'older than Christ' is appropriate for you?" Emily asked with raised eyebrows.

I nodded. "Can we leave questions until the end?"

"You were born in the age of Ancients," Emily said, waving me to continue.

"Yes, in England. In what is now known as York," I said. "To a tribe called Brigantes, who controlled much of northern England. My name was Sagillius. No last name. My father was a fisherman and hunter, and my mother a warrior of some renown. She'd come over to Britain from the continent. I was maybe six or seven when we left our home and headed south, across what is now the English Channel to Europe, stopping at Carthage."

Emily's eyes widened at the name and I saw she wanted to ask me questions, but she remained quiet.

"I was brought up in the city of Saldae, a port to the west of Carthage itself. My father taught me to hunt, my mother to fight. My parents fought alongside Hannibal; my father was a scout and my mother a general. When Rome destroyed the city, they removed all mention of the warrior women who fought against them. Rome was afraid that women would get ahead of themselves and start thinking they should be the ones running things." I sighed. "Anyway, I digress. My mother and father were highly regarded in Hannibal's military, and so I was brought up to hunt and fight. My mother taught me how to kill fiends."

"There were fiends then, too?" Emily asked. "Sorry."

"It's fine. Yes," I told her. "Quite a few. It was said that they were a punishment from the gods, many of them were never written about for fear that it would somehow displease them or please them too much. The Ancient gods of the time were fickle. But some, the chimera, minotaur, et cetera, they were mentioned. I killed my first at fourteen. It was a snake creature. Very much a lesser fiend, and probably only a quarter of the size my memory makes it out to be. Anyway, I killed it, and it was a big deal."

I didn't want to spend all night talking about my childhood, so I skipped forward a few years.

"In 218 BC, I was seventeen, and I joined my parents to travel over the Alps with Hannibal to fight the Romans. We won. I killed . . . I don't know, hundreds maybe. My father was a scout; my mother and her squad went with him, using guerrilla tactics that they'd picked up from the Gauls along the way. Lots more fights, lots more Romans dead. Lots of Carthaginians too."

I closed my eyes and took a deep breath, remembering the chaos, the noise, the blood. I had never seen anything like it before, and no amount of preparing had done it justice. Mostly people screamed, begged, pleaded to the gods, or shat themselves. There's no honour in war, that's for the people who stand at the back and get congratulated when their people died for their victory.

"Eventually, my band were sent to Cannae, and we won a big victory for Carthage. Sicily too. I was sent to Salapia, and we were betrayed by people who were meant to be loyal to us. I was killed in 209 BC at the blade of a priest who was meant to be my friend. He slit my throat, and spat on me as he watched me die."

"I'm sorry," Emily said.

"Don't be; I'll get to that," I said. "Anyway, I found myself awake in the rift. I didn't know where it was at first; I just knew it wasn't Salapia. I spent over a century in the rift; every riftborn does. It's to make sure that you don't immediately go back all evil-Superman and start tearing people's heads off to get revenge."

"What is the rift like?" Emily asked.

"Weird," I said. "Large parts of it are uninhabitable by anyone not a fiend, at least long-term. The Tempest in the north bleeds power all the time, so there are occasional fiends that come from the area surrounding it. And I don't mean like lesser fiends; I mean things that make Godzilla look like a pet in terms of temperament. These things are mean, cruel, and enjoy inflicting pain. There's a theory that the Tempest is made up of all the dead revenants and riftborn who were murdered with tempered weapons. I think it's horseshit, but no one is stupid enough to go up there and research it. Unless you like the idea of being worn as a hat."

"What did you do in the rift?" Emily asked, having seen an opening for another question.

"I learned how to fight," I said. "Properly fight as a riftborn. I learned how to use my power, how the world works, how the rift works. That hundred years went by in a flash, and when I returned to Earth, I discovered that it was 51 BC. I'd so wanted vengeance on those who had betrayed me, but my parents, Carthage were gone. I discovered that we'd lost the second Punic War and were given a treaty that made the one at Versailles look like a reasonable endeavour. It all but crushed us, but that wasn't enough for some in Rome, who went to Carthage and murdered everyone there just because they could."

"Did you find out what happened to your parents?" Emily asked.

"My father was killed in battle against Rome," I said. "My mother was hurt, and returned back to Carthage. She married a merchant and settled in Gaul. She never returned to Carthage after that. She never had more children. I don't know much more than that. The man who'd betrayed me was torn apart by horses a short time after my death. I didn't find this out until sometime after the fact; all I knew at the time was that everyone I loved was dead and the Romans had made sure that I had no home. I wanted them to hurt, so I joined the Gallic rebellion, which went about as well as expected, and then found myself in Rome. I figured hurting Rome from the inside was the next best option, and after Caesar's death at the hands of his own allies, I felt like I'd achieved something."

"You assassinated Caesar?" Emily asked.

I shook my head. "No, I just worked for some people who did. Put the right word in the right ear, and soon people were looking at Caesar like the tyrant he was.

"Anyway, after that, I moved around a lot, until I went back to the rift for the first time. As a riftborn, I have to return to the embers every month to keep the contact alive. If I don't, it causes issues, as I discovered recently, but I return to the rift regularly, too. I spent a lot of time in the rift over the centuries, and I always pop out a few hundred years after I left to continue whatever it was I needed to do.

"After centuries of working here and there for various people, I joined the Guilds. The Raven Guild. I was trained by a woman called Neb for several centuries more. The Raven Guild were the best of the best, and I was expected to be even better than that."

"Neb?" Emily asked.

"She's several thousand years older than me and used to be a queen, or a warlord, or a king, or a god, depending on who you ask. She helped create the Guilds."

"And she trained all of the Raven Guild?" Emily asked.

I shook my head. "No, just me and a few others."

"So, you were a Raven for centuries?" Emily asked.

"About seven hundred years," I said. "I did a lot of other stuff before that. I worked for Neb for a long time before I ever joined the Guild; I think that's why she agreed to train me."

"Why'd you change your name to Lucas Rurik?" Emily asked.

"I've been Lucas Rurik for a long time," I said. "First it was just Sagillius, then Lucius, and after a while I changed it to Rurik, and then I added them together."

"Why not keep Sagillius?" Emily asked. "Or amend it?"

"You can't use your birth name when you return," I said. "It's just something you don't do. We all pick a new name and go from there. I chose Lucius because Rome was everywhere like a bad rash."

"You're not a fan of ancient Rome?" Emily asked, eating another cookie.

"You ever seen *Star Trek*?" I asked her.

Emily gave me a look that suggested that was a stupid question. "Of course."

"The Romans were like the Borg," I said. "They assimilated you or they exterminated you. They were almost impossible to defeat, and even if you did win a battle or hurt them, there were millions more where that came from. They weren't all bad people, and I don't hate the Romans, and like Monty Python said, they did a lot for the world, but they did a lot via murdering everyone in their way. I probably wouldn't have strong feelings either way if I hadn't been in their way at the time."

"Anything else?" Emily asked.

"I'm also the Guild's Talon," I said. "Their protector, their . . . well, some would call them assassins. We don't generally assassinate unless we have to, but whatever we do, it's to protect the Guild."

"And humans?"

I nodded again. "The Guilds make sure to remove those who are deemed a threat to humanity, but we also remove those who are deemed a threat to the rift and its inhabitants."

"So, why has Mason been allowed to continue?" Emily asked. "Why has Callie Mitchell?"

"Both excellent questions I don't have an answer for," I said. "Both have powerful friends, and both seem to care little about the Guilds or Ancients becoming involved in their plans. They have backing. I just don't know who it is or why."

"The Ancients," Emily said. "I've heard that term before. They sort of rule over the Guilds, yes?"

"Among other things," I said. "They're meant to be the wisest and most powerful of us, but I can count on one hand the number of them I've ever met. And all of them considered themselves to be above it all. They would often say things like, 'See the long-term plan, Lucas.' As if I wasn't centuries older than they are. I think they're just scared to involve themselves in anything that messes with the status quo."

"You're not a fan," Emily said.

"The Ancients mainly live in the rift. They're all riftborn, they're all . . . well, ancient, and they're all emotionless assholes with the luxury of thinking long-term about everything. It's why they didn't get involved when the Ravens were killed; they've seen Guilds all but destroyed before, so why get involved with one more?"

"We've only known, *officially known*, about rift-fused for a few decades," Emily said. "I *know* you've always been here, but to really *know* you've always been here is a weird thing to think about. You've seen things I can only dream of, you've seen the ruins of Rome, and you know how it looked back then. Because you were actually there. I find that . . . difficult to comprehend."

"It's weird for us, too," I said. "Living alongside humanity but knowing you're not actually a part of it."

"So, do we have a plan on how we're going to stop Mason, Dan, and everyone working with them?" Emily asked.

"We're going to see someone with intel tomorrow," I told her. "We could use some assistance on the ally front."

"I might be able to help with that," Emily said. "A lot of my team were stood down, and none of them have been happy about it. I think most would want answers."

"Are you being swept under the rug or punished?" I asked. "By whoever stood you down, I mean."

"Bit of both," Emily said. "FBI agents died, and we've been taken off the case. It's been passed to the RCU, officially. Except the RCU is in tatters. So, who's in charge of it?"

"Dan is," I said. "Dan is in charge of the RCU. From what we understand, he's using Sky-High employees."

"How is that possible?" Emily asked.

"I don't know," I said. "But it means that the Ancients have either given him that control, or they're involved or they're waiting to see how things play out. Hopefully, we'll find out tomorrow when we see Booker."

Emily stretched and yawned. "I'm going to go down to see Gabriel," she said. "You staying here?"

"No, I need sleep," I told her. "Long day. Thank you for helping."

"My pleasure," she said. "I don't like to see the bad guys win."

I opened the entrance to the bunker and showed Emily down, leaving her with Gabriel as I went to find my bed.

I found it, got changed into something that I hadn't been in all day, lay down on the bed, and waited for sleep to take me.

# CHAPTER TWENTY-TWO

I don't know when I fell asleep; I just know that was pretty soon after my head touched the pillow. I was woken by Gabriel gently rocking my arm.

"I'm awake," I said, barely conscious.

"We need to discuss the plan," Gabriel said, handing me a mug of coffee that was the size of my head.

"You're a beautiful man, Gabriel," I said.

Gabriel left me to drink my coffee and get dressed, although the latter didn't happen until after I'd had a shower so hot, it was almost scalding. I padded barefoot through the bunker, finding everyone together in the main area.

"We don't have all day," Hannah said as I placed my now-empty mug of coffee on the table.

"Booker said Gabriel knew where to meet him," I said.

"Abbey Park," Gabriel told me. "Got an hour to kill yet. Emily is arranging to get some of her people to help. Officially off the books. The informant refuses to meet inside. Wants wide-open space, no people. Those were her requirements."

"Booker's informant had better have answers," Hannah said.

"At least it's outside of the town," I said, more to myself than anyone else. "You know this entire town is probably working for Mason's family. The police certainly are. Getting through Hamble is going to be difficult during the day. Especially considering all of us more than likely have a price on our heads."

"There's a tunnel that takes us out of the town into the park," Gabriel said. "There are tracks and a carriage down there; it's not exactly five-star treatment, but it's safe."

"Exactly what were the people who designed this place expecting to happen?" I asked him.

"It was extended during the Cold War," Gabriel said. "Some people were scared of invasion."

"So, they made a subway?" Hannah asked.

"Pretty much," Gabriel said.

"I will remain here until the meeting tonight." Nadia said. "I scare people."

"She's not wrong," Hannah agreed.

I picked up my two rift-tempered daggers and put them on. I was hoping I didn't need them, but I'm also a realist who understands that given the current climate, the odds were good I would. Before I left, I also took my Heckler & Koch P30L and a few extra magazines of bullets.

We followed Gabriel through one of the spokes to what I'd assumed was an old storage room, considering it mostly consisted of furniture with dust sheets thrown over them. We walked around to a large wardrobe, which Gabriel pushed aside, revealing a metal door. He opened it, the hiss of musty, warm air on my face causing me to cough, and stepped through, the old lights flickering to life inside a moment later.

We continued walking for ten minutes before the tunnel opened out into a cavern. There were railroad tracks on the ground and what looked like an old train engine attached to a carriage, both of which were hooked up to some kind of charging station.

"What is this place?" I asked.

"It's a modified train driver's cab and carriage from the 1940s," Gabriel said. "It runs on batteries that are linked to several solar panels that had been on top of the church. There should be enough juice to run it for a few weeks without them, but at some point, it's going to need fixing."

"You really went all out with this, didn't you?" I asked, walking up to the carriage and looking around it.

"It had already been done when I arrived," Gabriel said. "I just had it modernized and made safe."

"Are you some kind of doomsday prepper or something?" Hannah asked.

"I think I'm more of a realist," Gabriel said. "The church was meant to be a safe haven away from those who would use and hurt us. Sometimes, the safest thing you can do is escape."

"And this takes us onto the railroad tracks?" I asked.

"Disused but owned by the church," Gabriel said. "It goes from here to Abbey Park, and then up toward Lake Ontario and along past Rochester to Hamilton, before it goes up to Toronto."

"And no one questions the massive amount of disused track? I asked.

"Ninety percent of it is underground," Gabriel said. "The official records show it as an old subway route that was disbanded but is owned by about twenty different companies."

"You made it as hard as possible for anyone to check on it," Hannah said.

"I'm not sure if I've said this before, but you church types are crafty buggers," I said with a smile.

Gabriel nodded a thank-you as we all climbed on up into the carriage, which was remarkably less dusty than I'd expected.

"You come here a lot, I assume," Hannah said, taking a seat on a leather-clad bench.

"Once a month," Gabriel said. "It's relaxing down here, away from everything. Also, trains are cool."

No one said anything.

"They are; accept it," Gabriel announced, walking off toward the driver's cab.

"You're driving?" I asked him, sharing an expression with Hannah.

"Is there a problem with that?" Gabriel asked.

"It can't be any worse than when he drives a car," Hannah said. "This is literally on rails; it's not like he can go anywhere."

"None of you are funny," Gabriel said, opening the door and closing it behind him.

I sat back and closed my eyes, opening them a few moments later when the carriage jolted forward.

"He can't stall a train, right?" Hannah asked.

I looked over at her. "Having been in numerous vehicles with Gabriel over the years, he can stall anything."

The journey was peaceful and quiet. It took about twenty minutes as the train moved underground, occasionally venturing out into the daylight, only to be obscured by high banks and trees. A private railway for the church. I'd been alive a long time, but, like Hannah said, occasionally we were still surprised.

"You think Booker is still on our side?" Hannah asked me as the train stopped and Gabriel entered the carriage, looking very proud of himself.

"Yes," I said.

We all left the carriage and walked up the track. It was secluded where we were, with trees everywhere and denser woodland not too far from there. The park itself was a massive piece of land, with a large lake in the middle that you could walk around. A sizeable playground sat on one side of the park, just after the main entrance, although it was deserted now.

Gabriel took point and we followed him into the park, moving quickly and quietly, until we reached the rendezvous spot—a group of trees that were slightly elevated from the field around it, giving excellent views. Booker dropped down from one of the trees, landing in the snow as we approached. Zita did the same from a second tree, although she made no move toward us.

"She's the lookout," Booker said, shaking everyone's hand, leaving me for last. "Zita said that you're not what she thought."

"I get that a lot," I said. "Where's the informant?"

"Send her over," Gabriel called out to Zita. A woman of about thirty with pink-and-blond hair stepped out from the shadows of the trees. She wore jeans, trainers, and a thick black coat to keep out the chill that whipped across the park.

"This is Scarlet Harmon," Booker said.

The woman identified as Scarlet looked like a meerkat who had just come up to check it was safe; she constantly looked around the park, beyond where we were standing.

"You okay?" Hannah asked her.

Scarlet nodded for a moment, changed her mind, and shook her head. "No," she said. "My boyfriend was murdered, my life is in danger, and I just want to hide somewhere."

Part of me wanted to tell her that maybe she shouldn't have helped a psychotic doctor experiment on people before deciding she had a conscience, but I kept my mouth closed instead. Let's not alienate the person who wanted to help.

"Tell us what you know," I said.

Scarlet sighed. "There were six of us," she started. "Clive, Harry, Daisy, me, and two others. We all worked for Callie and Mason; I helped Callie with data that she'd found during her experiments. At the time, we didn't know about *people* being experimented on. We thought she was trying to save the world. We thought she was trying to find a way to use the tears in the rift to heal people. About four months ago, Daisy found out what was going on. She went to Mason, told him her concerns, and went home. She was murdered that night. *Break-in gone wrong*, the HPD said.

"We all got an email from Mason's pit bull; his name is William Stone. He's a . . . He's bad. Really bad. Anyway, we got an email to say that what happened to Daisy was awful and that we should all be more careful in the future, as it would be terrible if her death was the start of some crime wave. He actually advised us to make sure our doors and windows are locked at night.

"So, anyway, a week later, we're all shitting ourselves still, trying to find a way out. We get a timed email from Daisy telling us everything she'd found out. My boyfriend, Clive, contacted the FBI. Two weeks later, and three of us go to see a handler. They ask us to get intel on Sky-High, on Mason, on anyone who can help the FBI get a case together. So, we spent two months getting info. A little at a time, taking copies of data when we thought it was safe. Until Clive and Harry went to meet them just over a month ago."

"When they were killed," Gabriel said softly. "I'm sorry for your loss."

Scarlet nodded a thank-you before continuing. "The remaining three of the original six were called into Mason's office the day after Clive and Harry died. We were told that while it was really sad that Clive and Harry had died, it was clear that they had been somewhere they shouldn't have been, and that we should all take that lesson to heart and not go to dangerous places.

"I decided to keep my head down and just do my job. One of my colleagues tried to quit and was told why that wasn't going to be happening anytime soon. A few weeks later, I found all of this intel that Clive, Harry, and Daisy had acquired. I thought it had been with them when they'd died. There was so much of it, so much insane stuff. Experiments, people in positions of power being bribed, threatened. Murders. Most of it not concrete, just timelines matching up, emails, bank account details. So much data that they'd managed to acquire. Mostly illegally. They hacked the email server for internal emails, which they could do because it was their job to keep it working. They controlled every piece of info that went into the cloud; they build themselves back doors into every piece of software in Sky-High Security."

"Where is all of this data?" Hannah asked.

"On a USB drive," she said. "I gave it to Zita last night."

"A lot of it is encrypted," Booker said.

"I have the key to unlock it once I'm safe," Scarlet said. "Once I know these psychopaths aren't going to find me."

"We can do that," I said. "But I have questions."

Scarlet nodded.

"What do you know about Dan, the kidnapped RCU?" I asked. "Basically, everything that happened since three weeks ago."

"Not much," Scarlet said. "I didn't have access to external comms, and Mason is deluded, but he's not actually stupid. I'm pretty sure that one of the other techs working on the email server found out what Harry and Clive were doing and ratted them out. I know Dan. I've met him a few times. He used to say he worked for the RCU, but now he says he runs it. Dr Mitchell told me the same thing, that we'll have an easier time of it now that Dan is in charge."

"That confirms what I'd already heard," I said.

"There's an FBI person who comes in," Scarlet said. "Don't know his name. No other personnel are allowed in the labs when he's there, but he comes in once a month to talk to Dr Mitchell and Mason. I don't know why. There's no internal communications."

"What is Callie Mitchell doing?" I asked.

"Making hybrids," Scarlet said. "We were lied to."

"What does she want them for?" Gabriel asked.

Scarlet shrugged. "I just run the data, check for problems. For the first few months, I thought they captured fiends and ran tests on them, and I didn't mind. They're just fiends. Monsters. But Daisy found out about the prison under the Sky-High building. Rift-fused are kept down there, humans too, but mostly rift-fused. I realised I was working for a sadist too late and couldn't get out."

"We'll help you," Gabriel assured her.

"Do you know where the RCU agents are?" I asked Scarlet.

"Five are in the prison," she said. "Everyone was freaking out because the company had gone from working in the shadows to just outwardly kidnapping a bunch of agents and murdering more. It was all over the news. It's why I was shocked that Dan is now in charge of the RCU. He'd been a regular at the office over the time I'd worked there. He's . . . He wants Dr Mitchell's research to proceed as quickly as possible. We have chats with Mason about the data, because Dr Mitchell is too busy to bother with keeping the 'boss' informed, and I always got the impression that Mason and Dr Mitchell have different visions about what the experiments are for."

"What do you mean?" I asked.

"Mason wants to find a way to create a *super soldier*," Scarlet said. She was relaxing now and was quite animated with her hands as she spoke. "He wants to monetise it. He wants to get power and wealth and status, and that's his every aim. Dr Mitchell . . . It's personal for her. *Deeply* personal."

"You know why?" Hannah asked.

Scarlet shook her head. "She doesn't fraternise with the staff. She orders us to do stuff and we do it. Those who work with her on the experiments themselves have it harder. She threw a chair at one of them because he made an incision too deep on a fiend."

"Where do you get the fiends from?" I asked.

"Dan used to let us know when one had been found in the wild so they could go retrieve it."

"How long has that been going on?" I asked.

"As long as the data goes back," Scarlet said. "Two years, at least."

"And those things that attacked the RCU and FBI agents?" I asked.

Scarlet nodded. "They combine fiends with human DNA to try to make a greater fiend with intelligence . . . They're horrible."

"So, they killed the informants, dumped standard greater fiends near the cabin to make it look like they were responsible for the RCU and FBI attack to throw anyone off the trail as to what was actually behind the killings," Gabriel said. "Looks like you were right, Lucas."

"Had to happen sometime," Hannah said with a smile.

"Where are the other five agents?" Booker asked. "We know at the warehouse, but do you have a better location than that?"

"Main building offices, I'd guess," Scarlet said. "That's where they put people before bringing them to the offices. Or it's where they put fiends. It's big enough to house a few dozen people."

"I've heard rumours that Mason isn't very happy about what happened," Booker said. "About the attacks taking place without his say-so."

"I always thought Mason was in charge," Scarlet said. "But I don't think he is. I think he just found out that he was a smaller cog in a bigger machine than he'd first assumed. I saw emails he'd sent to Dr Mitchell a few weeks ago, calling her a Judas and asking how she could do it to him. Take something from him that was so important. I never saw a reply. That was when I knew I had to get out. At some point, people like me are going to be considered expendable for knowing more than we should, and I know *a lot* more than I should.

"I just want to go home," Scarlet said. "To Tennessee. Can you do that?"

"We can try," Gabriel said. "I think it's going to be a long time before you'll be able to walk around in public, though. Until we've dealt with Dan and his friends, the only way to stay safe is to stay out of the way.

To hide. We can hide you. The church has been doing that for a long time."

"I'm going to have to go to jail, aren't I?" Scarlet asked as we started to walk across the park as Zita brought up the rear, keeping watch, and Hannah did the same in front.

"I don't know," I said, trying to be honest but really having no idea. "The RCU are under the thumb of someone who appears to be using them to kill their enemies. The FBI have people working with the very people you're informing on, and the local police force are utterly corrupt. I think that's a question for Emily when we see her later."

"Who's Emily?"

"FBI agent," Gabriel told her. "She's definitely one of the good ones, so don't worry."

"Oh, good," Scarlet said.

I turned to check on her and saw Zita dive toward her, tackling her to the ground. They both rolled down a nearby hill, with Booker, Gabriel, and Hannah jumping down after them. I was last. A bullet whizzed by where Scarlet had been standing, impacting with a nearby tree.

"They've found me," Scarlet said, terror dripping from every word.

# CHAPTER TWENTY-THREE

Everyone had started yelling at once, and Scarlet had been half-dragged, half-pushed to the side of the hill, dropping behind an especially large tree. Zita had thrown up a wall of shadow behind us, hopefully obscuring us from view, but it wasn't going to work forever.

Scarlet looked petrified, her hands over her mouth, her eyes wide and full of fear. Hannah had her gun drawn, ready to fight. The difference between someone who has never been in a gunfight and someone who, by her own admission, had probably been in far too many.

"Can you see anything?" Booker asked.

"Not from here," Gabriel called back.

I scrambled up the hill, keeping low, to look through the shadowy mist that sat at the top, and hoped it would obscure me from view.

"Six incoming," I said to Zita as she joined me, lying down beside me.

The attackers had come in the park, using their large black SUVs to block the main entrance. They'd spread out, moving through the children's play area, taking up positions.

"How'd they track her?" Zita asked me. Her face was covered in shadow, her eyes giant pools of rippling darkness. Hooded revenants were masters of camouflage, stealth, and subterfuge.

I didn't have an answer for that. From the abject terror on Scarlet's face, she hadn't brought them there knowingly.

I moved back down the hill. "Get to the train and get out of here," I said to Gabriel. "You have cover for maybe thirty feet. Wait there, and I'll get their attention."

"And leave you here?" Gabriel asked.

"I'll give you time," I told him. "Look, we can't all die here, and we can't all get caught."

"Lucas, if you stay, they'll kill you," Booker said.

I stared at Gabriel.

"He'll be fine," Gabriel said.

"Are you all insane?" Zita asked as she joined us. "I count eight out there, at least one is decent with a rifle, and one looks like some deformed fiend . . . thing."

"Awesome," I said. "Even so, get going. They can't find that train, and they can't get hold of any of us. Everything we've done will be for nothing if they do."

"We can't leave you here," Hannah almost shouted at me.

"Look, I can keep them busy while you escape and then vanish into my embers," I said, avoiding Gabriel's expression. "It'll be fine. Just go."

"You'd better be right about this," Gabriel said, and ran after the others as they sprinted along the bottom of the hill toward the rear of the park.

The shadows that Zita had used to conceal us faded away, and I headed for the trees, which meant running across open ground for maybe ten or fifteen feet. I steadied myself and sprinted as fast as I could, hitting the tree line at full speed, tripping over a concealed branch, which sent me to the ground as a bullet smashed into a nearby tree trunk.

I drew my P30L and fired twice around the tree, hitting one of the soldiers and scattering the rest into the nearby trees. A sniper round slammed into the tree trunk about an inch above where my head had been, and I decided that whoever that was, they were my first problem. The fiend, though, all seven feet of skeletal limbs, muscular ape-like torso, and a head that appeared to be some kind of furry cross between a snake and a wolf, stood in the middle of the field and sniffed the air, its long dark tongue flicking around. Frankly, the whole thing looked monstrous and something I wanted no part of. I put it second on my list of things to kill. Because I'm optimistic like that.

I moved to the next tree along, but a bullet caught me in the shoulder, and I flung myself down to the dirt, rolling down another hill, stopping halfway down when I grabbed hold of some strong roots. I winced in pain but knew I needed to keep moving. I turned to smoke.

It's difficult to maintain turning into smoke at the best of times, but when you can feel a bullet tumbling through what used to be your body, it makes keeping things together much less pleasant. I kept in smoke form until I was safely inside the woodland, out of view of the sniper and, hopefully, of anything else that might be after me.

I stopped for a moment beside the remains of an old tree that had once been struck by lightning and reassembled myself. I hadn't long since left the embers, and had turned to smoke several times in two days, as well as having been shot. I wasn't even back to full power. It had been a long few days.

"This way," someone called out from close by, and I began to run through the forest, vaulting over low branches and trying not to maintain a straight line as I made a wide circle around where I'd been, hoping to come up behind my attackers. I assumed the sniper would stay where they were, just in case I tried to flee or some of my friends arrived, so I hoped that they wouldn't be expecting me to attack. My plan rested on hope and assumptions, neither of which were great.

Gunfire tore into a tree beside me, causing me to pick up the pace, but I wasn't watching where I was going, lost my footing, and tumbled down a large embankment. Leaves, snow, and dirt covered almost every inch of me, and the hole in my shoulder wasn't helping. Unfortunately, turning to smoke doesn't heal any injuries I've received. I've tried putting myself back together in my smoke form before, and . . . well, it went badly. I moved my arm slightly; it was stiff, but it wasn't broken.

I scrambled to my feet and ducked behind a tree trunk to catch my breath. I needed to even the odds a little, but whatever that fiend with them was, it appeared to be able to track me.

I peered between two interlocking tree trunks and got a view of the fiend stood beside the man I'd known as William Stone, a large metal leash in his hand. On the other side of William was a large man covered in a bone-like armour. Alexis Capan. They'd sent the big guns after us. That would have been almost nice if it weren't for the fact that they were trying to kill me.

As a riftborn, I can reach out and touch the rift, causing a small tear and using the power to detect rift-fused. It would have made my life a little easier. But with the fiend there, I wasn't certain if that was how it had tracked us, and if it was the way, opening a tear would have been like setting off a giant firework with an arrow pointing to me. Besides, with my increasingly painful wound, it was unlikely I'd be able to open a tear without being forced inside to my embers. I was going to have to do this the old-fashioned way.

I slowly backed away from the trees and threw myself forward as gunfire peppered the area I'd just been. I turned to smoke again and moved quickly through the dense foliage, re-forming a hundred meters away, as the sounds of my pursuers could be easily heard. I had to stop with the smoke; if I kept it up, I was going to pass out well before I was able to do any harm to any of them. I needed that fiend gone. Time to change plans.

The fiend was easily visible with William on top of the bank; clearly, William had expected me to be easy pickings.

I dropped to my knees next to a large tree and looked up at the thick branches above. I scrambled up the trunk—using claws of smoke to help—until I was concealed above my targets, fifty feet above the ground. There were three men, all with what looked like silenced MP5s, moving through the woodlands. They wore identical black outfits, with balaclavas and heavy boots that didn't make as much noise as you'd think. They were probably well trained and almost certainly versed in fighting rift-fused.

I kept low and moved along the branch, concealed from anyone below—it was large enough to support my weight—until I was almost directly above one of the men. The other two had gone around the trees. They were maybe fifty metres away by the time the one beneath me was where I wanted him to be. I was about to drop down on him, take him out nice and quietly, when I spotted the bone-armoured revenant moving through the forest, keeping low. The fiend was right beside him.

I spotted William walking back across the field toward the cars and wondered if he was going to get something that would make my life more complicated. I really hoped not; it was complicated enough.

The fiend was thirty feet away, fifty feet below me. It sniffed the air, growled, looked directly at me, and I shot it in the head.

The explosion of sound left no doubt as to where I was. I rolled off the tree, drawing my larger dagger as I fell, quickly turning to smoke to ensure I didn't slam into the ground at high speed. The soldier below was too slow to react, and I reformed just before landing in a crouch beside him. I stabbed him three times in the thigh as I stood and once more in the throat before taking his MP5 and moving away.

Bullets hit the tree beside me, and I fired back blindly, hoping to hit something, anything, as I ran into the densest part of the forest. I moved behind a stone wall that looked to belong to a long-since-overgrown hut and checked my ammo. The MP5 was almost full, and I had several bullets for my P30L, along with a few spare magazines, should they be necessary.

I spotted movement out of the corner of my eye, raised the MP5, and once I saw the balaclava-clad head of one of my pursuers, I fired a three-shot burst. The head vanished in a cloud of red mist, but the stone beside me exploded from gunfire, and I was forced to move away. My arm was sore, my shoulder too. I wasn't going to be able to keep this up for long.

I picked up a stone and threw it at a nearby tree, which was hit with gunfire a moment later. Trained but not that smart; that was good to know. I threw a second stone somewhat further than the first as I kept low, letting the moss and vines that covered the hut hang over me too.

The remaining soldier moved slowly past me, his gun moving left to right in a steady motion, tracking all before him. Turning to smoke was out of the question; I'd done too much and was too injured. I needed to get this over with. The soldier turned toward me, but I shot him through the head before his gun was aimed my way.

I moved low and quick to the nearby tree, next to the still-alive form of the fiend. I drew my rift-tempered dagger and stabbed it through the eye into its brain, killing it.

"There is only you and me," Alexis shouted out. "How about we settle this with honour?"

I ducked back down behind the tree. I wasn't about to let him know where I was, and I certainly wasn't stupid enough to stand up and throw my weapons away.

I looked behind the tree as Alexis tossed his rifle away, followed by his revolver and a dagger. "Just you and me."

I stepped around from the tree, my MP5 still in my hands. "I'll tell you what: you tell me what I want, and then we'll do this your way," I told him. We were maybe forty feet away from each other, and the smile on his face was easy to read.

"You did a good job with these," Alexis said. "With the tree, too."

"Thank you," I said. "Still got shot."

"We were after Scarlet. You were an added bonus." Alexis said. "That's how we found you, by the way. The fiend can track anyone."

"How?" I asked despite myself.

"Everyone who works for Sky-High has a medical," Alexis said. "Blood work included."

"It's a monstrous bloodhound," I said. "That how you tracked Harry and Clive?"

Alexis nodded. "The dog-fiends killed them both. I don't wish to watch something like that again."

"I'm sure they forgive you," I said sarcastically.

"How is Nadia?" Alexis asked, ignoring my comment. "I assume she has gone to see you. You're the angry smoke she's spoken about for the last few years."

"She's okay," I said, feeling that Alexis's question had been genuine. "Why'd you come after me and not Scarlet?"

"William thought you were more important in the long run," Alexis said. "He figured we could go after Scarlet anytime."

"That didn't work out so well," I said. "I killed your fiend."

"They'll figure out how to make another one," Alexis said. "It's sort of their job."

"This is very pleasant and all," I said, "but I assume we can't stay here all day and chat."

"It would be nice to think that we could," Alexis said. "Old warriors and all that."

"You have a romanticised version of what we are," I told him.

"Ah, I have done terrible things," Alexis said with a wave of his hand. "I know exactly what I am. I owe more than I can repay, so I hope one day to meet the person who will collect on that repayment. Maybe it's you."

"Maybe," I said.

"Dan told us that you were dangerous, but he thinks he's better than you," Alexis said. "Better than all of the Guilds, to be honest. He's in charge of the RCU now, you know?"

"I heard," I told him.

"Mason thinks you're just someone who can be brushed aside," Alexis said. "I don't think he truly understands what the Guilds do. What they are capable of. The training. The . . . camaraderie."

"But you do," I said.

"I think there are two options here," Alexis said. "I kill you and go back a hero, or I die. I can't go back empty-handed. I can't go back and admit failure. Not now. Maybe I could have taken you alive, but William thinks it's safer if you're dead."

"One of us has to die," I said, tossing the MP5 aside. "I'm not exactly in peak physical condition here."

"Your shoulder," he said. "Would you like to use knives?"

I removed the holster belt and placed it on the ground. "No, I'm good," I said. Knife fighting sucks for everyone involved. No one comes free from a knife fight without being cut up pretty badly.

I considered just grabbing the gun and shooting Alexis, ending it now, but he'd answered my questions, and I figured at the very least, he deserved what he'd asked for.

"There's a large spot just down there," Alexis said. "I think it would be the best place for this."

"After you," I told him.

He nodded and took off deeper into the forest. I kept twenty feet between us and hoped that no one would come along to find the small arsenal of weaponry we'd left behind.

Alexis stopped in the middle of the open patch of land, which was lightly dusted with snow but was otherwise thirty feet in diameter and with trees all around. It was a good size. I spotted several rocks and made a note not to get my head smashed onto any of them.

Alexis removed his jacket, rolling his shoulders. He started bouncing from foot to foot. He had the build of a heavyweight boxer, and almost on cue. He did some rapid punches into the air.

I stood and watched him for a moment.

"You're not going to warm up?" he asked.

I shook my head. "I'm pretty warmed up from killing your men."

Alexis laughed. "You are cold, Lucas Rurik."

"I have one last question before we start," I said.

"Sure," Alexis said.

"Where are Dan and Mason?"

"Mason is north," he said. "I don't know exactly where. I'm not that important."

"You know why?" I asked.

"Training exercise," he said. "Money. Power. That's always why Mason goes there. Dan might know more."

"I'll ask him when I see him."

"You are confident," Alexis said.

I nodded. "It was nice meeting you, Alexis."

"You too, Lucas. Abilities okay with you?"

I nodded.

Alexis charged at me, his bone armour covering his body in an instant. I dodged aside, rolled across the frozen ground, and came up in a fighting stance a few feet away while Alexis slowly turned around. The armour would stop a bullet, and being hit while he was using it would more than likely break bones and snap muscle, but he also had the turning circle of a small moon. Sacrificing speed and agility for power and endurance was never a sacrifice I would make.

Alexis strode toward me with purpose, his hands balled into fists. I couldn't out-punch him, and I couldn't keep rolling around the damned ground forever, either. I was hurt, tired, and needed to rest before I fell down, but I was also far too stubborn for my own good.

I dodged a cross and ducked under his jab, pushing his arm away and forming claws of smoke around my hands, slashing along the bone armour near his ribs before I put some distance between the two of us.

I'd cut through the bone armour, but it hadn't been deep enough to draw blood. He darted forward, surprisingly fast considering the armour, and lashed out with a kick. I didn't dodge in time, and he caught me in the shoulder with enough strength to knock me to the ground. I tasted dirt and leaves as Alexis stamped down on the bullet wound in my shoulder, causing me to shout out in pain.

Alexis reached down and grabbed me by the back of the shoulder, his fingers digging into the wounded flesh around the bullet hole. I tried to pull away, but he was too strong, and I was soon sailing across the clearing and into a tree with enough force that the air left my body in one rush as I crashed to the ground.

I had enough wherewithal to move out of the way in time to dodge a kick to my head, and continued to roll as Alexis stamped down where I'd been, the force of the blow leaving a deep footprint in the frozen ground.

I got back to my feet, feeling a little shaky. I was close to being done. I needed this over.

Alexis charged again and kicked out at my chest. Smoke poured out of my hands, wrapping around his foot and solidifying, pulling him off balance. The smoke outside of his body continued to grow and harden, until his hands, which he'd been using to try and pull himself free, were now trapped. He was strong and could probably have broken free after a few seconds, but that was all I needed.

His eyes, still visible inside the armour, went wide with shock as I grappled him into a chokehold, wrapping my legs around his back and placing a hand on the small hole he kept around his nose. I poured smoke into his body.

More and more smoke filled his nasal cavity, his throat, his lungs until the bone armour began to melt away from him. I continued to pour smoke inside of him until I felt something give. His lungs had burst. Only then did I stop.

With the smoke that had hardened and kept Alexis in place gone, he fell forward onto the ground. I didn't like to use smoke in such a way, it was difficult to control and even more difficult to watch someone suffocate to death, but he hadn't left me much choice.

I waited a few seconds, but Alexis didn't move. Even so, I picked up my pistol and put two bullets in the back of his head, just to make sure. Sometimes, revenants surprised you, and I wasn't in the mood for a second round.

I took a moment to get my breathing under control and heard the snap of a twig behind me. Nadia walked into the clearing, her chains dragging a semi-conscious William Stone.

"I thought you were staying at the church," I said.

"I thought you might need help," Nadia said, looking down at William as her chains uncoiled from around him. "I was right."

"And what are your plans for William?" I asked her as he began to stir.

"I thought we could ask him a few questions," Nadia said with a smile that was genuinely the most terrifying I'd ever seen.

# CHAPTER TWENTY-FOUR

William remained stoic and loyal to Mason for exactly the amount of time it took for Nadia to squeeze the chains around his body until he couldn't breathe.

"Guess who fucked around and found out?" I said.

"Whatever you need to know," William screamed.

"Good idea," I told him. "But I don't trust you, so the chains stay on."

"No," William yelled. Bullies really don't like it when they're the ones on the end of unpleasant treatment.

"I can use my chains to tell if you're lying," Nadia said. "I see the chains of your life. I don't see the exact events, but if you lie, I'll know. And I'll squeeze again until you tell the truth. A few broken bones are always a good motivator for honesty."

"I disagree with torture on principle," I told William. "So, we won't call it that; we'll call it **giving you an incentive**."

The fight visibly left William's body and he sagged forward. "What do you need to know?"

"We know that the hikers—Clive and Harry—were killed by Sky-High because Mason was concerned about the FBI getting intel on them," I started. "We know that Dan led the RCU and FBI into an ambush. We know your mutated dog fiends killed the hikers, and you deposited normal fiends near the cabin to throw us off the trail, and Dan was meant to be a hero and instead he got hurt."

"One of the hybrids lost it," William said.

"Truth," Nadia confirmed.

"One of the fiend-human hybrids Callie made just started screaming and flailing around," William told us. "They'd been used to kill the hikers, as they were used to being given orders. But then they just vanished, and when Dan turned up with his team to look for them, they went nuts. Killed everything in sight and ran off. We had to dump fiends as decoys to cover up the mess, and then more FBI turned up and we didn't have time to look for the real killers."

"We know that there's someone in the FBI who wants their involvement removed," I said.

"Only Callie knows who it is," William said.

"Lie," Nadia said, and started to constrict the chains.

"Fine," William cried out through haggard breaths. "Dan too."

"Truth," Nadia confirmed.

"No one else can know," William said, his voice hoarse. "There's an organisation behind Dan and Callie; I don't know who they are, no one does. They have several powerful people in their ranks."

"Why did Dan have the RCU teams in New York and LA killed?" I asked.

"Dan fucking hates the lot of you," William said with a croaky chuckle. "No idea why. He just does. It's not like we're besties. I work for Mason and Callie."

"That doesn't explain why he went after the LA team," I said.

"Callie needed more data," William said. "Field data. Dan suggested the LA team because he worked there and had some issues with those in charge. I think he wanted to go after every RCU team in the country, flush them all out, to be replaced with Sky-High employees, but he was talked out of it."

"By whom?" I asked.

"No idea," William said. "Whoever Dan works for. Someone powerful, that's for sure."

"You were tracking Scarlet with that fiend," I said.

"You killed it," William said, sounding vaguely sad about that, which surprised me.

"I did," I said. "How'd Callie make it?"

"She's been splicing shit together for years," William said. "She's trying to create something game-changing. She's really secretive about it, too. Mason knows, but I don't think he really *knows*. You've met Callie; she's kind of intense."

"I think *evil* is the word you're looking for," I told him.

"One man's evil is another man's . . ." William started.

"Evil," Nadia finished for him. "Evil is evil. Callie is evil."

"You're a traitor," William snapped.

"The code for the Sky-High building," I said.

William said nothing for several seconds, and as the squeezing became too much and I thought one of his eyes might pop out, he started to talk again. I used my phone to record it all and passed it to Nadia.

"Where's Mason?" I asked.

"Last I heard, he was going north," William told me. "Canada . . . with Callie. There's a meeting up there. I don't know where; I don't know why. I'm not privy to such things."

"Anything you want to ask him?" I asked Nadia.

"No," she said. "You always were an asshole. You should know that."

"You gonna free me or what?" William said.

"No," I told him, and shot him in the head.

"Take my phone to Gabriel," I told her. "I'm going to my embers to heal this bloody wound. I'll be a few hours, I imagine; the bullet is out, and it wasn't in anything close to a dangerous place. Besides, my body has already stopped the bleeding, so I won't be long."

"Riftborn are weird," Nadia said. "You want us all to do anything when you're gone?"

"Get ready for war," I told her, taking a deep breath, opening my embers, and stepping through into what I hoped was going to be a lot safer than it had been the last time.

"You look like shit," Casimir the stag said as I sat on a crumbling stone fence surrounding a longhouse.

"Thanks very much," I said, peeling off my jacket and shirt to find my entire upper torso covered in blood.

I placed the weapons in a neat pile beside me, and Casimir walked silently with me to the nearby stream, where I washed myself off. Sometimes when you were hurt and you arrived in the embers, you had blood and grime from the real world, and sometimes you didn't. I was never entirely sure why, but by the time I'd finished cleaning myself, the bullet hole was gone, and I could move my shoulder without gritting my teeth.

"I need new clothes," I said, standing up from the cold water of the stream, and was almost immediately dry.

"Maria is sat atop your old home," Casimir said. "Can I assume that you will not be staying?"

"I need to get back to the church in Hamble," I said. "My friends need me." I'd left my Talon mask at the church because it was an object of great importance to me. It meant I could go back there from my embers, and frankly, that was a better idea than having to return to Brooklyn each time.

"You are back to your old self, I assume?" Casimir asked.

I nodded. "Mostly. The power level isn't quite right, but I'll have to make do. Besides, people are going to die if I don't get back."

"You know that this will be twice in quick succession," Casimir said with an almost-chuckle.

"Yeah, I'm not actually new at this," I said as the pair of us walked through the village after I picked up the weapons I'd arrived with.

"My point is," Casimir said, "I would advise you to not be hurt enough that you need to come back here again. You will take much longer to heal."

I nodded. "I know, couldn't be helped. I got shot, and I can't be anything less than at full strength to go up against Mason's people."

We reached the longhouse and a raven landed on the wall beside me. "That's a little on the nose," I said to Maria.

"I thought it might remind you what you once were," they said with a short squawk.

"I remember," I said.

"You didn't remember to wear clothes," Maria said.

"I got shot," I said. "Had to wash the blood off. Any idea how much time will have passed? It wasn't critical, not life-threatening, so I'm hoping no more than a few hours."

"Half a day maybe," Maria said. "It's not an exact science. How's the arm?"

I flexed my shoulder. "Good."

"You need anything else?" Casimir asked.

"No, just a heal and run," I said. "Any trouble with the shadows?"

"Things appear to be back to normal," Maria said. "Or whatever passes for normal, anyway."

Maria landed next to a small stable, although there were no horses inside. "This the exit?" I asked.

"Take care," Casimir said. "Try not to come back injured for a while."

I opened the stable door and stepped into the tear inside, ending up beside the bed where I'd put my mask, close to the main area of the shelter under the ruined church.

"It's Lucas," I called out, unable to see anyone close by and not wanting to freak anyone out when they heard me moving about.

Gabriel's face was suddenly illuminated as the light beside him ignited, casting a glow as he holstered his gun.

"Nadia said you'd be back soon enough," Gabriel said.

"Everyone okay?" I asked.

Gabriel nodded.

Apart from Nadia and Gabriel, the former of which was sat beside a small fire, there was quite the group of people. Emily was sat cross-legged on a chair, frantically making notes. Hannah sat beside her, staring into space, while Zita was busy talking to Booker, occasionally looking around the room as if she was expecting an imminent attack.

"You stayed down here?" I asked.

"More space to move around," Gabriel said. "It was feeling a little cramped above."

The train had been returned to its former place, and as everyone looked up at me, Bill climbed down from the carriage, followed quickly by George and Dale.

"Glad you could make it," I told them. "We'll need all the help we can get."

"I'm not much of a fighter," George said. "I am a thinker, a litigator. I do not think I would do battle well."

"I am a fighter," Bill said with a beaming smile. "I'm here to hit people."

As the pair had been talking, several others had left the train, including Michelle, three other members of staff—two men and a woman whose names I didn't remember, and the two large bouncers who worked at the bar, Todd and Mikey.

"I'm here because I need to help," Dale said as everyone said hello and went to take seats around the fire. "We drove up after you called last night, got here about an hour after shit apparently hit the fan."

"What time is it?" I asked.

"Just after eight p.m.," Bill told me.

"We're planning to leave soon," Hannah said.

"A friend arrived at the church a few hours ago," Gabriel said.

"I came to save your ass," a familiar voice said from the entrance to the train carriage.

I looked over at Ji-hyun. She was a little over five and a half feet tall, with long brown hair that was scooped back into a high ponytail. She wore black boots, jeans, a white T-shirt with the word *kaiju* in bright red being eaten by Godzilla, and a black-and-red biker's jacket. She dropped down from the carriage, walked over to me, and embraced me in a tight hug. "I was worried," she whispered.

"Me too," I told her. "What happened in LA?"

"Same thing that happened here," she said, pulling away. "Team got attacked by people who could change into fiends. I'm the only survivor. They tore them apart, Lucas. Never seen anything like it."

"I'm sorry," I told her. "I'm glad you're okay."

"Me too," Ji-hyun said.

"So, Dan is working for someone else," Booker said. "Someone who was happy to have members of the RCU used as test subjects for their murderous fiends."

"And someone above my pay grade is working with them," Emily said. "Working to kill my agents."

"I'm sorry," I told her. "You manage to get any of your agents to help?"

Emily shook her head. "All being watched. Too conspicuous if we all run off at once. They have families; I can't do that to them."

"We'll be fine," Gabriel said.

"Zita and Booker, did you get anyone to help out?" I asked.

"We got a few people who owe us favours," Booker said. "What do you need?"

"Hannah, can you hack into the emergency systems of each of the four banks and get them all to show a bank robbery at the same time?" I asked her. "I've been thinking we need to keep the HPD busy. They're all corrupt, but that doesn't mean I want a bunch of humans getting steamrolled over by us."

"Certain parts of the media would eat that up," Emily said.

"Zita and Booker, I want your friends to piss the police off," I said. "Get as many of them away from that station as possible. I want anything you can do. But tell them not to blow anything up or start shooting people; just make noise, make it look like something big is happening."

"They can do that," Booker said, looking at a grinning Zita.

"Dale will accompany me to the warehouse," I said. "Hopefully, there won't be many of Mason's friends there. You know the cops, and if necessary, you'll make a good distraction."

"At least you're being upfront about it," Dale said.

"They rest of you need to get into Mason's building," I said.

"William's access codes are the real thing," Nadia said. "Scarlet confirmed them. Also, I know he couldn't lie, but it didn't hurt to confirm."

"You want me with them?" Ji-hyun asked me.

"We're the only riftborn here," I said. "They might need you if this thing turns ugly."

Ji-hyun nodded. I was pretty sure that anyone picking a fight with her had brought whatever she would do on themselves.

"And us?" George asked.

"No offence to you and your bar staff, but I don't think you're soldiers, are you?" I asked.

"Served six years in the British paratroopers," Todd said.

"And you?" I asked Mikey.

"Just some boxing and MMA stuff," he told me.

"Right, well, you're going with Ji-hyun and co," I said. "You're both revenants, so you'll be able to help, but Ji-hyun is in charge. You listen to her; you do as you're told."

"I'd already put myself in charge," Ji-hyun said. "But it was nice of you to do it too."

I smiled and shook my head. "Hannah, you're with Ji-hyun, so long as she's okay with that."

"George, I want you and your people down here," I said. "You're our eyes and ears. We need to know what's happening on police scanners and radios. If we need a quick extraction, we're going to need to know where and when we can get out."

"I'll get them everything they need," Hannah said.

"It's been a long day," I said. "It's not going to get any better this evening. You all need to be prepared to fight, to kill if necessary. Dan and those working for him won't hesitate. You can't either. I'm not losing anyone else."

I left everyone to get ready and walked back up to the shelter with Gabriel and Ji-hyun.

"I'm going to go make sure this place is secure," Gabriel said. "Give you two time to catch up."

"That'll have to wait," I said.

"Go talk to Ruby," Ji-hyun said. "I wish I could help, but . . . you're much older than me; I've never taken anyone into my embers before, and I don't think it would go well to take someone hurt in the first time."

"No," I agreed. "It would be . . . very bad." It would, most likely, kill Isaac instantly and kick Ji-hyun back to the rift for who knows how long.

"I need food," Ji-hyun said. "I guess it's too much to hope that you have kimchi here."

"Sorry, I don't think Gabriel got the fridge full of Korean food," I said. "You'll have to put in a request."

"I'll make sure I do," she said.

I smiled. It was good to see her again; it had been too long. But, as I said, our catch-up would have to wait. There were things that needed to be resolved first.

I found Ruby sat by Isaac's bed. She was reading to Isaac and looked up at me, placing the book on the table beside her.

"I know I told you I would take Isaac into my embers," I said. "And I will. I promise. But I can't tonight."

Ruby didn't look up at me, and just nodded.

"I got hurt," I said. "Shot in the shoulder. I had to go to the embers to heal up. Healing Isaac will take time and energy, and we don't have either right now. I know this is horrible, and I know that I told you I would do it, but I just have to delay it for a little while. I'm sorry."

"It's okay," Ruby said, looking up at me. "Isaac would understand. I understand."

As much as she said that she understood, Ruby's words still stung. I felt like it would have been easier if she'd sworn at me, or yelled, something. The acceptance was like a shot to the gut.

"I wish this hadn't happened," I told her.

"Me too," Ruby said. "I assume you're all going to save the others. The ones who were taken when Isaac was hurt."

I nodded. "That's the plan, yes."

"I don't want other families to go through what we're going through," Ruby said, looking over at Isaac and smiling sadly. "You do whatever you need to do to get them back safe."

"I will."

"No, Lucas," Ruby stared at me, steel in her eyes. "You do *whatever* it takes to get those people home. Isaac would tell you the same, wouldn't he? Take the gloves off; get done what you need to get done."

I thought about the Talon mask. I thought about how I had failed my Guild. I wouldn't fail my friends again. "They won't live through the night," I told her.

# CHAPTER TWENTY-FIVE

The teams were ready for their tasks within the hour.

Apart from Dale and Emily, Gabriel, and Nadia, Hannah also joined me on our trip to the warehouse in a black BMW SUV that I didn't ask where it was from, and no one told me. Plausible deniability.

Emily and Dale were wearing something resembling their FBI tactical gear that Booker had also brought.

I looked down at the Talon mask in the pocket of the SUV's door and retrieved it. Dan had been responsible for what had happened to my Guild, and I hadn't been able to stop it. Tonight, Dan would meet a Talon's justice. One way or another.

The weather had turned unpleasant on the drive over, heavy wind and freezing rain, cutting through the night. I lifted the hood of my water-proof coat up as I pulled the Talon mask down over my face, opened the door, and stepped into the night.

"We need eyes and ears in there," I said, looking beyond the BMW to the warehouse and its sizeable fencing.

"I'll go," Nadia said. "Be back soon."

She'd run off toward the warehouse before anyone could say anything, her movements becoming jerkier the closer she got and the more she accessed the rift. Nadia was soon up and over the fence and scrambling up the outer wall of the warehouse to the roof, where she vanished from view.

"Chained revenants," Gabriel said by way of explanation.

"Are we meant to just wait?" Dale asked.

"I believe so," I said.

I heard the dragging of chains along the ground and turned to see Nadia jerkily walking toward us.

"So, how bad is it?" Emily asked Nadia.

"Half a dozen hostages," Nadia said. "Let me show you."

Nadia's chains snaked around my wrists before I could say anything, and after the immediate explosion of sounds, smells, and, most unpleasantly, tastes, of what Nadia had encountered, I saw the hostages and the guards. There were six hostages, just like Nadia said, and six guards. I didn't recognize any of the hostages.

The hostages looked to be in relatively good shape, although one of them had a few facial bruises. They were sat together in the corner of the room, facing a window that had bars and was far too high for a human to safely use.

Nadia moved again, making her way through the warehouse, keeping high as she spied on the six guards. Three were on the warehouse floor, playing cards, while another stood at the bottom of the stairs; the final two were in the remains of the office room.

The images vanished, and I dropped to my knees as reality came back in a rush.

"You okay?" Emily asked me.

I nodded. "Little warning next time," I said to Nadia.

"Apologies," Nadia said. "I assumed expedience was the aim of the game here."

I got to my feet, feeling a little lightheaded, and saw Gabriel's concerned expression. "I'm fine," I said. "I do not like having memories dumped on me like that. It hurts."

"So, do we have a plan?" Nadia asked.

"I'm going up to the roof," I said. "Those bars aren't going to stop me. The biggest concern is that there could be guards we don't know about in the rooms that Nadia couldn't get to, and/or guards in the corridor."

"We're the distraction," Gabriel said. He'd brought his old 1950s Colt Peacemakers, both engraved in nineteenth-century patterns. They'd have been beautiful ornaments or exhibits in a museum, but Gabriel kept them well maintained and was steadily loading them as he spoke.

"That doesn't seem like a very cleric thing to own," Nadia said, with a huge grin.

"I wasn't always a cleric," Gabriel said, placing both guns in holsters against his hips.

"Emily, Nadia, you go with Gabriel and Dale," I said. "Hannah, we're going to need the security feed in that place on a loop."

"I'm on it," she said, throwing her rucksack onto her shoulder.

Dale tapped something on his watch. "Countdown," he said by way of explanation.

"Give me five minutes, then create hell," I said.

"I think we can do that," Gabriel said with a wink.

I ran off toward the warehouse, turning to smoke and walking through the chain-link fence.

There were no guards outside that I saw, which meant all of the trouble was contained within the warehouse itself. In many ways, that was the preferred scenario, as I didn't want to have to start running around in the car park to find people.

Climbing up the side of the building was easy enough. Much like climbing the trees earlier, I used my smoke to gain traction against the concrete wall and sort of dragged myself up it. It would probably look really strange to anyone below, but I wasn't doing it to look good.

I reached the roof and moved along it as quickly as possible, finding the edge from Nadia's vision and looking over. Smoke trailed out of my hand, snaking down around the bars in the window. I gave it a small yank, solidifying the smoke, and stepped off the roof.

There's always that moment of *Holy shit, I stepped off a roof seventy feet in the air* when I do anything like this.

I used my free hand to pour smoke out against the wall, making sure I didn't slam into it. When I stopped swinging, I retracted the smoke around the metal bars back into my hand, pulling me up the wall until I had hold of the bars with one hand, and the smoke anchored around it with the other.

I looked into the dark room and tried to make out exactly where the RCU agents would be. "Anyone there?" I whispered.

There was movement below, and the face of a male RCU agent came into view, lit by the dim moonlight.

"Who are you?" he asked. "How did you get there? Why are you there? What's going on?"

"Explanations later," I said, turning to smoke and pouring through the window, re-forming myself on the floor in front of the huddled RCU agents. "Name is Lucas Rurik; I'm here to get you all out."

"They made us wear these suits," the RCU agent said, showing the second-skin suit under his dirty clothes.

"Yeah, I'm familiar with them," I said.

"There's a digital lock on the back," a female agent told me.

"We'll get them done," I assured them. "Let me just go get rid of anyone who might be a nuisance. Be right back."

I opened the hatch on the door that was used to pass food through and turned to smoke, drifting through into the dimly lit corridor beyond.

I sensed the guard in the gloom before he saw me. A lone sentry sat on a chair between the two rooms of hostages, his eyes closed, his rifle held in a lackadaisical manner by his hip. I wrapped the smoke around his neck, nose, and mouth, solidifying it, choking him before he even had time to react. Another strand of smoke cushioned the AR-15 rifle from hitting the floor as I walked by. Threat removed without noise.

After checking the rest of the floor and finding no additional threats, I fished the keys from the dead guard and unlocked the makeshift cell used to keep the RCU prisoner.

"Stay behind me," I said. "You're all human if you're wearing those suits, and I'd rather not have Isaac kick my ass for not getting you all back home."

"Yes, sir," one of the RCU agents said.

I took the lead as gunfire broke out. I had just about reached the door when it was thrown open and a large bald man stepped through. He saw me, panicked, and went to raise his sidearm.

I moved quickly, stepping around him, grabbing his wrist, and bent his arm back up toward him. A small trail of smoke brushed over his trigger finger, forcing it down. The gun fired twice, removing a portion of the man's head and depositing it all over the wall behind him. I took his gun and slid it back toward the others before moving out onto the metal staircase.

Gabriel was a spined revenant, capable of growing huge spines all over his body and using them for both defensive and offensive purposes. He was currently firing them at two of Mason's people who had hunkered down behind some metal machinery, the spines tearing chunks out of it. They were safe for now, but it wouldn't last.

Dale and Emily were at the ruined entrance to the warehouse, shooting at two more guards who were returning fire.

I spotted Nadia crawling across the beams overhead; she dropped onto a guard who was trying to flank Gabriel. The guards' last moments on earth were filled with blood and screaming.

I vaulted over the metal stairs, turning to smoke. The smoke startled the two men as it moved past their legs, and I materialized again. I shot each guard in the head as they tried to turn toward me, and spotted that Gabriel had killed one of the two men he'd been engaged with, the second man screaming as his companion collapsed with a foot-long red spine where his eye had once been.

The distraction was enough, and Gabriel killed the other as Emily began to fire on two more guards who were now engaged with Dale.

It didn't take long for everyone to be dealt with, and despite the fatigue and injuries to the hostages, no one else was seriously hurt.

"These two were cops," Dale said. "Obviously corrupt."

"Not anymore," Nadia said, stepping over one of their bodies.

We found some digital cards and gave them to the RCU agents to get rid of those horrendous second-skin suits. We left the warehouse after Gabriel found several sets of car keys that had belonged to the dead guards. Emily joined Nadia, Dale, and Gabriel as we waited for the RCU agents.

Hannah left the warehouse. "All done," she said. "It's on a loop. It's not a lot of footage, but it'll do."

"Thank you," I told her.

"Now we get the others," Hannah said.

"You all have a choice," I told the RCU agents as they assembled before us. "Isaac is hurt. Badly. He won't be taking part in this fight, so we're going to have to do the fighting for him. If anyone here doesn't think they can do this, tell me now. No one will think less of you. You've been prisoners; you're beat up and exhausted."

Everyone stood where they were.

"Take a car," I told them. "We're going to Sky-High's main office. We've got more of these assholes to remove tonight."

"Booker and Zita called," Emily said, looking everyone over. "Apparently, their friends kept the HPD busy, but Mason's tower shut down almost the moment the rest of the team went inside."

"So, the whole second team is trapped?" Gabriel asked.

"I can't get hold of anyone there," Hannah said, trying her phone.

"They've trapped our people in Mason's tower?" one of the RCU agents said. "What do we do?

"Well, by god, we go get them back," Gabriel said, opening the car door.

"How?" Dale asked.

I looked around everyone. "We're going to do something extraordinarily stupid."

"Can I join in?" Nadia asked with a smile.

I thought for a second. "I'm going to need something to drive that's really big."

"Like a van?" Dale asked.

"No, more like *that*," I said, and pointed to several eighteen-wheelers in the warehouse car park and dangled a set of keys between my fingers.

# CHAPTER TWENTY-SIX

I'd never driven an eighteen-wheeler before, and after the initial difficulty of moving a vehicle so extraordinarily massive, I did a pretty good job. Or, at least, I didn't hit anything and managed to keep it from tipping over when going around corners.

Mason's tower loomed above and I spotted the SUV Emily had been driving parked up in front of it. There was a gentle slope from the road to the front of the tower, where the shutters had been closed. I stopped the truck and climbed out of the cab before running over to the shutters and looking for a way inside. Smoke poured out of me, but it found no entry apart from tiny holes, and it would take me ages to pour through and reform myself on the other side. And that was time I would be unable to defend myself.

"There's no one behind there," Nadia said from beside me, making me jump.

"You sure?" I asked, wrapping my knuckles against the metal shutters.

Nadia nodded.

I looked back at Dale and the others as they joined us. "Any other way in?" I asked.

"There's a loading bay at the back," Dale said.

"I know the codes," Nadia told everyone. "But they're going to expect us."

"What if they changed the codes?" Emily asked.

Hannah stepped forward, removing her jacket and tossing it into the open door of a nearby car. She changed before our eyes, moving from her usual self into her horned revenant form. She was nearly seven feet tall, with a two-foot-long midnight-blue horn jutting out of each temple.

Her skin was dark grey around her torso, while the palms of her huge hands were aqua blue. Her black eyes were like those of a shark, and when she smiled, you got to see the triangular saw-like teeth. Horned revenants were made for smashing. And Hannah was *exceptionally* good at that.

"We found a way in, then," I said, nodding to Hannah.

"Been wanting to smash something for a while," Hannah said, her voice now deep.

"What happens after that?" Dale asked.

"We find out," Nadia said, setting off in that direction without another word, Hannah quickly running after her to catch up.

Dale and Emily left with the two revenants, with Gabriel staying back. "You're going to drive that truck through there, aren't you?"

I nodded. "I figured you might like a distraction."

"Yes," Gabriel said. "And it's monstrously stupid."

"It is," I said enthusiastically. "I'm looking forward to seeing what happens."

Gabriel rolled his eyes.

"When you're in the lab, you need to find Dr Mitchell's work," I said. "Hopefully, we can find out *exactly* what she was working on, but destroy her work. It can't get out of here, no matter what it is."

"We sure she's not here?" Gabriel asked.

I nodded. "William couldn't lie, although he could be misinformed without knowing it. But while that might be the case, I'd still bet Callie isn't here and neither is Mason. I think one of them would have at least informed William that they'd be gone. Either way, Callie's research and results are conducted without any regard to morals or ethics. They need to be stopped."

"She needs to go before the Ancients," Gabriel said. "If she's been conducting experiments on humans to turn them into fiends, she will need to be judged accordingly. Not by humans. Mason too."

"We'll find them both," I told him. "First, we do the job we're here for."

"Be safe, my friend," he said.

"You too," I told him.

Gabriel ran off after everyone else, and I walked back toward the truck as a black Ferrari pulled up and Booker and Zita got out, and I waved them over toward the rest of the team.

I pulled on my Talon mask, climbed into the cab, and switched on the truck's engine, taking it away from the building down the block, until I was far enough away that I could build up speed. There were sirens in the distance, and while I didn't want to know what Booker and Zita had done to get the cops' attention, I also hoped that attention was going to stay elsewhere. I didn't want HPD, crooked or not, turning up to cause complications.

I gunned the huge engine inside the truck, and the rear wheels spun as it gained traction. I wasn't sure how fast trucks usually went, but even at only forty miles per hour, I was pretty sure I was going to cause significant damage to whatever it hit.

I planted my foot on the gas, and the truck continued to gain speed, practically launching up the curb onto the slope, storming toward Mason's Tower. I kept my foot planted as we hit the front entrance, and the world became one of overwhelming noise.

I'd turned to smoke a second before the truck had hit, but the momentary lack of the gas pedal being pushed had done little to stop the momentum of several tons of truck smashing into steel shutters. The shutters tore like paper, and the truck barrelled into the pristine foyer, destroying everything in its path as I drifted away from the chaos and re-formed behind a pillar at the far end of the large foyer.

The truck hit the reception area, destroying the granite, but the truck flipped onto its side, taking out the wall behind the reception in a cacophony of steel, stone, and wood all coming together. Shrapnel pinged around the foyer, destroying even more of the area. I moved around to the side of the foyer, the smell of burning rubber and oil combining with the dust to make a noxious atmosphere.

The lifts still worked, and they were far enough away from the ruination I'd caused for me to not worry about them breaking and leaving me stranded in the middle of a lift shaft.

I removed my daggers and pressed the button for Mason's office, the lift starting its upward climb. The doors opened just after the lift stopped, and I darted out, becoming smoke, but quickly realised there was no one there and re-formed myself. I looked around the empty reception area, half-expecting a dozen armed guards to drop out of the ceiling or something, but it was pretty clear nothing was going to happen, so I opened the door to Mason's office.

"I thought you'd have more guards," I said, removing my hooded mask and placing it on a nearby desk.

"You took your bloody time," Dan shouted from the far end of the office. He was sat in Mason's chair, his boots up on his desk. "You're a Talon? You kept that secret."

I nodded. "Was," I said. "Haven't been one in a long time, though. Not since my Guild were murdered in an ambush."

"Looks like we both kept big secrets," Dan said, but there was an edge of concern in his voice. "You know it never needed to be this way."

"You helped murder my friends," I said. "It was always going to end up being this way. How long have you been working against us?"

"About twenty years now," he said. "You want to know why?"

"Not really," I told him.

"Tough," he snapped. "When I heard that the Ravens were going to die, I asked them to spare you. Believe it or not, I did actually consider you a friend. They did as I asked, and then you vanished from sight to go hide somewhere, and I hoped you'd stay away. Give the people I work with time to do what they need to do. And the second it starts, you pop back up to get involved."

"They gave you the RCU," I said. "Was that your price?"

"Part of it, yes," Dan said. "New York was always going to have to be removed; the LA branch was just a happy coincidence. Callie needed more bodies, and seeing how I disliked many of the people working there, it was a good day to be me."

"You going to tell me who you're actually working for?" I asked.

"No," Dan said with a chuckle. "I'm definitely not doing that."

"So, all of this, all of this misery you've caused, was so you got a little bit more power?" I asked. "More wealth, more . . ." I waved my arms around the office.

"You've been a mercenary," he continued before I could say anything. "You've taken coin over people. You've taken coin over principles. At least I took the goddamn coin and have the principles to back it up."

"What? The principle to be an asshole?" I asked.

"The Ravens had to be killed," Dan said. "They *had* to be. Someone in your precious Guild discovered something they shouldn't have, and so there was a scorched-earth policy. I don't even know what that information was. I just get told to arrange the deaths of people, and I do my job."

"Like a good little assassin," I said. "You helped murder my friends. That's the crux of why I'm going to kill you."

"Do you ever hear yourself?" Dan asked, a chuckle in his voice. "You sound like you're the arbiter of life and death. The one person who gets to decide if I live or die. Fuck you. You don't get to decide shit."

"Dan, you don't really know much about me," I said. "You didn't know that I was a Talon for the Ravens, you didn't know that I've killed people bigger and better than you, you didn't know my history. We *were* friends, Dan, but it wasn't like we were besties talking about our hopes and dreams. When I walk away from your corpse—and I will be the one walking away—I'll feel disappointment more than anything else. You traded morals and ethics for cash and hurting people to get more cash. How many people here were innocent?"

"No one is innocent," Dan snapped.

"Oh, grow up," I said. "How many, Dan? How many people did nothing to deserve whatever monstrous shit you did to them?"

"We got them from prisons," Dan said. "Mason had a deal with a few. We get prisoners; they get paid. The prisoners were all long-term criminals, violent thugs who didn't deserve to be allowed to breathe. Who should have been put down when they were arrested!"

"So, you tortured them to death?" I asked. "You had Dr Mitchell experiment on them for profit. Not sure that's any better than being a violent thug."

"Yet you're going to kill me, so who has the moral high ground here?"

"I don't care," I said. "The moral high ground doesn't interest me, Dan. Don't you get it? You're going to die because you betrayed me, my friends, and hurt people I cared about. I'm not interested in a philosophical debate about morals; I care about putting your head through that wall."

"You want to fight me?" Dan shouted, rage on his face, spittle flying out of his mouth. "I'm an arcane revenant. You can't do a *goddamned* thing to me."

"I think you'll find I can," I told him.

"Your Guild thought the same thing," Dan said, shrugging off his jacket and making a big deal of removing his cufflinks and rolling up his shirtsleeves. "Guess how well that worked for them."

I took a step toward Dan as I thought back to that horrific day, of waking up at the bottom of a hill, of having to scale it with one badly damaged hand, drenched in blood. I thought back to seeing the bodies. I couldn't be sure it was everyone; I was sucked back into the embers before I could check, my body giving out on me.

"You know, I stuck the knife in Isaac myself," Dan said. "I figured it wouldn't be the same coming from someone who didn't know him. It was so easy, too. Like slicing through butter."

I sheathed my daggers and ran toward Dan, tendrils of smoke billowing out before me, wrapping around him. He smiled and grabbed one, and an electrical surge flooded back into me, throwing me back, my smoke vanishing.

"Arcane revenant," Dan said smugly, as if I might have forgotten somehow. "We're each unique, a bit like riftborn themselves. You ever met an arcane that can use a riftborn's power against them before?"

I blinked, pushed the pain aside, and got back to my feet, rolling my shoulders, which ached. "Lucky you," I said. "You're unique."

"I always wanted to know if I was better than you," Dan said. "You got to be a Guild member and I never did, people liked you, people looked up to you. I looked up to you. But I always wondered who was better. I guess we're going to find out."

I drew my H&K and shot him in the chest. I kept firing as I walked toward him, until the gun was empty, and I replaced it in my holster. The bullets weren't rift-tempered, and neither was the gun, so it wouldn't kill him, but I was pretty sure it hurt like hell.

Purple rift-power flooded over Dan's body as it sought to heal itself as quickly as possible. I drew a dagger as Dan rolled to the side and tried to get back to his feet.

"This isn't fair," he shouted at me, spitting up blood as he fell to the ground.

I shrugged, and stabbed him in the back, pulling him upright and stabbing him twice more. The rift-tempered blade hissed as it left wounds that would almost certainly be fatal should Dan be left alone. I dragged a badly bleeding Dan to the door that led to Mason's museum of stuff that didn't belong to him. I opened the door, pulling Dan inside, and closed it behind me.

I left Dan on the ground and walked over to where the Raven medallion sat, inside its glass case, amongst a hundred other artefacts that Mason probably had no business owning. I smashed the glass with the butt of my dagger and removed the medallion. I didn't know who it once belonged to; I just knew it wasn't Mason's.

"Do you know who you killed for this?" I asked Dan, who spat blood onto the floor.

"You didn't fight fair," he said, indigently. "I knew you were a killer, but you always fought fairly."

"Fight fair?" I asked. "We're not *children*. You ambushed and murdered my friends; it's not my fault you were so blinded by your need to be better to get one over on me that you ignored the fact that I just wanted to kill you. There's no such thing as fair when it comes to battle. There's winning or being dead, and you never were much of a winner."

Dan placed a bloody hand on a table and hauled himself to his feet, making unpleasant noises as he did. I watched with a sort of detached interest. There was no way he was going to survive the night, and I wasn't into torturing people, but I had to admit a level of being impressed that he hadn't simply curled into a ball and died.

"I will die on my feet," Dan said, his tone now hard and determined.

I looked down at the bloody dagger in my hand, and then over at Dan again, before pocketing the medallion. "Sure," I said, happy to oblige.

"Send me to the rift," Dan said.

I showed him the blue-tinted blade. "Nope," I said, and darted forward, plunging the blade into his chest.

Dan screamed in pain and I twisted the blade until he began to whimper. Only then did I drive my second blade up into his throat, puncturing his brain. I twisted the dagger, took a step to the side, and pulled it free, avoiding the gushing blood and falling body of Dan.

"That was for Isaac," I told him. "You deserved a lot worse." I stepped over the body and out of Mason's museum to find Ji-hyun sat on Mason's desk.

"He dead?" she asked calmly as she cleaned a bloody knife.

I nodded. "How about downstairs?"

"A few dozen guards, nothing major," she said. "We grabbed the surviving prisoners."

"Surviving?" I asked, not sure I wanted to know the answer but knowing I had to find out.

"Some," she said. "Found four of the RCU agents and a few human survivors. Ten in all. Dr Mitchell had over two dozen people down there; most of her experiments were done on people who were originally human, trying to change them."

"Damn it," I said.

"Hannah downloaded a lot of intel from the servers," Ji-hyun told me. "Hopefully, we'll get answers to pinpoint Dr Mitchell's exact location."

Ji-hyun passed me my Talon mask.

"Thanks," I said.

"Well, I think they'll know we're coming," Ji-hyun said. "We made quite the statement here. But I'm thinking that we need to make sure." Blue fire ignited over Ji-hyun's hands. She walked past me into the museum, and I heard the crackling of flames as she ignited everything she could. She left the room, flames flickering out of the doorway behind her, trailing in her wake as she walked through Mason's office toward me as I stood next to the office door.

The flames incinerated Mason's desk, and by the time Ji-hyun reached me, the office was on its way to becoming an inferno.

The fire alarms went off, and sprinklers started to try and put out the fire, but it would be a losing battle. I'd seen Ji-hyun's fire burn through metal. I left with her, taking the stairs down, as the lifts had shut down the second the fire alarms went off.

We reached the outside just as the glass on Mason's office was burned through and flames began to lick the outside walls of the building. It wouldn't move to other floors; it would stay exactly where Ji-hyun wanted it to stay, behaving like normal fire but not being normal fire. Ji-hyun clicked her fingers and the fire extinguished immediately.

"Now, that's a statement," Ji-hyun said.

# CHAPTER TWENTY-SEVEN

Ji-hyun and I ran a few blocks away from Mason's tower before being picked up by Booker and Zita, who were driving around in a large Mercedes SUV.

"Thanks for the lift," I said, climbing into the back of the vehicle, with Ji-hyun beside me.

"We've had a long night," Booker said from the front passenger seat. "I now owe a lot of powerful people some favours."

"Whatever you need, Booker," I said, "I'll be there to help."

"I will take you up on that one day," Booker said. "Just don't get killed before we get to that point."

Zita drove us to their underground casino building and parked around the rear, where the rest of the group were already waiting. "Figured the church might not be safe," Gabriel said as I got out.

"You okay?" I asked him.

Gabriel nodded.

"Anyone hurt in the attack?" I asked. "On our side."

"Bill got a nasty cut to his temple," Gabriel said. "Dale took a round to the chest, but he was wearing a vest, so he's mostly bruised. A few of the others have scrapes and bruises, but it looks like most of Mason's staff were absent."

"We closed the casino floor for the night," Booker said. "We've put Isaac in our office."

"What about those who we got out of Mitchell's lab?" I asked.

"Bill and Gordon sent everyone to the same hotel you were staying in," Booker said.

"They're safe; Isaac might not have mentioned," Gabriel said, "but we used the hotel as a sort of halfway point for the newly returned."

"Sounds like we owe you a lot, then," I said.

"The amount climbs ever higher," Booker said with a smile.

We all entered the building and found space on the casino floor to sit down and relax for a few moments. I sat next to Dale and Emily, both of whom looked exhausted.

"Glad you made it back okay," Dale said.

Ji-hyun went to grab food.

"Dan?" Emily asked.

"He won't be bothering anyone again," I said.

"Your friend is quite the fighter," she said to me.

"Ji-hyun was a Talon too," I said. "She walked away from the life about a century ago."

"She's as old as you?" Emily asked.

I shook my head and took a seat next to Gabriel. "Not even close."

"Still don't know who's working with Mason and co, though," Emily said.

"A problem for tomorrow," I said.

"They think I've absconded," Emily said. "My boss phoned. He was told I'd lost the tail that had been put on me; his response was to ask why there was one on me. No one had a good answer for that. He told me to help you however I can but that there'd be no backup. Can't risk it."

"So, everything you just did was all by the book?" I asked her.

"Retroactively," she said. "I think officially we were never there and it never happened. That seems like the safest way forward."

I nodded. "My lips are sealed," I told her. "I'm going to see Isaac."

"You sure you're up to it?" Gabriel asked. "Hannah is combing the information we took from Dr Mitchell, trying to figure out where she's gone. We can leave at a moment's notice."

"I promised," I said by way of explanation.

"And if it goes wrong, you're out of commission for a day, maybe longer," Gabriel said. "Isaac will understand. I'm pretty sure that Mason is going to want vengeance for the fact that we just killed his remaining staff, stole his research, burned down his office, and . . ."

I removed the medallion from my pocket. "Took back what wasn't his."

"Got the bastards," Hannah exclaimed. "Mason and Dr Mitchell went to Baffin Island."

"That's a big place," I said.

"There's a research station in the northeast," Hannah told me. "Well, it's more of a research village. It's big enough for a few hundred people. I'm working on getting a satellite image of the place, but it's going to take me a while. The old codes we used as RCU aren't something I want to use again unless I need to."

"Isaac's awake," someone shouted.

"Wait, what?" I asked, suddenly awake and looking around as Ruby ran into the room, tears in her eyes.

"He wants to talk to you," Ruby said to me. "He says it's urgent."

I practically sprinted through the casino, taking the stairs two at a time, and bursting through the office door to find Isaac lying in a hospital bed, hooked up to things monitoring his vitals.

"Hey," Isaac said. "You look tired. Miss me?"

"No," I said, walking over and hugging him. "We managed just fine without. Honestly, I think you'd have just made it all worse."

Isaac laughed, coughed, and took a drink of water. "You told my wife you could take me into your embers and you could heal me, give me time with my family."

"I did," I said.

"You left out a few bits of that story," he said.

"I did," I admitted.

"We both know if I come into the embers with you, you're going to be useless for a while. This is more important."

"I know," I said. "But . . . damn it, Isaac, you're my friend, and I can help."

"Dan stabbed me with a tempered-blade," Isaac said. "You take me into your embers, you take on what was done."

I nodded.

"You can remove the poison," Isaac said. "And then what? What is the safest option? For you, I mean."

"I open a tear into the rift, and you walk through," I said. "It's still exhausting, and I will have to spend a few days in the embers to heal, but it's more likely that both of us would be okay. Going in, taking your poison and bringing you back here . . . it's dangerous. For both of us.

"That's what we'll do, then," Isaac said. "I'm not going to die today. I can spend time with my wife, see my children."

"But I can try," I said.

"No, Lucas," Isaac said, sounding more like his old self. "I don't want you to. Ruby wouldn't want you to. Damn it, man, you don't have to save everyone. It's not your job."

I sat there with my mouth open, unable to formulate the words I wanted to say.

"If I'm still here in a few days when this is done, we'll talk about taking me into the rift," Isaac said. "In the meantime, I'm going to go with my wife and see my children."

"You're okay to travel?" I asked.

"Booker has a van we can fit all of this in," Isaac said. "We're going to Ruby's sisters; I can see my family, Isaac. It's what I want. That rift-tempered blade didn't kill me; Dan knew what he was doing. He wanted me to suffer."

"He's really dead, if that helps," I told him.

"It really does," Isaac said with a smile.

"I'll come find you in a few days, then," I said.

"If I go to the rift, will I remember my family?" Isaac asked.

I nodded.

"I love her, Lucas. So goddamned much," Isaac said with tears in his eyes. "The kids, too. How the hell am I going to tell my kids what happened?"

"I don't know," I said. "But most people don't get a few days to spend with them. They'll remember that more than anything else you do."

"That's what's important," Isaac said with a nod. "Can I ask you something I've always wanted to know?"

"Sure," I said.

"The Guilds," he said. "Why the birds?"

"That's it?" I asked with a laugh. "Your big question is why the Guilds are named after birds?"

"Yeah," he said, elbowing me in the ribs, as I wouldn't stop laughing. "Don't be a dick."

"Sorry, but it's not an interesting story," I told him. "You sure you want to know?"

Isaac nodded.

"Okay, thousands of years ago," I began, "Neb was one of the first rulers of Inaxia, who became Ancients over time."

"The woman who trained you to be a Talon," Isaac said. "See, I remember stuff."

"That's her, yes," I said. "Anyway, they couldn't agree on what to call the Guilds. They knew they needed something; they needed a group who would keep the balance of power from ever going in one Ancient's favour or one species' favour. They tried naming them after weapons, and that didn't go down well, because according to Neb, no one wanted to be a shield when someone else was a sword. Anyway, they tried all of this stuff and it just wasn't getting anyone anywhere. It lasted weeks, and no one budged. In the end, Neb said, *Right, my Guild is going to be the Ravens.* No one disagreed. Then everyone started to pick the names of birds of prey. Falcon, Owl, Eagle, et cetera, each Ancient thinking his bird was the ultimate predator. No one thinking about the Ravens. No one giving the idea of having a smart bird a second thought."

"Are you serious?" Isaac asked, disbelieving.

I nodded. "I am. And it really is as stupid as that. Sometimes, when you get a bunch of powerful people and try to get them to agree to something, you need to give them a gentle push in the right direction. So Neb said, anyway. I guess she would know."

"That was a lot less exciting than I'd expected it to be," he said. "I thought it was going to be some huge secret laid bare."

"Sorry," I said with a shrug.

"Do you like being a Raven?" He asked me.

"I do," I said immediately. "Or I did. I guess it's up to me to re-create the Guild now, being the last and all. I need the medallions first, though. Or at least I need to make new ones. Although I'm not even sure how to do that. I'm sorry I wasn't part of your life while you got married. I will always regret that. I wish I'd been there for you, and I'm sorry I wasn't."

"You don't need to be," Isaac said. "I'm just glad that you're okay— mentally and physically. I'm glad that you've buried your demons, at least for the time being. Heaven knows, we all get them sooner or later."

"I've fought battles almost my entire life," I said, "but most of the time as a mercenary, fighting for a cause but not its people, or fighting for coin and nothing else. I never knew just how hard it was to lose so much when you care about the people you're fighting alongside. I mean really care. Even when I was fighting for Carthage and I was killed and came back, everyone was dead. It had been so long since the war that I mourned them as one group. Being alongside the Guild, and surviving after so long of not facing defeat like that, it shook me up more than I'd ever wanted to admit."

"I'm glad you came through the other side," Isaac said.

"Me too," I told him, feeling somewhat relaxed now that I was able to talk about it with him.

"Okay, go end this," Isaac said. "I'll see you in a few days."

"In a few days," I told him. "Don't do anything stupid until then."

"Same to you, Lucas," Isaac said with a smile. "Same to you."

I left my friend alone, to find Ruby waiting outside. "You didn't tell me the toll it would take on you," she said tearfully.

"I know," I said. "I wasn't sure how to. I *needed* to help."

"We have a few days together," she said. "A few days as a family."

"I'm glad," I told her. "It was a pleasure to meet you."

"You too," she told me.

I left them alone and returned to the casino floor, where I answered a million questions all at once about Isaac and his condition.

When I was done and several of the group had gone to see Isaac and say their goodbyes before he left with Ruby, I found myself sat alone in the corner of the casino.

Nadia walked over to me. "I'm coming with you," she said.

"I never said I was going anywhere," I told her.

"I know," Nadia said. "But when you do, I'm coming with you. My chains are linked to you now. Where you go, I go."

She sat down beside me and picked up a bag from the floor, removed a ball of crochet from inside it, and set about continuing something that looked like the world's longest scarf. Chained revenants are full of surprises.

A few hours later, I stood outside of the casino as Isaac's bed was wheeled into an ambulance, with Ruby sat alongside him. They both waved to the group who saw them off, but as the ambulance pulled away, I stayed outside and watched it disappear over the distance. It felt like I'd been kicked in the gut. My friend was going away to die; nothing I could do about that. But he was going to give his family hopefully some peace before he did. That meant a lot. I just had to hope that he could hold out for a few more days before I could peacefully see him off to the rift. He deserved that.

"Ruby and his kids will want for nothing," Gabriel said. "I'll make sure of that."

"You're a good man, Gabriel," I said. "A better man than someone like me deserves as a friend."

"Nonsense," Gabriel snapped.

"Gabriel, I've spent a long time balancing those scales back to my favour," I said. "Making sure I did good things to counteract the bad. I had finally got it to a place where I felt balanced when the Ravens were killed. And then I spent a long time just tipping those scales in one direction."

"You did a lot of good today," Gabriel said.

"I know," I said. "But what comes next is going to tip the scales so badly, I'm not sure there's a way back."

"Meaning what?" Gabriel asked.

"I'm going to kill every single fucker in that northern outpost. I'm going to end this, Gabriel."

"You know, some people are put on this Earth to help by caring for people, by showing kindness," Gabriel said. "And some are put on this earth to eradicate evil."

"That's not a very cleric thing to say," I said.

"Yes, well, it's true," Gabriel said with a dismissive wave of his hand. "You were brought here to be a warrior. To remove the evil and infected parts of this world. Neb trained you to do it, trained you to be a force for good, even if it means doing bad. I think the scales have been in your favour for a long time. I just think they measure differently to others."

"You think me killing people tips them in my favour?" I asked with a laugh.

"No," Gabriel said, serious. "I think you removing those who would prey on the weak and innocent, who would hurt people, that is what tips them in your favour. Sometimes, that means you have to have blood on your hands. Sometimes a lot of blood. You are one of my oldest friends, Lucas, and I have never seen you act in a way that betrays who you are. Even when you were lost and didn't know who you were, there was that spark of good inside of you. It's always there, Lucas. I've seen killers, I've seen murderers; they don't have it. You're not like them."

I stared at Gabriel for several seconds. "Thank you."

"As a cleric, I will tell you that whatever you need to make the world a better place, it's yours," he said. "But as an ex-warrior, I'll tell you to eradicate them. They are a stain on this world and the rift."

"Let's go get ready," I said. "I have a feeling that I won't be going as alone on this trip as I'd originally planned. Nadia already told me she's accompanying me."

"She's already told everyone," he said. "She also told everyone they weren't allowed to go."

"She's right," I said as we walked back into the casino.

"People won't like that," Gabriel said, opening the shelter.

"I know," I replied. "But this isn't like the Mason tower. This isn't to save people or gather intel. This is an extermination. That's something I know how to do."

"And then what?" Gabriel asked after he'd shut the shelter entrance with a clang.

"And then?" I asked with a shrug. "I'll figure that out when I'm done."

# CHAPTER TWENTY-EIGHT

When Gabriel and I reached the casino floor again, everyone had reconvened.

"I managed to crack the data that I took from Mason's tower," Hannah said. "Emails between several of Dr Mitchell's associates. They thought they'd deleted them. They were wrong."

"Gloat later," Emily said. "Where are they?"

"North-east Baffin Island, just like I thought," Hannah said, with no indication that Emily's words had irritated her. "A place that used to be called Sam Ford Fjord. There's snow, mountains, the ocean, and a village with its own runway. There's a lot more in there, so I'm still going through it all."

"How are we meant to get to the middle of nowhere?" Emily asked from the corner of the room.

"How are you meant to land a plane in an area crawling with enemies?" Bill asked, sporting a rather unflattering bandage across the top of his forehead.

"With difficulty," George said, as he sat beside his husband, drinking something warm, judging from the steam coming up from it.

"I assume there's no direct flights," Gabriel said.

"There's nothing there," Hannah said. "You'd need a helicopter to fly there."

"Hannah, you're grinning," I said. "Do we have a helicopter?"

"The RCU does, yes," Hannah said. "And an airplane."

"And hands up if you know how to fly either one," I said.

Gabriel and Bill put their hands up.

"Seriously?" I asked both.

"Learned a few years ago," Gabriel said.

"Learned in Vietnam," Bill said, and everyone turned to look at Bill.

"You were turned into a revenant in the Vietnam War?" Gabriel asked him.

"1972," Bill said. "I flew a Huey, we crashed, I died, I came back. I sort of kept up with the changes in flying over the years. I prefer helicopters, but I can fly both."

"Okay, so, we have a pilot," I said. "If you're willing."

"I am," Bill said.

"Okay, but isn't the RCU under Dan's order?" I asked. "I know he's dead, but I assume the people he was working with won't let us take an airplane."

"Good job they're mostly dead too," Hannah said. "I've already arranged for the jet to be ready. We're good to go."

"I'll come along to help," Gabriel said. "I know you said you were going alone on this one, but you're not."

George looked up at his husband and reached out to hold his hand, squeezing it slightly. "Where you go, I go," he said.

"Not this time," Bill said, kissing George on the lips. "You'll have to wait for me."

"I am not incapable of taking care of myself," George said, but the smile on his face was one that said *Just try and argue with me.*

When everyone started to look between themselves, I figured there was more going on. "Okay, what?" I asked.

"You know I said I've cracked the intel we got from the tower?" Hannah said. "Well, I found something."

"Something bad?" I asked, knowing that it couldn't possibly be anything else.

"I know why they're on that island," Hannah said. "I spoke to Ji-Hyun and Emily, and we all agreed that it's something you need to know, but it's a concern to me about how you might take the news."

I took a seat opposite Hannah and crossed my arms. "What is it?"

"The Ravens weren't all killed," Hannah said almost tentatively, as if I might fly into a rage and start throwing things around.

"What?"

"Four survived," Hannah said. "They were taken to a facility that was called Netley Asylum."

Everyone stared at me. "Dr Mitchell experimented on my friends in that place?"

Hannah nodded. "There's more." Hannah turned her laptop around to show me an open file. It was well over a hundred pages long and called Caladrius.

"They named it after a bird that cures the sick?" I asked. "Any chance someone has read all of this, so I don't have to?"

"They've been experimenting with a serum for a number of decades," Emily said, taking a seat next to Hannah. "Trying to find a way to give the powers of the riftborn and revenant to humans without dying. They were unsuccessful. They took plasma, marrow, and DNA of riftborn and revenants, and spliced it into humans. There's a lot of data in that file that tells us about 250 people they got from prisons and the homeless. All of them died. Either the body wholly gave up immediately, or parts of the body were . . . ejected into what they assume is the rift, but it could well be an embers."

"Neither way sounds all that nice," I said.

"No, it really doesn't," Emily said. "They couldn't figure out why their methods weren't working. They tried splicing the formula with animals, and nothing, and then they tried using fiend DNA and splicing that with the riftborn and revenant serum."

"Success," Hannah said with a wave of her hands. "Although now it somehow gets worse."

"What did the serum actually do?" I asked.

"According to the notes, it was meant to give humans the powers of a revenant or riftborn," Emily said. "It didn't at first because it killed everyone, and then when they spliced in the fiend DNA, it turned them into inhuman monsters and then killed them."

"Enter Belarus," Hannah said. "1996."

"What happened? I was in Russia in '96," I said. "There was a revenant who thought it was fun to murder people. I was out in the field for almost the whole year, and I didn't hear anything about Belarus."

"Well, in '96 there was a fiend in Belarus," Emily said. "It was an elder."

"Wait, what?" I asked, finding the world *elder* in the file and going straight there.

"It was hushed up at the insistence of one of the Ancients," Hannah said. "Doesn't say which, but the body was handed over to Mitchell's predecessor." Hannah took the laptop back, clicked a few things and then passed it back to me. "Who looks identical to Callie Mitchell."

I stared at the photo of Dr Callie Mitchell. She wore a Russian uniform, and the photo was apparently taken in 1941, the name on the photo said Valentina Ermilova.

"She's been doing this a long time," I said.

"Centuries," Meredith said. "By my reckoning. She's a riftborn, I think."

"Okay, so, what happened after '96?" I asked.

"The fiend went to Mitchell, and she used the genetic template to create a new serum," Meredith said. "One that worked. At least for a while. It turns humans into those human/fiend hybrids we've seen. Originally, it turned them into super powerful elder-fiend hybrids, but Mitchell was almost killed by one, so she knew she had to tone down the power. That's what she's been working on."

"Why does she want to give humans this power?" I asked.

"She wants an army," Hannah said. "No idea why, something to do with a Project Blessed."

"What the hell is Project Blessed?" I asked.

Hannah shrugged. "There's nothing more on it. Just the name and the idea to create an army. I wonder if she's been working on it for so long that there's no digital footprint of the idea. She might have notes about it, or she might have put it on a flash drive and taken it with her, but that's all we know about it."

"So, what is Mason's angle?" I asked.

"Mason wants to sell the serum to everyone," Hannah said. "There's a ton of information about it. He wants to give the serum to humans, security, the military, the police. Imagine having all of those people taking this serum. They're meeting someone in Canada to discuss the deal. It looks like Callie has agreed to take several people to this meeting to show them the benefits of this serum."

"And the serum itself?" I asked.

"No idea where it is; a few samples will be with them, I imagine," Hannah said. "But from Callie's notes, I think there are two serums. One given to Mason for use, and a second, more potent one. Nothing about what that's being used for. We know that the first one unravels people, but the second doesn't seem to have similar issues attached."

"None of this sounds good," I said.

"It's not even slightly," Emily said. "They've made a serum to allow a group of people to just hulk out and turn into monsters."

"Until they got it working, they used prisoners to test it," Hannah said. "The idea appears to be that they want to inject the subject with this shit, drop them behind enemy lines, and watch the fireworks and dead bodies mount. That's what Mason is involved for. His money is buying that serum, but the second, more potent version, there's no information on it, but even more, there's nothing to suggest that Mason has any clue it exists."

"Callie is using Mason's money to create a better version of a serum he's paid her to make," I said.

"The weaker serum is a problem in itself," Emily said. "We need to stop this deal or at least find out who it was sold to."

None of what they'd told me sounded like something that I wanted to be accessible to anyone, let alone governments and militaries. "Okay, so, how much can you tell me about this fjord and how to infiltrate it?"

"I did some more checking," Hannah said. "It's now called Kangiqtua-luk Uqquqti, and was a popular destination with climbers before Mason essentially made a home there. There's an Inuit settlement by the name of Pond Inlet a few hundred kilometres from there."

Hannah took the laptop back, clicked a few things and showed me the screen again. This time it contained satellite photos. "Mason's people have built a sizeable structure there."

There was one large building and a dozen smaller that surrounded it. There were gates, fences, several guard towers, and it was going to be tough to get in in any way except climbing up the almost-sheer cliff face that sat close to one side. There was a ramp that went down to the water, and a small dock had been made. A large yacht was anchored there. "When were these taken?"

"Two hours ago," Hannah said. "I have friends who I now owe an exceptionally large favour to."

"Boat is out," I said. "They'd see us coming for miles. Can't land there on that airstrip. What about Pond Inlet?"

"There's an airstrip there," Hannah said. "But you'd have to rent snow-mobiles and go hundreds of kilometres through the harshest of condi-tions. Maybe five or six hours, depending on speed."

"I'll manage," I said. "Whoever else is coming can stay at the settle-ment with the plane. Can you arrange snowmobiles for us? Let's say four, just in case."

"A lot of people there work for the Canadian government," Hannah said. "Some people there owe the RCU. I can get it sorted. You're going to need someone who knows the area, too. You can't just get on a snowmo-bile and go there without almost dying."

"Then we'll need a guide," I said.

"I'll go get everything sorted I need to," Hannah said, and stood to leave.

I went back to where I'd been sitting before Ruby had entered, and found my Talon mask on the floor. I picked it up, placing it on the chair, and went to get ready to go end the misery that Mason, Callie, and Dan had started.

# CHAPTER TWENTY-NINE

The plane was fuelled and ready for take-off when we arrived, and while there were considerably more of us going than I'd expected there to be, the jet was big enough to seat us all comfortably. Gabriel and Bill went up to the cockpit to fly the thing, while George sat in the back.

There were warm clothes on board, and everyone grabbed what they needed.

Ji-hyun sat opposite me and had gone to sleep the second the plane had taken off. A trick she'd always been able to do, and frankly something that I was quite envious of. I found a small library at the rear of the jet, picked up a book by an author I hadn't read before, and settled in for the several hours of flying. The book, as it turned out, was pretty good. A fantasy story about gangsters, and I'd finished it well before we were due to land, picking up a second—this one about a siege and a blood cult—and settled in to get through that one, too.

I hadn't even made it halfway when the announcement of landing sounded throughout the cabin.

The jet landed with an unpleasant bump and Ji-hyun woke up, looking around.

"Nice dreams?" I asked her.

"No," she said, without elaborating. I'd known Ji-hyun a long time, and she'd had nightmares about her childhood in Korea for a lot of it. I knew bits and pieces about what happened to her—about her family being murdered, and her being the only survivor. She wasn't someone you pressed for further information unless you wanted to have her thumb pressed into your windpipe.

The jet came to a stop and Gabriel entered the cabin, opening the door and letting in the frigid air from outside. I was glad that I'd worn one of the thick, black coats that had been provided, along with a hat, trousers, and boots. Even with several layers of clothes, I still felt the cold.

We climbed down the steps to the tarmac and were met by a large Inuit man in a huge dark grey coat that would have fit me and Ji-hyun without any problems. "I'm your guide," he said.

"Lucas," I told him, shaking his hand.

"Peter Irniq," he said.

"You human?" I asked after he'd met everyone, and we walked away to the control tower and large building beside it.

Peter nodded. "I hear you're after Mason and his people."

It was my turn to nod. "He's a danger to everyone."

"People used to come here on their way to Kangiqtualuk Uqquqti," he said, opening the door to a rush of warm air and motioning for us all to get inside to the waiting area beyond.

"What happened?" Ji-hyun asked.

"Mason arrived and the people weren't allowed there anymore," Peter said, closing the door and pulling back his hood.

I would have guessed that Peter was in his forties, although I have a hard time guessing human ages. He was clean-shaven and had long dark hair that was tied back, although some of it still spilled over his ears.

"We've got four snowmobiles," Peter said. "They're pretty high-spec and will go about a hundred and fifty miles per hour if you push it."

"Sounds like fun," Nadia said from the corner of the room.

"Don't push them," Peter warned. "You stay behind me, and you go where I go. I've lived here my whole life, and it's still dangerous out there. You go too fast too quick and you hit something you didn't see, you're going to get hurt. Hurt people out there do not fare well. The weather is harsh, but the bears are just as deadly if they get close."

"Bears?" George enquired.

"Polar bears," Peter said.

"Everyone understand the plan?" I asked, wanting to steer the conversation away from the danger of polar bears.

"We stay here," Gabriel said. "It's going to be a long journey."

"Five hours to get there if we're lucky," Peter said. "Once there, we're going to want to find shelter."

"Once the research outpost they've created is under our control, we'll use it for the night," I said.

"Come back tomorrow morning," Ji-hyun said.

"You've got me for three days," Peter said. "There's a hunter's spot between here and there, about two hours in. We can stop, rest, warm up and head out again."

"Can't we just go straight there?" Nadia asked.

"I'll need food and water," Peter said. "We can't be stopping for toilet breaks on the way there, so we're going to have to stop somewhere."

"You do this a lot?" I asked.

"In winter?" Peter asked. "No, because it's stupid. I understand that this is important and that lives are on the line, but it's still reckless and dangerous to do this."

"I understand," I said. "We still have to do it."

"I'll make sure everything is ready, and once you're prepared, we'll head out. If at any point I think it's too dangerous to continue, we don't. That's the deal I made and the deal I'm sticking to. Human or not, you don't want to be out there in the middle of nowhere if a storm hits. We find shelter and you find another way."

"Agreed," Ji-hyun said before anyone else could speak.

George and Bill remained behind, waving us off as we loaded up any weapons and gear we'd need onto the snowmobiles and set off. It didn't take long for the town to vanish behind us, and I quickly understood why this place was so dangerous. There was a mountain range in the distance, but there was also a second, smaller one in the opposite direction further away. Actually finding your bearings would be next to impossible if you got lost out there, especially if a storm hit.

While we followed Peter on the snowmobiles I had very little concept of time. I had a watch on, and there was a digital clock on the snowmobile, but it kept getting frosted over, and I didn't want to keep removing my hand from the handlebars while in conditions I wasn't used to being in. I might have walked over the Alps, but that was walking. If Hannibal had used snowmobiles over the Alps, I think the war would have been a whole lot different.

We'd been given small communication devices to stay in contact with one another, but apart from Nadia shouting *Wheeeeeeeeeeee* every few minutes until Ji-hyun told her to either stop or be buried out there, no one said much of anything.

"We're stopping up ahead," Peter said, moving slightly to the right and continuing on until we reached a large cabin.

We all stopped and waited while Peter made sure that the cabin had heat before we entered. The cabin was essentially two rooms, one large room and a smaller bathroom. The larger room had a bunk bed in one corner, a table in the middle next to a sink and small stove, and that was it.

I felt the heat come up through the floor. "This is the best place ever," I said.

"It was used by scientists and people coming to see the cliffs," Peter said, filling the kettle with water and boiling it.

"Who keeps the water fresh and power on?" Ji-hyun asked.

"Me," Peter said. "Or, rather, I'm one of three who come up here once a week to make sure it's all secure and there's enough supplies, water, et cetera. There are still scientific experiments being run here; there's another hut about two hundred metres north that's measuring something to do with the ice and underground nutrients. There hasn't been anyone there for a few months now, but we still go and make sure it's not overrun by bears."

"Bears overrun cabins?" Nadia asked, looking out of the window at the vastness beyond.

Everyone turned to look out of the nearest window.

"They'd get in if food was there," Peter said. "It's why everything here is in tins and why the door is reinforced steel. They don't usually bother us unless they're hungry or sick."

"How far to Mason's settlement?" I asked.

"About the same distance as from town to here," Peter said, pouring four mugs of coffee and putting sugar in each.

"I don't take sugar," Nadia said as Peter passed her a mug.

"You need something sweet," he said.

Nadia shrugged and drank the still-far-too-hot coffee in one long gulp. "Nice," she said, the skin around her mouth now a little red.

Peter looked back at Ji-hyun and me.

"You get used to it," I said.

"He's lying," Ji-hyun said, blowing on her coffee. "You never do."

We drank our drinks, used the facilities we needed to use, and returned to our snowmobiles.

Peter raised his hand for everyone to wait and pointed ahead. I followed his arm, not seeing what I was meant to be concerned about, and then the polar bear moved, along with the small cub beside it.

"Is this a problem?" Ji-hyun asked over the comm.

"No," Peter said. "Not yet."

"Cute bear," Nadia said. "I want to pet it."

I looked back at Nadia, who had a beaming smile. "You know it would kill you?"

Nadia appeared to be considering it for a moment. "I guess," she said eventually. Her chains jangled as they wrapped around her body, and I wondered if they helped keep her warm.

We set off again, making a large circle around the bears, the mother of whom was watching us every time I looked over. I wasn't concerned that they'd be able to kill us or even do any real damage except to Peter, and we wouldn't let that happen, but that didn't mean I wanted to hurt her or her cub just for doing what came naturally.

Soon, we were back in the never-ending void of snow. It was beginning to get dark as Peter's voice came over the comms: "It's about half a kilometre ahead, down a hill," he said, slowing up and pulling the snowmobile over to a ridge, where we all followed.

The darkness happened all at once. One minute it was light and then it was dark. It didn't feel like there'd been any gradually getting darker; it was just changed like someone flicking a switch.

Nadia, Ji-hyun, and I followed Peter to the ridge, looking down at the large compound ahead. I removed a pair of binoculars from my pack and set about looking for a good entrance.

At the front were two guards, next to a checkpoint. Forty-foot-high chain-linked, barbwire-topped fencing encompassed the entire camp, with two high guard posts, one near the entrance and one further in. There were only half a dozen buildings: a large warehouse-like structure at the far edge of the compound, and five smaller albeit identical-looking buildings between the compound entrance and the larger building. Guards walked around the camp, occasionally going into one or other of the buildings, and two more guards remained outside of the larger structure.

"That's a lot of firepower," Nadia said, using her fingers to create circles and holding them up to her eyes.

"You want these?" I asked her, motioning to the binoculars, which she took.

"Is she . . ." Ji-hyun asked, leaving the last word unsaid.

"I think she's been accessing the rift," I said.

"Does that make them . . ." Peter didn't finish the sentence but gesticulated toward Nadia.

"I'm not crazy," Nadia said, passing me the binoculars back. "When we reach a point where things can go in wildly different timelines, the rift makes me see dozens of different timelines, makes my head jumbled. I have to tune them out, pick the one with the highest probability. In dozens of those timelines, I'm already holding binoculars. In one of them, I did pet the polar bear."

"What happened?" I asked before I could stop myself.

"It was bloody," Nadia said with a smile. "But so worth the loss of limbs. Not for that Nadia; that Nadia screamed a lot. But for me. It was worth it for me."

I looked over at Peter, who just shook his head and went back to the task at hand. "You want me to stay here until you've secured the facility?" he asked.

I nodded. "You okay with that?"

"I am," he said, removing a rifle as the rest of us remained in position.

"How do you want to do this?" Ji-hyun asked as she went with me to the snowmobiles, where we both picked up silenced MP5s with rift-tempered rounds. It was beginning to snow, and it rapidly got worse. Whatever happened, we were going to be staying the night in the facility.

"Those guard towers and the two at the entrance need dealing with first," I said on returning to the ridge. "Preferably at the same time."

"I'll do the furthest tower," Ji-hyun said.

"I've got the gates," Nadia said, walking back to her snowmobile.

"That leaves me with the closest tower," I said.

Nadia returned shortly with a huge sniper rifle that she dropped the tripod on just before the barrel and placed on the ground before unrolling a mat and putting that down in front of it.

Nadia looked over at Ji-hyun and me, who were staring at her and the faintly purple glowing rifle barrel.

"Barrett M82, special edition," she said. "I had it custom built. Fifty-calibre bullets and a rift-tempered barrel. It'll kill revenants, humans, polar bears, probably most riftborn wouldn't feel too good about it. Also tanks."

"It kills tanks?" Ji-hyun asked.

"Not kill as such," Nadia clarified. "Fuck up. It'll fuck up tanks."

"How loud is it going to be?" I asked.

"The rift-tempered barrel absorbs noise," Nadia said. "Also, I can use my chains to wrap around it, absorbing more sound and enabling me to control the speed and power of the shot."

"I didn't see that in your kit," I said.

"I had it in a bag," Nadia said, looking through the scope. "Built it here. It's my toy."

Ji-hyun and I shared an expression of part terror and part admiration.

"You going or what?" Nadia asked without looking up.

I vaulted over the ridge and started sprinting down the bank, hitting the flat at high speed and keeping low as I raced toward the fence. Search-lights moved slowly around the area, but clearly whoever was in charge of security didn't think anyone would be stupid enough to attack the place, so they hadn't used many of them. It left large parts of darkness that I used to my advantage until I reached the fence and spotted Ji-hyun already scrambling up toward the unsuspecting guard in the tower.

I turned to smoke and billowed up, tendrils of darkness wrapping around the guard's body as more and more of me arrived in the tower until smoke tightened around his neck and I rematerialized beside him, driving a rift-tempered blade up into this throat, killing him instantly, and he fell lifelessly to the floor of the tower. A bright blue flash in the opposite tower signified that Ji-hyun had finished with her own guard.

I wiped the dagger on the guard's thick winter coat, picked up the rifle that he'd been using, and looked through the scope to the entrance of the compound, where one of the two guards fell to the ground. The second guard raised his gun, and his head vanished in a plume of red.

"All done," Nadia said through the comms I still wore. "I'll keep watch up here."

A guard who'd been passing by the entrance ran out to see what had happened and soon found his own head matching those of his two dead companions. At this rate, we could just let Nadia kill everyone.

I dropped down from the tower, partially turning to smoke to slow my fall, landing quietly and without harm, while Ji-hyun climbed down the ladder and ran over to me.

"Show-off," she hissed with a smile.

"Right, you want to go building to building?" I asked.

"If Mason and Callie catch wind of us, they're going to be a nightmare to get to," Ji-hyun said. "How about you go scout out that main building and I'll take care of anyone in the surrounding area?"

"I have to pass by that tent there first," I said. "I'll clear it out on the way. Leave you with a bit less to do."

"Thank you so much," Ji-hyun said with every bit of sarcasm she could manage.

I unslung the MP5 from my shoulder. "You ready?"

Ji-hyun nodded and readied her own MP5. "We're keeping this low and quiet, yes?"

I gave her the thumbs-up and set off through the camp as Ji-hyun made her way to the closest structure, losing sight of her as I reached the tent nearest me, and moving inside with my rifle raised. It was empty.

"This is weird," I said through my comms.

"No one there?" Ji-hyun asked.

"Yeah, that the same with you?" I asked.

"Yep," Ji-hyun said.

"You need to get to the main building," Nadia said. "It's important."

"You know what's there?" I asked her as I left the tent and headed that way, making sure to keep an eye out for anyone who might like to do me harm on the way.

"No," Nadia said. "It's just darkness. But it's a feeling. Something isn't right here, Lucas."

I reached the main entrance to the large building and found the door wide open. I stepped into the dimly lit building and found it to be a large storage area of some kind. There were several jeeps along the far side and wooden boxes on the opposite. A set of stairs were at the rear of the building, leading up to what looked like an office above.

Massive fuel cells sat at the far end of the compound. The work they'd done there must have needed a huge amount of energy to keep going.

There was gunfire from outside the warehouse, and I knew that whatever resistance Ji-hyun had encountered would be having a bad day.

A metal grate in the floor opened and four armed soldiers appeared, each of them carrying a SIG716, all of them aimed at me. They wore dark grey and blue uniforms, looking just enough like military, you'd think they might be unless you were aware of the differences. Mercenaries.

"Take a step back," Nadia said in my ear.

The bullet hit the first of the five guards just under the armpit, punching through and hitting the one directly beside him in the ribs. I turned to smoke and flew back behind the nearest jeep, but the guards started to fire, and a round went through the smoke, causing me to re-form immediately. I managed to roll to the side behind the jeep as pain laced my chest and ribs. Damn it, I hated being shot by tempered bullets, even when they go through my smoke form.

The guards stopped firing. "You're too late," one of the guards shouted.

"Don't move," Nadia said. "Keep low."

I readied myself as there was a shout, a small bang, and then the rest of the camp exploded.

# CHAPTER THIRTY

The fireball that had been created by the explosions after the fuel cells and been breached could be seen from where I was inside the warehouse. The heat rushed in through the open door, and the force of the blast tore holes in the warehouse's outer skin. For the first time in many years, I was a little concerned about Ji-hyun's well-being.

The cacophony of malignant sound that tore through the night made the remaining guards scatter inside the building. I peered through the wheel arch of the jeep I was behind and found that the guards from before had run back down into the building behind them. I would have to hunt them down. Fine with me.

I moved my rifle up and stepped around the jeep, putting two rounds in the head of one guard who chose that exact moment to move toward me. His friend opened fire toward me, and I backed around the jeep as the sounds of bullets slamming into the reinforced vehicle combined with the noise of gunfire from outside. Ji-hyun was not done. The knowledge raised a smile.

With gunfire still being aimed at my location, I crept around the rear of the truck, lay down, and fired twice through the gap under the larger truck that my adversary was crouched behind. It hit him in the shin, and he toppled to the side, where I put two more rounds through his skull.

I searched the ground that I could see for more boots that needed urgent ventilation and, when I found none, got back to my feet and moved quickly around the side of the warehouse. I stopped at the back of a large truck, the loading bed dropped down and empty. The truck had chains on its tires, and I thought back to how Hannah had said that there was a boat in the nearby ocean. I wondered if the truck had been here to take stuff from the boat or bring stuff to it. Another question to ask the guards.

I rushed to the staircase and quickly climbed it, practically kicking open the door and moving into . . . a small, empty room. "Well, that was anticlimactic," I said to myself, pushing the button for the lift that, apart from the light switch, was the only thing inside.

The lift arrived, and the metal doors opened, revealing a gleaming interior of polished wood and glass.

"I'm going in a lift," I said into the comms.

"I'll join you soon," Ji-hyun said.

"Me too," Nadia added.

I stepped onto the lift, and my comms cut out as the doors automatically closed and the lift began to move down. It was pretty clear that we were soon well underground, although when the lift didn't stop for some time, I began to wonder just how far underground we were going. There were no buttons to select a floor, or even a panel to hide them behind. No screens of any kind. It was the most minimalistic lift I'd ever been in, and it wasn't like they were known for their clutter in the first place.

After what felt like a solid minute of movement, the lift stopped, and the doors opened. I had readied the MP5, but the tiled hallway beyond was empty.

I stepped out of the lift and looked around. The corridor had glass partitions on either side of it, showing two huge labs, each one looking sterile and empty. The labs were white and silver, and everything looked incredibly pristine, like someone hadn't taken their new toy out of the packaging yet for fear it might lose value.

There were four doors inside each lab marked with AUTHORIZED PERSONNEL ONLY in big red letters. I wondered if they needed checking, but I figured that doing that alone was probably not the best idea, so I continued down the corridor.

I reached the end, where the corridor opened out into a large foyer-like area, with two metal doors—with an *A* or *B* on them—blocking whatever was beyond, and turned back to the corridor to make sure I was still alone.

One of the metal doors—marked with an *A*—was slightly ajar, so I figured that was the first place to go. I pushed it open with one hand, keeping the MP5 ready in case something decided to have a try.

The room inside was huge, easily as big as one of the labs I'd just passed, but unlike those, it wasn't empty. It was, however, filled with corpses. A lot of corpses. Probably fifty people in total, some in lab coats, some in street clothes that looked old and tatty. Prisoners and people who no longer held value. I was going to hurt someone for this.

I stepped inside and checked the room, discovering that the victims inside the room had been mown down with gunfire. They'd fallen all around the room, and there were dozens of bullet holes in the walls. Some had tried to escape through a metal hatch at the far end of the room and had died holding the circular locking wheel. Judging from the number of tables, and the fact the window on the door some of them had tried to open revealed a spacious kitchen, this was a mess hall.

I moved back to the entrance and stepped out into the foyer again, moving to the second door and pushing it open. It moved without any friction, opening into a dim hallway. Two doors sat along either side of the hall, and as I moved slowly down the hallway, I opened each one to reveal a different office. There was a lot of mess in each of them, with the contents of paper, computers, and furniture having been thrown around. Fingernail marks could be clearly seen on two of the doors, and there was a head-sized hole in one wall.

A metal door at the end of the hallway was open, revealing a room similar to the foyer except for the two dead mercs inside wearing uniforms identical to those I'd killed up on the warehouse floor. Both had been torn into by something big. Apart from the dead bodies, there was a desk, which was still intact, and a door behind it that, from the looks of things, led to some kind of break room.

The only other thing in the room was the large open door that led into a blue-lit tunnel going down. "Great, more down," I said to myself, stepping over one of the bodies and entering what I hoped was the end of my searching for something that might tell me where Mason and Callie were. Or who they'd sold to.

The tunnel had metal rails down the centre of it, a bit like the tunnel under Gabriel's church, although I doubted it was for as wholesome a reason as to go see a train.

It turned out I was right. The tunnel opened out and I followed around a bend, directly into a large cart. It had an engine on the front, the key still in the ignition, and at least ten bodies piled up on the flatbed at the back. They all looked to be in various shapes and forms of not human, although most of them had at least human parts, so they could be identified.

Beyond the cart of death—which I decided there and then that if it wasn't already an eighties horror film, it really should be—was a large cavern with twenty cells all around the exterior. The walls were made of stone, and it was exceptionally warm. It also stank of blood, shit, and death, not necessarily in that order. The floor was dark stone, but there had been a thick layer of something placed over it. I looked a bit like a clear film you put over phone screens, but in gigantic size. There were little bubbles of air in places where the stone underneath didn't quite sit level, and a lot of the film was tinged pink. I got the feeling this thing was washed down a lot, considering how many drains there were around the outside of what was essentially a giant icosagon.

There were several bodies in the room, all looked fresh. One was half-way through a door, a set of stairs behind it leading up into a room that overlooked the icosagon.

The lights in the room were dim, little more than spotlights from above, shining unpleasant and harsh light down on the icosagon floor. I ignored it and watched as the creature that had once been human half-walked, half-pulled itself out of the open cell at the far end of the room. It was seven feet tall and naked from the waist up, its skin purple and blotchy, covered in what appeared to be boils. One arm was considerably longer than the other and ended in two long spear-like fingers. It had six eyes and a mandible where its mouth should be. The long dark hair on its head merged into fur across its back and arms.

The creature looked over at me and shrieked, fully pulling itself out of the cell. It had dark orange trousers on, but they were torn and covered in blood. I had no idea if the blood was theirs or not; it didn't much matter.

I fired two rounds into the thing's head, which snapped back with force. The creature shrieked again, so I put four more in its chest and another two in its head. More shrieking. *Goddamned rift-tempered bullets*, I thought to myself and tossed the rifle onto the ground, unsheathing my two daggers and readying myself for the inevitable.

The creature shrieked again and charged, moving much quicker than I'd anticipated. I dodged aside and slashed with one of the daggers, catching it across the side of the abdomen and opening a nasty wound. The creature stopped, put its fingers in the wound and licked the dark green goo it had for blood. The wound bubbled and hissed before closing shut.

"Well, that's new," I said with the sigh of a man who knows his crappy day is about to get much worse.

The creature ran at me, its deformed arm dragging along the ground, flicking it up at the last moment to try and spear me in the chest.

I'd turned partly into smoke, letting me move quicker than I had before while not having to worry about using too much power too quickly. My daggers flashed as I moved, cutting through the creature's spear-like fingers. They made a horrible sound as they fell to the floor and the creature shrieked once again.

I darted back to finish things when I saw a door directly below the glass window open and the soldier stepped out, raising his rifle and firing twice. I threw myself to the ground, the bullets hitting air as the creature pounced at me, landing on my chest, its mandibles clicking loudly as its bloody stump of a hand tried to hold me down.

I grabbed hold of the creature's arms—one in each hand—and turned to smoke.

Turning to smoke when someone is holding you, or you're holding someone, is not fun. It's something I try exceptionally hard to not do for two reasons. One, it causes me pain that tears through my body like water down a stream, and two, the aftermath is less than pleasant.

My turning to smoke filleted the creature's arms where I'd touched it. The creature looked like it had been peeled. Its legs, groin, and arms were all torn apart, leaving long wet pieces of flesh and muscle to hit the floor as the creature rolled around and screamed, causing even more blood to spill over the floor.

I'd looked for not even a second when the three bullets hit me in my smoke form, forcing it to disperse. The problem with dispersing my smoke form was that it became harder for me to think straight. It was like my brain was in a thousand places at once, each piece experiencing different sensations, different sights, and different sounds. The bombardment on the senses was unpleasant at best.

The bullets kept coming, forcing me to disperse more and more, each time my senses becoming more and more overwhelmed, my brain trying to keep everything together. I focused on the soldier, who ran out of the stairwell, jumping over the body of his comrade, firing the whole time. I felt all of those senses, all of those tiny pieces of consciousness, snap into focus with pure distilled rage.

The soldier had emptied a magazine and was sliding in a fresh one when all of the parts of my smoke moved toward him in a rush, re-forming myself and driving my fist into his face with terrifying speed and power. The soldier hadn't anticipated the attack and had left himself open, his magazine clattering to the ground as I kicked out his knee and drove my own into his stomach, forcing him to drop his rifle, which I kicked away with one foot.

I turned to seek out my daggers as the creature, still dripping gore, leapt at me.

I used the creature's own momentum against it and threw it behind me, into the soldier, who was turning into a shadow, the darkness having already covered his head and chest and moving down toward his legs. The creature's arm got lost inside the soldier's shadow form, and it began to kick and scream like a trapped animal, only making things worse as the soldier tried to disengage himself from the situation.

If the soldier had turned into a shadow, the fight might have been much more complicated. Hooded revenants who can become shadow are hard to pin down, and with the amount of shadows that were created over the floor, it meant he could pop up from any of them or merge his own shadow with one to leap out of.

I picked up both daggers, ignoring the squealing that had begun from the creature as the soldier continued to try and get away from it. The creature's blood began to bubble and boil as it was sprayed all over the floor, its flesh trying to heal and then begin torn apart again and again.

"Get off me," the soldier screamed, the shadows over his face now gone, the creature's mandible trying to snap at the shadows, to tear it away, and only resulting in the mandibles themselves being stuck in the shadows.

"It's a real catch-twenty-two situation you've got going on there," I said.

The soldier stared at me, turned completely into shadow, decapitating the creature, and vanished into the ground.

I really should have just kept my mouth shut.

The head of the creature came flying out of the ground a few feet from where the soldier had vanished. I avoided it easily, but it was enough to move me a step closer to where the soldier exploded out of the ground, punching me in the face and kicking me in the chest.

I drove one of my daggers up toward him, but he vanished again, the shadows on the floor around me moving and merging, giving me no clue as to where the bastard was about to pop up from.

I moved back to the corner of the icosagon, kicking my MP5 as I went, picking it up when I was completely in the darkness of the edge of the room, and using the rifle to shoot out the lights that sat all around.

It didn't take long for the soldier to figure out what I was doing, and he exploded from the shadow directly in front of me, grabbing the rifle and head-butting me. I saw stars for a moment, which was all he needed to pull the rifle away and smash the butt of it into my face.

"I will be rewarded when I bring Dr Mitchell your head," he snapped as he drove his knee into my stomach. "Nothing to say?"

"Made you look," I said with a wink.

He turned around as Ji-hyun grabbed him around the jaw and ignited her flame.

If the soldier had been able to use his mouth, I was pretty sure the screams would have been deafening.

Ji-hyun kicked him in the chest, sending the soldier to the ground. He tried to cover himself in shadows again, but Nadia fell from the ceiling, her now blue-and-purple glowing chains wrapping around him like snakes, constricting him, pinning his arms to his sides.

Ji-hyun walked past me toward the soldier, the smell of smoke filling my nostrils. Blood was on her jaw, which I was pretty sure wasn't hers.

"He can't use his power while the chains are here," Nadia said, almost whispering it into the soldier's ear. "Good to see you again, man whose name I never bothered to remember."

"Traitorous bitch," the soldier snapped.

One of Nadia's chains coiled around the soldier's throat and instantly tightened as the soldier fought to breathe. "Be nice," she whispered, and the coil lessened the pressure but didn't move it from his neck.

"Where's Mason and his staff?" I asked.

"Where's Dr Mitchell?" Nadia whispered.

"And why blow this place up?" Ji-hyun asked.

Nadia's chains snaked around the soldier, who fought to breathe.

"Mason isn't here," he said.

"Wait, what?" I asked. "Where is Mason?"

The soldier laughed. "New York, I imagine. Mason was no longer useful, so Dr Mitchell made a call to give his location to the authorities. About an hour ago."

"He's been arrested?" I asked.

"By now, I imagine, yes," the soldier said. "Poor little rich boy never figured out that he was never the one in charge. His money paid our wages, paid for the research done here, but we believe in Dr Mitchell. She's going to change everything."

"Where is Dr Mitchell?" Ji-hyun asked.

"We were to destroy it all," he snapped. "We were here to remove the lab people, blow the whole place. Kill anything that remained. Dr Mitchell knew you'd come sooner or later. They wanted you to get here, to find this place, so we could kill you all at once."

"That did not work out how you'd planned," I pointed out.

"Where is she?" Ji-hyun's tone left no room to suggest she was anything other than getting seriously angry.

"Gone," the soldier said. "Don't know where; she didn't tell us."

I tried to get reception on my phone, but there was nothing.

"It's a few hours back to anywhere with a reception," the soldier said smugly. "You're stuck here."

"I'll go back to New York," I said. "If Mason has been arrested, he might be more willing to tell us where Callie has gone to."

The soldier laughed again. "He's not going to do a damn thing if he has any sense."

"We'll see," I said, turning to Nadia and Ji-hyun. "Get back when you can."

"And this soldier?" Nadia asked.

"Where's the intel you got from the viewing point up there?" I asked. "That's what you came in here for, isn't it? Make sure there's nothing left? I assume some of the things got loose and you all had to fight your way in."

"The intel is gone," the soldier said.

"Kill him," I said. "He's useless now."

Nadia punched a hole through his head with one of her chains, killing the soldier.

"Keep safe," I said to Ji-hyun and Nadia, opened the embers, and stepped through.

# CHAPTER THIRTY-ONE

Y ou're back already?" Maria the hawk asked as I left the longhouse in my embers.

"Yes," I said, walking past them. Despite the fact that it was dark in Canada and would be in New York too, it was light outside in my embers. "In a hurry, though. I left my Talon mask in New York, need to get back there."

Maria took off and landed on my shoulder. "You can't heal here."

"I'm not here to heal," I said, stopping and turning my head to find my face less than an inch away from the beak of an animal designed to rend flesh from bone. It was a little disconcerting.

"So, you're here to just run though, is that it?" Maria asked.

I wanted to nod, but it would have involved head-butting Maria, so I just smiled instead. "Need to get from northern Canada to New York, fast."

"You're going to feel it when you leave," Maria said. "That's a big trip."

"I know," I said. "But it still needs to be done. If I have to crash for an hour after, so be it. I can't wait a day to get back there."

"What the bloody hell are you doing back here?" Casimir the wolf asked as they trotted into view.

"He needs a long journey done in a short time," Maria said.

"You're not hurt," the wolf said, sniffing me.

"No, I'm not hurt," I said, feeling slight frustration. "Seriously, I just need to get back to New York."

"It's a bit of a walk to the exit," Maria said. "Let's go."

I set off at a jog, and Casimir ran beside me. I knew Casimir wasn't really a wolf, but it was still pretty cool to have one running beside me.

And having once had to run from a real wolf—long story—having one not trying to bite you is a much more pleasant experience.

We ran for five minutes with Maria flying above, until they landed on a hut that was some distance outside of the main village. I didn't remember ever having seen this hut before. The embers changed as they needed to, and despite having been back hundreds of times, it was something I'd never quite gotten used to. We were close to a set of foreboding woods that I most certainly had been in before and never wished to again. These particular woods in my embers signified the furthest reaches of them. Stepping inside was bad. Really bad. I'd done it once and vowed never again.

I opened the door to the hut as dusk began to settle in the skies above. The embers weren't keen on me returning so often. Sometimes nightfall takes hours, but sometimes, if you keep making trips to the embers, it hurries it along. A warning to not overuse it, maybe. Who knows? Either way, it was my cue to leave.

"This is going to be the longest jump you've taken in a long time," Maria said. "You will not feel good."

"No, I don't suppose I will," I said.

"Take care," Casimir said. "Try not to vomit."

I stepped into the hut. "Thanks," I said as the door closed, and my embers kicked me back out to the real world.

I vomited. It was neither heroic nor pleasant, and I was glad to find a metal bin in the middle of the room I found myself in. I was also glad I hadn't eaten for a while.

I stood up and realised I was in the medical bay of the church shelter, just as Gabriel rushed into the room, weapons ready for fighting.

"Hey," I said. "This sucks ass."

At that point I fell over. You can't damage your pride and dignity if you're not conscious to remember it.

I woke up in bed, with Gabriel on one side and Hannah stood at the foot of the bed.

"This was not how I assumed today was going to go," I said eventually, after remembering that I shouldn't just lie still and stare. "How long was I out?"

"Two hours," Gabriel said.

I swung my legs out of the bed. "Had to come back from Canada pretty sharpish, no phone reception in the middle of nowhere. Mason has been double-crossed."

"He was arrested about an hour ago," Gabriel said. "Emily told us. He tried to run, ended up being detained in the Grand after he got spotted and led the police on a bit of a chase. He had put on a disguise and tried to pass himself off as one of the victims of Callie's experiments."

"There was a high-speed chase?" I asked.

"A slow, plodding chase," Gabriel told me. "It was on foot. Mason tried to take some hostages. It didn't work out so well; last I heard, he was being detained in the Grand waiting for his lawyer, or someone to take him to lockup. Turns out money still buys you some privilege, even after getting caught red-handed."

"So, I didn't even need to rush back and tell you," I said with a sigh. "Everyone okay here?"

"All good here," Gabriel said. "Or it was until a vomiting man passed out in our medical bay."

"I thought you'd be staying at the casino," I said.

"We are," Gabriel said. "After you left, Scarlet was finding it a little bit too overwhelming being around everyone, so Hannah and I took her here to collect some of her things. Then you burst in. Good timing, by the way."

"Sorry about that," I said, getting up.

"We needed to see you," Hannah said. "We found something. Something really bad."

"Any chance I can get something to eat and drink while I get the bad news?" I asked.

We went by way of the kitchen and a grabbed half a dozen apples and an entire pack of sliced chicken to eat while Hannah and Gabriel went through what they'd found. Scarlet walked into the room after Gabriel called her over.

"Dr Mitchell was working on a serum that let people turn into monsters," Hannah said.

"I know," I said. "I remember that bit."

"Well, we learned a lot more about the serum that Callie was working on in secret," Hannah said. "Scarlet told us about the hybrids that Mason got; she didn't know about the ones done in secret."

"The hybrids that Mason got were part greater fiend, part human," Scarlet told me. "They also have animal DNA in them, and honestly the whole thing is a giant dice roll as to what attributes you get with every vial. Also, the effect fades quicker, but the more doses you take in a short space of time, the more likely you are to suffer . . . problems."

"Problems like peeling apart?" I asked.

Scarlet nodded.

"Okay, so, what about the secret serum?" I asked.

"I didn't know about it," Scarlet said. "But reading through Dr Mitchell's notes, these hybrids are part elder fiend."

That got my attention.

"Seriously?" I asked. "How is that possible?"

"Dr Mitchell got it to work," Scarlet said. "I'm not a genetics expert to the level of Dr Mitchell, but the notes say it worked well. They kept the intelligence of the human part, but the level of power is off the charts. Dr Mitchell notes that she had to make tests away from the confines of the Sky-High facility because they were in danger of being discovered by Mason. She took them to a facility in Canada, left Mason behind."

"Yeah, she discarded him," I said. "Also, they just blew up their facility."

"Well, she did a lot of work there. In secret."

"You ever go?" I asked Scarlet.

Scarlet shook her head. "I didn't even leave the lab; I wasn't allowed to see the progress on stuff like this. None of us knew this was a thing."

"So, we officially have two types of serum, neither good, but one much worse," I said, summarising. "Brilliant. And Callie just sold some of that serum to a buyer we don't have the identity of."

"We know that she was handing over the good stuff," Hannah said. "There's a lot of emails from her to someone I can't identify about it. None of her notes say what their name was, though, or even how she knew them."

"More information she probably kept on her," Scarlet said. "She used a journal. A physical one. She was always asking about security for personal stuff."

"One thing at a time," I said. "Did Mason find out about the two serums?"

"No idea," Hannah said. "He's at the Grand; ask Emily to ask him."

"Excellent suggestion," I said, getting out my phone and calling Emily. The phone went to voicemail.

"That's not great," Gabriel said. "Maybe he's being questioned and she can't get to her phone."

"I'll head over there," I said. "I'll ask Emily myself. Besides, I have a bad feeling about him."

"He's not a warrior," Hannah said. "What's he going to do, set lawyers on us?"

"Fear my litigation," Gabriel said.

"So, what happens to you?" I asked Scarlet. "When this is done, I mean."

"I've spoken to Emily and agreed to testify against Mason in exchange for reduced sentencing," she said. "I didn't know what I was getting into, and by the time I did, it was too late, but I still worked there. There needs to be recompense for that."

I walked into the armoury and picked up a rift-tempered H&K P30L and enough ammo to hopefully give something a bad day. After the last few days, it was better to be prepared for any eventuality. If Mason's people had no qualms about killing FBI agents before, there was always a possibility they'd try to break him out.

My daggers were still in their sheaths, along with the throwing knives. At some point between arriving in New York and waking up, my jacket had been removed, so I grabbed a thigh-length leather jacket to keep me warm and also hide the weapons I was carrying. It looked a little Matrix, but what was good enough for Keanu is good enough for me.

"That necessary?" Gabriel asked as he walked with me up the tunnel to the bunker exit. He tossed me a set of keys to a Chevy truck that was parked nearby.

"Probably not," I said.

"You want us to come with you?" he asked me.

"No, get to Booker, notify him," I said. "If something is going on, he'll need help."

"What about you?" Gabriel asked.

"I'll be fine," I said. "If trouble is there, and that's a big *if*, I'll contact you; you can all rush over. If it's a setup, I don't want any of you near it."

"The injured RCU were going to be housed in an event room at the rear of the first floor," Gabriel said. "That was the initial drop-off point so they could be kept safe by the guards in the hotel while Emily interviewed them. Emily's people should still be there, will be able to tell you what's happening."

I practically jumped into the truck, started the ignition, and set away into the night at high speed.

The hotel came into view. It was nearly the witching hour and I didn't expect anyone to be out and about in the winter night, but the complete lack of anyone at all set my nerves on end.

I got out of the truck, checked I was ready for whatever was going to happen next, and walked casually across the road to the outside of the hotel. I stayed a little down from the main entrance and drew my gun as I moved up toward it.

There were no lights in the reception area inside the hotel. No movement of any kind, although the darkness, combined with the mirror sheen of the glass, made it difficult to determine exactly what was going on inside.

I remained low and moved up to the revolving door, pushing it slightly, but it didn't budge, so I pushed open the door beside it and stepped into a horror show. The entire front desk was caked in blood. It was dripping in a slow, methodical way over the edge of the desk into an ever-growing pool.

There were five bodies that I could see, although none of them were whole. Most were missing heads and limbs, and all five wore the uniform of the hotel.

I checked my phone, hoping for a signal, but got nothing. I replaced it, reached out, and touched the rift. Vapor-like trails of almost transparent purple and blue filled the entire room, moving through the hotel. Whatever was there was big. Really big. And incredibly powerful.

I stepped around the bisected body of a young man in a hotel uniform. The contents of a leather briefcase were thrown about the place—paper and pens stuck to the blood-slick floor. I moved toward the lifts, where there was another body. This one had a gun in his hand, which was several feet from where the rest of his body lay.

The blue and purple trails mixed together, twisting into one another as they went through a slightly ajar door opposite the lifts. The pale wood had bloodstained handprints over it, several of them smeared together as if people had sprinted through the door one after the other in quick succession.

I pushed the door open with the butt of my gun, but beyond was a calmness that didn't exist in the foyer. The hallway was thirty feet long, with two doors inside. One opposite the entrance and one that, as I opened it, revealed a small office. It was empty except for the radio jammer that had been placed on the desk.

After switching the jammer off, I phoned Gabriel.

"Lots of dead; send everyone with everything you have," I told him.

"Don't do anything stupid," he said.

"No promises," I told him, and ended the call.

I left the office, letting the door close behind me, and moved toward the door at the far end of the hallway. There were smears of blood along the hallway itself, as if people had stumbled while running, but whoever had made it into the hallway had made it through the opposite door in one piece.

They hadn't made it very far beyond that.

There were several dead just after the door, which led into what I assumed would at some point have been a gleaming white kitchen. It now looked like someone had produced a horror film there.

The dead I saw first were all in pieces, each one discarded around the room. The entire kitchen had been torn apart. Someone huge had killed the people inside, but it hadn't done any damage to the walls in the hallway. It had changed its size.

Considering the exit at the far end of the kitchen was now just a giant hole, it looked like whatever had killed the people had remained that size when it left.

I moved through the kitchen, fully aware of just how much noise I was making with every step. As I reached the far end, there were two men wearing Mason's security uniforms. Apparently, some of Mason's people had tried to get to him after all. Both had died from gunshot wounds to the head and chest. One of them had been partially crushed by something.

I stepped through the ruined exit and found Dale's head pinned to the wall with a butcher's knife. His body was nowhere to be found.

"Fuck," I snapped, stepping past the head of a man who had tried to do good. He hadn't deserved to go out like that.

I pushed through the large set of swinging double doors and found more bodies in the hallway beyond. All three had jackets with *FBI* in big yellow letters, although most of them were spattered with blood now. All of them had been cut through by something large and sharp. I wondered why they were there; maybe Emily had arranged to get backup after all.

There were more of Mason's guards in the hallway, too, one on the bottom of a set of stairs that led up to the rooms above, and the other two next to a giant hole in the wall where flickering lights revealed it to be some kind of function room.

I reached the hole in the wall and peered inside. Chairs had been stacked up on either side of the room, although on one side those had toppled over onto one another, forming some weird pyramid, the legs jutting out all angles.

The lights, I discovered, were from the set in the ceiling that presumably were used for parties. They occasionally changed colour.

There were no bodies inside the function room, but the sound of something hissing turned me around, my gun ready.

Emily's face appeared beyond the hole, her hands frantically gesticulating for me to get out of the function room. She looked bloody and battered but was otherwise alive. Another noise, this time from the raised stage at the far end of the function room, behind heavy curtains, drew my attention. It sounded like someone was trying to get the last bit of milkshake out via a straw.

I took a step back toward the hole as Emily hissed something I couldn't hear. I was waiting for whatever was behind the curtain to show itself.

The curtains began to move, and Mason appeared between the two, dragging something in one hand. He was completely naked and practically bathed in blood, his hair matted to his scalp. He licked his fingers and casually tossed the item he was holding off the stage.

The item in question was Dale's body, which hit the floor with a sickening sound as Mason beamed with pride.

Mason had thrown a two-hundred-pound body like it was a bag of flour. That could not possibly be good.

"Luca . . ." Mason began.

I shot him twice in the chest and once in the head, the latter sending him crumpling to the floor.

I kept the gun aimed at Mason, who didn't move. It couldn't possibly be that easy.

"They won't work," Emily shouted, finally getting into the room. "I was trying to tell you: bullets from a rift-tempered gun do nothing but piss him off."

"They shut him up for a bit," I said, taking the little wins where I could get them. "How many of your people are alive?"

"Don't know," Emily said. "We arrested Mason here, contacted my boss, arranged transport, but some of Mason's people attacked us, trying to get him out. In the fight, he turned into . . . something. There were five of us and a whole bunch of people who'd been rescued, not to mention the guests in the hotel."

"I saw three bodies with FBI jackets," I said. "I'm sorry."

"Me too," Emily said. "Mason isn't . . . He's just not human anymore. He's . . ." The dark red spear hit Emily in the chest, throwing her back and pinning her to the wall ten feet behind her. I barely had time to react as she let out a cry and died.

"Oh, don't spoil the surprise," Mason said, getting to his feet.

I shot him again, emptying the entire gun, reloading a new magazine, and doing the same as Mason laughed.

"It'll take a bit more than that," he said. "Callie betrayed me, but I knew she was going to. I knew she was making a second serum, a better one, so I took one of the vials. I was going to get it reverse-engineered. I managed to take the vial serum before they could stop me. It's soooo good, Lucas. Is this what you feel like all the time? The power running through my body. You ruined my building; you killed my people. I'm going to kill you, and then I'm going to hunt that traitorous cow down and tear her head off."

Mason's body transformed all at once, his legs growing three times their normal size, his arms too. Two more legs sprouted out of his abdomen—one either side. His torso became elongated and swollen, turning a deep shade of purple as his skull became misshapen and lengthened, his jaw audibly breaking as two sets of piranha-like teeth jutted out of his gums. When he was done, he looked like part insect, part fish, part human. The ends of each limb were still hand-like, although there were claws where the nails had been.

"Surprise," the thing that used to be Mason screamed, laughing as it climbed down from the stage. He roared and a second dark red spear flew from the spines on his back. I dodged aside as it smashed into and through the well behind me.

Horror and fear filled me. I'd never seen any human do what Mason had done, and for good reason. It was beyond monstrous. If he got away, and if Mason could turn from human to creature at will, a whole lot of people could die.

It was time to kill an elder fiend.

# CHAPTER THIRTY-TWO

In my entire two-and-a-bit thousand years of being alive, I could count on one hand the number of times I'd gone up against an elder fiend alone. Not a single one of those encounters had been anything close to a good time, and I'd almost died in at least half of them.

Despite that, there are two things I knew when it came to fighting one. The first was to not get hit, which might sound obvious, but it's much easier said than done, and the second was space. Get into as much space as possible. If you're fighting a creature that's faster and stronger than you, you want to be able to move away when you need to. I'd once fought an elder fiend inside a network of cave tunnels. Never again.

Elder fiends are as smart as a human, but the more damage they take, the more the animalistic parts of their brain took over. I hoped that Mason would be the same.

Mason laughed as I turned and ran out of the hole in the wall, bounding up the stairs three at a time, letting my smoke make me more agile. I was out of sight of the hole when I turned to smoke, billowing back down to beside the hole, through the wooden bannister, using it to anchor myself above it as Mason's long legs came out first, almost probing the darkness of the hallway for danger. A spine crashed through the bannister beyond, destroying several of the stairs. The sound was deafening as Mason's huge head poked out of the wall.

There was a brief moment when I thought my plan was working. That moment died a death the second his head turned a hundred and eighty degrees—which from the shape of it looked impossible—and his mouth opened wide in a horrific smile. Two eyes, both several times larger than when he'd been human, stared at me. They were nothing but darkness, and occasionally, I thought I saw them ripple.

I pulled back the smoke anchoring me in place and dropped down, my daggers in my hands, aiming for his head.

Mason's head moved too quickly for me to hit, but as I fell, I changed targets, slicing through his left leg. The rift-tempered daggers sliced through flesh, muscle, and bone like they were made of paper. I landed on the ground, immediately turned to smoke, and billowed past the howling Mason, back into the function room. I'd have rather had the space, but I didn't want the thing chasing me through the damned hotel.

Blood spewed from Mason's severed limb, spraying the noxious smelling, tar-like substance all over the floor and walls as he turned back to me, his eyes radiating hatred. He put the limb in his mouth and sucked for a moment before I heard a crunch and he spat out a chunk of his own leg. The bleeding had stopped.

"Well, aren't you just a big old bag of tricks," I said.

Mason took a step toward me, testing the fact that he now only had five legs. I wondered if I could get a few more removed and really limit his mobility. I couldn't go blow for blow with him, and I certainly couldn't keep dodging him. I had to fight. I just had to fight smart.

I sheathed my small dagger and sprinted forward, which, judging from the expression on Mason's horrific face, wasn't something he'd expected. I slashed at his other leg, but he moved it out of the way, almost scurrying back to put distance between us.

Which was exactly what I wanted him to do.

I reached for the rift-tempered throwing knives on the back of my belt, grabbed one, and spun away from Mason, throwing the knife at another leg. Mason batted the knife away, but I'd already drawn and thrown a second. This one hit home in one of his two huge eyes.

More blood, more screaming as he tried to remove the dagger, but the slick, tar-like blood made it all but impossible. He moved his hand ever so slightly, and I threw a third dagger at his remaining good eye. He dodged it and charged, his roar reverberating through me.

I turned to smoke, trying to dodge the lunge from his one good front leg, but he fired another spine at me, tearing through my smoke and forcing me to re-form as pain exploded through my body. I threw myself aside at the last moment, but he grabbed my ankle and tossed me across the room, firing a second spine at me, which I only dodged at the last second by turning to smoke and allowing it to rip through me.

I re-formed on the wooden floor and coughed up blood. The spines on Mason's body were almost pure rift energy. I could not afford to be hit by any more if I wanted to come away from this fight anything close to still breathing.

I drew another throwing dagger as Mason edged toward me. He moved with menace but also some caution. He didn't know what other tricks I might have.

I had two throwing knives left and my knuckledusters, the latter of which required me to get a whole lot closer to Mason than I really wanted to be.

When there was twenty feet between us, Mason took the chance and closed the distance between us in a huge leap, firing two more spines from his back that smashed into the wooden floor where I'd been standing, throwing up debris all over. I turned to smoke and moved back up onto the stage, re-forming as Mason leapt up at me again. I turned to smoke once more, moving back down to the function room floor, re-forming myself just beyond where the two large spines were jutting up from the floor.

Mason roared and leapt off the stage, landing just in front of the two spines. A swipe of his remaining hand sent them flying across the room. He smiled like he'd spoiled some particularly wonderful plan.

I threw another dagger at his face and darted toward him. He swiped at the dagger and moved to the side, showing me one of his side legs, which looked like it was made of his ribs. He stamped down with the sharp point of the leg, but I turned to smoke, moving between his mid and back leg, re-forming myself underneath Mason and slamming my dagger up into what was essentially Mason's thorax. I ran up toward Mason's head, keeping hold of the dagger and slicing through his abdomen, turning to smoke, and moving out the other side as green and black gore fell out beneath Mason's body.

Mason slid on the gore but hit me in the chest with his hand, sending me sprawling as he used his two middle legs to hold himself together.

I was just getting to my feet when he barrelled into me. I flew across the room, impacting with the wall before I could do anything about it. I hit the ground hard, all of the breath knocked out of me, as Mason grabbed me around the throat, lifted me off the floor, and repeatedly smashed me into the wall until pieces of plasterboard covered me.

I drove my dagger up into Mason's arm, but he jerked away, taking the dagger with him. I threw my last dagger at his face, which hit him square in the mouth, but he backhanded me quicker than I could move, and I saw stars as I hit the ground a dozen feet away.

My head swam as I managed to get to a kneeling position, only to be hit in the back again by a charging Mason. It took me a moment to realise that Mason had quite literally run over me. Blood poured out of the wound on my back, trickling down my arm, over my fingers. I didn't know how bad it was, but I think when a semi-elder fiend runs over you, it's probably not good.

Mason's hand wrapped around my throat and lifted me off the ground again, bringing me closer to his face and the snapping maw that awaited.

I'd already slipped the knuckleduster onto my hand before Mason had steamrolled me, and waited until I was only inches away, Mason's foul breath making my stomach flip, when I punched him in his good eye.

The eye burst like a water balloon, which is exactly as disgusting as that sounds, but Mason dropped me and I put all of my strength into a punch that broke his jaw, leaving it hanging uselessly. I walked away from the blind, thrashing Mason, grabbed one of his spines—being very careful not to touch either end—and ran with it like a lance back at Mason.

The spine pierced Mason's throat and I pushed it up as far as it would go, pinning his bottom and top jaws together.

Mason made a noise that I'd rather never hear again. I staggered away to pick up the larger of my two daggers.

I turned my back to Mason, who was trying to remove the spine from his neck, and ran over to the second spine, throwing it like a javelin at Mason. It wasn't a particularly good throw, but it hit him in the shoulder of his good arm, giving him something else to worry about as I ran at him, past his flailing arm, and cut through the middle leg that was still keeping the contents of his thorax from spilling over the floor. I carried on, hacking at his rear leg and darting away as Mason toppled onto his side, his guts spilling out onto the floor.

I was beaten, bloody, and would no doubt feel like a sack of warm crap in the morning, but as I placed my boot on Mason's throat and forced the spine further up into his head until it burst free from the top of his skull, I felt a sense of relief as he stopped moving.

I spent a little time removing Mason's head, just in case. It was unpleasant work, but the dagger made it easier, and when it was done, Mason's body dissolved into mucky brown water. I tossed his head to the side of the room, where it too dissolved. One dead Mason the elder-fiend wannabe.

My knees hurt as I fell to the ground, reaching around to my back to find the hole where Mason had punctured me was healing, but like every other part of me, it would feel like shit sooner than later.

I looked over at Emily, her body still pinned to the wall. She'd been a good agent, had tried to help people, and like everyone else with her, she had paid the ultimate price for that. I winced as I got to my feet and walked over to her, pulling the spine free and lowering her body to the ground.

I removed my phone and found there was a signal, so I called Gabriel.

"Lucas," Gabriel said, sounding more than a little concerned. "We tried to contact you."

"Yeah, had a little trouble with Mason," I said before explaining what had happened.

"Are you okay?" Gabriel said. "We're on our way."

"That's good," I said. "My body wants to fall down, and I don't think that's a good condition to drive in."

"We'll be there as soon as I can," Gabriel said. "I assume Mason is definitely dead, yes?"

I nodded, realised Gabriel couldn't see me, and sighed. "Yep. If I ever have to fight an elder fiend alone again, please shoot me. It would be quicker than what just happened."

"Keep safe," Gabriel said. "We'll be there soon."

"Cool," I said, dropping the phone to the ground and crashing to the floor beside it. "Ouch."

During the fight, and immediately after, my adrenaline had overridden the need for my body to scream at me, and with the adrenaline gone, my body decided to make up for lost time. Healing would take a while, but I shouldn't need a trip to the embers now that Mason was dead. I sat, and it was then that I saw a briefcase in the far corner of the room.

With much cursing, I got to my feet and walked over, picked the briefcase up, and sat down to empty the contents onto the floor. There was a binder, a phone, a set of car keys for a Bentley, a money clip with hundreds of dollars in it, and an empty hypodermic needle.

I tried the phone, but it was protected by a thumbprint, and seeing how Mason's thumbs were now puddles of goo, that wasn't going to work. Instead, I opened the binder. It contained maybe fifty pieces of paper and looked like a sort of sales pitch for the vile shit that Dr Mitchell and Mason had been working on. It advertised that there were going to be a few dozen vials of the same monstrous stuff that Mason himself had taken. Dozens of those bastards. "Fucking hell," I said aloud.

The phone rang, which made me jump, and then promptly made me curse myself for being an idiot. I looked at the screen on the phone. Callie Mitchell.

You didn't need a thumbprint to answer it, so I swiped the green button across to the right.

"Mason?" Dr Mitchell asked.

"Your friend isn't able to come to the phone right now," I said. "What with him being turned into goop and all that. You know he stole one of those second serums you were working on?"

"You killed an elder fiend?" Dr Mitchell asked, sounding somewhat impressed.

"He wasn't an elder fiend," I said. "I've fought elder fiends before, and they don't go down that easily." I tried to sound full of confidence and bravado, but everything hurt, and I just wanted to sleep.

"You sound hurt, Lucas," Dr Mitchell said. "Did he hurt you? I can help you; I can make you stronger."

"No," I said. "You can't. I wonder, though, how long have you been peddling this shit? You're a riftborn, yes? So, why are you so determined to create monsters to try and kill so many of us?"

"What I am is of no consequence to you," Callie snapped. "Although I find it fascinating that you were able to disconnect yourself willingly from the rift when we last met."

"Yeah, I'm full of surprises," I told her. "So, you've sold a shitty serum that makes people peel apart. I don't think that's going to end well for you when the people you sold it to find out."

"I was never selling that serum to anyone but Mason," Callie said with a laugh. "I could only have perfected it by making an inferior product first. Mason was just stupid enough to buy it. You won't stand in my way, Lucas. No one will. I will have all I need. I imagine this isn't the last time we'll speak, Mr Rurik."

"I'm going to find you, Callie," I said.

"Dr Mitchell," she snapped.

"No," I said. "You're Callie. You don't get to act like a monster and be called *doctor*. Doctors are meant to help. I'm going to find you, Callie, and I'm going to kill you and destroy everything you ever worked on. I'm going to reduce your influence to zero."

Callie laughed. "You really have no idea what's going on. But by the time you do, it'll be too late."

"We'll see," I said.

"You were their Talon, yes?" Callie asked, her tone becoming hard. "Their protector. You failed them. You'll fail your friends, the innocents who will die, and everyone else who stands in my way. I will get what belongs to me, Lucas. You can't stop that."

"And what is it you want?" I asked to a dial tone. "Goddamn it."

I picked up the phone, resisting the urge to smash it on the floor. I placed the phone and binder, along with everything else, back in the briefcase. Maybe Hannah could figure out what was on the phone before anyone else had to die. As I walked across the room, I wondered exactly who Callie Mitchell was. I wondered who she was so angry at that she would cause the deaths of countless people. Even people of her own kind. Riftborn weren't numerous, so it was odd that in all of my years on Earth, I'd never met her until that day at her asylum. I wondered how she'd managed to stay hidden while clearly working on her anger and rage issues by murdering and experimenting on people. It needed looking into.

I had reached the ruined doorway to the function room when I heard a gasp. I dropped the bag, turned, and drew my two daggers in one fluid movement. Emily was on her knees, staring straight at me. Her ruined clothes showed that the hole where the spine had struck her was healed.

"What the fuck is going on?" she asked me, her words tumbling out without pause, her eyes wide and full of fear.

I walked over to her and knelt beside her, taking her hands in mine. She was weak and cold, a normal quality for those freshly returned as revenants. The whites of her eyes flickered aquamarine.

"Welcome to the world of the rift-fused," I said.

# EPILOGUE

Isaac died four days after I killed Mason in the hotel.

I'd gone to the safe house they were staying in, I'd taken him into my embers, and I'd walked him through to the rift. It had been hard to see him go, and I'd had to spend two days in the rift, healing the effects of the poison, but it was worth it.

Two days after his death, we all got together for his funeral. Ruby had asked Gabriel to give the eulogy, so we all stood in the graveyard on a drizzly winter's day, listening to Gabriel make a heartfelt tribute about our friend. I drifted off, thinking about all the time I'd spent away from everyone, how pleased I was that Isaac had asked for my help. I'm glad I'd come back, even if it meant losing a friend. At least I got to see him again, to say goodbye.

I looked around at everyone gathered. Emily wasn't there; she was still back at the church, trying to come to terms with the fact that she wasn't human anymore. Her powers hadn't quite manifested yet, so no one was entirely sure exactly what kind of revenant she was. Not chained, that much was certain, but for some people it's a slow process, and for others their powers manifest immediately. Another mystery in a host of them when it comes to revenants.

As the funeral finished, I walked over to Ruby, who was with her parents and children.

"Thank you for what you did for us," Ruby said after hugging me.

"I'm glad you had some time together," I said. "I'm glad he got to see you all."

"When you see him in the rift, tell him we love him," Ruby said.

I nodded and smiled. "I will."

Ruby put her arm through mine and led me away from the rest of the mourners. "Are we safe?" she whispered when we were far enough away.

I stopped walking and looked up at the dark clouds above. "I hope so," I said. "Emily said that the FBI are rooting out their problems; she's taken some time off to deal with what she's become, but she seems to be optimistic."

"Are you safe?" Ruby asked.

"Probably not," I said. "But I'm used to it. I doubt Mason's family are going to be thrilled, and it depends how much they're involved with Callie Mitchell. She certainly wants me elsewhere, preferably after being allowed to dissect me for her own amusement."

"Please take care of yourself, Lucas," Ruby said. "You're always welcome at our home. I want you to know that."

"Thank you," I told her. "I'm sorry I never got to know you and Isaac as a couple."

I left the graveyard and made my way back to the ruined church, finding an alcove that kept the increasingly heavy rain off me while letting me stay outside. After a while, and with my thick coat wrapped around me, I drifted off, the sounds of Hamble traffic not enough to keep me awake.

"You know there's a warm place beneath us," Gabriel said. "It has beds and everything."

I opened my eyes to find Gabriel, Nadia, and Ji-hyun stood before me.

"I like the fresh air," I said as Ji-hyun sat beside me, giving my hand a slight squeeze of camaraderie for a fallen ally.

"I will miss Isaac," Nadia said, her chains wrapped around her like a security blanket.

"Me too," I said.

"What are your plans?" Gabriel asked me.

"I plan on finding the vials that Callie sent out," I said. "I plan on making sure that things like Mason don't happen again. If something like him happens in a crowded place, in a mall, or a football stadium . . ."

"It doesn't bear thinking about, does it?" Gabriel said.

I shook my head. "Revenants and riftborn are already viewed with suspicion. You throw one capable of mass murder into the mix, and the news is going to have a field day. The Guilds have done everything they can to make sure that doesn't happen. Callie is actively making our lives harder, Mason not so much anymore, but I'm hoping Callie is soon behind him."

"We don't know where she is," Ji-hyun said.

"I plan on finding the people she sent the vials to and asking them . . . nicely," I said.

"Very nicely?" Nadia asked.

I nodded. "If that's what it takes, yes."

"Maybe with cake?" Nadia asked.

Everyone turned to look at Nadia.

"I think maybe we're mixing up our metaphors here," I said.

"I like cake," Nadia said wistfully.

"Hannah still hasn't broken Mason's phone security," Gabriel said. "She's not sure she can break it, or that it'll reveal anything useful. Callie did everything with the goal to betray Mason in the end. His money was his downfall. We need to find every vial of that serum he had made and destroy it, though."

"Hannah will figure out a way," I said. "Or we'll move on without the information inside."

Emily arrived, looking around at the four of us from underneath her umbrella. "You all out here for a reason?" she asked.

"Lucas wanted fresh air," Nadia said. "I want cake."

"Do you have cake?" Emily asked.

Nadia looked over at Emily. "I'm going to find some cake," she said, putting her arm around her. They both walked away to the shelter entrance, despite the fact that Emily had only just left that way.

"She'll be okay," Ji-hyun said.

"I hope so," I told her.

"I'm going to go help Nadia find cake," Gabriel said. "Also whisky."

"I second the latter of those two," Ji-hyun said, getting to her feet. "We will find those people Callie sent the vials to."

"I know," I said. "Or they'll find us."

"And then we'll kill them all," Ji-hyun said, and I got the feeling she a hundred percent believed that one of those two things were the only logical outcome.

"That we will," I agreed.

I reached my hand out into the rain, turning it to smoke, feeling the tingle as the water drops fell through it before re-forming my hand and bringing it out of the rain. The church needed fixing. It was an important part of helping those newly turned into revenants and riftborn. There needed to be sanctuary for them.

I looked over at the entrance to the shelter and sighed. "I guess we'd better get to work, then," I said, getting to my feet. There were bad guys to find, people to save, and wrongs to right. I chuckled to myself. "And then they lived happily ever after."

# ACKNOWLEDGEMENTS

Being an author is a fairly weird job. You are, after all, pretty much on your own for the majority of the time. It's your ideas, and your words that bring them to life, but it's not as solitary a job as you might believe, and there are a lot of people to thank who got me to this point, with this book now in the hands of anyone who finished it and decided to continue reading the acknowledgements.

As always, my wife and children are the most important people in my life. They are a big part of the reason why I decided to start writing in the first place, why I decided to take it seriously. Without their support and love, I never would have gotten my first book published ten years ago. Thank you for everything.

A big thank-you to my parents, who have supported me in my writing since day one and have a wall full of covers of my books. Sorry, Mum and Dad, but after fifteen-odd books, you're gonna need a bigger wall.

My family and friends, all of whom know who they are and why they're important to me. I could list them all individually, but these are acknowledgments and they're not meant to be dozens of pages long.

I will single out Sarah, who read an early version of this book and loved it. Her opinion on my writing is one I greatly value.

A huge thank-you to my agent, Paul Lucas, who is awesome and has always had my back. One of the coolest people I know, and someone I consider a friend as well as my agent.

To everyone at Podium, you have been so welcoming and great to work with. To Victoria, Leah, and Nicole, it's been a genuine pleasure, and I'm looking forward to continuing to work with you.

My editor, Julie Crisp, who is one of the best editors I've ever had the privilege to work with. She makes my writing better every single time she's ever edited me, and I hope to work with her again in the future.

And last, but by no means least, to every one of you who read the book. To those of you who have followed my work over the years and continue to support me and the craziness my brain comes up with, you're all awesome. And to those newcomers who have never read my work, I hope you enjoyed your time and will stay for the ride that awaits.

# ABOUT THE AUTHOR

Steve McHugh is the bestselling author of the Hellequin Chronicles. His novel *Scorched Shadows* was nominated for a David Gemmell Award for Fantasy in 2018. Born in Mexborough, South Yorkshire, McHugh currently lives with his wife and three daughters in Southampton.

# DISCOVER
# *STORIES UNBOUND*

PodiumAudio.com

CPSIA information can be obtained
at www.ICGtesting.com
Printed in the USA
LVHW032114181022
731001LV00003B/112